A Gargoyle's Vow

The Dragon Roost
Bed & Breakfast Series:

Book 2

Betsy J. Bennett

Ahead of the Press Publishing
St. Louis, Missouri

Library of Congress Cataloguing-in-Publication Data

A Gargoyle's Vow
The Dragon's Roost Bed and Breakfast Series: Book 1
Betsy J. Bennett / author

ISBN   Paperback   978-1-950392-14-8
ISBN   KINDLE   978-1-950392- 15-5

This story is a work of fiction. The names, characters, places and incidents are products of the authors' imagination. Any resemblance to actual events, locals, or persons, living or dead is entirely coincidental.

Ahead of The Press Publishing
St. Louis, Missouri

TABLE OF CONTENTS

SUMMARY of Previous
DRAGON'S ROOST BED AND BREAKFAST SERIES
BOOK 1
:

A Dragon's Tea

Nothing made sense...
To hide from her ex-boyfriend Lori Lawrick runs to her
Aunt Jan. Jan runs a bed and breakfast, and Lori decides
that might be what she needs to put her life back in
order. *She will help her Aunt cook and plant vegetables
while she decides what to do with her life.*
He said he was born to make tea...
At her Aunt's B&B, Lori meets Byron, a handsome jeweler
who creates incredible works of art in gold and precious
stones, but he says it is his duty to make tea. While the tea

served in a fancy dragon-shaped teapot is excellent, it is not what she would
consider putting him to his best use. *She dreams of him, and when he kisses her,
she wants to chop into a tree the statement "It happened here" explaining the
magnitude of the effect the kiss had on her.*
The B&B stands at a nexus of several different worlds...
Lori comes to realize nothing is what it seems at the B&B. There is a witch who
threatens Byron's life when she asks for tea. Plants grow overnight when watered
by the tea, and then there is Byron himself who infuriates her and at the same time
makes her pulse throb who is never around when the tea is served. *When Lori
discovers a real dragon who terrifies her, she must find the strength to save
Byron, the B&B and maybe the entire planet from evil sneaking in from a portal
from another world.*

CHAPTER 1

"I don't know how you do it," Sal DeLuca said.

"Me?" With a casual hike of her eyebrow Brenda Larwick pretended she had no idea what her partner was talking about. She knew him better than to give him the canned "Police officers work as a team," liturgy, yet by the same token, she wasn't about to provide him with the truth. Or rather, she would willingly offer up the truth, if she had any idea what that was.

She wasn't a big fan of lying and her relationship with the man riding in the passenger seat had always been based on mutual respect and trust. Since she didn't understand what was happening, she didn't want to tell him what she suspected and thereby come across as some raving lunatic. Instead she said "We're in this together."

"Yes, darlin' that's true." DeLuca had Southern Alabama roots, although he'd been cruising the streets of New York's capital city for decades. He was hard, tough and coarse, and the drawl was selective. It only appeared when he knew it would rile her most. She looked over at him, her eyes hard for the moment, a biting retort sizzling on her tongue, but his eyes twinkled back at her, and instead of taking offense, she flipped back her head and laughed.

"You are so annoying. I don't know why I put up with you." At even intervals they passed under street lights, the illumination brightening the interior of the patrol car before shifting them back into shadow. "Are you sure you're not ready to retire?"

There had been no sexual connotations to his 'darlin', but she loved him desperately, this grizzly old man over thirty years her senior. He was wise, street-educated and his reflexes were honed. He was everything she wanted in a partner.

He chewed a fresh piece of gum a bit then met her gaze. "If I retire, who will watch your back?"

"Who indeed," she whispered, and suppressed the shiver that crept down her back. With her gaze alert, Brenda scanned the dark alleys, the hidden recesses, the parked cars looking for anything suspicious, anything warranting further investigation. Although the area was quiet, she had learned her lessons the hard way: danger could erupt from anywhere.

They were on routine patrol, no destination, just driving, keeping the streets safe by showing off the black and white squad car. He looked out the window toward the street well on its way to becoming part of a neighborhood. "You've got the touch."

Brenda wasn't certain all police officers were as superstitious as Sal DeLuca, but "the touch" to him was the highest of compliments. It was a second sense, a knowing of when danger lurked.

Brenda would have argued, but how many major busts had her name on them as arresting officer? She was beyond lucky, she was phenomenal, and lately it looked like criminals from as far away as New Jersey were driving up to Albany, just so they could be arrested by one tawny haired cop and her disbelieving partner.

He worked the gum a bit more before he spoke. "You just let me know if you have any more premonitions."

"You're the first."

Premonitions, like now. As her hands tightened on the steering wheel, she said, "Drug dealers. Call it in. We'll need backup. A lot of backup."

"Where?" His eyes scanned the streets with a professional's glance. This was not the place he would have pegged for a major drug bust. For decades this neighborhood had been steadily declining, then recently it had gone through a major upheaval, as if the worst was over, and it was clearly headed toward rejuvenation. Sal recognized the signs of families filling many of the houses: two wheeled bikes and lawn mowers and the occasional rose bush in full bloom. None of the windows were boarded up, and white paint covered decades of graffiti, so fresh they could almost smell it. Even more telling, an entire armada of derelict cars had been removed, and trash along the sidewalks and blown against the fences had been carted off, leaving the streets clean enough for an impromptu ballgame. Yet, there was trouble here. If she said so, he was certain.

Without taking her hands off the wheel, she inclined her head. "Two story house on the corner." She drove up slowly, passed the house, then made a right, and parked down the street under an elm. She exhaled to a ten count, not so much a sigh of despair as clearing her lungs so she could gather herself, prepare for what was about to go down. "It's going to be ugly."

DeLuca methodically blew a large pink bubble, then popped it. He could work a single piece of Bazooka for a full fifteen hours. He had to have the toughest jaw in the state. He clicked his seatbelt off, and studied the street ahead, wondering what kind of collateral damage they might incur in this quiet neighborhood.

"What tipped you off?"

Brenda knew, from the tone of his voice, from her own twenty-twenty vision, that there was nothing to see, at least not with his eyes.

He spoke into the radio, adding the address, the urgent need for reinforcements. "Drug dealers," he said.

She nodded, then added, "And more weapons than we're able to deal with." There was not much else she could admit.

His teeth worked the gum, making her jaw hurt in sympathy. "We'll never get a warrant."

Brenda grinned, feeding off the blast of adrenaline that made her feel alive. She opened her door silently and slipped out. "We don't need one. We are just going to knock on the door, all nice and friendly." But as she spoke, she knew that option would land both of them in matching body bags.

"Nice and friendly," Sal agreed, "with backup." He cracked his crusty smile. His nose had been broken two or three times and combined with that grin he could stand on porch stoops and frighten trick-or-treaters without a costume.

He replaced the microphone. When she wanted a hunch called in, it was called in.

Although it wasn't late, only approaching ten, traffic was light to nonexistent, with no pedestrians in sight. Dogs must have healthy bladders in this neighborhood. That was the one reason she leaned toward cats. Even carrying a badge and a gun, Brenda wasn't too fond of the idea of pet potty breaks in the dark.

"All things considered, this doesn't look too bad," DeLuca said.

"Yeah," Brenda grumbled, making sure he could hear her sarcasm. "This is a fine place to raise a kid." She notched her head toward the house, a universal 'move out' signal.

He blew a bubble, let the air out without popping it. "I wish I knew what you are seeing that I'm not."

She trusted him implicitly. Lately she'd been to hell and back beside him. These warnings of hers were never for spry little old ladies driving on a suspended license. "I told you what I can see. Drugs, about a truckload. Enough weapons to reach the Axis of Evil list."

"Terrorists?" he asked. Terrorists they would leave to another agency. Their manpower was limited. He didn't like to walk away, but years of experience taught him to recognize when he was out of his element.

"No."

"How many?"

She huffed a puff of air up, fluttering her shade-too long bangs. "I haven't a clue." Then, as if the image sharpened, said definitively "Five. Not kids. These guys have experience. We can handle them, if we're careful. This one is hot."

She slipped past the patrol car, keeping to the shadows as she reached the old, detached garage belonging to the white house on the corner. A peek in the window confirmed it was empty, except for a brand new F150. Sal reached out, tugged her back to the garage, when she would have done preliminary reconnaissance around the property. "You gonna tell me what prompted this one?"

"Darlin'" she said, picking up his word and turning it back on him, "you don't want to know."

She had a guardian angel. Patrolwoman Brenda Larwick suspected that was what the unseen voice was. She was too old for such fantasy, and if anyone at the police station ever found out she thought she had a guardian angel she would never hear the end of the ribbing, Brenda kept her ideas of divine intervention to herself and quite pragmatically thought of him as simply The Voice.

Hearing voices was never a good sign, but while reluctant to accept it at first, she had definitely become a believer. Still, for all the times this disembodied voice had helped her, she had never seen its owner, and how he managed that, she had no idea, for it was becoming almost a nightly ritual for them to talk. She thought of him as shy, a ventriloquist who could throw his voice, as opposed to a ghost, or the more reasonable explanation of a brain tumor or encroaching insanity.

The smooth, deep masculine voice brought her all kinds of luck, and it was her impression, without concrete proof, that he'd saved her life more times than she cared to count—or admit. As a police officer, she hadn't needed a guardian angel, for most of her work had been routine: speeding tickets, traffic accidents, domestic disputes, the occasional school visit and her life, while not dull, had been slipping into a quiet routine. While a quiet routine was not what most people wanted when they joined the force, there was a lot to be said for it: especially now, with an army of drug dealers settled in the innocent white house across the lawn.

High with dual jolts of adrenaline and fear, Brenda laughed silently, and with her left hand pushed back the mass of curls from her eyes. Her right hand was wrapped around her automatic. Seconds later, three additional squad cars drove up, sirens blaring. The response was immediate. Glass broke three feet to her right, a window shattering as a long barrel weapon was thrust out, pointing toward the line of flashing squad cars.

Brenda remained still, flush against the house. She heard the Voice, and this time it whispered that all would be well. She would have muttered "Yeah, right," but she had learned over the past two weeks to trust this internal communicator.

She checked her service weapon out of reflex. She had a full clip. She made eye contact with her partner, waving two fingers indicating she would go around the back if he would give her cover.

The light was poor, all but nonexistent, but he nodded his agreement, and she watched while he made similar motions to other officers, relaying their positions. A lot of communication could pass between cops with only a few hand gestures and nods.

She crept along the base of the house, an old building that should have been torn down two or three presidential terms ago, except, like the rest of the neighborhood it showed signs of new life. Without warning, two things happened simultaneously—something black swooped in front of her, huge, or she would have suspected a bat, and bullets started raining all around.

The gunfight didn't last long. A second later, Brenda was eight feet away from where she had been. Confused, annoyed, and obviously unhurt, she rolled, planted her elbows in the grass and aimed, but did not fire.

Sal rushed up beside her. Although he kept his gun aim focused on the house, he whispered, "You all right?"

"Fine, you?" They were both communicating on an audible level lower than a whisper. They knew each other well enough, trusted each other, so a look, a glance, was enough to get their point across. She almost asked if he had seen what had knocked her to the ground, for it had been a something large and solid, but she had learned through experience her benefactor was never seen, and to bring the topic up now would involve having DeLuca question her sanity. "You saw what?" he would ask. "You felt what?"

Unexpectedly, a weapon was thrown out the back window, followed by a second.

"I'm coming out," a voice shouted, in badly accented English. Later it would be established the suspects were from a Central American nation. "Don't shoot."

Her hands on her weapon were sweat soaked, but Brenda gave no other indication of her racing pulse. She rose flush against the building, a small target. Her partner had the other side of the door. "Who else is in there with you?"

The answer wasn't long in coming. "We are all coming out."

Three more weapons were tossed out, adding to the pile below the window. Brenda and Sal were joined by six other officers, and she knew every other exit from the building was being watched, but here was where the action was.

The first drug dealer arrived at the door, his shirt off, his hands in the air. She held her arms out straight, her grasp on the handgun steady. "Get on your knees," she shouted, and he moved forward, onto the grass, where he followed her orders, and from there he dropped to his stomach. Within seconds, four other drug dealers lay beside him.

She kept him covered, while others cuffed the rest, and others ran into the house, with shouts of "Clear" and hooting at the discovered bounty, heroin this time, a dozen kilos of the stuff. And guns. Crates of guns.

"A good night's work," DeLuca said a few hours later, as they were wrapping up. The suspects had been hauled off to jail, but this was a clean bust, with their rights read to them in English and Spanish. One cop had been wounded, a bullet to his foot, but although painful, initial reports indicated after surgery and some physical therapy, he would be good as new. Brenda and DeLuca had returned to the precinct, pounded out the paperwork and the thousand odds and ends of a solid collar.

"Going home to bed?" Sal asked. He was a good partner, a friend and a confidant, but right now she didn't want him, she wanted the Voice, for what she had come to think of as an almost nightly rendezvous.

"In a little while," she said. The yawn was real, and luxurious. Funny, how when filling her shifts, she never experienced exhaustion, but as soon as the adrenaline had worked its way through her system, tiredness hit her, and all but knocked her flat. She wondered if she could keep her eyes open long enough to drive home. "See ya later."

"And Brenda?"

She looked back at him, raising an eyebrow, indicating he should continue.

"No major busts tomorrow. Let's take one day off, huh?"

"Anything you say, boss." She laughed, getting behind the wheel of her Honda and starting the engine for the short journey home. "Works for me," she said with a grin, "since I'll be on vacation. You're on your own."

She had bought the house only three months before, a rundown bungalow which almost qualified as a shack. It had several advantages. It had incredible potential, for although she had a foot-long to-do list which took every free minute of every day off, she was making great strides to getting it in shape so she could sell it and make a fortune or keep it and relax. It was also close to work, close to her parents, and offered a bit of land in the back where she could feel comfortable while she watched rotund groundhogs and fat squirrels. Hers was a neighborhood of gardeners. The wildlife made out like bandits.

She parked in the drive, but did not approach the door, instead settling on a glider on the open porch which was probably the main reason she had bought this house. She loved the idea of sitting on the porch in her old age, not that twenty-five was anywhere near retirement.

Now she would wait. He would come, she was certain. He always came after a warning. Brenda felt her pulse throb. Although she supposed she looked relaxed, anticipation rose, as if this was a clandestine meeting between forbidden lovers.

"Good evening."

It was the Voice. The shadows were thick around her. While her first impulse had been to reach for her gun, over the past two weeks, she'd been able to temper that desire.

"Good evening," she responded. His was a courtly, formal voice, sounded European, perhaps Spanish, as in Spain, or from another small countries not easily found on a European map.

She shut her eyes, let relaxation fill her as she listened to the sound of squeaks from the swing. "I want to thank you."

"It was nothing."

The words wrapped around her, a caress as gentle as if he touched her with his hands. She wanted him to touch her. Although over the past few weeks nothing which had passed between them could be considered sexual, or even something as innocuous as flirting, she wanted him to touch her to see if the feeling of her heart tripping, from her breath hitching would be magnified with his caress. She was growing desperate.

"You saved my life tonight, didn't you?" She had never crossed this boundary before. She had kept her impressions to herself.

A pause developed, filled only by crickets chirping. When he spoke, it sounded as if he offered apology. "It was my fault you were in danger."

"How did you know?"

"Know?"

She opened her eyes, stared into the darkness, although, as usual, there was nothing to see. "About the drug dealers. The house. Any of it. All of it."

She heard a shifting, a rustling so light she suspected she imagined it specifically because she was listening for it. Then after a hesitation, as if he did not wish to make this confession he spoke. "I know evil."

She shivered, although the night was not cold. There was no fear here, nothing she could consider dangerous. Still, although sitting on her own porch swing, speaking with a man who had saved her life who knew how many times, there was no comfort either.

"You know evil and it fears you." This was a leap, taken specifically because the drug dealers had tossed out their guns, willing gone down on their knees when that shoot-out could have been far longer and much more bloody.

"Yes."

Was there regret in his one word answer? Or was it simply inevitability? "I don't fear you."

His response was slight, an exhale of breath or a "Ha!" expulsion, she had no idea which. Still, she was sick of the gentleness of their evening conversations when all she was left with was desire and no information.

"I would like to see you."

He cleared his throat, let long seconds pass, time counted by the lowing of the breeze, the rumbling of leaves. "It is better for you if you do not."

"Better. Who are you to say what's better?"

At night, laying in the darkness, her hand not far from her service weapon, Brenda's mind had dredged up all kinds of equally implausible scenarios of why he would not allow himself to be seen. He was badly scarred. He wasn't human. He was invisible. When she was thinking about the Voice, Brenda tried not to take herself too seriously. "Is there a secret?"

"A secret?" His response, although posed as an echo to her question, also sounded like part of a confession. Who knows? Maybe he wanted to confess, to tell her all of his undisclosed past.

"You can tell me." She waited, tried to come up with the words. Why was it so much easier to be eloquent the many times she'd had this conversation in her mind? To be insightful? To be sympathetic? "I won't be afraid and I won't tell anyone."

She did want to see him, to put her own fears to rest, the worst a worry she was somehow psychotic, there was no tangible being associated with the Voice, she was hearing things, and it was all in her imagination. Brenda didn't mind being lucky. She refused to think of herself as psychotic experiencing some kind of mental breakdown.

She heard the rustle, knew he was restless. "Not tonight. You must trust me. Too many things between us remain unsettled."

She stood, searched the blackness to her left, where his voice came from. She saw nothing, although the evening really wasn't that dark. Stars still shone. She could walk to her car, even take a stroll around the block without worrying about tripping or running into a parked car, but she couldn't see him. "How can these issues you mention be resolved if you don't share anything?"

"We are sharing trust."

Yes, they were. She felt petty for belittling that. She sat back down, hoping he would read the action as a concession on her part not to pry. "Ok. I respect that. If you won't show yourself, I'm willing to listen, talk about anything that might be bothering you."

She heard rustling which was probably fabric on fabric and knew it was deliberate, for he could move silently when he wanted. "Are you leaving?"

She heard a sigh, but in it she heard regret. "I cannot give you the answers you require."

"You could if you wanted." She touched her hair, all the fly-away strands which had escaped her braid. "Don't leave me like this, with only impressions. I want to see you. To touch you."

Even as she spoke, she knew she'd crossed a line. Although the rules between them had never been verbalized, they were real. And she hated that it sounded like she begged. She wanted to be strong for him, for herself.

"I don't even know what to call you."

"To tell you that would be to tell you too much."

"Yet you're real?"

"I am."

She couldn't let him go like this, with everything between them unsettled. "Well, I did want to thank you. They were nasty customers, and I'm glad they didn't have a chance to get too imbedded in Albany."

New York's capital city had enough drug problems without additional groups moving in. And from the quantity of the drugs recovered, she knew this was a hub, the start of new distribution routes, and the drugs recovered tonight would not find themselves on the streets of Chicago, Manhattan or Detroit in the morning.

"One other thing—" she waited, hoped he hadn't left yet. "You won't see me for a few days," she blurted, having no idea where the confession had come from. It wasn't what she intended to say. Still, since he helped her, she felt she owed him an explanation. If he were not some facet of her imagination, a schizophrenia-induced hallucination he deserved to know her plans.

"Why not?"

"I'm taking a few days off. My sister got married, and I'm anxious to meet my new brother-in-law."

He was silent, but she rarely heard him move, not a scratch, not a twitch or a growl from his stomach.

"It's upstate, near Plattsburg, a small town called Au Sable Forks. My aunt runs a small bed and breakfast. My sister and her husband are apparently going to stay there, at least for a while."

"Ahh," he said, as if that explained a lot, but she had no idea what he meant.

"Anyway, it was a good, clean collar this evening. For your help, thanks."

"It is my honor."

She walked away, shut and locked the door behind her. Aching, and somehow unsatisfied, Brenda went up the stairs to her cramped home, where she crawled under layers of blankets and hugged a pillow to her chest. She would dream about him, for although she had never seen his face, she could imagine him very clearly.

CHAPTER 2

"This is my aunt's home. I'll be safe here."

Brenda had serious doubts, not of the first part, for that was true enough. Jan Pikorski did live here, but there had been monsters here before.

Head back, shoulders straight, almost marching, Brenda Larwick boldly approached the front door, but then her courage deserted her and she stood for a long minute, staring at the brass knocker while panic crept up her legs, down her arms, and around and through her insides. She had never had a panic attack before, and only knew fear as a memory, something from her distant past.

"I've got commendations for bravery, for heaven's sake." Neither the words in the air nor the thoughts mutating in her gut, did anything to encourage her to simply lift and release the knocker.

She looked around, seeking, pleading for some major distraction: a drug bust, an obvious homicide, or some fool teen with the ink still wet on his driver's license, sailing though a stop sign. Nothing. Where was the Voice when she needed him?

Her surroundings looked innocent, almost pristine, resin rich pine trees edging the gravel drive and towering almost as high as the stone house, a pride of chipmunks chattering over a find of what could not be naturally occurring raw peanuts, and any number of unseen birds, singing their traditional mating calls. The air was heavy with the sound of lust, and standing there, Brenda felt her body turn edgy, not meshing well with the fear she also felt.

"I'll never hear the end of this if I turn tail and run now."

It bothered her very much that what her aunt, her mother and her partner thought of her in this particular instance held far more significance than she wanted it to. She had never been a person who put much stock in what other people thought.

Brenda reached out and prepared to announce her presence to anyone—or anything—inside, but it shocked her to realize she couldn't force her hand to make contact with the knocker.

"This is foolish. I can do this," she muttered, then dropped her hand, wiped her suddenly moist fingers down her buff colored pants.

She was afraid. Petrified was a better word, because since she dropped her hands, she hadn't been able to move. She wondered if some creature had put a spell on her, taken away her capacity for voluntary movement, perhaps even her free-will. She wondered if in a year or two some Girl Scout selling cookies or some intrepid youth seeking Halloween candy would find her here, rooted to this spot on the front steps, perhaps with leaves growing out her fingertips, branches sprouting from her ears and eye sockets.

The problem started seventeen years ago when she had been eight. Brenda had been sent to spend her summer vacation in the pristine Adirondack Mountains of upstate New York with her aunt.

Her mother and father had no idea about her trauma. She had tried to tell them, begged and pleaded and screamed, but no one had believed her claim that there were monsters chained in the basement and one of them had bitten her.

She had nightmares for years, harrowing visual images of greenish gray demons who walked on two legs with claws at the end of their hands. The monsters had a long, devilish snout which snapped and snarled, and dark round eyes which missed nothing. When she returned home, her parents tried to convince her the nightmares had no basis in reality and were merely the result of her anxiety at almost losing her father to cancer. They were kind, patient with their youngest child, and had tried everything: stories, warm baths, and nightlights. They limited her snacking after supper, kept her away from most television programs and movies, yet the nightmares continued. They refused to accept there might actually be grotesque winged monsters chained in the basement of her aunt's house.

For years they made her visit a pediatric psychologist who added her expertise to her parents' testimony, refuting Brenda's tale of hairy creatures, dripping carnage. Finally fearing for her own sanity, she had lied, said she made them up, used her imagination because she felt so helpless, frustrated with her father so sick and not being able to help. She learned the right things to say. Her parents were grateful to the psychologist, called her a miracle-worker, pleased they had their youngest daughter back from the nightmares which had been disrupting their entire family.

Eventually the nightmares faded and Brenda worked very hard to convince herself she had imagined the whole thing, and hadn't almost been eaten. She made it through high school because of the cross country team, and concentrated on her college courses, taking law-enforcement, refusing to admit she only felt safe with a gun strapped to her side. She took personal self-defense classes, far more than the police academy required. She learned how to defend herself against armed and unarmed assailants, denying that she was gaining skills to help her battle monsters knew instinctively she would face again...

As soon as she could knock on the door.

"Are you here?" she asked the voice in her mind. First she spoke silently, then, embarrassed she needed the extra comfort of his presence, she whispered: "Am I alone?"

Brenda did not expect him to answer. She hadn't needed someone to hold her hand in ages; then she decided to consider him backup. A police officer never went anywhere without backup, even if it were just radio contact, someone to answer an emergency call for help.

"Are you here?"

"I am."

She jumped back, startled. "You followed me?" She had no idea if she should be flattered or annoyed.

He must be telepathic, for he read her mind. "I mean you no harm. I am interested only in protecting you. If you ever need help, I will be there."

"Will I need help here? There are monsters."

"No monsters."

"You don't understand. There were—"

For the first time in their relationship, he cut her off. "You will find peace here, comfort."

She thought it telling that he did not deny the monsters a second time. "Where are you? I would like to see you." They could sit somewhere, drink coffee. She would face this door tomorrow...or next week.

"Eventually we will meet. I guarantee."

"I'm afraid."

She doubted she had ever admitted that to anyone. Not since the bite, since she realized no one would ever believe her.

"Darlin'" it was her partner's word, spoken with Sal's inflection, but with a completely different meaning. Darlin'. Just Darlin'. Her heart thudded, racing, and she searched the area under the dark trees, the gravel drive, the hidden recesses. Insane, yes, but she knew then that she would go with him if he asked, whatever that meant.

"The house is—" words failed her, but they were apparently not needed. He knew, or read her mind.

"You will be safe within this Inn. Should danger approach, I will protect you. This I promise. Brenda, although you were hurt here once, there are worse things than being bitten."

"Bitten?" Her voice rose an octave. "How did you know I was bitten?"

The door opened immediately, forcing her to step back, to almost stumble. A man towered at the opened the door, a broad smile on his face. "I thought I heard you here."

He was not the Voice. She was certain. She wondered, half afraid, if he was the unnamed threat the Voice had promised to protect her from, but he looked friendly enough. He was a tall statue of a man, six foot two or three, with broad shoulders and narrow hips, an athlete's body, a swimmer, perhaps, although it was impossible to judge while he was clothed. Brenda considered herself a connoisseur of attractive men, and this one would triple sales, if only some entrepreneurial advertiser would set him against a sand and surf background modeling swimming trunks or space age razor blades. His hair shone raven black without a trace of gray, and it was long enough to curl at the edges of his green plaid flannel shirt. From there it fanned out, soft and inviting. His clean-shaven face was long, angular with sharply defined cheekbones, with a nose firm and stately. His eyes were magnetic, drawing her attention, and his pupils were changeable, mutating from green to blue, then even bronze so quickly she thought all colors imagination. When he spoke, she noticed his teeth, which were far too long for his features. Until then, he appeared friendly, approachable, now her impulse was to stand back. Canine teeth. He looked far too feral for her tastes. Remembering the monsters chained in the basement, Brenda decided she could try this next weekend, regardless of the fact her voice had promised her safety.

"You must be Brenda," he said, reaching out, grabbing her, thrusting her over the threshold. "We've been expecting you. Lori will be so happy you're finally here."

She stepped into the house, although, really she was pulled before she could react. Speechless, still not certain she wanted to be there, she followed the force of his magnetism and gave in to the grasp of his fingers on her arm, until he shut the front door behind her with a resounding thunk.

"There's someone out there."

He shrugged. "There always is. You will be safe inside." His promise was not nearly as comforting as the one from her Voice.

She turned around, her eyes wide, her breathing irregular, and stared at the door now irreparably shut behind her. Rationally she knew all she had to do was turn the knob and she'd be free, it was a standard door knob, and he hadn't locked it. Why did it feel as if she were trapped, like she had entered the Tower of London or the Bastille or whatever torture chambers were put to use for the Spanish Inquisition?

He raised his hand, not for the standard handshake, but to cup her cheek, stare deeply into her eyes. "Yes, you have Lori's beauty about you." His eyes narrowed, turned fuzzy, and looked quizzical, the "But," at the end of his sentence hanging off unsaid yet clearly present.

"But I've never seen her look so terrified," Brenda completed silently.

His hand on her cheek had stayed less than a moment, but she felt burned, seared. His next words confirmed how cold her flesh must have felt. "Come to the kitchen. It's warmer there. There is stew; Jan has been simmering it all day. You must be famished."

Hungry? He thought she'd eat something in this living house of horrors? She'd been mesmerized by his good looks, but now looked past him in order to study the corridor. She had hoped like all childish perceptions that it would have matured—gotten narrower, the ceiling less high, or the closed doors less imposing. That didn't seem to be the case.

"I...um..." She was a police officer, used to going into buildings where literally anything could and often did happen. She would rather face a crack house or a drug cartel hit gone bad than take two more steps down this corridor—let alone approach the stairs to the basement.

There were monsters chained to a wall in the basement. She almost got her nerve up, almost found her voice to ask this brand-new brother-in-law of hers if the monsters were still there. She wondered too, what would bother her more—if he lied and said "No, there's no monsters, never has been," or if he looked her straight in the eye and said "Sure, wanna take a peek?"

Brenda had no time to formulate her stupid question for her sister Lori appeared at the far end of the long corridor. "Byron, what are you doing down there? How could you get lost between the front door and the kitchen?"

Byron's eyes sparkled with unsuppressed amusement. Brenda knew without a doubt what tickled his fancy. There were probably more than a dozen secret corridors branching off from this hallway, leading not only to other parts of this house, but to other worlds as well. Brenda wasn't a big science-fiction reader, because like so many others she believed truth was stranger than fiction. Sci-Fi writers only had imagination, while she had seen the real thing. There were portals to other dimensions all through this house and she doubted any of them lead somewhere pleasant.

Instead of questioning him or her own recollections, Brenda banked her fears and ran headfirst down the long corridor, into her sister's arms. "Lori, it's so good to see you." She wrapped her older sister in a secure hug. It was the first time she had felt warm since Albany.

Lori laughed and cried and returned the embrace with unbounded love as if it had been five years since they had seen each other. It had.

Through the comfort of the embrace, Brenda studied her sister. "You look so happy. Marriage seems to agree with you."

So it was with love, holding her sister, with her new brother-in-law following behind that she entered the kitchen. Much better than storming in, with both hands on her service weapon, which was how she'd suspected she would enter.

"Sit," Lori insisted, but the command would have to wait, for her Aunt Jan turned around from the stove and she was again embraced in the warmth and love of family. The first thing Brenda recognized was her aunt's scent, cloves, she thought, cinnamon, both of which she equated with security. When she was recovering from her bite, terrified by monsters, and her sleep was stabbed with visions of the attack, just her aunt's scent was enough to comfort her. It was why, she decided, she was drawn to bakeries, even when she wasn't going to buy anything.

When she pulled away from the embrace, Brenda gave her a long glance. "Oh, Aunt Jan, you look exactly the same, exactly, even down to your mismatched socks!"

Jan's blue eyes sparkled, showing traces of silver, matched by the color of her hair. "Well, I've got to wear the odd pair, or none at all."

"Oh?" Brenda asked, trying to be enchanted.

"The dryer is old, and it complains about all those towels, particularly the yellow ones. To keep it working, I have to give it the occasional treat."

"A sock," Lori said, giggling.

"Yes. Nothing else will do. I've tried everything, even fruitcake—"

"I'll bet that was messy," Brenda muttered.

"It wasn't too bad. The imps cleaned everything up. It is occasionally useful to have imps on the property."

"Imps?"

"I'm sure she means the kittens," Byron said, rubbing his chin with a massive hand. Funny how she had not noticed how large his hands were.

"Anyway, to get back to my story, I feed the dryer socks to stay on its good side. It will only take one of a pair. Never both. I just wish its memory wasn't so long, so I could sneak in the other."

"As they always say," Lori said wiping her eyes from the tears her giggles had brought, "a dryer never forgets."

Jan sighed, long suffering, yet resigned. "True enough. A dryer never forgets."

Brenda was annoyed with this foolishness, spoke flippantly. "I would have thought you would have a dragon on the premises, blowing warm air over your clothing to get them dry."

"The dragon," Byron said, showing teeth a shade too long, "generally has more important things to do."

"And of course," Jan added, laughing it off, "we don't like our clothing charred. A dragon cannot be trusted to only dry."

"Not when a dragon likes to burn," Byron responded, but his gaze was locked on Jan, and Lori moved closer to him, fitting herself, like a puzzle piece, under his arm.

"And really, when you think of it, don't you believe it is easier to feed the occasional sock to a dryer, than to try to get a dragon to do your bidding?"

"There is always that," Byron agreed.

"I think I could get a dragon to do my bidding," Lori said, snug against her husband.

"Yes, but you are the exception, my love. Remember, I told you everyone else gets eaten."

Jan curled her top lip at Byron, then casually asked, "How was your trip up the Northway?"

Brenda shook herself, putting the fantasy of sock eating dryers and charring dragons aside for the more practical concerns of small-talk. "Fine, the traffic was light. It's a relief to be away from work for a few days."

She realized that was true. She was glad for the vacation. The other officers were starting to take bets, wondering when she would find the next major bust. She just wasn't pleased to be here.

Jan wore her gray hair long, in a single braid down her back. Brenda's memories of her Aunt were mixed. Her aunt was kind, always knew what food to serve to satisfy a craving, when a hug was needed or a long talk by a blazing fire. She was like a fairy godmother, turning the dullest rainy day into an incredible adventure, with nothing more than pot lids and long handled spoons for weapons. While blowing bubbles she made up stories about pixies, and while baking loaf after loaf of bread told about tunneling dwarves with such realism Brenda had almost been able to hear the hammering of picks.

She had also lied, repeatedly, about the things chained in the basement. She had refused to allow Brenda to go back down those steps, and had refused to acknowledge that something had bit her. Monsters, demons, hell, whatever they were, they had been real.

Brenda would not sleep well tonight, did not suspect she would sleep at all while she remained a guest in this house. And it was too much to hope all the bedrooms were filled, and she could use that to her advantage, begging to find a convenient hotel. There were literally any number of floors in this bed and breakfast, at least ten, who knew how many more? It was another facet of the house her parents had refused to believe. "What do you mean, the number of floors in the house change? Do you really think that's possible?" Yes, she really found it possible. She had been an inquisitive child, had wandered away whenever her Aunt Jan's back was turned. Jan had been extremely busy during her stay here. Brenda had done a lot of exploring.

Lori led her sister to the highly polished solid oak table with the same spunky grin she had had growing up. "There's tea!" She held up a beautiful decorated dragon-shaped teapot, flashing silver and copper and a rich bronze color. "A cup of this and you'll be feeling better in no time."

"That must be new," Brenda said, indicating the pot.

Jan sighed then set out heavy mugs. "It's been around a long time."

"And now it's mine," Lori caressed the teapot, rubbing her fingers teasingly along the dragon's wings. "Although I don't get to enjoy tea from it that often."

"You can have tea any time you ask," Jan said, "but I suspect there are too many other things keeping you occupied." The wink was clearly meant for Lori alone. Brenda noticed and attributed it solely to the joys of being a newlywed.

Then she noticed there were only three mugs on the table.

"Where's Byron? I did want to question my new brother-in-law, in order to be sure he's going to treat you well."

"He'll be back in a little while. He had something to do." Lori shared a conspiratorial look with her aunt, and although both women looked happy, Brenda could only shiver and wonder at what they shared that she could not, in this house where her nightmares originated.

"I've chocolate éclairs," Jan said, putting a platter on the table. They were fat things, dripping with chocolate, and when Brenda lifted one, she knew they would be exquisite, for they were heavy, and therefore loaded with custard.

"I do remember the food here being the best I've ever tasted," Brenda said but Lori's next words had the éclair on her tongue tasting off.

"It's the magic."

"Magic?"

"Well," Jan corrected, "mostly sugar, chocolate, cream and butter." Jan shook her head once, sharply, renewing the secret non-verbal conversation Brenda realized was meant to exclude her.

"Tea?" Jan asked, but the question was asked to Lori.

"It's your home. You've done the honors so long I don't mind, and I'm sure Byron won't."

"Tea, Brenda? It's good to be welcomed back into the arms of family with a cup of tea."

Lori's eyes brightened and she opened her mouth to speak before she clamped it shut. More secrets. But being a cop was too deeply ingrained for Brenda to ignore the fact she was missing more of this conversation than she participated in.

She set the éclair on the dessert plate, wiped her fingers with her napkin, needing the time to compose her thoughts. "What were you going to say?"

"Me?" Lori asked, hands to her chest, all innocence.

"Yeah, you were about to say something about the tea."

"Only that it's very good," Lori answered, and if she didn't share a glance with Aunt Jan, it was because both of them clearly avoided it. The action couldn't have been more deliberate if it had been choreographed.

"Well then," Brenda said with forced gayety which she hoped would pass for genuine, "let me try some of this excellent tea guaranteed to warm me up." She held out her cup.

Jan poured the steaming amber liquid into three mugs. Brenda lifted hers to sniff the rich bouquet, finding it both pleasant and enticing. Smell, she knew, was the strongest of the senses, the one most likely to remain long after other impressions had vanished. The scent was welcoming: orange, a mixture of spices and an over-all rich tea essence. Brenda sniffed again, noticed although Lori and her aunt were trying to look casual, her reactions were being closely monitored.

"Try it plain first," Jan said, picking up her cup, breathing in the fragrance exactly as Brenda had done, then sipping with obvious enjoyment, "even if you normally take your tea with milk and sugar."

"Black is fine," Brenda answered. She was a cop, used to police stations where the coffee was so old and thick it could be considered a lethal weapon, and more often than not, if present, cream and sugar were considered signs of a wuss. She had been very tough as a cop. She did nothing which would make anyone think her soft.

Brenda took her first sip and visions exploded in her brain, like an assault, and before she could swallow, she spit, splattering the liquid against the slate flooring.

CHAPTER 3

"What? What happened?" Lori stood, the color drained from her face, and her eyes grew wide, showing far too much white. She grasped the teapot, as if protecting it. The reaction was far out of proportion to the action which preceded it. "Why did you do that?" Her voice was high pitched, trembled significantly.

"I saw something," Brenda confessed, rubbing her eyes and shaking her head, trying both to erase the images and bring them into sharper focus. She set her teacup down, pushed it away from her. The greater shock at the moment was not specifically her reaction to the tea, but Lori's terror-filled response.

"It's all right, dear," Jan said to Lori, putting firm hands on her shoulders and forcing her to sit. "You drink your tea and enjoy it, and I'll finish my cup too. No harm done. I promise you, he's fine. We'll just enjoy this while we find out what your sister saw."

Jan waited until Lori drank her tea, then sipped from her own cup. She nodded, once, slightly, an acknowledgement to herself, which stated "nothing here which shouldn't be," as clearly as if she had shouted. Lori, still cradling the teapot, also hugged her mug.

"What is that stuff?" Brenda asked. Hints of visions still swirled around behind her eyes, ghosts of things she couldn't quite focus on. If it had been hallucinogenic and she was certain it was, she would have had to swallow first, give the drug time to get into her bloodstream, then travel to her brain. This happened instantly, the moment the tea hit her tongue. She stood, reached for the teapot in Lori's hands. "I want a sample of this. I'm going to take it to a police lab, see what drug is in it."

"No!" Jan and Lori shouted together. Then Jan put a comforting hand on Lori's arm, an 'I'll handle this,' gesture. Lori nodded, but her mouth hung open, and her bottom lip trembled.

"Brenda," Jan said firmly, as if she were a trained interrogator herself, "I would like you to tell me what you experienced."

"Not until I get an explanation of what this is." She picked up her mug, getting to her feet. "It didn't affect you two, so I have to assume whatever drug you added was in my cup alone."

"No drug, I swear," Jan said. To prove it, she picked up Brenda's cup and downed the contents. Across the table, Lori was petting the teapot.

There was no other word for it, she stroked the wings back, scratched under the dragon's neck, the spout, as if what she held was a pampered lap cat instead of a ceramic teapot. Still, Brenda, who was an expert at reading emotions, knew her sister had been affected strongly, and the primary emotion visible in her blanched face and flared nostrils was fear.

"Lori, will you calm down? I told you there was no danger," Jan said.

Lori's bottom lip trembled. "He only wanted to welcome you. That's what he does. It's his penance, but it's also his pleasure. He loves—"

"That's quite enough. Why don't you take Byron a cup of tea?" Jan's voice carried enough command that both sisters took notice.

"Byron?"

"On the landing—there by the back stairs. Take the whole pot. You can see for yourself he hasn't been hurt."

With firm hands, Jan raised Lori to her feet and before she could protest, turned her to face the stairs, gave her a light push to get her moving. "There, on the landing. For Byron."

Brenda shifted so blocking Lori's escape. She wasn't about to let the evidence vanish. "Will someone tell me what is going on?"

"Lori, are you leaving?"

Lori was clearly in shock, and Brenda had been to enough accident scenes to recognize the dulled responses. Lori clung to the teapot as if it were the only thing keeping her afloat.

"Go, Lori."

"I'm afraid." Her bottom lip quivered.

"Then have another cup of tea. It will calm you. I tell you he is fine, and as the sooner you see for yourself, the better."

"He is just so vulnerable."

Jan poured Lori another cup of tea, a task made more difficult because Lori refused to relinquish the teapot, then waited while she drank it. "Better?"

"Yes."

"Landing?"

Lori walked, dazed, to a door off the kitchen, shutting it behind her. She still had the teapot with her.

"Was it something I did?" Brenda asked. She tried to follow Lori through the back door, only to find herself restrained by Jan's surprising strength. Her initial impulse was to fight against her aunt, to gain her feet and thereby acquire answers, but an image flashed across her brain, a vision of two monsters chained in the basement and that superseded everything else. She would bide her time. Consciously she forced her body to relax, knew Jan felt the easing of the tension in her shoulders and neck when her aunt eased the pressure she had on her, until it changed to a friendly family pat on the back.

"Eat. I can see you're hungry. And I'll put the kettle on, make you a nice cuppa coffee. You're probably a coffee person yourself."

Brenda kept her silence, reliving the impressions stamped on her brain. She wasn't fooled by Jan's actions for a second. If the police force had taught her anything beyond the patience she knew she would need, it was when a suspect relaxed that quickly, after a misdirection, there was definitely something worth pursuing. She would let Jan think her placated, regain her aunt's confidence. She would get more information that way. "Yes, I'd love a cup of coffee."

Brenda leaned back in her chair, stretching out her legs, shifting the long cord of her braid off her shoulder. "It was such a long trip. I guess I'm more tired than I thought."

But the vision from the tea remained and she set it beside the older image of monsters. She would find her answers.

Jan slipped behind her to the oven, returning almost immediately with a heavy pottery bowl. "Here is a nice plate of lamb stew. I can promise you there is no drug in it."

"That's what you said about the tea," Brenda said but she forced a smile to her lips to indicate she only kidded.

"And there wasn't. Here, I'll eat some myself, show you it's fine."

Brenda fiddled with her fork, entwining it in her fingers. "Aunt Jan, what's going on here?"

"I can't answer that until I know what it was you saw."

The back door opened and Lori stepped through, Byron's arms wrapped around her.

"Him," she said pointing to Byron. "I saw him."

"Certainly that couldn't have been so bad?" Jan asked, as color drained from Lori's face.

"It was, because he transformed into a monster."

Lori sagged, but with Byron's arms around her, wasn't able to dip far. Byron all but carried her to the kitchen chair. He looked across the table, apparently not finding what he was seeking. "Why isn't there ever any tea in this house?" he asked briskly.

"A question you should be able to answer far better than I," Jan responded, but if she had been tense earlier, it had vanished with his reappearance and her statement had been wrapped more with humor than sarcasm or accusation. Leaving Lori, he went to the cabinet, found a standard blue teapot.

"She's had a shock," he said, and Brenda, holding a fork, still hadn't taken a bite of the delicious smelling stew, wanted to shout, "She's had a shock? What about me?"

Byron set the kettle on to boil and came back with a plate of the same stew Brenda had in front of her and placed it before Lori. "You should eat."

She looked up at him, as if she might protest, then picked up a fork and started eating, blindly. People in shock often did what they were told, because they were too removed from their own life to cope.

"Brenda, perhaps it was a mistake to give you the tea, but you loved it when you were here before and I didn't know you would be so sensitive to residuals."

She picked up only one part of the sentence. She twirled her tongue around her teeth, giving herself a full minute to calm down then annunciated very clearly. "You gave me that tea before?"

"Yes. There are different brews for different purposes: for strength, for peace, for pleasant dreams and a solid night's sleep, for insight."

"There's even a brew that works as an organic plant fertilizer," Lori added. Her eyes had lost their earlier sparkle, and she grasped her husband's fingers in her own.

Byron shared a private glance with his wife. "I prefer to call it growth enhancer rather than fertilizer."

"Now," Jan said brightly, coming back from the stove with the blue teapot, "here's some fresh herbal tea, and it won't do anything, not even keep you awake. You should have a cuppa Lori. Brenda, do you want to try this?"

"Sure. How much worse can it be?"

"Tell me what you saw, Sis," Lori pleaded, holding onto her sister's hands. "You saw Byron?"

"If you would rather not talk about it—" Jan started while Byron spoke simultaneously, saying, "There's no need to go into that right now."

"I'd like to tell." Brenda pushed aside her plate, clearly ignoring the steaming tea cup, "I'd like to get your reactions. There are secrets here. I don't know what they are, but I think I'll be able to judge better when I see your response." She took a deep breath, then looked to each individually before speaking again.

"I didn't notice the taste of the tea. The visions exploded so sharply, almost painfully, that I had no sensation of taste. I expected to like it, since it smelled delightful. It is cold outside and I was chilled from the drive, so I had no qualms about trying it."

Across the table Lori grabbed Byron's hand and held on tightly, as if to a life raft. To show he was not as concerned as his wife, in a deliberate act of nonchalance, he picked up a piece of lamb from Lori's stew with his fingers and casually ate it.

"I don't take hallucinogenic drugs," Brenda continued, "so I don't know what a true hallucination is, although I've been told they are so real, you can't tell the difference from reality, but this was no hallucination. It was like being stabbed in the eyes with two hot pokers, so the only thing I could do was spit. Could you imagine the shock to my system if I swallowed?"

"But what did you—" Lori started, and Byron's touch on his wife's arm turned to a gentle caress.

"But what did I see?" Brenda finished. "Not much really. It was the intensity of the experience that mattered, not so much what I saw. I was looking at the teapot as I sipped, impressed with the colors and the detail, so who knows if I'd been looking at the refrigerator or a kitchen knife what I would have seen."

"Brenda," Lori said, and the plea was clearly heard by all four at the table.

"I saw the teapot morph into Byron, then I saw Byron transform into the teapot, but it was different, significantly different. It was huge and it was alive. I saw the wings flutter and his eyes, well there was life and knowledge in his eyes. Then he opened his mouth as if to breathe fire, and I spit."

"That's all?" Jan asked, and she sounded relieved.

"I saw a teapot turn into Byron then Byron turn into a hideous dragon."

"He's no monster," Lori defended, but Byron hushed her with nothing more invasive than a touch to her arm and the look they shared was intimate.

"Was it a truth tea?" Jan asked Byron. "I thought I would have recognized the scent."

"No, it was just a standard family tea, with nothing special in it, except a dragon's powers are magnified by about a thousand percent when he's breeding."

A second passed before Jan shouted, "Breeding?" the word both high-pitched and intense. It was as if she'd never heard the word before and was about to run to the dictionary to look it up. Then her reaction was as abrupt and explosive as Brenda's earlier one. She reached for Lori, pulled her out of her chair and hugged her joyously. "You're pregnant!"

"We haven't had it confirmed by a doctor yet, but Byron seems fairly certain."

Jan spun Lori in dizzying circles around the kitchen. "When?" she asked.

Byron shook his head slightly and Jan looked to Brenda, and Brenda knew the glance was meant to keep secrets from her.

Brenda pasted a smile on her lips, decided in the face of Lori and Byron's obvious happiness she would be happy as well. "Congratulations," she said.

"Because of the pregnancy, Byron wants to get away for a while, before I'm too big to travel. We've been so busy we didn't take a honeymoon, but now I think we'd better. It means we'll miss your visit."

"I only want you to be happy and to take good care of my new niece or nephew."

"Then we'll leave tonight, after we get you settled."

"Why don't you leave now, while it's still light out? Those hairpin turns must be tricky in the dark." Brenda hugged her sister, then gave an equally warm hug to her new brother-in-law. "You've made her happy."

"I hope to keep making her happy. Jan, we don't know when we'll be back. You know how time does funny things when I fly."

"Yes, everyone finds time goes too quickly on vacation," but her tone was dry and long suffering, as if there was a reference there that again indicated Brenda was out of the loop.

"We are anxious to get started."

Jan kissed them both. "Go. Enjoy yourselves."

Byron grasped his wife's hand. With an arm wrapped around Lori's back, they headed toward the back kitchen door before Lori returned to hug her sister again.

"Enjoy your honeymoon. You know I wish you two all the best. And I've always wanted a handsome brother."

Lori grasped Brenda's hands. "You will be comfortable here, I promise. And Brenda, I hope you find peace. You look like you need it. Still, I am sorry to be leaving so soon after you arrived."

"Is there a way we can get in touch with you if we need to?" Brenda asked. Suddenly, in this house where all her nightmares originated, she realized she had been alone for far too long. She craved the comfort of family.

"I'm sure Jan can find us if need be," Lori responded. They had never been close. As a child, Brenda had had her own problems, and as adults, they went in different directions, Lori to the university and increasingly time-consuming degrees and field work, and Brenda immersed herself in police work.

"I can find you, or I know something that can." Jan looked amused with the thought. "I want you both to have a good time."

"We'll miss your cooking," Lori said. "Heaven help me if I have to eat something Byron kills."

Brenda felt the statement rhetorical, so she didn't respond.

Lori waved, then, hand-in-hand with Byron, headed out the back door. Watching them leave, Brenda remembered something. "Have the rules changed?" she asked with a gleam to her eyes. "You made me swear when I was here last that I would never go out this door."

"And while you are here this time," Jan said, shutting the door behind the couple, then herding Brenda back to the kitchen, so she couldn't even look out the window and wave until they were out of sight, "you will again promise never to go out this door."

"Am I not old enough?"

"Age has nothing to do with it."

"Not tough enough?" She could go an entire shift and not feel the weight of the weapon she wore at the small of her back, other times, like now, she was supremely aware of it.

The gun under her jacket was invisible, but Brenda must have made some movement toward it, must have indicated by some unconscious gesture that it was there, for her Aunt Jan had no problem divining its presence.

"And if you think that gun you wear is going to save you from the things which roam the forests outside the back door, you're sadly mistaken."

"I can handle myself," she said defiantly.

"I don't think so."

Brenda felt a cold shiver run down her spine and wondered if, perhaps, her aunt was right. She hadn't been here five minutes, and already she was having visions, seeing monsters. Worse, her sister and brother-in-law were escaping, leaving her alone in this huge house with her aunt.

Alone, except for the things chained in the basement.

CHAPTER 4

Fighting memories from her childhood, Brenda ran upstairs to put her suitcase in her room and use the restroom. She splashed water on her face, hoping to wash away the horrifying images with her exhaustion. Lori was leaving. Yes, she was due a honeymoon, Brenda wouldn't deny her sister that happiness. Still, irrationally, she felt abandoned.

A scented sachet rested on the pillow of her bedroom, lilacs or hydrangeas, she had no idea the specifics, but it was exactly the same as it had been all those years before. Perhaps it was the trace scent tingled with sunshine and somehow, innocence that helped evoke the past. Even the bathroom had its own aroma, sometimes woodsy and primordial, sometimes lemony and invigorating. The scents had been here before. It was as if they remained, awaiting her return, to work their insidious hypnosis to awaken all her repressed fears.

Scents. How significant they were, how much a part of sensuality. Brenda breathed deeply assimilating the aromas around her, finding in them, surprisingly, a deep seated feeling of home. She kept scented candles in her apartment, lit them when she was alone, looking for what she had now, this ambiance of comfort and belonging.

Annoyed at her fancy, being taken in so completely by the artificial impression of lilacs, she pulled her gun from the holster at the small of her back. She sniffed it, looking for familiarity, but only found the action invasive and somehow incomplete. It had almost no scent beyond the oil she used to clean it; no sharp tang of gunpowder, no aroma of heat stressed metal.

Replacing it, she thought of Hansel and Gretel, how they must have been beguiled by the sights and scents of the gingerbread house. Scents then, were not to be trusted. Although this smelled like home, it wasn't home. She would do well to remember that.

Instead of frightening her, her relative's actions annoyed her, for it was as if they had decided she still was a little girl who needed protecting, and they defined 'protecting' as keeping her in the dark about all the secrets she had come to discover.

"I don't believe in monsters." Whatever she had seen, could not be a monster.

With her courage firmly in place, Brenda skipped back downstairs.

Less than thirty minutes had passed, but when Brenda entered the kitchen, she stopped, stunned. The room, which had been spotless half an hour before was in shambles. Nine men unloading a delivery truck couldn't have made a mess this significant. Every pot was dirty, stacked higher than her shoulder. Actually, if she had to venture a guess, every dish, cup, bowl, piece of silverware and cooking utensil in the country was here, waiting to be washed. Bits of crusted food dripped from pot lips or dribbled from spoons, and the counters which had gleamed, were now caked with hardening gravy, bits of potato and a hundred types of crumbs. The floor was sticky in places, and it was impossible to walk on, for not only were the dishes and cooking utensils on the counters, they had taken over every spare inch of the floor in the massive room.

"What happened?" Brenda blinked, rubbed her eyes, knew she couldn't be mistaken. Thirty minutes ago this place had been spotless. She wanted to ask if spitting tea out caused this spontaneous disaster, causing dirty dishes to grow instead of, for example, Jack's beanstalk.

Instead of loading a dishwasher, which any sane person would have done, Jan stood at the sink, up to her elbows in hot water and suds. Some of her gray hair had escaped from her neatly plated braid, and fluffed around her face like an aura and she had high color on her cheeks, indicating she had been working very hard.

"Please, sit. You look like you need to rest. You never ate your stew or the éclairs. If you don't mind, I'd like to get some of these dishes done."

"No, I'll not eat while you slave away here. What happened?"

"Timing, that's all I can think. Every now and then these dishes have to be washed, but I will admit the timing could not be worse, with Lori and Brew off on their honeymoon…"

"And me here, when you're trying to keep all your secrets," Brenda finished for her. She stood between a dozen piles of teetering dishes, wanting to help, not having a clue where to start or what to do.

Oddly enough, in spite of the disaster surrounding her, the kitchen smelled heavenly, of rich lamb gravy and golden loaves of freshly baked bread. Her stomach grumbled loudly, a liquid gurgle she knew her aunt heard. Brenda rubbed her belly through her clothing, embarrassed. She had skipped lunch working, then had not stopped on the highway, in an effort to get here and face her fears.

"You're hungry. It's ready and hot. You might as well eat. It's not as if these dishes are going anywhere on their own."

"I've been hungry before, and I'll not eat while you work." Then a whim tickled the back of her mind. "Is this sort of like the Elves and the

Shoemaker in reverse, where instead of all the work being done in the quiet of the night, it must be done by people in the day?"

"An excellent analogy," her aunt said, with an inflection to her voice Brenda did not understand. "Now sit."

"Of course." Originally she had no intention of eating, but the food smelled enticing, and she couldn't resist. "When I finish, I'll help."

"Tomorrow will be soon enough. I'd be grateful for your help then, but you were not brought here to be a slave dishwasher. I want you to relax. Walk the trails and get some fresh air, sleep yourself out, and mostly, I would like to hear how your life is going. Is there a man in your life yet?"

Brenda speared a piece of potato with her fork, intending to do nothing more than move it around on the bowl, but instead she put it in her mouth, chewed thoughtfully. For a second, she thought of the Voice, a man she had never seen but who definitely intrigued her. There was nothing there she could admit to. What did she have, a one-sided attraction with someone she had never seen, who had some way of speaking with her telepathically, who knew where all the bad guys hung out?

"I haven't been as lucky as Lori. I really haven't been dating, if you must know. I've been working a lot of overtime and concentrating on my career."

In this kitchen, that sounded so lonely, so pitiful. She stabbed a carrot and something white which might have been parsnip, chewed thoughtfully before she spoke again, hoping to put her life in better perspective, both for her mother's sister and herself.

"I am rarely home but when I am I have a to-do list about a mile long. I bought a fixer-upper, and I'm really getting into it. Dad taught me how to grout a bathroom and sand a floor and mud drywall. I find it therapeutic."

"So, you've got a home then?"

"It's not much of one yet. No, I take that back. It is a home. It needs a lot of work, and frankly the kitchen in the thing should have been condemned fifty years ago so I don't do any cooking there, but there's a swing on the front porch and I rock there in the evenings, and I when I do, I can't imagine being happier."

Of course when she was there, she wasn't alone, for there was a Voice keeping her company, and a promise of a future.

"So, that's what's important to you?" Jan moved a stack of plates from a teetering pile to the sink. If this were a major restaurant, and they had an endless supply of pots, pans and dishes, none of which had been washed in over a year, Brenda suspected the resulting disaster would look much like Jan's kitchen.

"Yeah. It's great. A couple weekends ago I had all the guys on the force over for a barbeque, well, the ones who had the weekend off anyway, and their wives and kids. I made them work for about five hours first, cleaning brush from the backyard, putting in a garden, scrubbing down my gutters, taking a dumpster to the garage, putting in a fire pit, but then we feasted on ribs and corn and baked beans. Now that I think of it, that's probably the first thing I've cooked at home, and I've been living there for a couple months."

"You like your work."

Brenda set her fork back in the bowl, took a sip of milk, let the creamy liquid sit on her tongue for a moment before swallowing. How many years had it been since she had tasted milk with anything other than breakfast cereal?

In addition to the lamb stew, there was a platter of steaming garlic bread, a tossed salad with dark leafy greens, tomatoes, radishes, and other vegetables she couldn't identify. She decided one of the reasons she rarely ate was food had lost its taste for her. Most contained too many artificial chemicals and useless calories, not enough natural flavor, texture and substance. This was easily one of the best meals she had ever eaten.

Brenda took another bite of stew, finding it spicy and delicious. More than the taste, it was the completeness of the meal, as if something from within her had been missing a long time, and she had been craving it, and had only just discovered it.

"I like to keep the streets safe. While I am basically only a traffic cop, I answer domestic disturbance calls, things like that. There is definite talk I'll be promoted to detective any time. I've been studying for the test. I like to know that directly through my efforts, some scum-bag is off the streets, and people can go about their lives in peace."

Jan put a dripping plate into a dish drainer. "You have a strong sense of self-sacrifice."

Brenda laughed. "No. I am not sacrificing anything." Still, she appreciated the approval in her aunt's voice.

"Yet you chose a career that puts you in danger so other people can go safely about their lives."

Brenda gnawed over Jan's comments. She had never given a thought to the element of self-sacrifice in her actions. She always thought she did what she did to prove she was strong, that whatever monsters appeared she could handle, and the easiest way to accomplish that was to be a cop, with the backing of other trained officers.

As she sat, exhaustion crept in, filled her to overflowing, as if it had come with the stew, instead of something she'd lived with day and night for the past few years.

"Sit for a few more minutes. By the look of you, you don't have the strength to climb those stairs to reach your bed and I can't carry you."

"I'll be all right in a moment." Brenda was used to living with exhaustion, working through it. She plopped her elbows on the table, then rested her face in her palms. She wasn't sure if she fell asleep immediately, or if somehow she was granted a vision, but the images were so sharp, it was as if there were two of her, an eight-year-old girl and, invisible behind her, her current self, present only as a watcher.

Her father had not been expected to survive his cancer. While he was getting the best treatment, and while everyone believed the doctors competent and the hospital top notch, the cancer had spread. Initial results of treatments were not promising, the chemo ineffective, and the surgery, although successful by any definition, hadn't managed to provide a clean bill of health. For months everything had been in turmoil, dinners late, and even then it was something simple, pancakes or a bowl of cereal. Homework papers needing a signature were forgotten or misplaced and there was never a parent at soccer games or parent teacher conferences. As a family, they spoke in whispers, afraid of death, fearful it could be contagious and could come into their home so unexpectedly.

It was hard for the child Brenda facing a series of babysitters: neighbors and women from their church, but summer appeared almost unexpectedly, and things got worse. Her mother was so caught up in visits to the hospital that no one seemed aware school was about to go into recess for three months. Lori had been around then, but she was busy with friends of her own, especially a wealthy neighbor who invited her on a two month vacation to Martha's Vineyard. It looked like Brenda would be left alone. There was talk about finding her a summer camp, but Brenda had been shy as a child, and the idea of spending months away from home terrorized her. Yet she was not old enough to stay home alone, and she wasn't welcomed on the oncology ward at the hospital. The problem was solved the very afternoon Lori left. They had just returned from the seeing her off at the neighbor's when they arrived home and found Jan waiting for them. "I know you're busy," Jan said to her sister, Brenda's mom, "so I've come to take Brenda."

It was settled quickly. Within the hour, Brenda found her clothes packed in two neat suitcases, traveling to upstate New York with an aunt she barely recognized. "Are there other children there?" Brenda asked. The silence in the car was oppressive. No radio, no singing or the silly license plate games her family always indulged in while traveling for long periods.

The road was busy, the traffic brisk, but even then, tightly secured in a seat belt, she felt she was leaving everything familiar, and going to someplace not quite right. For a few minutes, she imagined she was kidnapped, being taken against her will by some monster, who in the daylight looked perfectly innocent, exactly like her aunt.

"No. I live alone." Not quite alone, but Brenda wouldn't find that out for a while. Although, too, perhaps the statement was correct. She lived alone where other humans were concerned. What the child Brenda found in the basement had clearly not been human.

"Any dogs?" Dogs could make any situation tolerable.

"No pets. They interfere with what I have to do." There had been a black cat, but it had been a haughty creature, independent and unwilling to be a child's plaything. Brenda clutched her doll, a big, soft, red-haired companion she named Abigail, and on whom she had lavished all her love and compassion. Brenda was beginning to think she would survive much better forgotten in her own home than as an unwelcome invader in her aunt's, and the impression was only highlighted when Jan parked the car in front of a huge monstrosity of a house, which looked definitely and completely haunted. Brenda gasped. She didn't remember crying out, but found her aunt rubbing her knee. "Are you all right, dear?"

"I don't like it here." She had not been an insightful child, had not had impressions of things right or wrong, but this wasn't normal.

"What do you see?" Jan asked softly. The adult Brenda watching realized something the child Brenda had not figured out at the time. Jan could have grabbed her, forced her into the house, dismissed her impressions and fears as childish. Jan was busy, had no need to be saddled with a niece she barely knew. But, here, still sitting behind the steering wheel, she exhibited kindness.

"The house, it's all..." she fought for a word, didn't have the vocabulary to grasp exactly the one she wanted. "It's all dusty," she finished.

It looked old, rotting, it looked like thirty or forty stories of decaying mausoleum.

Jan looked at the house long and hard, as if seeing it for the first time. She nodded her approval, then turned back to her niece. "It's really a friendly type of house, once you get to know it. It can put on airs, act like it doesn't want to play nice, but it will welcome you, I guarantee it."

"What if I don't want to be here?"

"I know you don't," Jan said. In the vision, she didn't look any different from the Jan who had welcomed her into the house a few hours ago. Whether because this vision was strictly a dream, and therefore was pulling recent facts to overwrite what had happened then, or because Jan herself had not changed by so much as a single gray hair, Brenda had no idea.

"But you're old enough, and I want you to think. You would do anything to help your father get better, wouldn't you?"

The child nodded helplessly. "I would."

"This is the medicine your father needs right now. He needs to have time to only worry about himself, and your mom needs the time to worry about him. I know you think presents are something you buy at the store, but that isn't always true. Some of the best presents you can give are sharing of yourself and making it so others don't have to worry about you."

Brenda puffed out her bottom lip. "It would be easier to buy a present from the store."

Jan nodded, agreeing. "It's always easier to buy a present. But, like I said, they are not always the best kind. Think how much your mom loves you. If you were home, she'd have to make your bed, wash your clothes, and make sure you have nutritious dinners. The present you are giving her is that she doesn't have to. She can concentrate on your father and on keeping herself healthy."

And Brenda looked at the house, and it no longer seemed forbidding and it no longer looked 'dusty.' It looked exactly like the kind of place where a princess would stay. Especially one who needed rescuing.

***

Brenda startled, coming awake abruptly, as if someone had touched her. The dream had been so real, she had to look at her hands, to ensure she wasn't the eight-year-old from the vision. She scanned the kitchen quickly, as if something had tapped her on the shoulder, and moved away so quickly she couldn't see what it was. The house felt cloying, confining, although she had no idea why, unless a direct result of the piles of dirty pots. "Did you have a monster party here just before I came?"

The response, "Monsters' party?" sounded just a bit strained coming from her aunt.

"You know, ten thousand people you had to feed?"

"Oh, the dishes…" Jan ended off on a sigh, as if she had just escaped a hangman's noose, a reprieve she had not expected.

"No, no, child. Nothing like that. Sometimes the dishes catch up with me." She laughed, as if it were a joke Brenda should understand. "I have to do dishes about once a year, whether I want to or not."

Brenda nodded, appearing to agree. "I know what you mean. I felt that way about my own apartment, when I ate there."

"It will take me a week or two to get a handle on this mess, but I should be able to make you chocolate chip cookies tomorrow. Do you still like chocolate chip cookies?"

Brenda was about to complain that she was an adult now, and watched, religiously, everything she put into her mouth, but at that moment, the thought of hot cookies, fresh from the oven seemed like just the pampering she needed.

Brenda waited until her aunt was shifting a heavy stack of dishes into the sink, before sneaking a peek at the basement door. The door to the dungeon, she corrected.

There came a time when every adult had to face—and eradicate—childhood fears. If she was sure of anything in her life it was this, there had been two huge, hulking creatures down there. She had no idea what they were. She had spent countless hours in libraries and searching the internet for representations of what her subconscious remembered. Brenda didn't want her aunt's permission to go down the stairs. She wouldn't get it, but mostly, she wanted to investigate when that would be the last thing Jan would suspect.

She would bide her time. The dishes would be done eventually and then her aunt would find things to do in another part of the Inn or even in town. The time would come.

The monsters would wait.

CHAPTER 5

"Aunt Jan, is Byron all right?"

"What do you mean?" Jan moved from the sink to the table, swiping the surface, ineffectively for with the dirty dishes piled, she didn't have access to a great deal of the tabletop.

Her aunt's response came too quickly to be causal. Brenda was a trained police officer, knew, instinctively what Jan was doing was not housekeeping so much as damage control. "I'm not sure. He offered me tea, then disappeared. He seems to be—"

"Seems to be what?"

"Hiding something."

Jan dropped the dish rag, reached out, wrapped her fingers warmly on Brenda's shoulder. Her touch was a step up from comforting, it was almost as if she could heal confusion with nothing more than compassion and warm fingers. "If he is, then it is something Lori already knows. She is very happy, Brenda."

Brenda shook her head, tried to remain objective as she slowly inched out from under her aunt's touch. "I can see that. I want her happy. For all we fought as children, I do wish the best for her." But she had enough experience on the street to know when something wasn't completely accurate. Byron had met her eyes as if sincere, but he had a cocky assurance that in Brenda's experience arose from ego, a type of 'you'll never guess what I'm hiding,' swagger.

"Byron is the best for her. Now I've got to run upstairs for a minute. I'll be back soon."

Brenda blinked, ineffectively tried to block a yawn. Exhaustion rippled through her, although her body was tired, Brenda knew she wouldn't sleep. Her mind was sluggish, but occasionally a thought poked through: Yeah, you invite no one to the wedding, and the second I get here, Byron whisks Lori off for a honeymoon. All this takes place in a location where I am certain there are monsters. Tell me there's nothing suspicious.

The kitchen felt different without Jan. She recognized the feeling, it wasn't emptiness, it was abandonment and it pricked her so sharply and clearly she wondered where the idea came from. There were times on patrol when she would enter an empty house, and it would be just that, an empty house. There were times when she entered a similar empty house and although there might still be furniture and knickknacks, the house itself would feel abandoned. There was no explaining it, except to think the kitchen wasn't at all pleased to have her here alone.

Brenda picked up a plate, the soil on it, some kind of pasta sauce if she didn't miss her guess, was fresh, although where it came from she had no idea. She had intended to throw it, express some frustration, but it had literally appeared from nowhere, and only added to her discomfort, so she set it back on top of a tottering pile. "If he hurts her—" she muttered to herself.

She would run his name through the system when she got back to work, see what she could turn up. Everyone left a trail. She would find out more about him.

Brenda stood, did a three-sixty around the room, looking at the high corniced ceiling, the slate floor, the cabinets and dirty pots and pans, and stopped when she faced the closed basement door. There would be a better time to investigate childhood nightmares. She needed a rest, eight hours if she were lucky, three to five if she wasn't. The stairs, and whatever secrets they held weren't going anywhere.

Still, curious about the depth of her own courage, Brenda put her hand on the doorknob.

"I've taken the liberty of drawing you a bath."

She jumped what felt like twelve feet in the air, came down to her feet in a karate ready position, not relaxing until she recognized her aunt. "Sorry. I didn't hear you come up on me."

"Obviously. Brenda, whatever ghosts you've come here to exorcise, whatever things are haunting you, save them for another day."

"I don't want—" Brenda started. She decided she would not share the invader with her aunt. At least not yet.

Jan chose to misunderstand Brenda's unfinished sentence. "I know you don't. You modern women, a shower is all you need, but indulge me this evening and soak for a while. Take all the time you require to fully relax. The water should stay hot."

Her muscles ached. A bath sounded heavenly, a luxury she never would allow herself at home, but she wasn't there.

"All right. Thank you. I know you mean well."

"I've left towels out. Brenda, I want you to be comfortable here."

She straightened from her half-bent position, massaging her aching back. "I don't see how that's possible."

"Go upstairs. Take your time. Find peace in this house."

"Peace, here?" Brenda scoffed. At the moment, there wasn't an inch of her that didn't ache, the deep soul ache, down to the bones. Her legs, her back, her shoulders, her elbows, her knees, all throbbed to the tempo of her headache. So exhausted, she doubted she could find the stairs, let alone climb them.

"Believe it or not, this is a good house for finding peace. And you are welcome here as a friend."

Brenda paused, her muscle aches forgotten. It was as if her aunt had read her mind. Hadn't just thirty minutes before, she wondered if she would be welcomed here as a friend, because she had her own agenda? She was too tired to follow through with an interrogation, but she would, in the morning, find answers.

Jan stopped her, put a comforting hand on her forearm. "I know what happened to you here when you were a child."

"You do?" The confession caught her off guard. "Maybe we could compare notes on it someday."

"I would like that. Brenda, no harm came to you."

"No harm? Perhaps we need to compare notes on that as well. I've been in therapy most of my life for something you say caused me no harm."

"Your mother doesn't understand."

"Neither do I. I suppose you do?"

"Yes. I would have explained it to you then, but you were too young, and you have to understand anything I said then might have made matters much worse. Your mother wouldn't let you return, so I really haven't had opportunity to explain."

Brenda pantomimed dialing. "There is such a thing as a telephone, you know."

"What I have to tell you is best told face to face."

Her spine straightened and she thrust out her chin. "How about now? If you have a confession about the monsters I saw, the monsters who actually bit me, I'm ready to hear it, right here, right now."

"I'll make a deal with you. Take your bath, try to get some sleep, and I will make myself available to you in the morning to answer all your questions."

"Fine. I suppose it would do neither of us any good to talk now. But answer me one question."

"Of course, if I can."

"Does Lori know what you are about to tell me?"

"Lori has her own concerns. Maybe she will share them with you one day. But no, what I have to tell you, she may suspect, but she doesn't know."

"Is Byron a monster?"

"That tea must have affected you far more than you said."

"Answer the question."

"Byron is good for Lori. He will make her happy all the days of her life. I would not have countenanced their union if I didn't believe that."

"If he is so good for her, why didn't you wait, allow the rest of the family to come to the wedding? Why wasn't there a reception and a notice in the papers? Mom got one quick phone call from an Au Sable public phone. Did Lori have to sneak out and call?"

"No. Brenda, until tomorrow?"

"If you insist. But before I leave, I will have my answers."

"Then enjoy your bath."

In the bathroom, Brenda slipped off her clothing, sitting on the edge of the tub to test the water temperature. A shade too hot, it was scented with herbs she didn't recognize, but which soothed. She knew the power of aromatherapy and she was grateful the scent cleared her mind. She wondered if it had been nearly boiling when Jan ran the bath, considering how long they had talked in the kitchen. She slowly sank into the water, breathing out, as she let the heat relax her. The dozen aches and pains vanished with her submersion, and she felt not lethargy, but calmness fill her body. Maybe Jan was right, maybe she did need to find peace. Brenda had no idea it would come so easily, from hot water and herbs.

She thought back to the Voice, wondering why she didn't find it strange he had followed her. She wouldn't think of him as her protector. She could protect herself, but she wasn't quite ready to think of him as a stalker either. With fingers starting to wrinkle, she rubbed her breasts. They felt sensitive and she thought again of her feeling that she needed a man in her life.

She scratched her ankle where an old scar itched, bending, to give the scar a closer inspection. It was where, as a child, she had been bitten by a monster...

***

...clutching her doll Abigail about the middle, eight-year-old Brenda looked both ways, then scurried sidewise into the kitchen, the fiddler crab walk of a child unaccustomed to secrecy. She was bored, wanted adventure. The fact it was pouring rain outside, visible through the few windows the house possessed, limited her options for exploration. Her aunt was always around. She ignored her, but was always watching, seeming to have eyes in the back of her head.

"Abigail, what do you say? Should we go downstairs?" She had been a child who had been raised in safety, with a mother and a father and an older sister, Lori. They owned a standard black and tan dachshund, a dog who was notoriously incontinent. She lived in a middle class housing subdivision filled with white picket fences and minivans with families almost identical both genetically and socially to hers. Because she had been raised gently, she was more susceptible to the lingering effects of urban legends and Halloween fables. She had an active imagination and the ability to visualize monsters in all shapes and sizes. Her exposure to ghost stories was limited to the occasional sleepover and stolen afternoons with her older cousins who had a penchant for scaring the life out of her.

Her aunt had forbidden her the basement steps. "It's too steep and dark. You could fall."

The risk only made them more enticing.

She had been in the house about two weeks, annoyed at the lack of television, and bored with the books she could find. There were plenty of those, but most had no pictures. Those which did have illustrations made her feel creepy. The text was impossible to follow, and when she got home and thought about it, she finally realized they were not novels, but non-fiction, and her failure at comprehension stemmed from that fact more than a difficulty of language. Even at eight, she had been a prodigious reader.

Because it was an adventure, she packed a lunch. No great explorer ever went traveling without sustenance, so she made a peanut butter and honey sandwich quickly in the kitchen, leaving crumbs and dripped evidence on the counter. She wrapped the sandwich in a linen napkin, the only thing she could find. In a hundred drawers and cabinets of the kitchen her aunt did not store anything as normal as sandwich bags. There were cookies set out, half a dozen moist, fat chocolate chip, but she gobbled those up while looking for the sandwich bags, so there were none remaining for her picnic.

"There's no need to be afraid, Abigail," she told the red-haired doll, which, with its blue eyes and round face resembled her 'mother' almost exactly.

Brenda opened the basement door and started down the stairs. Counting them, sixteen, seventeen, eighteen, to give herself something to do. She was also, for her age, a brilliant mathematician, a benefit from Lori who would come home from school and teach her math homework to her younger sister. Lori had wanted to be a teacher even then.

The trip down seemed endless. The stairs were firm, nothing rickety about them, for they were solid stone, as if carved from time itself. They were a bit depressed in the center, as if countless eons of travelers, going up and down, had smoothed the sharp edges.

It was dark. Brenda, holding Abigail and the sandwich in her left hand, held a flickering candle in her right. Any stray breeze, and the air did seem restless, and she would be lost in the stygian blackness. The air turned cooler as she went, and echoes bounced around her. Occasionally the noises sounded joyous, filled with life, occasionally menacing, as if repelling invaders took only indistinct whispers coming from all directions. Every dozen stairs corridors branched off guarded by doors which looked like they might be suspended in mid-air. The downstairs of her own house held no fear: only the washer and dryer, the hot water heater, her father's bench saw with boards part of more than a dozen half-finished projects. Her father tinkered. Even at eight, Brenda understood that meant an escape from his wife and two daughters, the women of the family. Also in her downstairs there were holiday decorations, boxes of other things that fit nowhere else, but which were good, on a rainy afternoon, for exploration. If there were spiders, they were the small, almost translucent kind, hiding in corners with their long legs spread out, and no bother to a child with worlds to conquer.

Thirty-four. Thirty-five. Thirty-six.

The candle flickered. There was light, and she whispered encouragement to Abigail, hurrying her steps. She would need her sandwich when she arrived. "It's cold down here, isn't it?"

The doll kept her silence, but her eyes looked wider, and her lips slightly parted. She no longer looked pleased, but looked just the tiniest bit startled.

Ninety-one. Ninety-two.

The sound of heavy chains rattling was the first distinct noise to reach Brenda, and it almost made her turn tail and run back up the endless staircase, but if nothing else, she was pragmatic, and it looked much easier to keep going down than to climb back up.

"Hello? Is anyone down here?"

There was no answer, although Brenda knew something was here. She heard high-pitched howls, coming from all directions, the sound of wolves—or werewolves. Looking into the expanse of the lower level, she missed her footing, and fell two or three steps to splat ignobly on a landing, a cold stone floor without seams. The howling increased in intensity and volume. Whatever it was had her scent now, and wanted her blood. She grew afraid and clutched Abigail tightly to her. The candle, now at her feet, had blown out. The remaining light was indistinct, she could see well enough to suspect spiders the size of army tanks in every dark corners, and chained dogs, with teeth bigger than dinner knives, waiting in the shadows to rip out her throat.

"Hello?" she tried again. She would have run up the stairs, but in her panic, somehow she had gotten turned around and could no longer see them.

It wasn't just howling any more. There was also the sharp, terrifying sound of jaws snapping and the ringing of chains, stretched to their full length.

In the faint light, she spotted the struggling creatures. She had the feeling the skin of these beasts was not normal people-colored. She thought their skin, for it was skin or something like it, not fur, was gray or perhaps green and maybe just a touch scaly.

Eight-year-old Brenda had no idea what they were, for there were two of them, but they were not dogs. They had long, broad, dog-like snouts, filled with snapping teeth, but their bodies stood on human legs, and they had human looking arms, although the hands were not hands at all, but claws of some kind. Most startling of all, both had a massive pair of wings growing out from their shoulder blades, coming to a clawed peak somewhere two or three feet higher than the beasts' heads.

They were chained three separate places, once at the neck, and by one wrist and one ankle. The chains ended in broad rings anchored to the stone wall. Whoever chained them really did not want them getting away.

Brenda was frightened, but she was also curious. She knew enough not to approach strange dogs, knew about the danger posed by wild animals, but she was a friendly child, and more, a lonely child. She would try diplomacy. She opened the linen napkin, tore off a piece of sandwich. She tossed her bribe to the first monster.

"My name is Brenda. Can you say Brenda?"

The monster sniffed, then gobbled the treat, making the second one snap and growl even harder. "I don't know if I have enough for both of you," she said, tearing off a piece for the second creature and tossing it in his direction.

That was a mistake, for the first then attacked the second, stealing the morsel for himself as well. They were male. Although their loins were covered with some kind of loose short pants, their chests were exposed, a broad muscled expanse in no way feminine. The fight was short but vicious. The second, bleeding from half a dozen bites, backed off, to lick its wounds while the first devoured the treat.

"That's not fair," Brenda said, a child who believed in fairness above all else. She broke off another piece, this one slightly larger than the first two she had shared. "You behave yourself," she said to the first, pointing her finger as sternly as she dared, with a dark stare, her bottom lip pouted, and her eyebrows lowered.

She tossed the treat to the second monster, as far from the first as she could manage. Fighting broke out, fresh and vicious, the second defending itself, and ignoring the treat the first could not reach but still coveted.

It was then Brenda recognized her own tactical mistake. She had crept closer to watch, when the first monster turned its attention from its companion, and ripped the doll from her arms. The monster bit deeply into its midsection, tossing it over its shoulder with a swift, abrupt swing of his head. A second later the second monster sunk its teeth deep into her ankle, and Brenda started screaming.

***

Brenda awoke, her heart tripping, her pulse loud in her ears. The bath water was still hot, almost uncomfortably so, so she couldn't have slept long. She rubbed the ankle again, with its puckered scar where four demon teeth had dug clear to her bone. She hadn't had the dream, vision, nightmare, that intensely in over a decade. It hadn't lost any of its punch.

From her vulnerable position in the tub, she checked on her clothing, where she had left it on the bathroom counter. She could see the weapon in its holster, could get to it if the need arose. When she approached the monsters this time, she wouldn't be armed with only a peanut butter and honey sandwich. She would have her automatic.

"As soon as that door is unguarded, I'm going down," she muttered. The dream this time was not a warning. It was impetuous, speaking of the necessity of getting down those stairs as quickly as possible. "I'm going," she promised herself, standing, dripping, in the water, and then stepping out onto the bathmat. "I'm going."

She dried off quickly, with a green towel which was soft and warm and very large. Her nipples had puckered, turned into hardened nubs. They felt sensitive as she rubbed the towel against them. Usually after exposure to hot water, they were soft, unformed. She rubbed her palms against them, liking the sensation. It would be better if a lover were performing the action, but there was no man in her life, and hadn't been, for the longest time. She turned, studying her naked body in the full-length mirror on the back of the bathroom door. Her breasts were high, firm, small. The tips looked pert, saucy. Sometimes during the bitter dregs of loneliness, after long, frustrating shifts facing the scum of the earth, she would return to the loneliness of her apartment where in the dark, she could imagine a different existence: a child nursing from her body, drawing nourishment from her breasts. She was a pragmatist and strongly suspected she would never marry, never give birth, no matter how often the impression she was meant to mother, to nurture, popped into her subconscious recently.

Her complexion was good, though she did nothing to it, not even make-up. Occasionally she wore sun-block, when the summer was in full attack mode and she didn't want to burn. Red-heads were notorious for burning, never tanning. It was the curse of the fair skin obtained from the Irish side of her genealogy. She didn't even freckle, at least not any more than she had. No, exposure to sun meant sunburn. The added time to slather SPF 35 was worth it, when she remembered.

She smiled, checked the change to her reflection in the mirror. She knew most of her fellow officers had never seen her smile. The occasional laugh at a joke, the shared comradery at a cop-bar after a long shift resulting in a good, clean bust, but beyond that, she rarely laughed. Not one for finding the good in people, she had been disappointed too many times.

Her waist was narrow, her legs long and shapely, deeply muscled. Her exercising over the years had paid off, resulting in a well-honed body which moved smoothly, and although it rarely granted her a solid night's sleep, on the whole it gave her no problems. She could eat what she wanted, never gain weight, not that she had developed the curse of all beat-cops: the donut-addiction. When she snacked, she ate cucumbers, raw carrots, raisins. "You eating rabbit food again, Larwick?" her partner would demand, over a jelly Bismarck.

"Only so I can eat lasagna with impunity," she would answer. When she ate real food, she could really pack it in.

***

The bath had drugged her with lethargy, a delightful, soggy, boneless feeling Brenda consciously hadn't let herself feel in years. She would have, she hoped, just enough strength to make it to the bedroom. Her eyes were only at half-mast and everything looked more than a little out of focus, fuzzy and indistinct. Shadows darted off to her left, but she couldn't get enough neurons to fire to comprehend what, if anything had moved. She had, when she opened the bathroom door, interrupted her aunt in conversation, but when she asked if she should apologize for the intrusion, Jan only patted her hand and said she was only talking to herself, the result of old age and living so long alone.

"Is there anything you need to help you sleep?" Jan asked, following

Brenda down the corridor, her arms piled with linen.

"I don't suppose you have a sleeping pill?" Brenda asked. She wouldn't take one, she didn't like ceding her ability to come instantly awake especially in strange circumstances, but she wondered at her aunt, her motives, and her hospitality.

"No, I don't have any drugs in the house. I was thinking more along the lines of cookies and warm milk."

Brenda ran her fingers down the robe she had found in the bathroom. She had thought she had brought her own, but her short, familiar robe was nowhere to be found when she stepped out of the tub, but this one was. It was floor length, high waisted, and with a long, pointed hood she didn't bother to put up over her damp hair. Forest green and softer than new moss, it made her feel elfin.

"I was eight years old the last time cookies and warm milk helped me sleep."

"That doesn't mean it won't work again."

"Then no." Brenda stood at the door to her room, hand on the knob.

"Brenda, I don't mean to be rude, but you look like you really need some rest."

Exhaustion rattled through her, her head was mushy with it, her bones throbbed with it. After the renewal of the monster nightmare, no matter how lethargic she felt now, it was highly unlikely she'd find sleep tonight.

"This is a good house for dreams," Jan continued.

She opened the door to the bedroom, stood just inside. A fireplace dominated the far wall of the expansive room, a massive thing, that through some wisp of fantasy, she suspected to be a portal into another world. The logs lay expectant, but the fire was not lit. Brenda could see clearly, as if she were watching a movie, stately godlike people walking through chest high blazes, without getting burned, people who disappeared and landed, presumably, at the location of their choice.

"Something the matter?" Jan asked, when she saw her niece mesmerized by the fireplace.

Brenda shook herself, clearing her mind. "No. I'm sure I'll be fine here."

Although it was full dark outside, the room glowed, cheerfully bright. On the end tables, on the mantle, on the desk, cream-colored candles burned, fat pillar affairs, with upright, well behaved flames providing the only light. The room smelled deeply, sensually of vanilla. The puffy comforter on the bed was pulled back, revealing sheets which had a satin-like gloss, again in the same yellowed, off-white that matched the candles.

"There are plenty of blankets on the bed. You'll be warm enough."

Brenda ached with the desire to pull the heavy covers up over her ears and nestle in the cold room. Maybe that, by itself was part of her insomnia problem. Her bedroom at home was not yet weather sealed and was always too hot or too cold. Her blankets never seemed to hit the right note, either too much or too scratchy or too noisome.

"I don't dream," she replied in a surly manner. No, her nightmares could not be called anything as gentle as 'dreams.'

"You should. It is good for the soul."

"I don't actually believe in souls," she snapped back. She rubbed her eyes, massaged the back of her neck where the tension had re-knotted. "I'm sorry. I don't mean to snap. I really do need a good night's sleep."

"Several good nights' sleep," Jan said with insight. She stood on her toes, spontaneously kissing Brenda on the top of her head.

Brenda shut the door behind her. The room was large, and by any definition, luxurious. A nook, to the left of the fireplace, was created by a window seat at a bowed bay window, the darkness outside hiding anything but Brenda's own startled reflection. Candles were clustered on a tray there and Brenda doubted she had the strength in her arms to shift them, should she decide to read. No, she was too tired for anything but the high, four-poster cherry-wood bed. The bed was huge, far larger, she suspected, than a standard king size. Brenda removed the gun from the pile of clothing she was carrying in her hands, removed it from the holster, checked the chamber and the safety, before she thrust it under her pillow. She sat on the edge of the mattress. It was firm, the covering soft. Silently she hoped she could sleep. She stripped off her bathrobe, then put on a new layer of clothing, covering her body as completely as if she had not bothered to undress at all. Sweat pants and a sweatshirt in addition to clean undergarments. Only bare feet indicated she wasn't about to go out running. Restless, she checked the closet, under the bed, behind the dresser, finding nothing out of the ordinary, not even a trace of dust. The floor was a dark hardwood, polished to a high gloss and looked like something stolen from the wisps of antiquity, some Arthurian boudoir or Rapunzel-like tower room. She wished she had been wise, brought a book, something gripping, to take her mind off her problems, but when she had been packing, filling hours of loneliness had not been a priority. She would ask her aunt in the morning for a trashy novel, or see if there was internet so she could download something from her favorite publisher. She needed to escape into someone else's problems for a while.

Brenda pulled back the covers, then slipped between the smooth, inviting sheets. She was breathing deeply, evenly two minutes later.

She awoke abruptly from, reaching instinctively for her weapon. Her palm wrapped around the grip, her index finger straight along the barrel, away from the trigger as she had been taught. "Who's here?"

No one answered, but she knew she wasn't alone. The window was open, the curtains billowing in the invasive breeze. She had been certain it had been latched securely the night before. Underneath the covers she was warm enough to have hibernated through the winter, but as she popped her shoulders and arms out from under the blankets, she felt chilled, but more so felt vulnerable, a feeling she hated.

Checking her watch, found it hours later than she suspected. After nine, when she was used to waking up a dozen times a night, at two o'clock, two-thirty, three, three-thirty, four.

"I really should work graveyards," she often thought, although she generally didn't sleep any better during the day. The hairs on the back of her neck tingled, and her grasp on the weapon tightened as she turned her head and her breath caught in her throat. She was alone in the room, but not alone. There, on the pillow beside her, lay Abigail, the doll she had not seen since she was bitten by a monster.

CHAPTER 6

Brenda left the doll upstairs in her suitcase, wrapped in a brown paper bag. She wondered what a good forensic workup would show, if, using modern technology, a technician could find trace amounts of DNA from the creature which had bitten it. If she didn't find answers any other way, it was definitely an avenue she was going to pursue. Although, if the monsters in the basement were werewolves, it was unlikely the Albany Police Department crime lab would have representative samples of their DNA on file. Still, there might be something she could use, some information to help erase her nightmares.

Before she put it away, Brenda had carefully inspected Abigail. The doll's cloth body had been painstakingly sewn closed, the wounds nearly invisible, sealed with a thread that matched exactly. Someone had taken care with her. After all these years, Abigail was not moldy, stained, dusty or deformed from having spent the intervening years locked into a small box, closet, or the corner of a damp and frightening basement. She was in such good condition, Brenda doubted the best police lab would find anything. Using only her naked eyes, Brenda noticed nothing that would help identify her 'kidnappers'. Still, there might be saliva at the point of stitches and trace amounts of all kinds of things from mold to blood.

Also, she considered how the doll had gotten into her room. She was on the fourth floor. The bedroom door was still locked. Yes, the window had been open, but there was no trellis, no convenient tree for climbing. A ladder would have made noise, and if someone had rappelled down from the roof simply to return her doll, the effort seemed a little extreme. After all, he could have left the doll in the corridor and she would have found it just as easily.

It was funny how she assumed the person—or thing—who had returned her doll to be male. And, even considering he had gotten into her room without her permission, there was no sense of personal invasion. Brenda would not charge him with breaking and entering. A good hour or two in an interrogation room would be nice, while she asked questions about werewolves and other mythical creatures chained in basements, but for now, oddly, she was charmed to have Abigail returned. Brenda had hugged the doll tightly when she discovered her, as if she, Brenda, had abandoned her to the monsters by seeing to her own safety.

Funny too, no matter how old the woman, how tough, how well trained, there always remained a little girl inside who cheered at the sight of a soft, red-headed baby doll.

Brenda dressed quickly, braiding her red hair into a single thick strand down her back. Once she had her hair cut very short, donated her hair to Locks for Love, a group providing wigs for cancer survivors, and her hair was long enough now, and enough of a bother, she was considering doing the same thing again.

She was a cop. She didn't have time for fidgeting with hair. She refused to admit vanity was the reason she kept it long. That, and the fact her ears were traditionally cold when she slept, and she liked to keep them covered with her blanketing hair.

The trip down the stairs surprised her. She must have been daydreaming, for it seems she was barely out her bedroom door when she reached the kitchen. She had somehow overlooked the three other floors. "I'm going to have to start paying attention," Brenda said, speaking to herself, but her aunt looked up.

"Oh, you're awake," Jan said, running past her. Jan wore a light jacket, and was sporting a rather heavy looking tote bag on her left shoulder.

"Is there a problem?" No progress had been made on the dishes and Jan looked more than a little frazzled.

"There's been an—" attack or accident, Brenda did not know, for Jan was unable or unwilling to finish the thought.

"Is there anything I can do to help?" she asked.

Jan gave a long glance toward the back door, then huffed in exasperation, a 'I-haven't-got-time-for-this' look which clearly indicated she would have to make time. She spoke sharply, each word distinct, staccato, as if with proper enunciation and rhythm she wouldn't have to repeat anything. "I have to go out for a few hours. Your breakfast is on the stove. There are books in the red living room, the second door to your right, as you come in from the front door. If you get bored, you can go into town, do some exploring. The tourist season is about over, well, that's not true, exactly. The winter tourist season is over, and the summer hasn't yet gotten into full swing, so you should find the shops quiet. There are even churches, one on almost every corner, if you would like attend a service."

Ahh, that's right. Today was Sunday.

Brenda shrugged, feigned a cheerful nonchalance. "I think I'll call my parents."

"There's not a phone on the property, nor a computer either, if you wanted to email them, and, I'm sorry to say if you have a cell phone, it's unlikely you'll get reception here. If you want to call, you would do better to go into town."

"I think I will," Brenda said pleasantly. "I would love a quiet day in a tourist town."

Jan tightened her eyes, as if weighing the statement, then breathed a sigh of relief as she decided to take it at face value. "There's anything you could want—ten thousand shops, and more than a dozen restaurants in the area. Or you could take the tram up White Face, the local ski resort. It makes a nice day trip. The view is well worth the effort."

"Maybe I'll stay here, work on trying to make some headway on this mess in the kitchen."

"No, there's no need of that," Jan said quickly, as she opened the backdoor, those words slurring into each other. "You relax. After all, this is the first day of your vacation. I will get to it when I get back. I have a system." With that, she slipped out the door, shutting it tightly behind her.

"Yeah!" Brenda said, peering out the back window to be certain her aunt would not come back, grabbing something she had forgotten. She was distracted for a moment by the black cat rubbing against her, and when she was able to look out the window again, she could see no sight of her aunt in any direction.

It seemed unlikely her aunt had to respond to an emergency by going out the back door when the only things there were a small, well-tended yard that ended in a hardwood forest, with steep mountains sprouting almost at the steps. But she wasn't one to look a gift horse in the mouth.

Brenda returned to the kitchen, where the scent of her breakfast reminded her how hungry she was. She ate the casserole, having no idea what it was, some baked affair consisting of eggs, cheese, huge chunks of delicious sausage, and something else she didn't recognize, bread, perhaps? She would need fortification for her foray down stairs.

After she finished, she ran up to her bedroom and retrieved her flashlight. She would be more prepared this time and wouldn't have to rely on a sputtering candle. This one was sturdy, reliable, and could be used as a weapon if the need arose.

Brenda opened the downstairs door, pleasantly surprised to find it unlocked. She had been expecting to have to find some way to force or pick the deadbolt. The black cat slipped around her feet, but Brenda picked it up, petted it fiercely for a moment, then set it gently back down on the floor. "You can't stop me, you know. I have to do this." The reassurance was as much for herself as for the cat. On a whim, she wondered if she should go back for Abigail.

She flipped the flashlight on. The beam was strong, wide. It was the only light as she faced the opening to the basement, for she couldn't find a light switch, and as she reached her hand around the inside wall, she felt nothing. In the beam of the flashlight, the stairs were just as she remembered them, about thirty-six inches wide, and about nine or ten inches deep, the next step down was always a little bit further than she suspected it would be, as if the architect and the builder had conspired to create this annoyance, making each step slightly further away than the one before it. The steps themselves were made of worn stone: marble, perhaps or a smooth granite, as if the staircase had been carted intact from some German castle built centuries before. Breathing deeply, Brenda discovered the air smelled musty, which she had expected, but with an underlying trace of something sharp, bleach, perhaps, or cleanser, which she did not.

What Brenda found the most disconcerting was the lack of walls. She was down ten or twelve steps when she noticed, and she cursed mildly wondering how she could have forgotten that detail. Certainly as a child she would have realized how difficult it was, going down a long staircase without a handrail or the perceived security of walls. The stairs went down, endlessly down, as Brenda recalled, but she had no idea what supported them, although there was no doubt they were sturdy. If claustrophobia was the fear of closed spaces, then what was the sudden, unreasonable fear of huge open spaces? It could not be vertigo, for she had no fear of heights. She flashed the light around her, first annoyed and then concerned when she could not detect the bottom, for the light only shone on, nothing in any direction limiting it. Suddenly Brenda realized how massive the cavern was. She had no idea how the house above her was supported, when this cavern apparently went on for miles.

She called out, a broad encompassing "hello!" deciding if the things were still chained, announcing her presence would make no difference. The greeting was swallowed up by the immensity of the cavern, as if it found no walls to echo against. Moving faster down the stairs, passing a landing, but not bothering to stop as she continued her trek downward, she directed her flashlight, first to one side of the staircase then the other, but the floor remained too far below for her to detect.

"Hello!" Feeling childish and immature, she wished she had prepared better, had brought her partner and a SWAT team. Barring that, she'd even be satisfied with Abigail and a peanut butter sandwich. It was best to do investigating with both companions and provisions. Still, she had her gun, her courage and an overriding necessity to find answers which had eluded her for years.

She stepped onto the next landing a moment later, perhaps the second or the third one she had reached. It was a ten by ten foot swatch of stone, which had, inexplicably, a closed door freestanding in a frame to her left. Brenda reached out, decided no matter what was on the other side, she didn't want to know, and started humming the Twilight Zone theme, as she took the stairs a little more quickly than before. She wasn't shocked when she saw another portal at the next landing, standing without support, leading, apparently, nowhere, for there was nothing behind it, but what appeared to be open abyss. She remembered the doors from when she had come this way as a child. Even then, holding a flickering candle, and willing to accept ten impossible things before breakfast, the doors which led to only a long drop-off and certain death had bothered her.

The air grew cooler, consistent with this being a cave. Of course it was a cave. With a free-standing natural staircase that went on forever. That made tons of sense.

She had dressed warmly, comfortably, a hooded gray sweatshirt covering a pull-over, jeans, white at the knees and other stress points and high top sneakers, offering both traction and support. She was ready for anything.

Brenda passed two more landings. She switched the flashlight to her left hand, kept her right free so she could draw gun should she need it. She should have come with a back-up plan, something, in case the flashlight was taken from her, in case the gun didn't work against whatever was down here. She knew enough about fantasy, about science fiction to know bullets didn't kill the really bad stuff.

The smell of bleach intensified, stung her eyes, the back of her throat. She had no idea how long she had been walking. She passed another two landings, another two free-standing doors. She could spend the rest of her life exploring this, except there might be another option: considering the number of people who played tourist at natural caverns, Jan could make a fortune with this cave, if she could find some way to put in an elevator and deal with the terrors Brenda expected to find at the bottom.

Curious, Brenda flipped off the flashlight, keeping her finger on the switch. The darkness was invasive, intense, and far darker than anything midnight had to offer, for around her, above her, it was unbroken. Not even a trace of light from the kitchen made its way down this deep into the bowels of the earth. Curiously, she detected an indistinct glow below her, too far away to make out any details. She turned the flashlight back on, and continued her descent, wishing for a handrail, hoping when she made her exit from this entrance to what might be hell, she wasn't being chased. It would be hard to climb up, at speed, with no walls, no handrail or cover.

A thought intruded into her consciousness. She had no idea how she had gotten back up the stairs as an eight-year-old child. She could not have climbed them, for she had been bitten, and in extreme pain. Her aunt couldn't have carried her, for she was big as a child, heavy boned, although not fat. It was a long journey up, without walls or handrails, made more difficult by holding an unconscious child. She had no idea why she would have been unconscious. When she woke, she was in her bed, her ankle wrapped in clean bandage, the pain only a memory. Whatever analgesic her aunt had used had been effective. She had no pain from the wound after waking up, none, ever. It occasionally itched, even now, after working a double shift, or when she was about to walk into a dangerous situation, but it had never hurt again.

It was the memory that hurt, the impression it should hurt, more than actual discomfort. She wished she could stop, rub her ankle. She wished whatever crisis her aunt had to deal with had been later in the week, so she could have put this off for a few more days. She wished she were a coward, so she could run back upstairs to the black cat, her doll, and the books her aunt left out for her. She would get in her car, take the tour up White Face, stop at a pizza parlor, eat fudge and soft pretzels with mustard. She would take a nap. Therapy, as a solution to her problems was appearing to be a more viable option.

However, the light was getting brighter, and her need to know won out.

"Hello?" she called, again expecting, but not getting an echo. "I'm a friend." She wanted to add: "I come in peace," like some astronaut making first contact, except she decided she would not lie, at least not any more than she already had with the 'friend' statement. She swung the tight beam of the flashlight around her, still finding no sign of walls. The cavern must be immense, as big around as the Astrodome, or a black hole, something Steven Hawkins or Stephen King would understand.

No one, and thankfully, nothing, answered her, not even the rattling of chains, which she both feared and half-expected. She reached the final landing, for here the floor went on in all directions. There were also four doors, three grouped closely together, like a Lady-or-the-tiger option, another off by itself. As a child, she had not gone through any doors. This Brenda remembered with certainty.

So, she would avoid those, but that did little to narrow her options. She tried calling out again. Oddly, she started thinking of the monsters possessively: they were her monsters. It would annoy her more than a little if they were not here.

They were not.

She gasped, startled, as she found the heavy iron forged link chains, each twenty-to-thirty feet long, bolted securely to two free-standing walls which met at a ninety-degree angle. She stepped forward, bent, picked up one end, discovering it ended in a link, not on the broad wide band the monsters had worn at neck and wrist and ankle.

The chain was heavy, rattled when lifted. The weight hadn't prevented the monsters from battling each other, hadn't kept their necks' bent, for example. She remembered the sound as the chain scraped against the stone, and it raised goose bumps on her arms. She'd heard that sound in her dreams over a hundred times, the latest only yesterday. In addition to being heavy, the chain was cold, as if it stole heat from her body. She tried to recall the creatures. They had a heavy ruff of fur at the neck, insulation from the cold, but their wrists and ankles must have been blistered, worn bloody from the wide bands.

"It was real." Now that she faced the evidence, Brenda found herself surprised at her doubt she would find proof the monsters had been real.

"I knew you couldn't keep away."

Brenda jumped, startled, turned, holding the flashlight two-handed, and faced her aunt. "You just scared me out of ten years growth."

Her aunt couldn't have come down the stairs behind her, for there were no hiding places, since there were no walls. Brenda's footsteps, on the stone, although not loud, were audible. She was certain she would have heard someone following her.

"I knew you would be drawn here," Jan said, this statement significantly different from the one which preceded it.

"Then you're not disappointed, are you?" In the wan light surrounding them, and in the sharp white light from the flashlight, Jan looked pale, ghostly.

"I told you I would explain, and you couldn't wait."

"Did your crisis get taken care of?" Brenda added an inflection to her voice, indicative that she questioned whether Jan had engineered the circumstances to make it seem to Brenda it was safe to come down. A false crisis offering her free rein to explore.

"No, it didn't. I had to drop everything and run down here, before something even worse happened."

Brenda kicked the chain, listening to the rattle as the metal resettled, then walked away, further into the shadows, because although there was no discernible source of the light, it was centered around the two sets of chains. Everywhere else, even the four doors, was in comparative darkness, even downright blackness.

"What is this place?"

Jan looked around, her pupils dilated, from the dim light, or from an increasing fear, Brenda had no idea. "I would rather not talk here. Although I let the creatures go, other things hunt down here, especially since these chains are empty and there is nothing to stop them."

"Are we in danger?" Brenda scoffed. The only danger she could see came from her aunt's secrets. Keeping things chained in a basement couldn't be a healthy hobby to maintain.

"Danger, where we are, is a relative term."

The cat, tail high, wove around between Jan's feet and Brenda's. "Your protector is here," Brenda said, "certainly we'll be in no danger now."

"Don't mock what you don't understand," Jan said. She grasped Brenda's wrist firmly. "We're leaving, now."

"And will I get the answers I need, when I go upstairs?"

"Yes. As I told you last night, it was never my intention to keep the truth from you. I'll put on a pot of tea. You can ask all the dirty little questions you want, and I'll answer them."

"I think I'll skip the tea, if you don't mind," Brenda said, pulling away to regain her freedom, "but I will get my answers. Although I think one or two before we go might show good faith. What were those things?" Brenda inclined her head and focusing the flashlight beam on the abandoned chains.

"Are," Jan corrected. "They are still alive. Up you go."

Brenda heard something behind her, an indistinct high pitched screech, and immediately the sound seemed to be answered in any number of directions. The cat turned-tail, started for the stairs, walked back, impatient, and moved again toward the stairs. Follow me. The feline couldn't have communicated any clearer if she spoke in unaccented English.

"We're leaving," Jan said, reaching out, grabbing Brenda by the forearm, this time with a force which brooked no refusal.

"All right. I'm coming. I've seen what I needed to see."

"I'm sure you have." Jan's response was mocking. She thrust Brenda ahead of her. The back cat was barely visible on the landing above. The urgency she felt was increasing; Brenda took the stairs two at a time.

"What are we running from?" she asked, when she reached the third landing. She stopped, panting. She was used to running, used to heavy exertions, but there had to be more here than stairs, more than fear.

"Don't stop. You can catch your breath when we get to the kitchen. Remember, if you're ever in trouble, the kitchen is usually safest. It's important you know that. No matter what is happening elsewhere in the house, not many things can manage to reach the kitchen."

"That's certainly reassuring," Brenda responded, hoping to match her aunt's disdain. "I suppose if they come to call, we could offer them tea."

Indistinct sounds of pursuit followed them, as if claws on stone, and a high pitched squealing, and a third sound: thumping as if from a hundred bats' wings.

When they reached the kitchen, Jan pushed Brenda hard enough she fell forward onto her hands and knees, against the slate floor, then slammed the door behind them. Before Brenda could complain about the rough treatment, before she could even reach her feet and snarl, something thumped against the closed door, one, two, three times, loud bangs which reverberated around them.

"What?" Brenda regained her feet, but stood bent, trying to catch her breath. They had been running and the distance had been long. She had the feeling she had just escaped something narrowly, but there had been nothing behind her, nothing which could have crashed loudly into the kitchen door.

"Sit," Jan ordered. "You might not need or want tea, but I do." She poured water into a heavy blue kettle, put it on the stove, then brought out a dark loaf of something which looked like date nut bread or pumpkin loaf. She sliced it, then, after shifting the heavy piles of dirty dishes on the kitchen table into even taller stacks, managed to clear enough space for two plates and tea cups. Regardless of the fact Brenda had said she didn't want tea, she was going to be provided with some.

"The monsters—" Brenda said, when her breath caught. She reached back, touched her weapon, for reassurance more than anything, but didn't pull it, had not had it in her hands as she raced up the stairs. "Was that the monsters?"

"To answer the question you think you're asking, no. Those things on the stairs behind us were not the creatures you saw as a child, the ones who were chained in the basement." Her breathing too was uneven and she stopped to pull in several deep breaths. "Brenda, know this, there are worse things than those monsters, far worse. You have no idea."

She thought of drug dealers, murderers who killed without remorse and slimy creatures who preyed on children to satisfy their sexual perversions. "I've been exposed to a lot of bad things. I can handle anything you tell me."

Jan's hands, as she added loose tea leaves to the teapot, shook. "I don't think you've been exposed to anything quite like this."

Brenda leaned forward in her chair, setting her chin and her resolve as she faced her aunt. "I suppose that thumping was my imagination too?"

"Regardless of what you remember, I never said your experience down those stairs was the sole providence of an overactive imagination." Jan rubbed her palms over her eyes, as if pushing back her hair or her bad memories. "You were a curious child. Curiosity is generally considered—"

"You're going to tell me curiosity killed the cat?" Brenda asked. She sneered, aware the black cat now lay blocking the basement door, busily involved with cleaning her front paws, her whiskers, and her ears.

"Nothing of the sort," Jan huffed, straightening her back. Her hands were steady as she set a crock of butter beside the quick bread and her color, which had paled as things unknown thumped against the door, had returned to normal. "Curiosity is an asset. The ability to question, to seek answers yourself requires intelligence, courage, understanding of consequences, and an awareness of how patterns merge, separate, and reemerge. You had no idea what those things were, but Brenda, you were not afraid of them until Longfellow bit you."

"Longfellow? Those things have names?"

"Of course. They are extremely valuable to me and were treated extremely well."

"So well that you kept them chained, neck, wrist and ankle."

"For their own protection."

"I'm sure they'd agree." Her words dripped sarcasm.

Brenda leaned back in her heavy oak chair. She'd been watching the basement door with her senses sharp, as if she would need to draw her weapon at any moment. There seemed no need for such diligence with the cat working her scratchy tongue on the long fur at her tail and Jan pouring tea as if this were any other morning and in a moment they would discuss distant relatives they had in common or books they had enjoyed.

Jan poured the tea, a fragrant brew that filled the kitchen with the allure of apples and cinnamon and nutmeg, which soothed before either of them managed a single sip. She set the teapot down, and sat heavily at the head of the table. She looked around the piles of pots and dishes and cups, then exhaustion which hadn't been present in her face the second before appeared, and she leaned back in her chair, her eyes shut. "I forgot the milk."

"I'll get it." Brenda rose to her feet. Adrenaline still coiled within her, keeping her muscles limber and her heart rate elevated and she was anxious and eager to do something physical. She would rather pound something into submission, or barring that, jog, but first she would question and cross-examine until she finished this interrogation with her aunt as a hostile witness. Good cop, bad cop. She could play both roles simultaneously.

"There, on the counter."

To say dishes were piled to the ceiling would be no exaggeration. Dirty dishes filled every nook and cranny of the kitchen and it was a huge room. She searched, until she found the cream, her left hand holding a pile of dishes which looked about ready to topple, her right on the pot.

She felt the claws dig into the flesh of her neck before she knew there was an invader in the house. A beast, she knew from scent, from size, from the shivers running up and down her spine where her body touched his. Not a man with rape or murder on his mind, a monster, from the depths of her nightmare.

"Put the HOLD spell on me, and the maid dies," the voice in her ear said. Paralyzed with fear, feeling the sharpness of the weapon at her throat, she didn't dare move.

"I can immobilize you." Jan's voice.

"If you do," her attacker said, "you won't free the girl, and my grasp will tighten as I slip into paralysis. Do you want that?"

"You'll never get away with whatever it is you want."

"I will. I only wish you to listen to me."

"Not while you hold her prisoner."

"Would you listen else? If I had come to you with my knowledge, would you have offered me tea? Would you have taken the time to analyze what I have to say? Or would I find myself regaining consciousness chained by my throat in the basement dungeon?"

"If you harm her, there is nowhere in the seventeen kingdoms or all the known worlds you can hide. I am not defenseless."

"At the moment you are."

"What do you want?"

"There is something I must show you. Something vital you must know, and I cannot do so if I am chained below the stairs."

"And the girl?"

"The maid will be safe, you have my word, if I have yours that no harm will come to me while I relay my message. If you swear, I will release her, and rid you of my presence as soon as my task is completed."

"Is there danger?"

"Grave danger, but not from me or my kind."

"The dragon—"

"Call him. He should know what has happened. It is against him the outrage has been perpetrated. I would have gone to him directly, but I cannot locate him. He is not on this world."

Brenda trembled. She had been in hostage situations several times before, all in training, but never as the victim. She could feel the sharp weapon at her throat, knew, although her skin was not punctured yet, it would take very little effort on his part to kill her.

She must have made some movement, some stiffening of her spine, for Jan spoke to her. "He will not hurt you, Brenda. He has never hurt a mortal." Perhaps the statement was as much for her assailant as for her.

Jan continued, this time speaking to the criminal. "The dragon will hunt you—"

"He has his own problems. Call him. He must know of this."

"He will, rest assured. Still, I will see what you have to say before I call."

"As you wish. Now, I need your word before I release the maiden."

"You have my word I will not cause you physical harm while you explain what you have come to say."

"Not good enough," the voice at Brenda's ear growled, low and feral. He shifted, and although she still couldn't see him, Brenda got the impression of height, at least six five and raw, brute strength. The weapon at her neck was held steady.

"I will not put the HOLD spell on you, nor attempt to recapture you for a period of twenty-four hours. Will that do?"

"It will. And the maid?"

"The maid," Brenda spat, despising the word, "will rip your miserable throat out the moment you let me go."

"I think perhaps that will not be in your best interest, my lady. You would be wise to grant me clemency for the same period your aunt has."

"And free a monster to rape and pillage? Not in this lifetime."

"I would not have come if it were not vital you have this information. I could easily ignore it and you, for I feel I owe this House no loyalty. I am willing to leave now, take my chances with the maid's ire, and keep my secret to myself. It might take you days or even weeks to discover what I have found. Then, it might be too late. And you will have to answer to the dragon. It will be no skin off my back."

"Brenda, I cannot believe he would risk coming if he did not have vital intelligence we could not get any other way."

"Aunt Jan, can't you see what he is? He is a monster. Do not negotiate with him."

"Yes, Aunt Jan," the creature agreed. "I am a monster. That I do not deny. Perhaps I will rip her throat out in repayment for centuries of languishing as your slave, chained in your dungeon."

"I have your promise no harm will become her."

"And I have your promise you will not harm me. All I require is the same from the maid."

"Brenda, do what he says. There will be time enough to hunt him down later."

"Never. I will not negotiate in a hostage situation, even if I am the hostage."

"Then we have a standoff. You will excuse me, if I take the maid with me, as insurance?"

"Brenda, give me your vow you will not harm him, and not use the HOLD spell against him." "I promise," she spat, not like she had a clue what the HOLD spell entailed.

He released her, and Brenda rubbed her throat, swallowing, for she had been afraid to swallow while the weapon had been pressed against the vulnerable skin of her neck.

Nothing casual about it, she reached behind her, pulled out her weapon, her finger on the trigger. She pivoted quickly, raised her gun, and took aim. "Put your hands in the air!" she ordered.

She gasped. For the creature she pointed her gun at was most definitely a monster.

CHAPTER 7

While Brenda had labeled him a monster, she had not meant literally. She had meant in the criminal, should be behind bars for the rest of his life sense, but she turned, and what she faced was something stolen from her worst nightmares. He towered above her, and while his torso, arms, and legs, were well muscled and human-like, there was nothing else human about him. His head had a long broad snout which ended with two wide nostrils, and was rimmed with wicked looking teeth. From under a thick brow, his wide-spaced eyes were black, beady and pupil-less. They stared at her without fear, instead with an amused tolerance. She gripped her weapon tighter. His long hair cascaded to his shoulders, and he had a mane or oddly shaped beard around his neck where he sported a broad metal collar. Similar restraints bracketed his left wrist and ankle. All three sported broken off, dangling chains. Except for what was on his head and neck, as far as Brenda could tell he was otherwise hairless. His skin looked thick with an overcast pallor between green and yellow. To add to the grotesqueness of the monster-image, he had broad wings rising from his shoulder blades that reached more than two feet higher than his pointed ears, and hung nearly to the backs of his knees. There were sharp talons at his fingertips, clearly the weapon he had used against her.

"I know you!" she said, gritting her teeth. Her breathing was erratic, but her hands on the weapon were rock steady.

"And I know you," he responded with a clipped bow, "but now is not the time for formal introductions. You must go upstairs to the dragon's lair. Immediately."

"Why?" Jan asked.

"Something has happened you must know."

"Is this a trap?" Jan shifted, trying to put herself between Brenda and the monster. Brenda prevented her with a sharp look, and an abrupt movement of her service weapon.

The monster ignored the gun, concentrated his attention on the innkeeper. "No trap, on my word."

"Will we see you there?"

"Yes. I will enter a different way, as those stairs are no friend of mine."

"Will we be able to pass?" Jan questioned.

"That depends on your control of the forces within this house. I have put no spell on them, nor would I if I could. My only interest is in getting as far from this place as I can, for I have been chained here too long. But I cannot leave in good conscience without showing you my discovery."

"Then we will meet you in the lair."

Jan pushed Brenda toward the stairs. "We must find out what he knows." Leaving the kitchen, they reached the landing, with the door leading outside, the stairs going up. Jan stopped beside a baking powder box, where the black cat slept peacefully. "Genevieve," she said, gently waking the animal. "Genevieve, I need you to find Byron and tell him to return immediately."

"Aunt Jan, what are you doing?"

"I know I said I wanted to see what awaited us upstairs before I informed the dragon, but I've changed my mind. There is no sense going into a particularly dangerous situation without backup."

"As a police officer, I agree," Brenda said. "Shouldn't we be dialing 911?"

"There is nothing mortal law enforcers could do to help us, and would you like to be the one to explain to them what you just witnessed?"

"A man in a Halloween costume," Brenda scoffed.

"Come now, you are far more intuitive than that."

"I am a trained observer. I know what I saw. I will not be stopped from reporting a crime because it sounds ridiculous."

"Trust me, the police cannot help us. But if Genevieve finds Byron, I suspect he can."

They reached the second floor landing before Brenda paused. "Aunt Jan, do you know what that monster is?"

Jan looked like she would rather not take the time to discuss it, but eyeing Brenda's gun, and the determination she saw in her niece's features, she stopped, leaned against the wall, apparently trying to determine how much information to impart. "Yes. His species is gargoyle, and he was chained in the basement of this house for centuries. That much is true." Jan continued as she climbed the stairs. "There was a major problem here a few weeks ago, and in order to save him and the other like him, I released them. I have been unable to recapture him."

"Why in heaven's name didn't you kill him? Can't you see what he is?"

"Gargoyles are more valuable than you can imagine. I couldn't risk having him hurt."

"I don't understand."

"Actually, it's vitally important you do understand. I don't know whether or not bullets can hurt him, but I don't want him injured or killed."

Brenda followed her aunt up another flight of stairs before she spoke again. "This makes no sense."

"Gargoyles have a specific power. With their magic, they keep this house free from evil influences."

"Don't you think he's evil influence enough?"

"There is no evil in him. Brenda, listen to me. He is evil looking, but not evil."

"Then why was he chained?"

"A good question. I suppose the answer is because that was how it was always done. They were chained when I took control of the house. I kept the status quo."

They had climbed three or four flights of stairs already. The climb did not making her breathless, but the thought of what she would face when she reached her destination. "How much further?"

"There is no telling," Jan answered.

"What do you mean?"

"I would rather not give you all of this house's secrets, but this staircase can lengthen or shorten distances for reasons I have never been able to fathom. And Brenda, I am not making this up. The gargoyle alluded to it when he said he couldn't pass these stairs and really, when I think of it, the only one who has never had any problems with these stairs is Byron. Their magic either doesn't affect him or his magic is stronger, I'm not sure which, but even I, who have dominion over this entire house cannot always pass."

***

Flying felt incredible. It was the grandest of pleasures, one which had been denied him for centuries. Still, his wings flapped effortlessly. He had not forgotten how to catch an updraft, how to struggle against a headwind, how to gain the altitude he needed to avoid being seen. Still, even in the ecstasy, he cursed himself.

"Fool. Idiot. Maniac. You finally get free and what do you do? Walk boldly into the kitchen, the bastion of her strength. You idiot."

He banked, pulling his wings in, dropping lower as he spotted the entrance to the cave, visible as a blacker void against the darkness of the mountains.

"You could still turn around, flee. There are seventeen kingdoms where you would be welcomed, and uncounted, endless worlds where a gargoyle could find refuge and wouldn't have to be chained to a wall."

Talking to himself had become second nature. Secured neck, wrist and ankle hadn't provided him with many varied social activities and his only companion had been his mortal enemy. Not much comfortable chatter had passed between them.

"They will find the problem on their own. They've probably already informed the dragon—and that's all I wanted: for this outrage to be brought to his attention." He should leave now. It was the only thing that made sense and as a gargoyle, he was nothing, if not logical.

But every time he tried to imagine turning aside, he recalled her scent, that sharp tang of sex which made his mouth moist and his loins respond in a way he hadn't imagined possible. She was a cool one, with her long hair the color of dragon-fire often tied in that thick corded braid down her back. He felt his body flush and harden as he imagined his fingers boldly reaching out, undoing the band she restrained it with. As clearly as if he had already accomplished the feat, he saw her facing him, welcoming him, wearing only the flame colored hair, a shield he would have no trouble penetrating. It would be soft, cascading, tenting around them as he brought her to a bier and found his home in her body.

Ahh, but she was cold, facing him without twitching, both hands on the weapon, which although he didn't recognize it, had no trouble understanding what it was. It would give him pleasure to warm her, to bring her to boiling. He brought his wings in, and landed at a run on the dragon lair's ledge.

Yes, he planned to warm her.

"I hate to sound like some whiney child in the back seat of a car," Brenda said, pausing half-way up yet another flight of stairs, "but are we there yet?"

The house didn't look that big from the outside and she was beginning to wonder if they were in some kind of hellish loop they would keep climbing forever and ever, never reaching the top.

Jan, beside her, didn't look winded, but she was taking the steps slower, certainly not even attempting the two-at-a-time they had climbed to reach the kitchen from the dungeon.

"We're almost there, but before we reach the top, I should prepare you for what you're going to find."

"There," said Brenda, who was ahead and sprinted the last dozen steps until she reached the top landing. It was small, no more than six foot square, unadorned with bare walls and a rough surface, as if made of quarried limestone no one had bothered to polish. The door was wooden and shut.

"Brenda," Jan said and Brenda stopped, her hand poised on the doorknob.

"Secrets?"

"Secrets," Jan admitted. "This is Byron's lair, where he and Lori live."

"I hope Lori is in better shape than I am, if she has to make that trek a couple times a day."

Jan put her hand over Brenda's, preventing her from opening the door. "It…um…won't be what you expect."

"I won't like the way she's decorated the place?" Brenda scoffed. "Probably because there is a creature there which should be chained?"

"I suppose it would be safe to say you'll probably find it shocking the way Lori has the cavern decorated, and it might be best to keep your comments to yourself about what should be chained."

"Cavern?" Brenda asked, but then she turned the knob, opened the door and stepped through the threshold.

Into Oz.

It looked like a huge cave, as big as the one she had been in that morning, but it had been downstairs. From the way the muscles in her thighs were protesting, she knew she had been climbing. This was upstairs. She stopped, taking stock of her environment. There was a major difference between the two. The one downstairs, except for the two walls, and the free standing doors, was completely empty, as if a vacant warehouse. There was nothing but darkness as far as her flashlight could penetrate. This was far more cave-like. It smelled like a cave, and occasionally there were stalactites and stalagmites, even a beautiful display of flowstone. But before she had time to completely come to terms with what she witnessed, the gargoyle appeared.

He came in, running, on his feet and knuckles, his wings outstretched behind him, as if he had been flying, and arrived at a dead-run. Brenda reached for her weapon and arrogantly he met her gaze and held it with a brazen, conceited dominance which indicated he believed she couldn't hurt him. Brenda left the gun in place, and Jan, coming up behind her, studied the cave with an invasive look. "You said there was a problem here?" she asked defiantly, and more than a trifle annoyed. "I don't see anything out of place. From the way you spoke of devastation I thought at the very least there would be cracks in the wall, gasses seeping up from the bedrock."

"What I have to show you is here."

He moved off to one side, his body and broad wings hiding

something, and Jan and Brenda looked down and saw a nest with three eggs, each roughly the size of a football.

Brenda looked at the nest and only felt revulsion. "You've laid eggs? There are going to be more of you?"

"No. This is important. These are not eggs, they are ne-chakra and they belong to the dragon. There should be four."

A massive roar sent Brenda dropping to her knees and rolling for cover, her hand drawing her gun with one smooth, fluid movement. A dragon, twenty feet tall, stood at the back of the cave. Brenda, who had never screamed in a dangerous situation before, screamed, then noticed Lori climbing down from the dragon's shoulders. The dragon roared again, and a blast of fire engulfed the gargoyle, causing her and Jan to take further cover, both inching to the sides of the cave.

The gargoyle's wings fluttered as the dragon lunged, his broad jaw snapping.

"HOLD!" Jan ordered, holding out her hands, as if evoking a spell.

The gargoyle instantly turned into stone.

One second it was a living, breathing monster, the next it was a statue, poised with wings unfurled, in the exact position it had been in when the word was uttered.

"Byron, stop it. He can't hurt you now," Jan ordered, and Lori ran to the dragon, pelting it with her fists.

"Byron, what's happened?" She had tears in her eyes. She was also, massively, incredibly pregnant.

"Byron," Jan said. "We need to talk. I need to know what happened here."

Brenda aimed her weapon. This dragon was an even greater threat than the gargoyle.

"Don't shoot him," Lori said, running to her sister, using both hands to deflect Brenda's aim. "He was wounded a few months back. I don't want him hurt again."

Bullets cannot hurt me. She can shoot as much as she wishes. I will be safe.

"Will someone please tell me what is going on?" Brenda demanded.

There is, however, danger that the mortals in this cavern could be damaged from stray bullets bouncing off my scales or shrapnel cut from the cave face.

"The dragon is right. Put the weapon away, Brenda," Jan ordered again. "The time for violence has passed. And Byron, I would rather not have to deal with you in this form."

But it was Lori, on her hands and knees, over the nest, weeping, which drew their attention.

"One is missing. One is missing," she said.

Almost instantly the dragon morphed from a huge fighting reptile into the man Brenda knew as Byron. He reached out, tenderly took his wife in his arms.

Jan situated herself between him and Brenda. "There is no more danger here, except perhaps from you. Brenda, I am not telling you again, put the weapon away."

"Do you know what he is?"

"A dragon. We were going to tell you, but your sister asked to be the one to break the news. I think she wanted to before she left, but something happened, and they embarked before you two could have your conversation. Now, Lori, are you all right?"

Lori looked up, she had been leaning heavily into her husband's arms. "No. One is missing."

Byron's look hardened. "And if this demon is responsible, an eternity in hell will not be long enough for him to suffer."

"Then these belong to you, not the gargoyle?"

"They are ours."

"Good. Because I was certain both the gargoyles I kept chained were male."

"There should be four."

"Four what? Eggs?" Brenda demanded. None of this made sense. She didn't believe in dragons or gargoyles or caves that appeared at the top of long staircases. She rubbed her eyes, wondering if she were insane or drugged.

"Come downstairs to the kitchen. I will make tea. Byron, you look like you could use a cup."

"I cannot leave the nest. I will stand guard here, until I determine how to deal with my loss."

"Well before you do, can you bring this," Jan said, indicating the gargoyle, "back to the dungeon? I can chain him there so he will cause us no problems and you'll be able to question him."

"Yes. That is a valid request. He will not escape."

Brenda replaced her gun in the holster. "What happened to him?"

"The HOLD spell. It turns him into marble. All gargoyles are susceptible to it."

And if he has harmed my ne-chakra, I will turn him into marble, and crush him beneath my jaws, until nothing remains of him but dust, and I shall scatter that to the winds on ten different worlds. Byron was gone. In his place the dragon reappeared. It lifted the statue, leaving out a back entrance Brenda could not discern from where she stood.

"Come downstairs."

"I won't leave the nest until he returns," Lori said.

"Could you explain to me what this is?" Jan asked, pointing to the eggs. "Milton called them ne-chakras? I know what chakras are. But this is something different, I think."

"I am not used to the idea myself," Lori said, rubbing her extended abdomen, and then wiping the tears which still flowed freely down her face. "My tiny babies," she said, touching the three eggs and rubbing her rounded stomach. Only five minutes later the dragon returned.

He is secure. He will not get loose again. I have made certain.

"One is missing!" Lori said again, her tears resuming.

I see no indication of shards. He did not crack the shell. There is nothing inside for him to eat, was that his intention.

"Eat!" Lori said collapsing, but Brenda, rushing to offer her sister support was gently pushed aside as the dragon reached out with its small forearms, and raised her up. A moment later, it wasn't a dragon holding Lori, but Byron.

"Creatures of darkness have been known to feast on dragon eggs."

"These are not eggs."

"Perhaps he did not know."

"Is the gargoyle still alive?" Jan asked.

"Except to chain him, I did not harm him," Byron answered. "I will take my time with that. He will know pain. And if I find out he was directly responsible for the loss of the ne-chakra, then I will make certain his life is short, no matter how desperately you need him for your protection spells."

"I'm not feeling well," Brenda said. She had been standing silently, for the most part watching the procedures, and except for trying to help her sister, once she had put her weapon away she had not moved. Now she swayed on her feet. Jan caught her.

"All this is new to her," Jan explained to Byron, "and most of it is new to me. I am taking Brenda downstairs and Lori, I suggest you come too. You've had a shock. We can leave Byron here, guarding your nest for the time-being. When our heads are clearer, we can question the gargoyle. When is your baby due?"

"Babies. Byron told me there are four. At this point I don't know. They are half-dragon, and who knows how long the gestation period is, and it has been a long time since one has been born on this planet."

Shock set in, and Brenda started shaking.

"Byron," Lori asked through her tears, "is there anything we can do?"

We must question the gargoyle, the dragon answered.

"Is there any way you could—we could—get another ne-chakra, if that one is ruined?"

No.

"You couldn't make another?"

It is impossible. If we cannot find it whole, one child will suffer. One child will have to go through life incomplete. I would give up my own, if it would help, but it would not. Lori, I need you to go downstairs with your aunt. You need to eat. Then come back, and I will let you sleep, here, by the three remaining ne-chakra. The children in your womb will be comforted by their presence.

"Three children in my womb will be comforted."

No, all four will. It is what they are. It is what they need to be whole. We will find it. All will be well. We have to believe that.

Lori went to the dragon and hugged him, looking so small and defenseless against so huge a beast. "We should never have gone on that honeymoon. We should never have left them. I'll carry that guilt for the rest of my life."

Go with your family, little one. We will talk later.

CHAPTER 8

A few moments later, the three women reached the kitchen. Lori wiped at her tears. "I've been gone seven months and you still haven't finished the dishes?"

"On our timeline, you left only yesterday, and there has been trouble," Jan said from the stove, where she was moving the tea kettle over a bright blaze.

"And these dishes, where did they all come from?"

Jan looked at Brenda, cleared her throat. Brenda, still in shock, stood, angry. "Yes, this is a good time, I think, to continue keeping secrets from me. I suppose I should go back up to my bedroom while you two talk about gargoyles, dragons and eggs?"

"No, Brenda. Save your anger and your sarcasm and sit. You have as much invested in this as any of us. It really was my plan to let you know, certainly about the gargoyles. If you hadn't ventured downstairs, I would have found a way to tell you this morning."

"You went downstairs? You led whatever it was up here—to take my ne-chakra?"

Brenda looked to Jan who answered for her. "Brenda did nothing to your eggs. I promise. Brenda was seeking answers of her own. When she was here as a child, she found out about the gargoyles, and wanted to see if they were real."

"They are, apparently, real," Brenda said dryly.

"And Lori, as to the dishes, I can explain. There is magic in this house. Some makes it so I don't have to do everything all at once. It is easier for me to do one thing over and over. I get in a rhythm, and things move much faster. For example, when I am canning peaches, if I had to stop, make the beds, cook the breakfast, and do the dishes, I might get only two or three hours of canning in a day. This way, I can prepare my fruit and throw them in jars from morning to night, uninterrupted. Then, when canning season is over, I may spend a month washing dishes, a month just making beds—"

"That must be a thrill," from Brenda.

"And a month scrubbing the bathrooms and the floors. I generally like the time I spend washing dishes. And before either of you scoff, I'll explain. It's mindless work. I get to think things through. I don't have to worry about anything. And it really does make my cooking easier. For example, when I am cooking and I need a chopped onion, I don't have to stop and do it, it's already done. My time is used very effectively. Without this time stretching, I wouldn't get a fraction of the things done that I do."

"This makes no sense at all."

"It makes perfect sense. Your suitcases brought up from the car, the cheery fire in your rooms, those are all done another time, in the past or in the future. Sometimes I can tell who will be staying at the Inn by the sheets I'm washing and the beds I'm making."

"Is there anything you have to do in the here and now?"

"Many things. Feed the gargoyles. I had to do that daily. Planting and tending the garden must be done by the seasons here, no matter what other jobs I have. And the crisis I had this morning, was one I could not put off."

"And what crisis was that?"

"Something not resolved yet. I will have to get back to it, when we get some breathing room here."

Brenda looked to her sister. "So, that monster said you carry four babies?"

"Monster, the gargoyle?" Lori questioned.

"The dragon."

"The dragon is my husband Byron."

"Great, my older sister is married to a dragon, and my aunt, for all practical purposes, manages a haunted house. Is there anything else I should know?"

"Oh, quite a bit, actually," Jan said cheerfully, bringing the teapot to the table, as well as three bowls of a baked pasta casserole, dripping with white cheese. "We all will feel better after a bite to eat. And right now, before we go into other secrets, we need to discuss the ne-chakras."

"Those eggs are your babies?" Brenda asked, looking at Lori's rounded stomach. "How is that possible?"

"Apparently for a dragon he is very fertile."

"When you left here, yesterday you didn't look pregnant."

"I was. A few days only."

"And your children grow this fast?"

"Byron and I have been gone seven months. We were planning on leaving in a week or so when Genevieve found us. That is how we got here so quickly."

"Seven months?" The thought made no more sense than anything else she had witnessed in the past hour.

"Where we were time flows differently. Byron found us a beach, where he could stretch out his wings and bask in the sun, and I swam and slept and feasted on the most glorious food imaginable. Except for fish and birds and the servants we kept, we were the only living creatures for miles. It was heavenly." Her face crumpled, and tears began again. "Then we came back, and found one of the ne-chakras have been stolen."

***

Early the next morning, Brenda crept down the stairs, to the kitchen, annoyed to find her aunt already there, washing dishes.

"I know you feel better if you can sneak down—" Jan said, indicating with a flip of her head the basement door.

"Well," Brenda said, "I suppose." It bothered her she was so transparent.

"But if you want to bring his breakfast down, you're welcome to. It would be a help to me."

"Will he hurt me?"

"I wouldn't get too close if I were you, but I doubt Milton will hurt you."

"Milton, is that his name?"

"Yes."

"How long had he been free?"

"A few weeks only. I hadn't been able to find a trace of him or the other one. I thought he was long gone. It really is in the best interests of this Inn to have him where he is."

"The best interests for the Inn," Brenda repeated, "but not for Milton?"

"He is a living creature, like any other. He enjoys his freedom."

"And his captivity is the price for your Inn being safe from evil influences?"

"Yes."

"Has anyone ever asked him in the centuries I've heard that he's been here, if being chained to a wall is his idea of a good time?"

"No. There is no need. He would be free if he could."

"How dare you keep a creature like that chained? What gives you the right?"

"You said it yourself, he is a monster."

"That may be. He certainly looks like a monster, but yesterday when he was in the kitchen, it sounded like he only wanted to help. It sounded like, if you would recognize his freedom, he would share his information."

"He had his claws at your neck at the time."

"I wasn't hurt and if I'd known what to expect, I doubt I would have been frightened. Would the ne-chakra have been stolen if he had still been trapped downstairs?"

"Probably. I don't know. Byron's lair is not specifically part of this house. Actually, most of this house is not specifically part of this house."

"I suppose that makes sense to you?"

"No, actually, it doesn't. For all the years I've been here, I'm still fairly amazed at what's going on. Also, Brenda, I spoke with Byron this morning. He made an appointment with their obstetrician and is planning on taking Lori later this afternoon, while I watch over the nest."

"Then her babies are all right?"

"As far as we can tell, the babies in her womb are healthy. Now, here is Milton's tray. Can you manage the stairs?"

"It's dark. I'll need a flashlight."

"There is a light spell. And Brenda, if he does anything to frighten you, anything at all, yell HOLD, and it will turn him to marble."

"I doubt that will be necessary."

"I want you to be protected."

Going down the stairs, carrying the heavy tray, Brenda thought over the last evening's events. They had spent yesterday rehashing Milton's capture, and had filled Brenda in on Byron's background and how he and Lori met. Brenda still wasn't certain how much she believed. She had a brother-in-law who was a dragon, and her aunt lived in a house built at the nexus of several worlds, where magic reigned.

She heard the chains rattling long before she reached the bottom, continuous movement indicated the monster was restless and paced the length of his captivity.

"Bitch. Traitor. Liar!"

The monster strained to the length of his chains, his claws extended as he swiped at her. "Come closer, little girl. Let me get my talons into your neck yet again. You will not escape so easily."

Feeling foolish, she set the tray down. "My aunt said you would be hungry."

"I take no handouts from those without honor to keep their own word."

"How freely you use the word honor. Yet you should realize I would have promised you anything because at the time you had your claws digging into my neck. I also promised I would shoot you."

"Pull out your gun. Aim for my heart. You have me trapped here. I am sure it will give you pleasure to murder a creature chained not once but three times."

"No," she said, surprised at her own honesty, "it would give me no pleasure to kill a chained animal."

"Yet I am no animal. Regardless of what I look like, I have a soul."

"You would say anything, I think, to get your freedom."

"No, for although you think I use the word honor lightly, my word has always been true."

"You should eat while it is hot."

"I took food from you once, honey on bread, with something else."

Brenda sat down on the cold stone, pushed the meal closer to him, then reached out, swiped an orange from the tray, which she peeled, and ate slowly. "Peanut butter. It's called peanut butter."

"The Innkeeper has never brought it to me. I did not know what it was. Is it rare?"

"No. Not so rare."

"You have not lost your naiveté have you?"

"To creatures from the depths of hell, how could I?"

"Yes, I have been to the depths of hell and I like it better than being chained and used here."

"Then you are evil."

"Like your aunt? No. When I give my word it means something. I believe in honor, integrity."

"I find that unlikely. If true, why would my aunt keep you chained?"

"A valid question, one which I have been trying to answer for centuries."

"Gargoyles are evil-"

The beast snarled, and the chains rattled with increased intensity. "We have each committed a single act of great evil, but centuries ago. Since then, there has rarely been a gargoyle turned evil, for we strive daily for repentance. We are the most holy of creatures."

Brenda scoffed.

"You do not believe? Then why are we set to guard the most sacred of buildings? Gargoyles keep cathedrals free from evil. That is why we were placed around the greatest monuments to your religions over the millennium. We feast on it."

"Gargoyles are nothing more than decorative water spouts."

The gargoyle howled, and it took Brenda a while to realize it was laughing. "Do I look like a decorative water spout to you?" Before she could answer, he continued. "Gargoyles have a divine assignment to prevent evil and in our presence evil cannot exist. Because of that your days on this world are numbered, little conniver. I will taste your blood before I am through."

You will not harm the mortal.

Brenda looked and five feet from her, the gigantic dragon stood. She startled, went for her gun.

There is no need for that, sister, for I will not harm you, and regardless of his threats, the Gargoyle cannot either.

She left the gun alone. "Byron?"

Yes, we must talk later, we three. It is what Lori wishes. But now I must question the prisoner.

"Prisoner," the gargoyle snapped, "when I have done no wrong to you."

The dragon moved closer, walking upright on two huge, thickly muscled legs. *After extensive questioning, Jan has confessed what she understands to be your role in the loss of my ne-chakra.*

"Then you've come to kill me? I can hear when I am turned to stone. Did you know that? I cannot respond, and I cannot react, but I can hear. What is it you plan to do, crush my marble into dust, and spread it across a dozen worlds?"

I will listen to your explanation.

"I have none to offer while I am prisoner for a crime of which I am not guilty."

I will not release you. You are too valuable to the Inn.

"I was not given mortality, but because I retain my soul, I was given agency, the greatest of LORD's gifts. I choose not to answer you. Then you will suffer for all eternity, wondering what happened to your ne-chakra, for you will never get the information from me."

"Yet," Brenda said, speaking to Byron and to the gargoyle, both which, to her eyes, were monsters, "you knew of the loss of the egg. You wanted to warn the dragon. Byron, if Jan did not tell you, I will. He—" she pointed to the monster, "said it might be months before we discovered the missing egg and it was vital that we know."

What were you doing in the lair?

"Release me, and I will tell you."

There will be no release for you.

"But I will find release, eventually. For I have a soul. When I die, I am promised heaven. The same is not true for you."

I am willing to hasten you on your journey, but for two things. The Innkeeper needs this House evil-free, and at the moment I require answers no other can give me.

"I owe no allegiance to the witch. She betrayed me."

What were you doing in the lair?

"Answer him, please," Brenda said.

"Never."

Brenda moved closer. "If I release you, can I have your word you will tell Byron what it is he wishes to know?"

"You have my word. I do not have all the answers, but I will tell him what I witnessed."

"And if I release you, will you hurt me?"

This is foolishness. He will answer me, and you will leave his chains alone.

Brenda ignored him. "How do I release the chains?"

"You have only to pull on any link. They are enchanted to respond to mortal touch."

"And the metal bands at your neck and your wrist?"

"Will not bother me, once I am free. All of us wear some form of our servitude. Some more obvious than others."

You will not do this thing.

Brenda reached out, and the link from the chain at his wrist opened. The gargoyle howled and Brenda feared for her life, until she realized it was celebrating the breaking of the bonds and the noise was not a prelude to attack.

She reached out, again, severing the links at his ankle.

"I am free. I am free."

CHAPTER 9

HOLD!

The dragon's roar echoed around the huge chamber, reverberating over and over causing Brenda to nearly go mad. She covered her ears, clamped her eyes shut, terrified. She was a cop, trained to deal with dangerous situations, and now her only response was to cower. She felt like a fool, until she opened her eyes, saw the massive twenty foot dragon which she still didn't believe. He was the monster—the dragon her sister had married, not the creature chained to the wall.

Yet, when she straightened, she saw the gargoyle kept moving, unaffected.

"I thought—" she said, but it was a sentence she couldn't finish, because she had no thoughts on the subject at all. It was all too new, far from her range of experiences. This was nothing she had run across while driving a squad car, and it had not been discussed in morning meetings.

The chains rattled as the creature moved but the sound didn't echo as the roar had. The jingling metal chains sounded not only defiant, but a tad cheerful, like Christmas bells. Then the monster smirked, slowly, showing a great number of teeth in that long animal snout which topped a human-appearing body. "You have no effect on me, Beast," the gargoyle said.

The spell no longer works?

"It works, but as an immortal and one without a soul, you have no authority over me."

The dragon shifted, not retreating, not coming closer, just moving its heavy weight from one colossal hind leg to the other. For an instant Brenda studied her brother-in-law, from the light, almost feathery green scales at its eyes, to the long copper-colored tail which dragged down behind it, but her concentration and her interest was riveted not on the dragon, but the gargoyle. It might be captured, chained, even perhaps, debased, but was not defeated. Standing there, with heavy bands securing his neck, his ankle, his wrist, he looked noble, dignified. He met her glance and his spine straightened. He still looked alien, but not nearly as frightening as he had a few moments before. The gargoyle's ears twitched. They were big, upright affairs, like a Doberman's, not small, coming from the side of his head like a human's. Brenda looked to the dragon, comparing. It did not look like he had ears at all, at least none she could discern.

I should have dominion over you.

"Because you have no soul and thus were not granted the blessings of death, you have no control over me."

Blessings of death, Brenda thought, but the dragon interrupted, before she could mentally pursue that line.

But I can still rip you to pieces. You will not stand a chance against my strength.

The gargoyle stopped moving, smiled slowly. "Kill me now, and you'll never get what you want."

His ears were expressive, twitching with his curiosity, but it was his eyes which fascinated her, for they sparkled with intelligence, or perhaps conniving. There undoubtedly was an excellent reason why he was chained to the wall.

In defense of my infant's ne-chakra, it would be a pleasure.

"Byron, leave him alone."

Stay out of this, human. You have no conception of the ramifications of what he has done.

Brenda bristled. She was not used to being spoken to like that, had trained with weapons and field procedures specifically so she would be at no man's mercy. She would take lessons from the gargoyle and not be alarmed by the dragon's size and imposing arrogance. She straightened her spine, faced this monster who was, inexplicably, her brother-in-law.

"He was imprisoned unfairly by my aunt who gave her word he would not be harmed. I will not stand by while he is kept chained, regardless if this house needs his protection. If history has taught us anything it is when you take freedom from one group of people, you start taking freedoms from all. I am willing to take responsibility for releasing him. I was there when Jan promised not to HOLD him. He did nothing to break his end of the bargain."

She took a deep breath, moved closer, wondering where she had gotten so foolish all of a sudden and wishing even in her own mind she could call it bravery.

She turned, met the gargoyle's gaze, his dark brown eyes clearly visible in this area of light which came from no discernible source. "Now, you said if you were set free, you would tell the dragon what he wanted to know."

Brenda, you make a mistake.

"Gargoyle, can the dragon hurt you?"

"With his fire, no. Yet, I think I am vulnerable to his strength."

"Byron, I need you to promise me you will not hurt him. I don't know how he got freed the first time, but this time, I will let him go to right a wrong. Besides, after centuries, don't you think he deserves time off for good behavior?"

"I will not forget your kindness or your actions." The gargoyle bowed, honorably, to Brenda. "Dragon, change into your human-form."

I will not make myself vulnerable to you.

"As an indication of goodwill and trust, Byron. If he attacks you, I will put the spell on him."

Yet, I think you cannot be trusted to do so. I will listen to what he has to say, but I will remain in this form while I do so.

"I will tell you what I know. I was in the forest, stretching my wings, as I had not done in centuries, basking in my own freedom, when I noticed Evil. It was moving through the forest, clandestinely moving from tree to tree, and it had your ne-chakra. I have never seen one before, but I knew what it was, and I knew the creature, whatever he wanted the ne-chakra for, could not be planning on using it for Good."

Did you try to stop this Evil?

"I could not do so without endangering the ne-chakra. I weighed my choices. Sometimes destroying evil takes precedence over harming good, but that is the rarest of occasions. I could not take the chance of having your ne-chakra damaged."

The gargoyle stood, stretched his wings, but it was only an exercise, movement, for he did not take flight. "I followed him for a few minutes, but he saw me, and shot something from his hands I recognized as a weapon: a bright colored flash of light."

Powerstrand, the dragon said. *That means he is a wer-wizard or necromancer. Probably a wer-wizard.*

"I avoided injury. I am not certain it would be fatal if it hit me, but I did not want to take the chance during my first month of freedom."

There is a possibility it would be fatal, or if you were only wounded, then the second would surely be fatal. And this is interesting information, for I battled with a wer-wizard only a month ago—as time is reckoned in this sphere. I wounded him, although I am certain I did not kill him.

"Do you think he is after your egg for revenge?"

"That is a valid question," the gargoyle said. "What would he do with it?"

*You are correct in labeling him evil. I believe if revenge were his only motivation, he would have destroyed the ne-chakras where I would find them, or perhaps destroy most of them, leaving me hope that one survived, so I would hunt him down in an attempted rescue and thereby put myself in jeopardy."

"He was carrying it very carefully. I cannot think like an Evil, but I imagine if it were only to lure you, he would not be so careful. He also took only one, because he could carry only one safely."

Still, I have something he wants desperately. It is possible he either lures me, or he thinks he can get what he wants from the ne-chakra he has.

"Could you tell me what the ne-chakra is?" Brenda asked. "I want to know why it is so valuable to you and my sister."

The ne-chakra is a term for a fetal dragon spirit.

"Not a soul," the gargoyle said emphatically.

Not a soul. It is what will make the children in Lori's womb complete dragons. It is something my wife and I want desperately, for our children to be whole.

"Let me see if I understand this...when the ne-chakra hatch, or whatever term you wish to use, they will merge with the children Lori gives birth to?"

Yes.

Sitting, Brenda stole an apple from the gargoyle's tray and crunched into it. "Could it be possible the ne-chakra the wizard stole could merge with something else? Something evil?"

Brenda did not need to hear the dragon's confirmation. As soon as she asked her question, he hung his head, and dropped from his legs to the floor, as if he had been mortally wounded. *Yes.*

The gargoyle too, looked shocked. "Should the wer-wizard have access to any number of minor forms of evil beings: demons, sprites, certain types of lower-elves, and if that creature could bond with a chakra, the resulting creature would be very powerful."

And under the direct control of the wer-wizard.

What happened after you were attacked by the powerstrands?

"I came immediately and told my jailor what I had witnessed. I would have told you, as it affects you directly, but I could not catch your scent."

I was away, and if you had not warned Jan, the possibility exists that I would still be away, and unaware of the danger, perhaps giving the wer-wizard the opportunity to return and steal the others.

"Have I then, fulfilled my end of the bargain? I told you all I witnessed."

Brenda, this is your last opportunity. Stop him before he leaves.

She set the apple core on the tray, wiped her hands on her jeans. It had been a fresh apple, extremely juicy, exceptionally delicious. "Byron, answer his question. Has he fulfilled his end of the bargain?"

Yes.

"You may go," Brenda told him, releasing the third chain, the one at his neck. "We thank you for your information. You were right when you came to us in the kitchen upstairs. This was information we could get no other way."

"And I beg your forgiveness, for baring my claws against you."

She rubbed her throat. The only pain she felt came from the memory of being at his mercy. "Now I understand why. I hope the next time you have information we can communicate without bloodshed."

Wait, before you go--

The gargoyle stood tall, majestic. Even though he was ugly, deformed, there was a dignity in him Brenda recognized. "Yes?"

Could you hunt the wer-wizard? Find his trail?

Milton's monstrous talons clicked on the stone floor, but with the question, he stopped and turned to face Byron. "I am not sure. I have been trapped down here for centuries. I do not know to what extent my abilities have atrophied." The dragon warbled, a strained sound of pain. "But, to give you comfort, I know evil. I would know his scent again should I come across it, and I could track him. He would not escape. Whether I could kill him, I do not know. But the trail is fresh. I should be able to at least track him, and if I found him, also find your ne-chakra." Then his wings flapped, and he rose with dignity, flying into the darkness of the cave, disappearing from sight.

The dragon waited until the monster had completely vanished, then turned his dark, invasive gaze to Brenda.

That was a foolish thing to do.

In the presence of this twenty foot monster, her impulse was to run, to quiver, but the gargoyle had met him with dignity. She would face him in strength. "No, it was a noble thing. If it were foolish, you'd be flapping your own wings, chasing after him. You may refuse to acknowledge it, but I did what was right."

***

"You let him go?" Jan screamed. The force of her expression was almost as loud as the dragon's bellow an hour before.

"I did. You have no right keeping a living creature chained in your basement."

"You have no idea of the consequences."

"I'm sure that is true. Why don't you tell me?" They sat on a mat on the ground, in the upstairs cave, beside the ne-chakra nest. Lori was there, her eyes swollen with tears, her body extremely pregnant. She and Jan were drinking tea from the dragon teapot, an exact miniature likeness of the huge dragon. Brenda, having had enough experience with the food from this house, was drinking water from a sealed bottle from her car.

Brenda held her sister's hand. "What did your doctor say?"

Lori caressed her stomach. "The babies are doing fine, I should rest, and the longer I can prevent myself from going into labor, the better. Byron thinks they will be born soon."

"Seven months?"

"He says once they merge with their chakras, they will be strong. He does not fear for the children."

"Only for the missing egg."

Gingerly Lori set her teacup aside, took the napkin from her lap and rubbed her swollen eyes. "Yes. Jan, there is something else you need to know. Since I arrived here yesterday, I started having contractions. I don't want the babies born, until—"

"Byron will find some way to get it back."

"No. He won't. He won't leave the nest. Now that there are no gargoyles in the basement and creatures of evil know ne-chakra are here, he says the nest is in danger. He will not, or cannot move it this close to my confinement, so he must stay on guard."

"I don't see him now," Brenda said. Although most of the cave was very dark, she felt certain if the dragon was there she would sense him, hear him, smell him.

"He is close," Jan said. "I doubt he will let Lori or the other ne-chakras out of his sight until the babies are born and united with their chakra."

"I don't see how we can find the missing egg and return it, if Byron won't. Aunt Jan, is there anything else you could send looking? Another dragon?"

"Dragons are not that common. And no. No one can help."

"I will. But you will have to tell me where to go, and what to do."

"A gun will not suffice against this Evil. Brenda, even Byron in dragon form fought this wer-wizard, and was almost killed. You wouldn't stand a chance."

"Then I am going downstairs to bed. I suggest you get some sleep, too."

"I don't want my babies born, without—"

"We will find it, Lori. We will get it back."

***

Brenda did not go directly to sleep. As was her habit, she went running, and as she hoped, she met the gargoyle at the bench beside a small ringed campfire the gargoyle called dragon fire.

Her heart gave a strange flip as she saw him, recognition, she said to herself, refusing to believe it was anything more. She grinned, and realized she was no longer terrified in his presence. If anything, she was pleased to see him, almost enchanted. "I thought you would be miles away by now."

He did not touch her, but moved close enough for her to reach out and caress those huge wings if she wanted. They looked leathery, soft, but not with feathers, more like a bat's wings. "I have been. And I intended to stay away, but you often go running at night and I wanted to see you."

"Did I do the wrong thing in letting you go?"

"I am unlikely to ever say yes to that. However, if you wish a different perspective, you should speak to your aunt."

When he smiled, his face no longer looked so alien or feral. He was becoming familiar to her, and she liked that.

"I have. And to the dragon. They were both ranting."

The gargoyle laughed, then stretched his wings before folding them up behind him, he sat beside her. "I would imagine, when he gets a full head of steam up, he could rant for several centuries. I wish your sister happiness with him."

Since she heard only sincerity in his statement she said, "You do?"

"Of course. Marriage is sacred. And their marriage is already blessed with children. Such covenants should never be taken lightly."

She looked up, but with the brightness of the dragon fire, few stars were visible, so she returned her attention to him, and asked the question foremost in her mind. "Are you evil?"

"Not as you understand it."

"Why did my aunt keep you chained?"

His palms rested on his thighs, and he spread his fingers and those huge, dangerous claws, slowly. Brenda was not threatened, but fascinated. "Do you want the simple answer, or the involved one?"

"Start with the simple. And you do know I will ask for my aunt's version of this story?"

He laughed again. "You may. I doubt it will differ significantly from mine. The House your aunt watches is unique. There have been only two others like it on this planet, and at the moment one of those two is under reconstruction, so I can say honestly, there is only one other."

"And what makes this house so unique?"

"Besides the fact that there is a dragon in residence and generally it has gargoyles chained in the basement?"

She nodded her head in acknowledgement. "Point taken."

"The work your aunt does is good work. The magic she controls is good magic, and those she helps generally fight for the Light. Generally. Not all elves can be trusted at all times, not all faeries can be relied on to remember which side is good, and which is evil, but on the whole, your aunt supports the Good."

"By washing dishes?"

"And cooking and cleaning and baking and gardening. Her tasks are endless. She offers sanctuary to those who need it, and comfort to those in pain. There is nowhere else for creatures of faerie go. If you stay, you should support her. Lori will help, it is in her nature, but her pregnancy limits her, and after their births, she will be too occupied with her four children to be of much assistance for decades. Raising dragon children is no easy task."

"Apparently why there are so few of them."

Brenda meant to be flippant, but he answered her soberly. "Exactly. But I have not answered your question yet. I serve Good. By my Vow, a promise I made long ago, I can do nothing else. Evil cannot exist in my presence. It can flee, or it can die, but it cannot remain unscathed. So, my companion and I were kept downstairs to keep the house and the area vermin free. It was a good plan, and for a while I even enjoyed it. The food was plentiful and I was useful."

"But not as useful as you could be, in eradicating evil."

"That is my impression. Chasing and destroying evil is my vocation. For centuries I felt I should take a more active role. And I do like to stretch my wings."

"Did you speak to my aunt? Ask her to let you go?"

He bent down, picked up a stick from the ground. Slowly he broke it into pieces, added them to the blazing pyre. "Daily. Not an opportunity went by when she delivered our food that we did not ask for release. But something changed, and she could not let us go, even if she wanted to."

"What?"

"My companion grew to love the darkness. He had made the same covenants as I, but he found them wearing, and he sought the kind of excitement Good cannot provide. And so, for centuries we fought. And it was better, overall, for us both to remain chained so he could not perpetrate his evil, than that I be loosed to bask in my freedom."

"But you did get out."

"The wer-wizard, the one who has stolen the ne-chakra, opened a portal to an evil world and as a result, the House was falling. The dragon was wounded and could not help, so rather than have us die, your aunt released us. Longfellow would have killed her then, but I prevented it. I was looking for him when I spotted the wer-wizard. I did not know then he had opened up the portal, for he had never been allowed in the house so I hadn't been able to sense who he was."

"Will evil take over the B&B, now that you are gone?"

"I cannot say. I cannot read the future. Although Evil is powerful, it is not more powerful than Good, for in most instances they are fairly well balanced. Your aunt will defend the Inn, and the dragon is a force for Good, though we see things from different perspectives. If I can control and restrain Longfellow, I am willing to stick around and work here. I like the area. I am used to it."

"Just not chained."

"Exactly." He moved his hand, and she wondered if he were scratching, but it was not his own body he approached, but hers. He did not touch her, and dropped his hand before he made contact. "You enchanted me from the first moment I saw you."

Brenda grew uncomfortable, inched away. "I was a child."

"You are not a child now."

"Milton—that is your name, Milton?"

"Yes."

"Don't, please."

But it was too late. With hands grown remarkably gentle, he completed the motion he had started the second before and lifted her chin. She had felt his claws at her throat, she had known his strength and his power so she stiffened, eyes, jaw, muscle, but when there was only tenderness, she opened her eyes and forced the tension from her body.

Brenda didn't know what to expect. He looked so alien, so frightening and she was not used to trusting even normal looking men. She felt only confusion, and hated that in herself. She wanted to make a sharp, quick decision to hate him, but then Milton nuzzled. The soft fur from his neck rubbed across her cheek and she felt herself falling. The action was seductive and very erotic. Her body tingled in places she had never allowed it to tingle before. Her mouth and her palms became moist. She wanted to push him back, thrust him away, but somehow, far beyond all logic, she enjoyed his caress.

"Touch me." His voice was low, whispered.

Brenda thought for a second that she was feeling fear and tried to tap the emotion down. Fear, because her breath was quick and her pulse was tripping. She lifted her right hand, toward his strongly defined snout where it tapered to a point, but refused to touch him. If she had to think, she could probably come up with a dozen reasons why she should not, but at the moment there was only one. She would not because she wanted to. Caressing him was an impulse she would never give in to.

"No."

"Because I am a beast?"

Brenda moved her head away from his touch, then inched away from him, her emotions twanging. She prayed he could not read her mind as easily as he could put his thoughts in hers. "Because you look like a beast," she corrected. She would make no mention of his soul, no statement about how her own heart thumped loudly in her chest and her palms ached to reach out.

He nodded and she accepted it as an acknowledgement. He was a beast. He did look monstrous. But she wished desperately that she had waited a minute before moving and could trust her own emotions when she was with him.

He stood, stepped back, gave her a courtly bow. "I must search for Longfellow, but we are not finished, you and I."

She shivered once, at the threat inherent in his last statement. "Will you look for the wizard?"

He shook his monstrous head. "That is not for you to ask, but for the dragon."

"If I did?"

"I will help you. You know I enjoy helping you, but in this, you have no right to ask."

She stood silently as he lifted from the ground, as he took flight. His wings flapped noiselessly, and the fire sparked as the breeze caught it. As she watched him go, she thought of what he said, and the statement echoed in her brain. "You have no right. You have no right."

She wondered what it would be like if she did have the right, what she would have to do to earn it, and if his wings were as soft as they looked.

And Brenda stood there long past when she could see him. And now it was not her mouth and her palms which were moist, but her eyes.

***

The babies were born exactly one week later. Lori had been on bed rest, but the four were active, ready to enter the world. There was panic in the Inn, for although as a police officer, Brenda had all kinds of first aid training, it was ineffective when it was her own sister crying out in pain. Without a word Byron lifted Lori into his arms and disappeared from the cavern, leaving Jan and Brenda to travel by more mundane means to the hospital in Vermont.

As Byron promised, all four boys were born healthy, with the proper number of fingers and toes. Their weight was respectable for a multi-birth, all at least five pounds. The labor and delivery went quickly. Lori brought them home from the hospital in Bennington after staying only two nights. Brenda, who up to this point had never been attracted to pregnant women or babies was enchanted. She couldn't stay away, holding an infant whenever Byron or Lori would relinquish one.

"Thank goodness they do not look like their father," Brenda said, rubbing the soft pad of her index finger across Raphael's downy soft cheek. The baby was nearly asleep, and Brenda found herself surprisingly, sharply interested in what pregnancy was like, and wondered what it would be like to hold her own child. Lori's hormones should be in flux after birth, but not her own, so she was not given the comfort in blaming her maternal instincts on biochemistry.

"No claws," Lori said, laying on the couch in the red living room, trying to nurse two babies at once. It annoyed her that she would not be able to nurse all four. She had decided she would pick the first two crying at any one time and nurse those. The other two would get a bottle. The routine seemed to be working well, with the babies satisfied with either nipple.

"During the latter part of labor, I was certain they were growing claws, and they were going to find a way out, even if they had to dig their way through."

Brenda giggled. "The doctor did mention you said something like that. He thought it was hilarious."

"Only because he didn't understand I was serious."

"Their claws won't come in until they have developed a bit more," Byron said, but when pressed, he could not give a date. None of them were certain if he meant two months old, two years old, or even, knowing him, two hundred years old.

Then Byron cocked his head, listening to something none of them could hear. "We have to go upstairs, immediately." He picked up Lori, before she had a chance to even gasp. "Hold onto our sons. We must go now."

"Their chakra?" Lori asked, standing. Raphael, in Brenda's arms, and Dominic, the infant Jan was rocking, were suddenly both extremely alert, looking around and, for want of a better word, anxious, as if knowing something marvelous was about to happen.

"Yes. Now."

"Jan, if you would bring Dom, and Brenda, you do not mind?"

"I'd be honored," Brenda said. She cradled the infant gently against her breasts and gently kissed his soft, fuzz covered head. The boys had been born with a dusting of dark hair, and it was too soon to tell if it would stay dark, like their father's or mutate into the deep red of their mother. Their eyes were already turning copper, showing distinct heritage from Bryon. They were alert babies with strong grips and already easy natures.

The staircase was compassionate, and they only had to travel the equivalent of two flights. Byron changed immediately into his dragon form, and held Lori tightly. Brenda and Jan behind him stopped. The gargoyle was standing over the nest.

"I would be honored to witness the joining," Milton said, his hands palm out, not so much in entreaty, as to show he was unarmed and meant no harm.

Be welcomed, then. Of all the things I have taken pride in over the length of my life, none has been as great as my sons.

Milton moved back, and Brenda could see the eggs rocking. Beside the nest, four small, soft cradles lay on the ground, and as Byron set his wife down, he put a hollering baby boy into each.

"They sure have healthy lungs," Brenda remarked.

"That they do," Milton said. "They will be magnificent dragons."

But then, except for the wailing of the children, there was silence, as if none of the adults could think of an appropriate answer. For only three would grow into magnificent dragons.

The first egg cracked. It started as a tiny fissure, which grew as the shell separated, then an instant later, split into shards. The creature inside was a dragon, a miniature dragon, which would fit into the palm of an adult's hand, with the tail long enough extend down the forearm, and wrap along the upper arm. But it was transparent. Brenda gasped. She could see right through it.

"Is that normal?" she asked.

Yes.

The tiny dragon chakra raised its snout, trumpeted into the air, then on very wobbly legs, started walking toward the four screaming, red-faced infants. It passed the first child, smelled the second for a long time, then passed him by, before waddling to the third. This time, as he started sniffing, the baby stopped crying, and the trace of a smile lit his features.

"Byron—" Lori said.

Hush.

The infant reached out, as if it would embrace the chakra into a hug, and the tiny, transparent dragon walked forward, stepping on its body, then, was adsorbed into the child's being. The baby transformed for a split second, into the form the chakra had held, a complete miniature dragon, not transparent now, but fully developed with a pale orange color, a shadow of his father's magnificent gold, then reverted back instantly into its human form. It cooed for a second, lowering its eyelids, plopped its thumb in its mouth, and went to sleep.

"Amen," the gargoyle said with bowed head.

The women made no comment, but all three felt the same, like they had witnessed something holy.

The second chakra hatched, and the third, merging with their respective babies in exactly the same way. Three babies slept. And one continued crying, flailing its arms and legs, unsatisfied, unable to console.

Lori picked up the infant, her face wet with tears. "Lorenzo," she said, cooing to her son, trying to offer comfort. "We'll find your chakra. I promise you. If it's at all possible, we'll find it." The baby kept crying. Incomplete. Alone. Not a dragon, not an infant, but a half-being.

The gargoyle stretched his wings. "I leave now."

Wait, Byron said.

Milton looked to Jan, as if seeking her permission. But if her impulse was to yell HOLD, she refrained.

I need to ask a favor of you.

"Ask, Dragon. After what I witnessed this morning, I will listen."

I cannot leave my children. They are vulnerable this young, and without a gargoyle to keep the Inn safe, I dare not absent myself.

There was no question, so he waited.

"Would you hunt for the missing ne-chakra so my fourth son can be made whole?"

Lori, still grasping the screaming infant, looked to him as a savior. "Would you? Could you?"

"Do you think it has hatched?"

I do not know. Perhaps.

"If it has merged with something evil, I would be forced to kill it."

The dragon lowered its head, bowing. *If it has merged with something evil, it will need to be destroyed. If you cannot handle the resultant creature, come tell me, and I will do it.*

"It couldn't be…removed…so it could merge with Lorenzo?"

No. If it has merged with something evil, then it will be Evil. We wouldn't want such a thing in our son. If it has merged, it would be no true dragon, but would be a corrupted version of whatever it had merged with.

"Are you sure you couldn't just lay another ne-chakra?"

That too is impossible. Four ne-chakras for my four sons. There is no possibility of another.

"Well, Gargoyle," Jan said. "Would you undertake the quest?"

"I have thought long and hard on this question. While your babies cried through the night, I could think of nothing else."

"Then you'll do it?" Lori asked, over the sound of the squalling infant. "You will seek out his chakra?"

"Perhaps. But with anything important, the cost is high. I doubt if you will pay."

What do you require, Gargoyle?

"Two things. First, never for any reason will I be chained in your dungeon, or otherwise forced to remain here."

"I agree readily," Jan said. "You have my word. If you can return Lorenzo's chakra, or kill the beast which has corrupted it, then not I, nor any Innkeeper of this House, so long as you live, will ever have claim on you or your freedom."

I too consent. I will do whatever is in my power to see you maintain your freedom, should you return undamaged my son's chakra, or destroy the beast who has adsorbed it. There is a second thing?

Milton looked at Brenda, all six-foot winged arrogance. "Yes, there is a second requirement. I wish to take the maid Brenda as my wife."

CHAPTER 10

The gargoyle raised his broad snout and sniffed the air, relishing the different scents which reached his nostrils, a feast after being chained for centuries. Aromas assaulted him from a hundred different sources, a thousand. Each creature left its own mark on the air, traces of its passing: squirrels, rabbits, skunks, raccoons, deer, dogs, even bear. For a long moment he feasted on the cornucopia of delight before taking the time to separate old from fresh, prey from smaller creatures not worth the bother. His nose twitched and he felt salvia pooling in his mouth. The claws at his feet dug deep into the underbrush, anxious, almost antsy, ready to pursue his next meal. This was what freedom was.

The air hung heavy with early summer, hot, sultry, and thick with biting black flies and mosquitoes seeking blood. He flicked his tail and stretched his wings, but they were too mindless to understand their danger. Because his blood was not mortal, no insect could use that nectar, even if they could break through his tough hide. They buzzed around him with fruitless intensity but he ignored them as he inched from the heavy woods into a broad, natural grassland.

The scents were different here, closer to the ground, as if the June heat kept them weighted. Even though he had been imprisoned for centuries, he hadn't forgotten the scents of morning: pollen from the flowering plants, moss, mold, even distantly, the hint of roses.

But it was prey he was interested in. It had been centuries since he had feasted on fresh caught, still twitching meat. Then, of course, it had been a necessity, the only way he could obtain food, now it would be a pleasure: for his taste buds, his sense of exhilaration, and what remained of his soul.

The gargoyle stretched his fingers, enjoying the feel of the talons at the end of them, talons which were far more than appendages, but weapons. He was used to fighting. This would be the first time he would be able to enjoy the fruits of battle. He salivated, thinking of bloody meat.

The Inn stood, tall and imposing behind him, until recently his prison. It was heavy with the woman's scent. He had tasted her blood once, long before. Her flavor lingered. Over ten years, he hadn't forgotten the sweetness. It would be different now, more mature. Definitely he would play with her. Another thing he had not done in centuries was mate. The rising pressure in his groin indicated the depth of pleasure he drew from the mere thought. She would top his list of victims soon enough, but for the moment, he was interested in mindless conquest.

He picked up a trail from the shore of a languid creek. His prey had come to drink, and not long ago. Pleased, he raced on legs and knuckles, closing in on his quarry. He could fly, but for the moment he wanted the sensation of the ground under his feet. It was more sensual somehow. His heart raced, anticipating. Pleasure rippled through him as the scent grew stronger.

He caught the doe unaware, feasting in a meadow on thin, pale green grass. She did not hear him coming, did not spook. Her death came quickly, almost too easily. But he was too hungry for remorse, or to search for more difficult and satisfying prey. He ripped out her throat, let the blood flow over his hands, bathing him, almost anointing him. He dug his tongue into it, lapping the salty tang, feeling, as he did, her heart stop beating. He howled his pleasure.

"Beast—"

The gargoyle looked up, carnage dripping from his fangs. Neither friend nor foe, the man standing in the waist high grass was at the moment, only an annoyance. Still, the gargoyle recognized power, knew that to survive away from the witch's clutches, he might do well to court those who also fought her.

"What do you want?" he demanded. Then, to show he was being inconvenienced, he lowered his face into the doe's abdomen, let his teeth sink into the warm flesh.

"Gargoyle," the wizard said, with the hint of a growl, a trace of anger.

He rose, faced the wizard, and sensed enough about his power to know he was no match for this one's, at least not yet. Let the wizard grow cocky; let his guard drop for an instant, and he would be prey as well. For now he would bow. He would grovel. "Master."

"I have something which might interest you." The wizard wore his black flowing cape as a sign of his vocation. The garment covered his body completely below the neck. The hood was thrown back, so his features were visible, and in this light, the evil radiated off him in waves, like the powerstrands he liked to play with.

The gargoyle would be subservient, but he would not forget and he would get his revenge. He bit again into the hot flesh, tearing muscle, tendons. He swallowed, and then he deigned to look up again. "What?"

The wizard parted the cape, held out his hands, which had been hidden. In them, rested a large egg, as big as an ostrich egg, except even in this light, it appeared to lack substance. It seemed more holographic, visual more than physical.

"What is it?"

"Ne-chakra."

"Pre-chakra?" Longfellow asked, all interest in the deer and in annoying this wizard passing. "Where did you get it?"

"The dragon lair."

"Then he will not be pleased to find it missing. Do you seek to be slaughtered? Even I, with all my power and experience, cannot expect to win against the beast."

The wizard laughed, dominance and arrogance finding form. "I think you are missing the bigger picture. I am not doing this to enrage the dragon. He has been no friend of mine, and where possible I give him wide berth." He remembered dragon fire, and the agony of his recovery, how close he had come to death. "But if an evil creature could assimilate this chakra, if he could corrupt it—"

The possibilities became evident. Longfellow stopped, prevented himself from showing enthusiasm. He slowly licked his talons clean of salty blood. "Such a being would be nearly indestructible. But, chakras are selective with whom they bind."

"Ahh, there is the rub. I have sent word to all the imps in the forest, to the demons of any world which borders this one, to all who wish to be great. Any who would like to try, may have access to this ne-chakra."

The gargoyle grinned, thinning its long, hideous lips. "Any?" he asked.

"Any." The wizard turned away, bided his time before he spoke again, taunting. "But you have a soul. I doubt it would find interest in you."

"I won't have one much longer, as I intend to pull the black thing from me." He hadn't yet. Even a black soul was better than none, but to have opportunity to merge with a chakra, a real chakra, was an unparalleled opportunity.

He straightened, spread his wings. "You will let me have a try?"

"You think you can manage?" The response was tinged with sarcasm, with scorn.

He dug his claws into the blood-soaked grass. "I think it would rather a large fighting beast, than a mere imp."

"If you can catch it, Gargoyle, it is yours, with the understanding of course, that I rule, and your allegiance is to me."

"Of course," Longfellow said, his lips thinning further. "Master." His thoughts continued, words he would not speak to this fool: And the chakra will be mine, and we will see who rules all the evil in this land.

His wings fluttered in leathery anticipation, and the talons at the ends of his fingers flexed, anxious. *And then we will see indeed.*

***

Before Byron, Lori, or Jan could react, Brenda screamed. "You cannot mean that."

The cave was large, but the shout had been loud, and the echo surrounded them, "mean that, mean that." Mean, a word with two definitions: to intend, and the opposite of kind. The offer fit both.

The gargoyle stood without moving, looking exactly like a statue of a corrupted beast at home on a large European cathedral. It was a creature stolen from antiquity, with no place in the modern world, still wearing the bands of his subjugation at his neck, one wrist, one ankle. He had been a prisoner. Now he was seeking revenge.

Brenda shut her eyes, tried to ignore the nightmare surrounding her, but it was worse in the dark, for she feared he would reach out, take what she would never offer freely with his alien claws and prehistoric manners. He didn't move, he didn't flinch, giving her to wonder how many other monstrous gargoyles watched the penitent seeking absolution enter their churches, while they sneered down from above, supremely arrogant.

The lair was dark, especially where the gargoyle stood, but Brenda could almost swear his eyes glowed red, ugly burning coals adding to his feral, untamed look.

Milton ignored the dragon, dismissed the innkeeper who was said to have magic of her own, and paid no attention to the woman on her knees, weeping with a child who wept. With a slow, meticulous smile, he concentrated on the police officer.

"It is my price to rescue your sister's child's ne-chakra." He made eye contact with her, his laser gaze locking with her frightened one. When he spoke with Byron, his attention remained centered on Brenda.

"Now, understand, even should she agree to my terms, I cannot guarantee I will be able to find the ne-chakra, whole or corrupted. I only offer my pledge to search with all of my ability until I find it, or until I die, even should it take the remainder of my life."

Dizzy, Brenda tried to pace, but there was nowhere she wanted to go, so her movements were jerky, a step forward, a step back. She did not want to be closer to the gargoyle, but at this point, she did not want to be any closer to the dragon or her sister either. A stairway rose from the cavern floor, higher than she could see, disappearing into the black void. Would she find escape if she went that way? Probably there were other monsters above, other painful choices. She would stay, she would fight this battle.

"That is absurd. Insane."

Beyond the crying of the infant, there had been silence, the other adults absolutely motionless, until the dragon shifted its weight. *There is nothing else you require? I have wealth, jewels.*

The gargoyle's look sharpened, as if the dragon were beneath his contempt. He lowered his chin, looked down his snout. "We do not value gold or the things dug from this earth. The only thing important to us is our integrity. There has never been a gargoyle who took breath who had use for possessions."

Swallowing her revulsion, Brenda glared at his heavily muscled chest and extremities, so virile and so masculine. She studied his horrendously grotesque head and at the claws at his hands and feet. "You seek to possess me."

The gargoyle crossed his arms against his chest, cocked a hip. "I seek only what your brother-in-law has. A child or children."

"You can't be serious. You can't expect me to…to…" to speak the word would give it possibility, and she wouldn't give the creature even that much power, "…with you?"

Milton nodded and his gaze warmed as it rested on Brenda, as if already he feasted on her flesh. "It is like for like. I will try to save his child; in return, I only ask for the opportunity to father a child."

"You can't honestly expect I would wish to give birth to a monster?"

"Brenda, listen to me, for I am speaking true. Any child of mine will be fully and completely human, in every respect. It will have a soul, it will be mortal, heir to all the blessings LORD gave humans, free agency, joy, pain and suffering. It will look as you do, for it will be human. The curse of the gargoyle, although we who are gargoyles do not consider it a curse, will not extend to the next generation. It is our penance to look like this. No child born from my seed will bear the shame I wear."

"Brenda, please," Lori said. Not knowing what else to do, she held out her arms, with the tiny infant still wailing. "To bring peace to all of us."

"If you do not wish to raise my child, or my children, for I do expect a marriage in every respect, I will do so. But no child of a gargoyle has ever been born a bastard. I require marriage."

None of the adults could meet the gaze of the others. Each found their feet, or their claws, suddenly fascinating, until the dragon spoke, his voice ringing over the bellowing of his son. *It is too high a cost. We will let the infant suffer.*

"Byron, couldn't you search?" Jan asked.

No. Now that the children are dragons and until they are strong enough to defend themselves, they are in danger from the evil forces of the world. Were the children kidnapped now, eventually they would take their draconic form, and if slaughtered, there is much wer-wizards could do to create immense evil using their carcasses. It is a question of numbers. I will stay and guard the three, forced to sacrifice the one.

Lori snarled. "Byron, you can't mean to let Lorenzo suffer."

The dragon morphed, quickly. One moment it was twenty feet tall, the next, Brenda saw a lean man with long arms reach out and caress his wife. Because Brenda was so close, she heard the words he whispered. "Beloved, this is not an easy decision for me to make, for I know what the boy is missing. I know why he aches, and he will never find peace without his chakra. I want to search. I want to find the demon who is making us suffer and rip him to shreds, yet I must consider the others. They are vulnerable. Jan cannot protect them. Only I can. Taking one chakra might be a ruse to draw me away, abandoning our other sons. Think of the evil the wer-wizard Andrew could cause with three dragons in his possession. We know he had no trouble entering the cave. We don't know how yet, but I promise you I will find the entrance he used and close it for all time, gargoyle on the premises or not."

Wrapped in her husband's embrace, in his love, Lori cried, and the infant she held wailed louder still, as if, Brenda thought, being so close to a real dragon made the infant realize what he was missing.

"And Lorenzo will never find peace? Never?"

Byron changed back into his draconic form, an action so swift this time, in a blink a man was gone, replaced by a gold colored reptile. *To answer your question honestly, I do not know. I have never been near a half-dragon before, for, what few there were are shunned among us. I would imagine eventually he will not cry as much, and will become resigned to his fate. If he survives, I doubt he could ever be productive as a human, for he never will be human and never be whole. Brenda, I do not require you to make this sacrifice.*

"I do," Lori said, her face ravaged by grief.

Brenda swallowed, then wiped her eyes. She had no idea how long she had been crying, although she suspected it had been a while. She had been so touched by the beauty when the first chakra merged with an infant that her eyes had watered and the depth of her expression had only heightened as the other two merged, as comfortable and complete, the children fell asleep. Since, she had been watching Lorenzo suffer. While Byron had been speaking to the gargoyle, she had been watching her sister weep. She had been praying silently for something she could do to help ease his pain. "Certainly someone else must have a gargoyle chained in their basement...a female."

"No, that is what made them so valuable to me," Jan said. Her face too, was drenched with tears.

"I am willing to help—as a cop. I am willing to face danger. I will hunt the thief. I will find him, if you are unwilling."

The gargoyle had been motionless for so long she had almost forgotten he was still there, until he spoke again. "You would be slaughtered. This Evil fought a dragon in his prime and was nearly victorious."

Lori nodded, conceding the point. "True, Andrew almost killed both of us."

The wer-wizard is not a creature you can fight, even if you found him.

The gargoyle licked his lips with his long, slender, evil-looking tongue. "The danger you will face from me will be of a different nature. You might even come to enjoy it."

"I doubt that."

The dragon hissed, then his voice rang through the cavern with bell clarity. *Do you seek to harm her?*

"No mortal of clean heart has ever suffered at the hands of a gargoyle. That is documented. You may research it through the archives, if you wish. Her heart is pure. I would like a wife. I will cherish her as a mate, perhaps even come to love her."

Brenda swiped her eyes. She found her dignity as she searched for her stoicism. "Then you admit you do not love me?"

The gargoyle's long pointed ears twitched and his enormous wings unfurled, before folding back down. "How could I? That emotion takes decades to set. But, in honesty, I am in lust with you. I desire to mate with you."

His head was so animal, so hideous. He had a beast's snout and horns. For heaven's sake, he had horns. She lowered her gaze, down his perfectly formed chest, to the loincloth he wore over his hips.

He understood where she looked, knew what it would take to embarrass her. He sidled closer and raised her chin, his hands on her jaw remarkably tender. "That part of me you would consider normal. I could bring you pleasure."

"You sicken me."

He met her gaze and held it, for she did not have the strength to look away. "I do not believe that."

How long before you require an answer from the maid?

"I put no time limit on it. But every minute we delay is a minute I could be searching for the chakra."

"And you would never do this thing for the baby?" Lori asked. "For Lorenzo?"

Milton's gaze softened as he shifted his look from Brenda to Lori and her suffering child. "No. And I will explain my rational so you not think me heartless. I have been chained for centuries, locked in a dungeon with a creature who for all practical purposes is my mortal enemy, when I should have been out fulfilling my destiny. I have my freedom now, but if I agree to do this thing, it is naught but another type of prison for me. I will have no rights, no agency until the chakra is returned or destroyed. You have my word. I will do nothing, literally nothing, but search for the chakra once I have given my Vow to search."

"Nothing, but impregnate me."

"You might not find it so repulsive."

"I find you repulsive."

"Then your sister's child will suffer." He raised his wings, stretched them out, a wingspan of twelve or thirteen feet. They sounded leathery, dry, frightening. Every time she looked at him, she thought Halloween masks, as if this were some kind of macabre joke, and she had only to yell 'hold' and he would stop it. But also every time she looked at him she saw something obviously not human and completely beyond her frame of reference.

His wings flapped again, once, twice, as if in preparation for flight. "If you need me, to agree to my bargain, you have only to call my name. I will return." He turned his back, started walking to the far side of the cave, where, apparently, there was an exit someone with the capability of flight could use.

Brenda took a step forward, her knees wobbly. She had been standing motionless too long. "Wait! Don't go. You don't have to come back." She swallowed, then spoke quickly before she could change her mind. "I'll enter into your devil's bargain."

The gargoyle's response was immediate and considerable. His roar had the cavern walls shaking, throbbing. Falling to her knees, covering her ears, Brenda wondered if the bellow would ever end.

"I have literally made a devil's bargain, so I know what I am talking about. This, which I have offered you, is no covenant with Satan but an eternal pledge between you and I and which would be witnessed by the One God. I am no longer interested. Take your foolish ignorance and find comfort in it. I retract my offer. My apologies…" this with a bow to Lori and the crying infant she held, "…for I would have liked to attempt to ease your pain. I owe nothing to the dragon. And witch," he said, turning to Jan, "I will not even attempt to mention what I think you owe me. Adieu," he said. With a bow, and flapping his wings, Milton was gone a heartbeat later.

***

The next week lasted an eternity. Lorenzo would sleep for an hour or two and would occasionally stop crying when he was awake, but when he did, his eyes were dulled, glassy and sunken into his sockets. He lost weight and color and he became frail and while Byron assured them he would not die, it was obvious he would not thrive. His three brothers nursed heartily and when they tightened their tiny fists around a finger, their grip was firm and strong. Already, only a week after absorbing their chakras, they were visibly round, pink, and alert. Three boys could grin. Three boys could follow objects with their bright, inquisitive eyes, three boys could sleep untroubled. And with each day, the differences between them and their brother magnified.

The cavern at the top of the stairs was becoming second nature to Brenda, but she doubted she could ever get used to the dragon, who rocked a crying infant just inside the landing.

"Lori?" she asked the creature.

Finally drifted off to sleep. She is so exhausted, even Lorenzo isn't keeping her up, but I doubt she'll sleep long. None of us have.

In an effort to both make herself useful and keep out from underfoot, Brenda had been washing dishes, eight, ten, twelve hours a day, making no discernible progress on the huge stacks, but she figured it helped, for Jan always looked grateful as she slipped in or out through the back door. Jan, and a friend she called Arthur who Brenda had not yet met, had been looking for the wizard, but there were too many portals, too many kingdoms and from what Jan could determine, the wizard was keeping a low profile. If the chakra had merged with an evil creature or been destroyed, no one had any idea.

"I'm glad she's sleeping. Don't wake her. I just came to say I'm leaving, going back to work."

That is a decision you must make.

"Byron, I'm sorry. I feel responsible."

You are not to blame for the actions of one evil wizard. And put your heart to rest. Earlier this morning I found the imp who led the wer-wizard to the nest. It has been dealt with and will have no more opportunity to betray my trust.

"Imp?"

A small creature of lesser faerie. They have always had free rein over this cavern, for while they are annoying, there is rarely any evil to them. This one was caught by the wer-wizard, and made a deal to save its own life. I am certain the wizard had no idea the prize the imp was leading him to, or he would have come better prepared and taken all four. He planned to return for the other three, that much is obvious, for he did not destroy them. Because the gargoyle hunted the forest here and alerted Jan and me, he was unable to come back. Brenda, realize too, the gargoyle stayed in the area to be close to you. So rather than blame you for the continued loss of one, I must thank you for the safety of the other three.

"I...um...did nothing."

Be that as it may, Milton remained because of you. I wish you success in your career and happiness, whatever happens. I will tell Lori you have gone.

Then, before Brenda could react or respond, the dragon was gone and in his place stood Byron and he hugged her warmly, but her guilt was so great she could not stay. Fighting back tears, she ran, blind, down the stairs to her car and started for home, where she was needed, where she would not have to witness a tiny infant suffer.

***

"Larwick, is something bothering you?" Sal DeLuca asked. He was wizened and gray haired, a cop, she had once decided, since Marshall Matt Dillon held law in Dodge City, and who had simply moved eastward every century or so. She loved him as a father or grandfather, for he was more than a mentor, but was also a friend. They scrapped, battling over his donuts versus her salads, but there was no one she would rather have guarding her back, no one she trusted as much, even if she had not been able to share with him what she discovered at her aunt's upstate B&B.

"There's nothing bothering me. Haven't I been holding up my end of the shift work?"

"That and then some," he agreed. "But your shift ended three hours ago. You should be prettying yourself up, getting ready to go out on the town. Tell me, why aren't you trolling for some man to bring you pleasure?"

Funny, how with the line, some man to bring you pleasure, she hadn't thought of a man at all, but a creature of darkness, with a soft, deep voice, gentle hands. A monster who had once called her bitch, but who had cried when three infants became whole when they merged with their chakras.

And with Sal's line, she didn't remember the fear she had as a child, the terror she had experienced as she felt his talons at her throat. She only thought of pleasure and impossibility and an aching, enduring loneliness.

With a couple of key strokes, she turned off the computer, leaned back in her chair which was old and gave her low back pain, but which was so familiar she named it Fred and wouldn't trade it for the world. Fred creaked, aching joints, arthritis probably, and she could relate, for she felt aged and infirm herself. Although she still jogged, although her body was still young and in good shape, the spark seemed to have gone out of her. She felt ninety or a hundred, with gnarled fingers and throbbing knees, when in reality she knew all her pain centered around a decision she had made not to help an infant, even when she honestly did not know how she could have made any other.

They had been having a good week. It seemed every time they rode out, they came back with a clean collar. Yesterday they even picked up a fugitive on the FBI's Ten Most Wanted List, without a shot fired. They had been on routine patrol when that familiar Voice told her to stop in and check out a small, traveling carnival. Although she had not seen Milton since the Inn and he was not around to talk when she sat on her porch swing and she ached for the comradeship they had, he had still been whispering insight to her, an average of nearly once a day.

"What's in here?" Sal wanted to know as she flipped on her turn signal and pulled the squad car into the lot.

"Donuts," she answered.

"Do we need backup?" he asked, familiar now with her unfailing intuition.

"Probably. When do we not?" she asked, driving into a 'No Parking Police Only' lane and leaving the car.

"What is it?"

"Haven't got a clue," Brenda answered, "but whatever it is, it is at the carousel."

"Seems quiet enough," Sal said, wary. His hand wasn't far from his weapon, but there were too many people, especially families with young children for him to feel comfortable drawing. Brenda watched him silently pray this one wouldn't turn ugly, and with a nod she added her Amen. It had been early Friday morning, and although the crowds were not heavy, there were plenty of people about. Still nothing appeared out of kilter when who should they come across running the carousel but a three time convicted murderer, wanted two time zones away. He was in a cell now, awaiting extradition to Nevada.

"Nice hunch," was all Sal had said, as he filed paperwork. And her 'hunches' continued, early that same afternoon as they went for lunch. "Stop here!" she said, pointing to a donut shop and Sal had laughed, for donuts were his vice, not hers, when they came across a robbery in progress and a clerk who would have bled to death if they'd arrived even ten minutes later. They still hadn't eaten.

"You go home, Larwick. Any other bad guys will have to wait until Monday morning, or we can let the weekend shift have a go. We don't have to clean up the streets by ourselves."

"I'm going," she said, grabbing her purse from her locker.

"You are?"

"I'm driving up north. My sister and her husband have a sick child and I'm interested in seeing how he is doing."

"So that's what's had you distracted?" he asked, a gentle probe, but since they were friends, she took no offense.

"Distracted? Is that what you think I've been? I have been here with you, holding up my end of the duty roster."

"Sure you have. But every now and then, when you think I'm not looking, you're scanning the skies. What are you expecting, your guardian angel?"

"Something like that," for she wasn't a woman prone to inspiration and more than once she was certain she saw a large creature awing who could easily be telepathically offering her suggestions, even going as far as watching her back.

"Best wishes then to your nephew. Send him my love, if you don't mind. And, if there's anything I can do, give him a kidney or anything, be sure and let me know."

"I don't think a kidney would help. I should be back Monday morning."

"If you're not, I'll clear it with the captain."

"I will be," she said, but knew, as she pulled her keys from her purse, that if she went through with the absurd plan she was hatching, more than likely she'd be deeply involved with something else come Monday morning.

CHAPTER 11

It was a two hour trip up the Northway, an easy drive over excellent roads, with beautiful scenery, rolling hills and hardwood forests which sprouted "Deer Crossing" signs every few miles. Brenda might have felt better about the trip if her stomach had not been used by fifty Boy Scouts to practice tying knots.

"I wish you'd leave me alone," she said, having no idea if Milton could hear her or not, only knowing she had to speak to someone, even if it were herself.

The problem was he did leave her alone. She could hardly consider him to be stalking her, when all he did was whisper advice which resulted in apprehending criminals thus making Albany safer and putting her career on the fast track. Most police officers would be happy to have a major bust once in a distinguished career. She was having them almost daily.

She drove due north into evening for to the west, over her left shoulder the sky was adorned in russets and oranges, twilight colors. It would be a pretty sunset, if she could find a scenic overlook to check it out, and the night would be cloudless, giving stars free reign. She would like to take Lorenzo out and show him the constellations. Poor Lorenzo, she was certain he still had not stopped crying.

Brenda searched through her windshield for she suspected she was not alone, but she saw nothing except other drivers making the weekend commute as she was, families in minivans with kids piled haphazardly in the backseat, watching Shrek or Monsters Inc. or Beauty and the Beast on video. When she thought of monsters who only looked foul but which were really gentle, she had to pull off the road to hurl the burger she had bought as she slipped out of town. She still hadn't come to terms emotionally with what she had decided to do. She didn't understand this deep-seated need all of a sudden, to be a victim.

***

Brenda shifted the car into park, turned off the engine, and though the windshield stared at the B&B. From this angle it didn't look all that imposing or frightening, and she wondered how the cave at the top of the stairs fit in, for as far as she could tell, there were only five stories. The red tile roof was steeply pitched with gables and chimneys but the trees encroached so she couldn't tell. A cave. She would rather think of herself insane, or hallucinating. She would rather put the car back on Route 87 and head south, but she was not that much of a coward.

It no longer felt like her life was her own, but whether it was Lorenzo's or Milton's, or even possessed by evil spirits, she had no idea. Free agency, the hulking gargoyle had promised her, and now, sitting alone in the dark, she doubted that was true. Whatever agency was, and at the moment she had no definition, she doubted it was free. Everything good was hard won, everything evil was hard fought. Nothing came without a price tag. She only had to decide if she were buying or selling and if it were worth the cost.

She exited the car, locked it, then, because she didn't feel like she could face her aunt, her sister, her brother-in-law, or one tiny wailing infant, Brenda took off at an easy lope, jogging toward the pond. Crickets chortled, having the time of their lives, seeking mates. Isn't that what their song was for? Seductive music to lure the opposite sex? Lightning beetles, with their intermittent flashes were doing the same thing. Frogs singing along the shore, owls who-wooing. Spring was a time for forming alliances. She thought of the sheets on her bed and the hulking, deformed Milton and she couldn't imagine anything at all.

She drew up short as she approached the bench, not the slightest bit winded, for the jog hadn't been long and she had paced herself. The exercise after being cramped in the compact car felt good. It was the first thing in weeks to feel good, and if she went through with her plan, likely to be the last time she would feel good for ages to come. The flame still burned, although she thought it might be a tad smaller. It provided heat, which she didn't need, and light which she did.

The bench was occupied.

His profile was bathed in dragonfire, and gave a ruddy appearance to his complexion, healthier looking than his gray to green normal skin tone. "I knew as soon as you took to the highway what your destination would be," the gargoyle said. He stood, bowed, courtly and oh so politely. "If you wish to be alone, or you wish never to see me, I will bid you a pleasant evening and leave."

"No, that's all right. I wanted to see you." Perhaps she should not have admitted that. Perhaps he was not there, and instead she was insane. Brenda would have believed that, had not his tips been so accurate.

Fighting revulsion, for he was repulsive, she forced herself closer, sat beside him, although she left a good two feet distance between her body and his.

"Lorenzo?" she asked. After all, he was what this was all about.

"The ne-chakra has not been returned. The infant remains incomplete."

"Has he…is he eating?"

She read his sorrow. It floated off him in waves. "Only enough to stay alive. Lorraine and the dragon suffer as their child suffers. They get very little sleep. The dragon has not even left to hunt food for himself. The innkeeper must bring in meat, adding to her burdens."

"And the dishes, are they finally clean?"

"I do not know. I have not been inside since the day the three chakras merged." The day he had asked, or rather demanded, she become his wife. A question of semantics.

"Have you looked?"

"For the ne-chakra? No. I meant what I said. This is not my quest and I do not wish to get involved without compensation."

"Compensation." She swallowed, but her throat was dry so the action was without purpose. The whole point in coming was without purpose.

Silence rattled around them. Funny how loud silence could seem when there was too much to say and no way to say it. She jingled her keys, needing to hear something before she could put into words what haunted her. "You said you made a deal with the devil?"

His chin had been lowered for he suffered for the child, but with her question he dropped it further and spoke to his chest. "I did. It is not something I speak of lightly, nor discuss at all with those who choose only to mock."

"And do you work for him now?"

"Because you are ignorant, and because you are only seeking information for a decision you must make, I take no offense at your question. I serve LORD, and have since before this world was formed."

"The devil…" she asked, still needing clarification.

"There is a literal devil. He is not corporeal as you and I, but believe me when I tell you he exists. The creature who stole the ne-chakra is his servant, though perhaps both would deny the relationship."

"Then you were, by your own definition, evil at one time?"

"A very short time, but the answer is yes. It is the reason the HOLD command was laid upon me, and those who were with me."

"Punishment?"

He started to nod, then shook his head instead. "It is not punishment so much as acknowledgement. We erred, sinned," he corrected, "and we take responsibility for our actions."

"House arrest?"

"A close analogy."

"The HOLD spell, will it always stop you?"

He met her glance. His pupils were black, fathomless, but while his earlier demeanor spoke of sorrow for the infant's plight, there was aggression in him now, and perhaps more than a slight measure of self-defense. "Do you wish to know or do you only mock?"

Because he was right, she did intend to mock, she spoke quickly. "Does it make a difference?"

"It does. I do not speak of sacred things with those who seek only derision or a diversion."

Brenda curled her top lip. "How easily you speak of sacred things."

"Believe me when I say I have the right."

She did not like the direction the conversation was veering. "We were talking about the HOLD spell. Are you always susceptible?"

He let the silence develop while he debated whether to answer. Silence, except for mating crickets, mating frogs, mating owls.

"Yes and no." His fingers were long, tapered to stiletto points, curled and inhuman. She watched while he folded them together, a movement indicative of prayer. "I will explain. I have a soul and therefore I have free agency, so I can decide not to let the HOLD spell affect me. In doing so, I would have to break covenants I hold sacred. Yet, I cannot imagine a time or place when I would consider such an action."

"But you could ignore the HOLD spell?"

"Yes. Anytime I wish, I can ignore it, but listen clearly: I have been alive centuries and have always fallen under its jurisdiction. It has always stopped me."

She stood, moving closer to the dragonfire, her hands out for warmth, but she didn't need the heat, so she turned back to face him. "Then the day you told us the chakra was stolen, when my aunt had you rechained, you could have ignored her command and escaped with your freedom."

"Yes."

"Yes? As simple as that?"

"I admit for an instant I was tempted, for I know how sweet freedom feels on my wings now. And I had her promise she would not so restrain me. I could have argued to myself that she had broken the verbal agreement first—she was in the wrong to yell HOLD, but I would rather be chained in her dungeon for all of eternity than break my covenants. And Brenda, if I neglected to thank you properly for releasing me, do know I am grateful."

"I don't want your gratitude." She never had. She only wanted to be left alone. "But what you're saying is the HOLD spell will always stop you?"

Milton raised his jaw, met her gaze, and she wished she could read his emotions, for his eyes were alive and there was something there, but Brenda did not know what it was for he was still a mystery to her.

"With one exception, or perhaps two, I give you my word it will always stop me. Does that satisfy your curiosity?"

"I'm not sure."

She waited, having no words. He waited, having only patience, until he spoke and Milton realized he could not feel patient and sit beside her. "What do you want from me?"

"Now?"

"Now," he agreed, "with your questions."

"An out, I suppose, some reason not to consider what I'm considering. Or barring that, answers to questions that make no sense, I guess. That's obvious, isn't it? I'm a cop. I'm used to the answers not making sense. This is the first time the questions don't make sense."

She looked to his lap, where his hands were still clasped. His thighs were huge, broadly muscled. She could see scars, faint traces, one upon another, looking like worm trails in soft mud after a rain. "You fight?" she asked, indicating the scars.

He pulled his hands apart, rubbed his thighs, giving her the opportunity to see anew the curved claws at the end of his fingers. "It was why the Innkeepers kept me chained. I kept evil out. Evil which has made it that far into the Inn never left quietly."

"And you're a gargoyle?" she asked. Even the obvious suddenly needed clarification.

"I am."

"A living gargoyle?"

"For as long as time is left me, a living gargoyle. I told you that earlier. Did you not believe me?"

Brenda was restless. She shifted, squirmed. "It's not that I don't believe you. I'm trying to understand. I did a Google search and came up with tons of hits on gargoyles, but only those for sale, nothing having to do with devil's agreements or HOLD spells."

"I do not know what a Google search is, but if you are using some tool to hit gargoyles, I should tell you—"

She would not let him finish. "No, nothing like that. I used a computer, tried to research gargoyles."

"The witch has mentioned a computer. She believes knowledge is power."

"And you?"

He stretched his fingers long, then coiled them back toward his palms. "I see things differently."

Her sister was an academic. No doubt Lori too felt knowledge was power. While Brenda did not disagree, as a policeman, she realized there were too many other ways to amass power.

"What I'm saying is I didn't find any answers from the computer. I, umm, were you watching me?" If he knew all this, she would feel the fool confessing it.

"No. I seek evil. When I would find it, I would deal with it myself, or if it were in Albany, I would let you know. I did not have the time to follow you during those times when you were not in danger."

In front of her a fire burned. She had no idea how or why, did not know that once, to give her sister comfort, a chakra had created it.

"I have never been close to my sister." This was a confession which was painful, and she wiped at her eyes, but there were no tears. "As an adult I see her differently than I did as a child. I want to be her sister, and I want our family to be healthy, but I don't know whether or not that is possible when she is married to that...thing."

"You do not approve of the dragon?"

"I do not know him. He looks—"

He knew why she broke off, would grant her no pity. "He looks as evil as I do."

"Yes. I mean, I know enough not to judge a person by their looks. I've been on the streets. Looks mean nothing to me when I have evidence. But for all practical purposes, we're not talking people here."

The gargoyle said nothing, and Brenda knew she had hurt him. "Lori says Byron makes her happy. I was there as she suffered her labor, as she fought to bring his children into the world. I saw how she loved him and how much he loves her. And children, whatever else they are, are a blessing from God."

"That they are." His words spoke of reverence.

"I have a decision to make, although I also understand if I do not make a decision, I am in fact making another decision." She smiled in derision of her own statement. "I don't have any information. I don't know who or what to believe, and anything I thought before seems to be wrong."

Stars popped out, first one bright, bold one, then others, more shyly, until there were thousands. "Wrong? The tenets your life is based on are true."

"Is it? I thought dragons were fantasy. I thought gargoyles waterspouts," he curled a lip, but made no noise. "I never heard of a chakra, or an imp and the only wizards and witches I knew came from inventive fiction. And, I want to feel love. I want to cherish the man I marry, be his equal and his friend and his lover, sharing everything between us without deceit or deception."

"There has been no deceit," he said, which only forced her to think there might be deception.

"Lorenzo's life is at stake, so I searched for answers. I found a Catholic church, which had gargoyles outside. They were not—"

"No," he agreed, "they are representatives of my kind, as if having a statue of something of power will provide the same power."

"I spoke to a priest. He didn't know either. I'm sure he thought me a lunatic, asking after living gargoyles."

"If it would ease your mind, I can give you names of religious leaders who could help you, should you give me time to compile a list. While they would not know of me personally, they would know the religious significance of gargoyles. Would that be of benefit?"

She twisted her head, her thick braid whipping around her shoulders. "Yes, no, I have no idea. Will they know why you need a wife?"

"If they are sensitive, they will understand every living creature at some time feels the need to procreate."

"You're not teasing me, are you? Torturing me?"

"I don't understand the question."

"You're not doing this deliberately, forcing me to choose between my happiness and Lori's?"

"If by your words you mean do I seek to cause you pain, through my actions or the bargain I am willing to enter into, the answer is no. I have been a prisoner for centuries longer than you can imagine. Now that I am free, I wish a family. There is nothing unusual about that. I have not been able to seek a wife before this, and your aunt never thought to address the subject. And you, Brenda, have you ever thought of having a child?"

She wanted to lie, but he had been honest with her, so she felt constrained to do the same. "Yes, of course I want a child. But my career has been important to me, and there never has been a man I have been attracted to seriously enough to get careless." She wiped a tear, hated that it made her look weak, pitiful. If the guys on the force could see her now she would be crushed, not that it was any better for Milton to witness her humiliation. "Lately I've been thinking being an aunt to Lori's children might be enough."

"Enough?" he questioned, "When they are not even human?"

"They cry. They suck their thumbs. Their diapers need changing. They are human enough for me."

"Based on that logic—"

"No, I refuse to consider you human. Look at yourself. How can I think that?"

"You are right. I am not human. But this is the truth, Brenda: I am heir to all the blessings LORD gave humans. Do you not want to share in those blessings? Do you not want a child of your own?"

"That's the problem. I do. I want to feel my body change. I want to suffer through morning sickness and pick out tiny outfits of blue or pink. I want to plan a college fund, and worry about car insurance for a new driver. I want…the list is endless." Before meeting Milton, she had only wanted to be a cop. Strange since meeting him she had become so needy.

The wind kicked up, a stray breeze, and with it the sound of something large hunting the night. Milton's ears twitched and he raised his nose, scenting the night. "Do not be afraid. I will protect you. While I am here, nothing will approach us."

She returned to the bench, sat and faced him, putting her right ankle under her left knee. It was the closest she had ever willingly approached him. "Is it foolish to want a child? I know how hard it is. I've heard the talk. No sleep, tons of bills, ear aches, orthodontics, play dates and after all that, the child will never be what you expect."

"That last at least is for the best," he said, and she grinned.

"If you were human, and you made that request of me: marriage in return for helping someone I love, I'd slap handcuffs on you so fast you wouldn't be able to turn around, and I'd have you in front of a judge for extortion or at the very least, sexual harassment."

"But I am not, and I have no other way to find a mate other than a bargain. I could hardly do a Google search."

She laughed at the fact he had picked up her phrase so readily. He continued. "I would not be welcomed in a single's bar."

"I don't know. You might fit right in. Not a lot of single's bars have a dress code."

He moved his lips in what might be the gargoyle equivalent of a smile, but the light was bad and Brenda could not be sure.

"I think it is significant you are already comfortable enough with me to joke. Our relationship would not be bad for you. I could give you a human child. You could work or not work as you wish. Although I told the dragon I have no need of his jewels, I could support you. I have no wealth, but your children would never go hungry, and I swear you would never be without everything you need to make your life bearable."

It stunned her she was starting to think she would enter into this bargain and even wanted to. "Maybe I'm greedy. Maybe I want more than a bearable life."

"With me, you could have all you desire. I could continue to assist you at work as I do now if you wish. After our child is conceived, I would leave you at night, if you prefer to sleep alone. I will not be a demanding husband.

"Having said that, I do require a marriage from you—should you agree to my terms. Should we become husband and wife, I would ask as much as you are able you do not treat me as an object to be switched off should I no longer appeal to you. I will require your honest participation in the marriage if it happens. And Brenda, your birth control pills will not prevent conception if conception is destined to occur."

"How lightly you speak of destiny."

"If you believe that, then you know me not at all." He stood, and in the evening breeze, his wings fluttered. "You are not ready to make the commitment, so I bid you a good evening."

"Wait, Gargoyle—"

"Yes?"

"May I see you again?"

"Should you wish it, I will be here, at this bench anytime you are or if you call my name from the dragon's lair, I will come there."

"I don't like to be frightened."

"Then I will keep my distance."

"Then," Brenda said, "you know me not at all."

***

Longfellow stroked the ne-chakra, rubbing it gently with the pads of his hands.

"You think to get it used to you?" the wizard asked.

"I do. Will it harden before it is set to crack, or grow softer?"

"There is nothing written in the lore. If the dragons know, they have not told my kind and if other wizards have successfully controlled one, they have kept that information to themselves. Wer-wizards do not share power."

"Still," the gargoyle said, "I would like it to be used to my feel and my scent. When it hatches, it will accept me."

CHAPTER 12

Brenda kept away from the gargoyle during the day. That was easy, for she told herself she wasn't thinking of him every minute, and proved it by staying in the kitchen, washing the endless supply of dishes. When her fingers grew wrinkled from soapsuds, when her back ached from standing over the sink, when she could not face another filthy pot or she felt she would scream, she kept herself busy by holding, changing and loving the other three boys.

That would have been a delight, except she was always aware of the sorrow permeating the cavern, for there was one child she did not feel comfortable holding, one she found every reason to shy away from.

The other three infants needed attention too. Holding one, or two, she would read to them, silly children's picture books Jan had bought in town, letting them get used to the cadence of her voice, the sounds and the rhythms and the music of the words strung together. She looked them in the eye, and told them they were fabulous and handsome. She nuzzled their bellies when they were sleepy, for they were soft, and she could pretend she was helping, as she avoided looking at the far corner, where the darkness reigned, and one child wailed.

It was unbelievable how much Lorenzo could cry. And with each tear, with each second, a part of Brenda died too.

Lorenzo lost weight. His bones looked rubbery as they started to stand out in stark ugly exposure covered only by a thin layer of skin which had a sickly pallor. His eyes took on that hollow look, always so expertly depicted in paintings of ghosts or others who were damned. Brenda had always thought such artwork overdone, excessive, but now whenever she caught a glimpse of the baby, she realized how macabre true pain could look.

After a while, his cries grew weaker, but everyone in the cave knew that was not a good sign. No one said anything to her, or mentioned with her sacrifice she could ease the baby's suffering, not Jan, Lori or Byron, but she knew she was responsible, and minute by minute her heart shattered.

She was a police officer, trained to keep her emotions under strict control to face whatever nightmares the street regurgitated on her shift, but such stoicism was impossible with a baby suffering, with the sharply delineated differences of the three others who were soft and smelled so sweet. It was also impossible to keep her heart locked up when always, whenever she turned, there was a possibility of facing the huge, winged monster who wanted her for his own.

Brenda was able to avoid Milton during the day. It was harder to keep away at night, for any number of reasons: Jan refused to let her wash dishes then, saying even she needed time off, and the three babies slept quietly in their cribs, while Lori and Byron and her aunt tried to snatch a few minutes rest for themselves, staying in shifts, for one person was always needed to hold the infant who could find no peace.

And her insomnia was back, raging, full force. So she returned that night to the bench, although she hadn't wanted to.

He stood, the rustling of his wings no longer frightening and offered her a slight bow, not of welcome, and not even of arrogance. This time she read only humility, or perhaps disgust, with her, with himself. Brenda decided the distinction didn't really matter.

"I will leave, if you wish." His voice was low, rich, almost seductive. There had been a time, in the not too distant past, when she had welcomed that sound, almost cherished the comfort of it.

She raised the tongue on her jacket, zipping it to her neck although the night was warm and she didn't need it. She could not decide on what she felt, when there were so many emotions caustically traveling through her bloodstream, so she decided on disgust. "You act like you have such decency, like you care about my feelings, yet you let that baby suffer."

"It is not I who causes Lorenzo agony."

The breeze freshened, carried a taint of something rotting. "Still, you would hold me to your bargain."

"Yes and no," the beast answered, for he looked even more repulsive in the dark, heavy shadows of night, his wings bigger, more deformed, his hands—his claws--more alien. "I do care about your feelings, and I understand decency and no, I do not hold you to the bargain. I only offer it. The decision must be yours."

Even in the shifting light of the dragon pyre, his eyes were dark. She could not see the pupils. When Brenda looked at him, all she could see was deep, fathomless holes in his head.

She thought of the dungeon at the base of the Inn, of the chains, and her stomach twirled. Since Milton offered his deal she had been unable to get much food down. Beautifully prepared meals still appeared on a regular basis but she could not chew, could not swallow, and whether because of the condition of the kitchen or the condition of her heart, she had no idea.

Unsettled, she walked toward the fire, dropped her chin to her chest, her long hair cascading around her. "And if I cannot decide?"

Milton moved closer until he stood behind her, a hulking monster, a creature from antiquity, but she was not afraid of him so much as of herself: what she might choose, of the decision she perhaps subliminally wanted to make.

His voice was a whisper, and again, spoke of comfort. "Then you cannot. It has and always will be your choice."

She was cold and hot and trembling. Her eyes stung as if bathed in lemon juice. Blinking did not help, seemed only to exacerbate the problem. She breathed deeply, hoping to fill the emptiness inside her with something, only if it were air. "The baby is suffering."

The gargoyle shrugged. "I can hear him. Do you think I am insensitive to his plight?"

She twirled around until the fire was at her back, found that a tactical mistake, for now he was only inches from her, not touching, but close enough that the air they breathed was the same. Now she felt heat down her spine, and heat of another sort facing her, yet, oddly, she remained chilled to the marrow of her bones.

"Yet you could help."

He shook his head, the long, broad snout traveling side to side. "That is perhaps, not true. I have offered to look and I do have some ability to locate and destroy evil, but as to the quest, the finding of the chakra, I can make no guarantees."

"Then I could marry you for nothing."

He stopped moving as if she had paralyzed him, with hope or despair, Brenda had no idea. "That is not how I would see it. We would have a marriage that could last decades, something holy."

Brenda still found him repulsive, and she moved away, cursing herself, and cursing him, and escaped back to her room, stared out the window into the darkness and wondered why she wished she were back out there, by the dragon pyre, sitting on the bench, when she despised him so.

***

The next night she was back, for she had a decision to make, and if the answer were no, she needed to return to the police force and her interrupted life. She could not, would not, stay here, the way things were.

The sound of snarling reached her long before she reached the bench, vicious growls and the snapping of teeth and the ripping of flesh which accompanied it. A dog fight, she thought, for it always amazed her how loud those things were, but there were no dogs involved. The night was dark, the constellations unfamiliar, but the dragonfire was bright and in its shadows she could see movement.

Brenda moved carefully, inching closer. Dogs she thought again, but the creatures which could walk both on four legs and on two, were not dogs. Dozens of them were moving, shifting, attacking, so it was impossible to get an accurate count. And in the middle: Milton. By himself, the gargoyle fought ten or fifteen black, bear-like monsters, and he was clearly outnumbered. She noticed about five of the demon-like creatures dead or dying on the grass which surrounded the pond and the bench, their throats ripped open, or with gaping wounds in their stomach, and it sickened her to realize how violent Milton could be.

But while she was nauseated by the violence, she also experienced increasing terror. The remaining monsters could see the gargoyle was tiring, and their strategy was improving, for they had learned not to attack him individually, but to fight as a unit, from all sides at the same time, and it would be only a matter of time before he was overcome, or forced to flee.

For he did have wings, and they did not, but perhaps he did not recognize that.

"Milton—"

He looked up. Before that moment Brenda was certain he was not aware she was there. "Take to the sky. Leave before they kill you," she shouted. She cursed, for she did not have her weapon, although she did not know if bullets could even hurt the black things.

And while she searched, looking for any help she could offer Milton in his battle, she noticed a second gargoyle, standing on the far side of the dragon's pyre, beside the weeping willow, watching, and he looked pleased with how the fight was progressing.

"I cannot leave." He was wounded in a half-dozen places, long, bleeding gashes along his legs, arms and wings. His blood, in the late evening, looked black.

The beasts continued to attack, leaping for his throat, latching onto his wrists and his legs, pinning him, so it mattered not if he changed his mind and attempted to flee. He no longer could.

Desperate to help, not knowing what the creatures were, but knowing instinctively they were evil, Brenda continued to search for a weapon. She had no time to run back to the house for her gun, or to inform her aunt for Milton had fallen down. He crawled on his hands and knees, trying to keep the beasts from his throat. Snarling, grappling, snapping, the monsters jumped all over his back, his wings, throat and legs. Milton bellowed, a cry of pain, and they howled, the chilled call of evil domination.

It was then she saw the pyre as something other than a source of heat and light. Brenda moved quickly. Silently.

Eleven. "Well, that's less than a dozen," Brenda whispered continuing on with her quest. She could feel the heat from the fire now on her face, her hands. She sought a weapon there, a branch not completely engulfed in flame, one she could hold. Adrenaline surged through her body. She knew this feeling of rushing into danger and liked it, even as she realized the odds were not in her favor. She could die here. But even that did not stop her.

The beasts were single-minded in their intensity, attacking only Milton, ignoring her, which left Brenda free to pull a burning brand from the flames, and raise it. Holding the branch two-handed, she caught two unawares, turning them into flaming infernos, torches which yelped and ran, but did not make it far before they dropped, dead. Then, without any form of communication she understood, the attack split, half of the large black monsters concentrating on her, the remainder staying with their original target and fighting the gargoyle.

Swinging her branch in a half-circle in front of her, her defense now looked insubstantial. Brenda recognized her tactical mistake, and muttered, only to herself, "What was I thinking?"

She was no match for them, and the she was liable to join Milton as a victim, but Brenda was pleased to realize they could take more than a few with them before they died.

"You fool," the gargoyle hissed, his breath ragged. "You could have saved yourself."

Brenda was concentrating too intently on fighting to state the obvious, that the same option had been open to him and he had refused. Although she was trained in hand-to-hand and weapons combat, a burning branch was no strong deterrent to the creatures attacking her, and a few minutes later she felt the sharp stab as teeth dug deeply into her shoulder and she fell. The monster biting her flamed into oblivion, but it was not her branch that killed him, for a gigantic dragon had appeared, shooting a deadly stream of acidic fire from his throat.

The dragon roared, and a second and third monster died. Then Milton finished one, while the dragon killed a fifth. The battle was over in an instant.

"Byron?" she asked, her voice weak, her sight unreliable as pain rippled through her. She hoped it was her brother-in-law, not some other dragon cruising the demon-filled night, looking for a virgin to snack on.

I will take you to Jan.

"Byron—" she was losing consciousness, but noticed the gargoyle approaching her, pushing past the dragon who would have restrained him.

"Let me help."

See to your own wounds.

"The maid was wounded in my defense. That makes it my responsibility." The beast neared, crawling on his hands and knees, looking all the more alien, all the more frightening because how badly he was hurt.

The innkeeper has medicine, and I am not without an elixir I can offer to ease her suffering. But, having said that, the dragon moved aside, while the gargoyle approached. With his long, black tongue, Milton started lapping the blood flowing from her shoulder wound.

***

"What…what happened?" Brenda asked, returning to consciousness. Opening her eyes slowly, she found herself in the dragon's lair, surrounded by her aunt and her sister, Lori still rocking the inconsolable Lorenzo.

Jan's smile was medicine enough, her words only reinforced it. "Milton brought you here. You were wounded, but you will be fine."

Brenda felt her shoulder, where teeth had torn into her flesh, but although she could see a scar, it was rapidly fading, and she felt very little pain. She did not see Byron, except there was a large dragon teapot beside her which reminded her of his draconic form. The gargoyle was off to one side, busily licking his own massive wounds.

"Brenda," Jan continued, "there is tea. I don't know how you will react this time, but I promise it will help. If you feel up to it, I would like you to try some. Just a sip, in case you can't tolerate it, but it will speed the healing."

"I—" she fought, struggled for the images to reform. Her mouth was arid. Tea sounded heavenly, but there were things she had to take care of first. She pointed to the gargoyle. "He was going to kill me."

"Kill you?" Jan demanded. "Milton said you fought at his side and were wounded in his defense."

Her body felt numb, but images fought within her mind. "After I was hurt, after the dragon appeared, he attacked me."

"That is not so," Milton said, looking up, his snout covered in blood.

Jan needed no convincing. "Brenda, you are wrong in thinking Milton meant to hurt you. Gargoyles have healing in their saliva. He is in large part responsible for you being alive."

He inched closer, still on his knuckles and toes, an odd, alien crawl. One wing hung at an odd angle, and she could see vicious wounds across his naked chest and legs.

"But to an extent, she is correct. If she had not decided to help me, she would not have been wounded at all. I feel responsible."

"Nonsense," Jan said. She turned her back. Brenda heard the unmistakable sound of liquid being poured, then an instant later an intense scent of something rich, intoxicating reached her nostrils.

Her tongue was so dry it stuck to the roof of her mouth. "There was another gargoyle," Brenda said.

"Longfellow watched," he said. "He gave the creatures instruction. He wants the house."

"He, or the creature he serves," Jan agreed. She handed the mug out to Milton. "Try it."

Milton did not reach out his hand.

"Come, you have taken food from my hands before."

His eyes twisted, side to side, emotion rich. "Signs of my enslavement. I am free now."

"This is healing. I promise you it will help."

"I dare not. Creatures of faerie—"

"Byron will not hurt you, either. Did you not realize while the evil forces want this house for the power it will grant them, Byron could not have fought them by himself, not and guard the children. Drink his tea. It is all he can offer for thanks."

Milton accepted the cup reverently, bowed over it, then took a tiny sip. His eyes were lustrous as he looked up, and it appeared as if he were participating in a holy ordinance.

Jan poured a second cup, held it out. "The same goes for you, Brenda. I know you are nearly healed, but try a sip."

As Brenda struggled to sit, the blankets shifted from her shoulders and she discovered she was naked under the covers. Her braid was undone, and her hair covered her breasts, cascading nearly to her hips, but Milton watched her movement, and the look he gave her was lustful. He turned away quickly, but she saw how he wanted to possess her and was disgusted by it.

She held the blanket to her chest. "How long have I been out?"

"All night, most of the day. Garntz teeth have venom."

"One attacked me once," Lori said, struggling to be heard over the infant's wails. "Byron saved me. It was when I first realized I loved him."

"It was a brave thing you did," the gargoyle said, "coming to my defense, when it was obvious we would both be killed."

She thought back, sifted through her emotions, picked one, almost at random since there were so many raging inside her. "I could not let you die when I could help. I did not know the house was in danger, but I am glad the creatures you call evil did not gain control of it."

Milton took another sip of the tea, a small one, and he closed his eyes, letting the liquid sit on his tongue, savoring the bouquet before he swallowed. "Longfellow knows most of the secrets of this house. While we were chained and could not explore, we could hear, and we had centuries to learn the entrances and exits, to anticipate where demons would appear."

Jan handed Lori a cup, but instead of drinking it, her sister put finger in the steaming liquid, and let a dribble or two fall into Lorenzo's mouth. The baby lapped the tea, but his wailing continued.

Jan poured herself a cup, threw back her head and drank it quickly. "Longfellow cannot be allowed to roam free."

"Yet I fear he would do you no service, if you kept him in your dungeon."

While they spoke, Brenda took a sip of the tea. Again the visions exploded as they had before: huge, fire breathing dragons morphing into a man and into...a teapot? "Byron. This is Byron?"

"Yes. It is his gift to humanity, to serve them."

The tea was warming and the taste was complex so she could not analyze any single flavor, except to determine she found the combination delicious. As it coiled down her throat and into her bloodstream she could feel the healing strength. Aches, for she felt no real pain, vanished. Her thoughts, which had been a bit fuzzy, disjointed, cleared.

She took a second sip, taking the time to savor it, found the visions less, the comfort of healing greater. "Is there any danger to drinking this?"

Lori dribbled another few drops into her infant's mouth. "No danger. It is a healing blend. We could all use it."

"It is the only nourishment Lorenzo will take, although heaven only knows how a drop or two we manage to get him to swallow will sustain him," Jan said.

She had a traces of a dragon inside of her. Funny, now the image was not frightening or repulsive. And as she wrapped her chilled fingers around the mug, she looked at the gargoyle, then at the sleeping infants, for three slept peacefully. Finally she turned her gaze to the baby who could find no comfort and she spoke without thinking.

"If you are still willing to mount the quest, I will marry you."

CHAPTER 13

Milton put his mug down very carefully, although it was obviously empty. He looked to Jan and to Lori, checking to see if they had heard what he had, as if he needed witnesses. He had been crouching, but he straightened, rising to his full height, but made no move closer to her. "Would you repeat what you just said?"

Brenda swallowed, wondered if she could blame the tea for her statement, declare she was drugged and therefore not accountable for her actions. She decided that no, she would take responsibility for this decision; it had been inevitable since he made his offer.

She would do this with dignity, so she stood, pleased her legs held her, and she felt no pain anywhere. The blanket was warm, wrapped around her, she felt almost queenly, wearing a mantle, and she thought nothing of her nakedness underneath.

Fighting revulsion which she knew she could not hide, she met his hungry stare. "I am willing to give myself to you, in marriage, if you will enjoin the quest to find the ne-chakra or destroy it if it has turned evil."

"Be sure this is what you want," Milton said, and Jan seconded it, and whereas an instant before a teapot sat, there now stood a massive dragon.

Lori wept loudly. "Brenda, I wish I could tell you not to do this, that your happiness means more to me—"

Tenderly, she touched her sister. As children they had fought. Lori had never been able to understand her nightmares, Brenda had never had the carefree childhood of slumber parties and long giggling phone conversations about boys or homework secrets. That was behind them now. They were adults, but more, they were sisters with a joint heritage and a shared pain. For comfort, she looked to the three sleeping infants, their cheeks fat, already rosy. Their color much better now, pinker and healthier, than it had been when they were incomplete. She changed her touch, from her sister, to her nephew, caressing his forehead with the back of her knuckles. The wailing continued, uninterrupted. His eyes were scrunched shut, his pain so physical that all five adults in the cavern felt it. With her decision, there could be four sleeping infants. There could be happiness here.

She tried to define her own rationale, not only for her sister, but herself. "Lori, I have always fought against evil. That is what I do; I try to put the bad guys away. Now something evil has kidnapped my nephew. Although you hold the baby in your arms, his life has been stolen. I don't mind martyring myself to help him. That's why I'm agreeing. I would put myself in the line of fire for a stranger. I would take a bullet for someone I don't know, to protect the life of an innocent. Cops put their lives on the line every day for less. The least I could do would be to allow myself to be married to this creature to protect my nephew."

Milton spread his wings wide, then settled them back, His voice coming from deep within his barrel chest. "This is a sacrifice you should make willingly. You will be my wife."

She set her jaw and her resolution. She shivered once, wondered why the cave had gotten so cold all of a sudden. "I am going into this with my eyes open. It is a cost I am willing to pay."

I cannot allow you to do this.

Brenda craned her neck, ten feet, fifteen, twenty. The gold colored dragon filled the massive cavern, from the curled length of his spiked tail to his head with teeth as long as her forearm and eyes which seemed to glow a fiery copper. Brenda stepped away from him, aware as she did that she inched closer to Milton.

"Yet you are helpless here, Byron. There is nothing you can do, but stand by for years, and watch your son suffer. And if I do nothing but protect myself, I will ache, for I will know there was something I could have done. I think it would hurt more, in the long run, to watch Lorenzo suffer."

Brenda studied the cavern, from the impossibly high ceiling dotted with slowly dripping stalactites to the damp stalagmites stuck to the cold stone floor, to the sconces along distant walls which provided the only light. She looked at the creatures torn from her worst nightmares, dragon, gargoyle, and who knew what else, then at her sister. Lori's face remained ravaged with tears.

Nothing made sense. Since she knocked on her aunt's B&B door, her world had turned skiddly-wampus. She was cold and hot, rubbed her arms with hands which were uncharacteristically shaky.

"I don't understand what a wer-wizard is. Or a gargoyle or a dragon for that matter. They were just words to me, fantasy I read and thought about while growing up." She paused, try to find the words to help, as if in stringing together nouns and verbs she could find an agreeable solution. "I want the world to be quiet and peaceful. I want to find love and laughter with a man I can cherish the rest of my life. I have found too many other battles to fight that cannot be ignored: drug abuse, domestic violence, and murder that flows both hot and cold. If I had the chance to stop evil, and give you back your child and I did not, then I would suffer all my life."

She turned, faced the gigantic winged monster who had haunted her nightmares for years, then drawing in her courage, held both her hands out, palms down, fingers slightly curled. She waited until Milton reached out, touched her, and wrapped her hands in his own.

"Is there another reason why you are doing this?" he asked, softly. His voice was deep, gentle, non-threatening, and his hands, wrapped around hers somehow offered comfort she did not anticipate, but his teeth were long, pointed, sharp. His snout was broad, tapered to a point. She had seen those teeth rip the life out of monsters. She had felt those teeth imbed themselves in her ankle and remembered that pain for decades. She could not imagine kissing him. His nostrils were raised, twitched at the end of his snout, and his eyes lacked a center pupil, a colored iris. She recalled the feel of his tongue on her body, how it had healed, and how she had been terrified to be near him.

Wrapping the blanket tightly around herself, Brenda pulled him aside, walked with him to a far corner of the cavern, where they could be alone, hoping the privacy would allow her to open her thoughts. She would be honest. With herself. With him. "You need to understand, I do this thing for Lorenzo, but I am also doing it to thank you. You could have left when you found your freedom, taken to the skies and forsaken this place. The demons would have taken over, if not yesterday, when you fought, then eventually."

An eyebrow rose. "What do you mean?"

"I know so little about this, but you protect this house far better than Byron can, don't you?"

His head shook in the slightest negation. "My responsibility and his are much different."

"You could have saved yourself pain. You could have left when those things attacked, but you didn't, even when you were overpowered, even when it was obvious staying meant your eventual death—or are you immortal so they cannot kill you?"

"They can kill me. And you are correct in your analysis. If you had not come along with your burning branch, if the dragon had not intervened, I would be dead now."

At his statement, at the resignation in his face, her heart tripped. "And that does not bother you?"

Milton reached for her chilled fingers again. His hand was warm, and surprisingly tender. No claws met her flesh, no threat of danger.

"It does bother me, for I wish my life to be more than the sum total of my actions. I wish to leave an heir. If I had died a few hours ago, my soul would have been intact and I would have been welcomed to heaven, but I would have felt incomplete, and a significant part of my life would have been a failure."

Brenda tightened her grasp of his hand, then pulled away. She could not let him hold her so gently while she asked her question. "Will you hurt me? Before you answer, will you lie to me?"

There was a movement to his lips, so quick, that she could not determine what he meant to do, smile or snarl, or something else entirely.

"Because I am heir to human, I can lie. I am capable, although because I am a gargoyle, lying is never the first thought that comes to my mind. Because of promises I have made, and sacred oaths I have taken in the past, I will always try to be truthful. You have my word. So, to answer your question, it is not my intention to hurt you. You might find loving me not as unpleasant as you fear. And I will be a good provider. You will never be rich, for gargoyles have no interest in material wealth as dragons do. But as a husband, I will swear you will always have food, there will be a roof over your head, and I will protect you from what evil I can. I will never hurt you physically. I will make it my aim to see to your welfare before my own. I will not commit any sin while we are united. I will hold sacred what you call commandments. There will be no other woman in my bed or my thoughts, and I will neither do nor tolerate anything which you might consider a perversion. My child or children, if there are any, will be raised with all the love and protection I can manage."

Her toes curled on the stone floor, but she doubted it was the chill causing the action. "And me?"

He spread his wings again, then settled them back, and Brenda wondered if that was a movement he made when he was uncomfortable.

"Is the idea of the physical intimacies of marriage with me so repulsive to you?"

She spared a glance to his loincloth, the only clothing he wore. She thought of animals, of beasts. "Yes." Her answer was whispered, her head hanging, her eyes clamped shut against the possibilities.

Milton waited until she raised her eyelids, then sighed and his shoulders sagged, and his wings, which he normally held high, drooped. "Because I have no wish to hurt you, I will make you a promise. One time is required to consummate our marriage. If you find that intimacy repulsive, we need never join again. With or without our union producing a child, once is all I will subject you to. Is that acceptable?"

She glanced up at him, felt hope for the first time since he put his talons to her neck in the kitchen, weeks ago. "Only once? You would be satisfied with only once?"

"No, I would not be satisfied, for my body hungers for yours and I understand what a marriage is. I will hunger for you when the nights are freezing and you huddle under piles of blankets. I will wish to seek the comfort of your body on weekends, when you sleep in late, when your hair is tousled around the pillows and you smell of desire. In the afternoons, my body will yearn for yours, when your skin is warm from the sun, and you return home with laughter in your eyes, or sorrow in your soul. But I give you my word I will never touch you, after the first, without you being the one to initiate the intimacy. You need never even see me, should that be your desire. I will leave you alone, as long as you understand my thoughts will be on you always, and my heart will be committed."

"Love. You're speaking of love." She wanted to spit, found her voice quieter, softer than she intended.

"Yes. For I know what it is. All the years I have lived, I have seen it, but never felt it burning in my own blood, but you are mine, Brenda. Recognize it or not, you are my only love. You may call the terms of the marriage. After our union is consummated, I grant you that much power. Should it be your wish, I will leave you while I fulfill my end of the quest for the ne-chakra, and you need never think of or see me again, but with this marriage, I do require consummation."

She looked away from him, for she did not want him to see the relief in her eyes. She could get him to look for the ne-chakra and help Lorenzo, and the payment would be so slight. Certainly she could survive only once, mentally, physically, emotionally.

She studied her hands and her feet and the darkness of the cave, of which he was just another dark patch, and then she turned away, and he walked beside her, until she reached her aunt.

"Jan," Brenda said, "I have agreed to marry him." Then because that was impersonal, because she didn't honestly want to treat him like a thing, although that was how she saw him, Brenda continued. "I have accepted Milton's proposal of marriage. We wish to be married as quickly as possible."

"Are you certain, Brenda?"

"I am. He has asked, and I have agreed." When her aunt tightened her lips and looked as if she might protest, Brenda used the words he used, hoping it would be enough, to see her through the night, and all the miserable days to come. "I am doing it of my own free will."

"I wish this did not have to be so, for I can see you think of it as a type of penance." That statement and its insight, came from Milton.

"But I will not call it off, and I will honor my commitment," then she added her biting, limiting codicil, "tonight."

"I have been granted power, by the State of New York, and by the creatures of faerie, to perform wedding ceremonies."

"She married Byron and me," Lori said. Her eyes, still red and swollen, were no longer dripping, and there was hope in them, a brightness Brenda had not seen since before they stood over a nest with only three eggs.

"Now?" Brenda asked. She could not have swallowed if she had wanted to, for her mouth had grown unaccountably dry, and her word ended on a high, squeaky pitch. "Now?"

"At your convenience, My Lady," the gargoyle said.

Brenda cursed free will then, for it felt suddenly as if she had just made the greatest mistake of her life. "Now," she said.

CHAPTER 14

He still faced her, still held her hands in both of his. She knew there were terrible claws at the tips of his fingers, but she only felt flesh, and his hands were warm and already familiar.

"I am willing to wait until you are more comfortable with the idea, for I am a creature which has known much waiting. But, by the same token, I am eager for the ceremony, for I look forward to finding my pleasure in your body, and letting you find your release against mine."

"I, um," Brenda said, words and sanity escaping her. Her mouth was still dry, her thoughts confused, jumbled, for somewhere, deep within her, she thought he could bring her pleasure, and all things considered, in taking a lover she was not paying so hard a price. And she did want a child. Since looking at Lori's children this past week, since feeling Lori's swollen stomach before they were born, and watching the three sleeping peacefully now, she realized she had been hungry for a baby of her own.

Lori, be certain it is a price you can pay before you agree. Jan's marriages are not easily ended. There is no divorce.

"No divorce?" She hadn't been thinking of divorce, she had been thinking of sheets and sweat and crying out in pleasure. But she had also been thinking of never again granting him access to her bed, for he had given her that power over him. After this once, she had been thinking she would be rid of him and his uncomfortable lust.

"My powers of officiating at a wedding are not worldly. When I marry you, I set bonds that cannot be broken. You will be his—"

"And I, yours," the gargoyle interjected.

"Until you both shall die. Hear me, I said both. For if one of you should precede the other in death, there will be no remarriage, no second chance for happiness. You will grieve until you join him."

"I will not grieve at your death," she said.

He bowed his head and his words were low, spoken only for her. "Then you will be blessed, for I will grieve every minute of the remainder of my life, should you find your mortal release before I find mine."

There were no clocks in the huge cavern, and the watch at her wrist was digital and silent, but she could swear she could hear ticking, over the weeping of the one incomplete baby, over the soft breaths of the three who slept, even over the pounding of her own heart. Time was passing, time which would be better spent somewhere else, doing something else, which she was afraid to visualize at the moment, because the possibility now of them coming to fruition, was too real.

"Are you ready, gargoyle?" she asked.

"You may call me Milton. It is my given name."

"Milton." Paradise Lost. Was that what she was seeking when she agreed to marry him? Paradise? Or a long descriptive journey into hell?

"Milton." It too sounded strange, but when she thought of it, it also sounded right.

"I am ready," he said.

"I should get dressed and then I will be ready," Brenda said, copying his words, his inflections, for she had no thoughts of her own, lost the ability to do anything but follow the tide which was rushing around her, sweeping her away.

Lori swiped at tears, handed the screaming infant to the dragon who accepted him gently. "I can't do much to make this wedding a happy one," she said, "but at least I can see you properly dressed as a bride."

Brenda wanted to demur, to say old jeans and a sweatshirt would be enough, but her sister so desperately needed something to keep herself busy, something to show she was not being martyred for her, that Brenda smiled, reached for her sister in a hug. "Thank you. I would like that."

"We'll be back in a minute," Lori said.

"You honor me," Milton said, and he bowed low. Brenda hoped he meant Lori, her preparations to make this wedding outwardly appear happy, but she knew he spoke to her, and she was ashamed, for she could do nothing in return to honor him.

The women ran down the stairs, and Brenda smiled, then laughed, as if this were her wedding and she were happy, for her sister needed the pretense, and she did also.

"Give me that," Lori said, taking the blanket after they reached the room Brenda had taken. "It gets cold in that cave, and while Byron is always hot, I am not. Now, quickly, into the shower."

"Do we have time?"

"For a bride to shower? Of course. Besides, from what I hear, you battled for your life, and were bitten by a monster. You need to shower. If you would rather take the time for a bath, I am certain Milton will not mind."

"No. A shower." There was something too personal, too intimate in a bath, and if she took the time to think this decision through, she might change her mind. "I won't be long."

The towels which Brenda grabbed as she exited she shower dripping wet were a thick, rich, cobalt blue. Lori must have found them, for as she entered the shower, there hadn't been any. They were huge, wider than her outstretched arms, soft and thick. Brenda laughed as she picked the first towel up, because suddenly, inexplicably she felt like a bride and she loved the feeling. Brenda found a smaller one and wrapped her long hair in it, and set about to drying herself in front of a floor length mirror.

As she rubbed her body, as she dried her breasts and her thighs, she relaxed, for she could imagine a man caressing her in the same manner, as a way to express his love. The towels themselves were lightly scented, or maybe it was the residual of the soap or shampoo she had used for the aroma was musky and enticing. She felt more than clean when she dried off, she felt, unexpectedly like a bride.

A robe lay on the counter, a silky, regal affair that caressed her body and left her tingling. The collar was high, Oriental appearing, as was the multicolored pattern. The bodice tightened below her breasts, then fell, unobstructed, to rub at her feet. The sleeves were long and loose. The entire garment was fancy enough for a medieval princess to wear.

"Oh, is that stunning!" Lori said when Brenda returned to her bedroom. "You'll have to let me borrow it sometime."

"It's not mine. It was here when I left the shower."

"This house," Lori said, "does things like that all the time. Or maybe it was Milton, wanting you to feel beautiful."

"I prefer to think it was the house."

"Sit!" Lori ordered, and positioned her sister on a tall stool beside a roaring fire. "I spent some time in a tribal village once, I won't bore you with the details, but while I was there, I met a woman who could do incredible braids, and I begged her so long, she eventually relented and taught me. I can't do it on myself," she said, with a huff to her bangs, "but you have such beautiful long hair, I'd love to experiment."

"Please," Brenda said, "be my guest," and she cursed herself for her own impatience, for she wanted to rejoin Milton as soon as possible, yet emotionally, knew she should be in no hurry to bind herself to him forever.

"I wish we had a veil," Lori said, standing back.

Brenda stood, looked at herself in the mirror, almost not recognizing herself, for she looked so beautiful. "And cover this? It's magnificent." Lori had braided a good portion of her hair into a crown which encircled her head and some she had braided into thin strands, and those she hooked back up into the crown, so they looped and some of her hair she had left long, flowing down her back. "I feel like a princess."

"You look like a princess. I had no idea how much I would remember."

"Well, thank you," Brenda said, hugging her tightly.

"Now the dress. I've hunted all over the house while you were in the shower. That's one of the nice things about this Inn. You can usually find exactly what you're looking for, if you're willing to look long enough. Now, are any of these right?"

If she couldn't have jeans, she had been thinking of something black, nondescript, something to hide in, but her hair was beautiful and she felt so pretty after the shower, so Brenda carefully fingered Lori's selections, trying to find one which was exactly right. She reached out, knew by touch alone she had found the dress. "This one."

"There are fancier ones," Lori said, pointing to a pale rose colored silk dress. She held it up, under her own chin. Brenda felt the floor length, off the shoulder dress was something a princess would wear to a coronation, in she knew the color would complement her flaming red hair, yet she had no interest in it.

"No, this one. I'm not sure why."

The dress she selected was yellow, lighter than sunflower, darker than butter, a shimmery silk dress with cap sleeves and an uneven hemline. Brenda quickly fit a wisp of a bra over her tingling breasts, a small scrap of delicate lace on as panties, both flesh colored, both so tailored to her body that she felt more naked than she had been before donning them. Brenda laughed when Lori handed her silk stockings and garters. "For tonight."

"I won't know how to put them on."

"I'll show you. Nothing to it." Left unsaid was the fact Milton would know how to take them off. She did not want to think what this evening would bring, nor did she believe a suit of armor would guard her better. The slip, the same color as the dress, was a mere wisp of material, short, covering only her panties and her buttocks, leaving her thighs bare.

"He won't be able to keep his hands off you." If Lori thought that, she had the dignity not to say it aloud.

"Now the dress. Let's see how it fits." Brenda stood, raised her arms as she allowed her sister to put the light, cool material over her head. Lori tugged the hem down, then stood back, wiping a tear.

"Whatever the reason for this wedding, I've never seen you look lovelier."

"It's the hair, the dress." Brenda was all but speechless. She had no idea she could look this pretty for she was used to her police uniform, and when she was not working, she wore sweats to exercise, and grubby jeans to putter around the house. She did not even own a dress.

She fingered the silk material, enchanted on so many different levels. Whoever had designed this dress, whoever sewed it, had been an artist.

"I wish we had a camera."

"If we hunt, could we find one?" Brenda asked, suddenly reticent, wondering what Milton would think, what he would say.

"No. This B&B doesn't run toward technology, and even if it did, it makes no records of events. Probably because no one would believe what goes on around here. Come, are you ready to go back upstairs?"

"Yes." There was no sense in delaying.

"Then you will need these," Lori said, handing her dyed to match yellow strap sandals, delicate and stunning.

"I doubt they'll fit." But they did. She had big feet, had the hardest time finding shoes, but these slipped on as if she had Cinderella's luck with footwear.

"I'll always remember how lovely you are." Spontaneously the sisters hugged.

She would honor this commitment and pray he would not hurt her with his claws and his razor sharp teeth. She had seen him kill with those claws, had seen him rip bodies apart with those teeth.

She sat heavily down on the bed, dressed like a queen, and felt her body starting to tremble.

Lori touched her shoulder, gently, tentatively. "You don't have to do this if you don't want to."

"I do," she answered, but whether she responded to the first part of Lori's statement, or the second, Brenda had no idea. Whatever that meant, she would fulfill her part of the bargain.

"I know you're doing this for me, Byron and Lorenzo. We'll never be able to repay you."

"Milton can make no guarantees."

"I know, but he will try and that's all we can hope for. I had no idea when I carried my babies, when I gave birth to them, they would be in so much danger." Lori hugged her tightly, desperately. "Anything Byron and I can for you, anything, you've only to let us know."

"I will, I promise." Then, because she was not a coward, because she had put this off long enough, she stood, straightening her shoulders, raising her chin. "It's time."

As Brenda headed for the stairs, she only wished the dress she wore had a place to hide her service weapon.

***

Milton and Byron were talking, heads together, when the women walked into the room. Strategy, most likely, where to hunt, how to attack and kill the monster who had stolen Lorenzo's ne-chakra. It was unlikely it was wedding advice, one newly married man to another.

"Mercy, that's a lot of stairs," Brenda told her sister, slightly out of breath as they entered the cavern. For a moment, since the hair braiding, the dress, the stairs, she had felt like a bride, had enjoyed the anticipation of marriage, then she looked, saw him standing there, huge and imposing and virile, and grew frightened again.

The gargoyle raised his head, stared at her as if she had turned him to stone. Their eyes met, locked, and for a second she was not afraid, she was pleased to look nice for him, pleased she agreed to this marriage. Milton stepped in front of Bryon, then bowed deeply, to which Brenda grasped a thin handful of her dress and curtseyed in a way she didn't even know she knew how. For the moment there was silence, even Lorenzo stopped wailing, speechless and spellbound at the lovely bride.

"Mom will kill us, you know," Lori said, "now that she has missed a second wedding." It was an attempt to bring levity into a situation which had every participant thrumming.

"Then she can hold a backyard barbeque as a wedding reception. I'll invite all the policemen on my shift. Dad can invite all his cronies."

"That is not the best—" Byron started, but stopped. There was no need to finish. There would never be a backyard barbeque wedding reception. No friends from her police force would be informed. Milton inclined his head, an acknowledgement more than a bow, an apology that she could not have the things other brides sought.

"After the wedding," he said, "I will not keep you from your family."

She nodded her thanks, accepting that was all he could give her. And she wondered what her parents would say when she turned down their attempts at blind dates, or if she would tell them she was married and what she would say when they wanted to meet their new son-in-law and welcome him to the family. They had only daughters. They would welcome husbands. Well, they would have to be content with Byron. At least he could look human.

Milton reached out, took her right hand in his and gently kissed the back of her wrist. Brenda expected to feel repulsed, thought his flesh against hers would feel alien, invasive, but her skin tingled, and her anticipation rose.

She reached out her left hand, while he still held her right, gently brought it to his face. His snout was long, pointed, very feral, looked, if she had to compare it to anything, canine, but surprisingly, his skin was soft, and almost familiar.

He closed his eyes, tilted his head until he gently captured her hand between his shoulder and his elongated jaw. Then he released her, and she brought her hand back, so his hands tightened in hers, and she sought acknowledgement, reassurance, and perhaps, eventually tolerance, if love wasn't possible. Yes, she would pray for tolerance, for when he made love to her, she would hope she would feel more than revulsion.

"You were hurt," she said, her words a whisper, carrying the hint of a tremble.

"I heal quickly." He looked at the dress, and while she expected a leer, while she anticipated feeling abraded by his eyes, they were soft. "Did you know yellow was my favorite color?"

"No, how could I?"

His voice was as low as hers, this private interlude before the ceremony. "We had limited exposure to colors. Over the centuries, chained in the basement, we knew black and gray and the colors of the creatures we fought, green and blue, and the red color of blood. We always shed a lot of blood."

Brenda waited, fascinated by his confession. "Then one day an Innkeeper, one of your aunt's predecessors, came down the stairs wearing a blouse almost the color of your dress, and I remembered yellow, the sunlight, how it felt warm on my wings, for it had been centuries by then since I had seen the sun or felt warmth. And I remembered bright flowers, for Eden was draped in flowers, and even after they left the Garden, they planted flowers for their enjoyment, for mankind must always be surrounded by beauty. And I stayed chained in the dungeon, and there were times when because I remembered yellow I was able to continue fighting my battles and not fall into despair as Longfellow did. You honor me by wearing it, and you honor me by being here, by my side."

Brenda wanted to say she would honor him all the days of her life, but the words wouldn't come, for they would be false, for she thought him a monster and had not meant to honor him when she put on the dress. She had meant to please herself, to feel pretty, because after the Vows she expected to feel nothing at all, except revulsion, and perhaps pain. Maybe she would despise yellow all the days of her life.

"I am glad my choice pleases you," she said instead. She could blame the Inn for that.

She looked around, across the broad expanse of the cave saw hundreds or even thousands of creatures surrounding them, standing in the shadows, tall and short and solid and ephemeral. She startled, wanting to scream, but Milton stopped her, with a shake to his head indicating it was all right, and Byron spoke. "These are not imps, creatures of evil, but are denizens of the faerie kingdom: elves and brownies, and faeries and pixies. They come because a marriage should be celebrated. All through the night they will party, drinking to your health, your happiness and your future children, for to them, marriage is sacred. You are invited to party, should you wish."

"No," she said abruptly. There was only one thing worse she could think of than going to a party given by elves. "I—we will be busy this evening." With the quest, she hoped, but knew Milton would plan to delay his search until tomorrow morning.

Milton touched her hand again. "Your aunt waits."

Bridegrooms were always eager. Then, before it would be too late to back out, Brenda gasped: "My child will be normal?"

"I guarantee your children will be normal. The stigma of being a gargoyle will not pass into another generation. The sins of the father will have no bearing on the child."

"And have you sinned, gargoyle?" she asked. She let her tone turn sharp.

Jan gasped, but Milton ignored her. "It is as I have told you. I have committed the greatest sin possible."

She tried to pull her hands back, to find release from the sickness swamping her, making her nauseous and lightheaded and swaying on her feet. She wished he had lied. Two seconds before she married this creature, she did not want to know he had committed the greatest sin possible for she could think of a lot of horrendous sins.

Milton tugged gently against her hands as he fell to his knees, and Brenda, still clasping him, did the same. He bowed his head in reverence or perhaps in shame, but finding no comfort in looking at the faeries, Brenda stared at Jan, or at the dragon which she saw differently now, because she saw him as her brother-in-law, and not a monster at all, and she stared at all four children: three still sleeping contentedly, one who had resumed crying.

"I have no ring to offer you," Milton said. "I know mortals of your religion signify the covenant of marriage with a ring."

I can provide a ring.

"Gargoyles own nothing, except the bands we wear at our neck and wrist and ankle. I have no worldly goods to offer. But, if it is it your wish to have a wedding ring to remind you of this commitment, I will allow your family member to provide one."

She wanted nothing to remind her of this time. Nothing, except perhaps the baby in Lori's arms, whole and complete. "If I feel it is necessary to mark our marriage with an external token, then I will accept Byron's ring, but now, I will only require the words spoken, the power of the ceremony to join us."

And the gargoyle smiled, pleased, for he took her words to mean she would hold the marriage sacred, but Brenda meant exactly the opposite, for she wanted nothing to remind her of this night, no band on her finger tying her to him, as he wore his bands of shame and servitude.

"Marriage is a covenant between two people…" Jan began, and ten minutes later, Milton and Brenda were married.

At the end of the ceremony, Brenda waited, expecting her first test: the familiar closing statement of a wedding ceremony, 'you may now kiss as husband and wife,' but Jan did not say it. Brenda did not know if that were kindness on her part, or if it was not required when married by someone with the power of faerie, for Jan could not possibly have forgotten. But Milton did not look like he expected a kiss, and Lori and Byron certainly did not mention its lack.

You have mentioned you will not join the faeries, but will you stay long enough for some kind of celebration? I could provide tea. There is a happiness brew which is appropriate.

"Perhaps another time. There is much my Lady and I must do. I take her with me now, but I will return her tomorrow, for I do not want her traveling where I must go, and facing what I have to face."

"You're putting me aside already?" It annoyed Brenda when she heard the relief in her own tone, and was certain Milton heard it too, for he cringed.

"You will be safer here, with family. You could help your aunt with her Inn, and help your sister with her children. Four babies are a lot of work, bathing and feeding and changing. It is more than one person, or two, can handle."

"With your permission, I would like to go with you. I want to help seek out the wizard who has done this horrible thing. Yes, you said my gun won't work, but there must be something I can do, to support you in your quest."

That she could do. She would deny him conjugal rights, but she would be as devoted to him as she could be, for she had found the ceremony moving, even if she could not recall a single word.

"Then forgive me, all," Milton said to the dragon, Jan and Lori. "The lady and I will return as soon as there is something to report. You may pray if you like, but please do not try to hope, for the task we have set ourselves looks hopeless, and the outcome unlikely to be pleasant."

Quickly Brenda hugged her aunt. "Thank you for your kindness. It was a beautiful ceremony." She hoped so. The only thing she remembered was her own voice sounding strong, secure, stating that she would take Milton as her husband, and his voice, warm and virile promising the equivalent for her. Then she kissed her sister. "We will do what we can to bring Lorenzo's chakra back with us."

Take him with you.

"What?"

*Take Lorenzo with you. He will find no peace here, and if his chakra has hatched, there will be no way to transport it, without it merging into a living being. It is not corporeal. It will link or cease to exist."

"How long after it hatches will it cease to exist?"

I cannot say. It varies. It could be years. But I meant what I said. If the chakra has hatched, you will need Lorenzo, for there is no way to bring the chakra to the infant.

"We will take the baby. With your permission, Lori?"

"No, yes, no." Lori's tears freshened, and she ran to her husband, who transformed instantly into his human guise, wrapping her in his arms.

"Let them take him," he said. "It will be better for all of us if we do not have to watch him suffer, and he will help them locate the ne-chakra or chakra."

"Byron, he is my baby. I can't give him up."

"We have the other children and they are whole. If we have to raise Lorenzo as a half-being, we will do so, but for now, let Brenda take him.

"Byron—"

"Let me hold him, Lori," Brenda said. "I promise to be gentle." She held her hands out, for she found her emotions twisted, holding this half-being, which she had avoided.

"You will need this—" Jan handed Brenda a diaper bag.

She quickly scanned the contents. She felt a heaviness in her own breasts and she knew what was missing. "There's no food here."

"Lorenzo will not eat until he is complete. He will not starve, do not worry."

"It could take years," Milton said.

"Then it will take years," Byron answered, grimly. "But even as a half-dragon he is not mortal and cannot die from starvation."

"Certainly mother's milk," Brenda said.

"No. I wish it were so, but it is not."

"Then the tea, the dragon tea?"

"I am needed here, and a drop or two a day, which has been all he has accepted, will hardly make a difference, one way or the other."

Milton bowed, very deeply and respectfully to Byron and Lori. "My wife and I will be very careful with this gift you have given us. We will treat him as the precious being he is, and return him as quickly as we can to his brothers."

Lorenzo's weight was slight, but she wrapped her arms around him snuggly, and she felt a mother. For the longest second she wanted her own child, a baby born from her marriage, a child they could watch grow up healthy and active. She had ignored Lorenzo so far, but only because, since he was the neediest, he was the one she loved the best.

"Good-bye." Brenda accepted the diaper bag. Then she felt the monster sweep her up into his arms, and a second later she gasped, as they were airborne.

***

She had seen him chained, seen him kill. She had seen him wounded. Now, airborne, she saw another side of Milton. He could be tender.

"He should sleep for you," he whispered. "The rocking movement of flying should relax Lorenzo enough that the flight, at least, should offer him some relief."

Milton's words were prophetic, for after only a few minutes in the air, the infant whimpered once, then shut his eyes and slept.

"And I suspect he will find comfort where we are going. He should sleep for us through the night."

Through the night. She would have no excuse. Not that Brenda suspected he would offer her a reprieve.

"Are you frightened? Does the flight bother you?"

She wondered if that were two distinct questions, and if he meant them that way. Yes, she was terrified...of the night to come, but she answered, "The flying does not bother me."

Oddly enough, Brenda rarely flew on commercial airliners. As a police officer, her job was demanding, and all her vacation days lately had been taken up on trips back and forth to the hardware stores, buying supplies and fixing her bungalow. But with his question, she analyzed what she felt. She was secure in his arms. She knew Milton would not drop her, so there was no terror of height. It surprised her to realize she trusted him. All her fears were concentrated on the coming ordeal, but at the moment, they could fly straight on until morning and she would not care.

"Are we too heavy?"

"No. I like—" he started, but stopped. Brenda did not have the courage to ask him to finish. Some things, she thought, were better off unknown.

Oddly enough, flying in his arms he felt less alien to her, when by rights he should have felt more.

"Where are we?" Brenda asked, several minutes later as the gargoyle, who had been flying high, started banking, losing altitude, preparing to land.

"New York City."

"New York, New York?" she asked, as if there was another one.

"I can cross worlds, and we probably will before this adventure is finished, but there is one thing we must do on Earth first."

"My impregnation?" she asked, and the dread was back and it was big and frightening.

"Two things I must do on Earth, first," Milton said.

CHAPTER 15

Two things.

Swell. Was it too late to change her mind?

He must have had some psychic ability, for as his wings continued their rhythmic motion, Milton said, "You are the bravest person I know."

Brenda was in no mood to accept a compliment. He was so alien, so opposite from anything she had grown up believing in, she didn't know how she would survive her thoughts let alone what he had waiting for her in whatever pit he would find to consummate their marriage. All she could think of was how he fought those monsters, his teeth and his claws and the viscous sounds he made: snarling, growling, howling. One had bitten her. She could still remember the pain. The fact she had healed quickly and for some reason had no scar, mattered not at all. She suspected if he wanted, he could use his magical healing saliva to torture her, biting her, making her suffer, then healing her to repeat the entire horrific process again. The bravest woman he knew. Maybe he didn't have psychic powers.

Now, flying three hundred feet in the air with a monster, she came to a renewed comprehension of the magnitude of the mistake she had just made. But she held the baby against her breasts, a skeletal and suffering child, and she knew whatever awaited her, she would make the same decision again. Whatever a chakra was, she would do her best to make certain Lorenzo got his back.

Below her, the pristine Adirondack scenery had given way to an increasingly urban setting. Buildings grew taller, the traffic arteries more congested, intersecting at shorter intervals. They had followed the Northway down, she was certain. Now she was positive the road beneath them was the New York State Thruway. She should fly more often. All the benefits, none of the tolls. She would have laughed, had she not been so frightened.

Her body grew cold and she shivered. The only source of warmth was Lorenzo and the blanket Lori had wrapped him in, although honestly, where she pressed against Milton, where he held her, was warm.

"It will not be as bad as you fear." It was the first time he had spoken in an hour.

"I think I should be the judge of that. Is there no way we could delay...tonight...for a few days, until I get used to the idea?"

"No. This is all I have asked of our marriage."

"But I am only asking for twenty-four hours."

He looked at her, his face only inches from hers, and the intensity of his pupilless stare bored into her and if there was compassion or derision, she could not tell. "I might be killed during this search, and I would like the chance to leave an heir."

"I might be killed," Brenda said. Being reasonable was the furthest thing from her mind.

"Yes. If so I will grieve, but at least I will have known one night of passion in your arms, which is more than I ever expected."

He banked, coming in lower, the flapping of his fourteen foot wing span nearly silent against the night. They were low enough for her to hear the sounds of traffic, the rubbing of tires against asphalt, the occasional honk of a horn, blast of a radio.

"Can we be seen?"

"It is unlikely. Gargoyles have magic, so we are invisible to all but those who know how to look for us."

"The wer-wizard?"

"He will have the ability to see us. We won't come upon him unawares."

"Can you defeat him?"

"I do not know. I am used to battling evil. He will not find me an easy target. Also, should I not be able to defeat him directly, I am certain the dragon would leave his lair to offer assistance."

"Yes."

She hated to sound like a child, but he gave her no other option. "Are we almost there?"

"Yes. Our destination is that building straight ahead."

She looked where he pointed, saw a huge cathedral, massive and impressive, with stained glass windows lit from within, a Christian beacon against the dark proudly displaying brilliant colors of red, gold, and blue. She could not make out the pictures or the designs, for Milton did not pause, but continued flying closer, giving her little time to sightsee. As he landed, Brenda noticed gargoyles on the outside of the church, ugly parodies of his finely honed body, snarling monsters with their mouths open, frozen, for what looked like all eternity.

How easy it was to think of eternity when standing beside him.

As Milton landed at the bottom of the cathedral steps, two things happened simultaneously. First, Lorenzo woke. The rest had done him good for his eyes were clear of the puffy redness they had held while he cried, and his color seemed improved. He did not resume his crying, instead looked around, bright and alert. "Thank God," Brenda whispered, but when she looked back, she nearly fell.

The horrendous monster Milton was gone. In his place stood a gorgeous man, human in every respect, dressed in a gray suit, the silk tie hanging loose at his throat. He was tall, well over six feet, and powerfully built with broad shoulders and narrow hips. His eyes were the color of spring grass and his hair, as long as Byron's, but a light fawn brown, was spotlessly clean, for it glistened in the twilight, and it looked soft enough for her dig her hands through it.

"Milton?"

He turned, walked back down the stairs, for when she had stopped, he had kept moving. "What you see is my human guise. I can switch as easily as the dragon."

"I didn't know."

"I know you didn't, and it didn't affect your decision but it should make tonight easier."

She breathed a sigh of relief, knowing him correct, but she bristled as she realized what it said about her. "Do you think me so shallow that how a person looks determines whether I find a sexual encounter unpleasant or desirable?"

Milton showed no emotion as he called her bluff. "If you wish, I can revert back to my natural form while we consummate our union, but for now, I need to keep this shape, so I do not shock the parishioners inside."

"You have a human form?"

His grin was sardonic. "Yes. I am not human, but I am heir to human. I will explain one day."

She looked him over, trying to see if she could discern the traces of the monster in his countenance, knowing a snout, horns, and pointed ears were not the only criteria for judging a man's merit.

So many times she had seen evil manifest in the felons she arrested, insanity in their eyes, revealed in their actions, but she was equally aware of the number of people who were pedophiles, rapists, or murderers who looked like the guy next door, who you would have no problem asking to baby sit if you needed to rush to the grocery market for a gallon of milk.

Brenda couldn't make a decision based only on appearance, but she knew, no matter how flawed it made her in his eyes, she would be a lot more comfortable with him wearing this appearance tonight than if he were in his normal form.

While his body was powerfully built, she felt no fear in his presence.

No anxiety. She would rather what was to happen tonight, happen with this man than with the monster she had married.

"The chains," she said, indicating the broad ring he wore around his neck. It was the reason his tie was undone. He cocked a half-grin, and held up his left hand, pulling back the suit jacket and the shirt. The prison band was still about his wrist. She had no doubt he also had a silver manacle around his ankle.

"They don't come off, and never will."

"Another long story?"

"Related to the first, I'm sorry to say."

"Do they hurt?"

"Only when I strain against my chains."

In her experience he spent most of his time straining against his chains.

They entered the cathedral, walking down the center aisle, with Milton's arm around her back, Brenda carrying the alert and occasionally cooing infant. Inside, she recognized the lingering traces of incense and saw rows of small candles burning steadily in silence.

There was no service in progress, but a few people prayed quietly. As they passed, one man, kneeling in a pew got up and looking at Milton, left quickly.

"Evil cannot remain in the presence of a gargoyle," Milton said in a whisper.

"Evil?"

"The creature who just left. He does not affect us, for he has nothing to do with the ne-chakra, but he cannot remain here on holy ground, while I am here."

"It's a church. Perhaps he was here to pray."

"No, Brenda, only to prey on others. You must trust me. If his conscience were clean, he would have been able to stay. While I am here he could not remain with a black soul."

"You can tell a person's soul?"

"Always. It is one of my gifts."

Milton approached a robed priest. "We seek the elder in charge."

"That would be Monsignor Delahey."

"We will see him."

"He sees no one without an appointment."

"I will see him now."

"I am afraid that is impossible."

"I am St. Caspian."

Saint Caspian?

"Please give my name to whoever is in charge here. Then he will see me."

The priest bowed, disappeared and was back within two minutes, with an older, almost feeble priest.

"My God…"

"I am no god."

"I only meant to pray, not offer sacrilege. Saint Caspian. I have heard, of course. All who reach a certain level of authority in the church have heard."

Milton waited quietly, while the priest noticed the infant. "The baby is just a baby," he said.

"I do not believe that is an ordinary baby."

"If he is not, then it has nothing to do with your religion or mine." As if those were two separate things.

"How may I help you this evening?"

"I need two favors."

"Anything, Sir."

"I would like to be married here, on holy ground, to this woman. And then I would like a room with a bed, for about an hour."

"On holy ground?"

"Yes. I must consummate my marriage within a cathedral."

The monsignor looked at the baby in Brenda's arms, Lorenzo awake and staring wide-eyed at the stunningly ornate architecture. "Consummate your marriage?"

"That is what I said. You will be well compensated for your time. I require the authority you hold."

"But we are already married," Brenda whispered.

"By different rites we will be joined again. Trust me, Brenda, it is necessary."

"Yet you said—"

"What?" Milton asked, while the Monsignor waited.

"That you had sinned."

"So I have. I have also been…forgiven."

"Yet I think not completely," she said.

"Forgiven enough that no stain will reside on any child you provide me. Forgiven enough to be welcomed on holy ground. Will you marry me again, Brenda?"

She looked around at the opulence and the religious tradition. Formal wedding services often took hours. It would delay…the inevitable. "I will."

"Do you have a license?"

"I only require the ceremony by priesthood power. As my wife has stated we are already married by non-secular means. It is important we marry here, so all righteousness may be fulfilled."

"Come, Brenda, this should not take long."

"Your complete name?" the priest asked Brenda.

"Brenda Elizabeth Claire Larwick," Milton answered for her. "My given name is Milton."

The ceremony was over quickly. As with the rite her aunt performed, Brenda remembered nothing. It was as if as soon as the words were spoken, her mind shut off, denying her their meaning, lulling her with their sound.

She felt no more married at its conclusion than she had hours before, in a cavern at the top of a house in upstate New York. Kneeling beside her, Milton stayed very still, his head bowed, adsorbing the ceremony.

He squeezed her hand lightly as they stood, more an acknowledgement of the wedding than a prelude of what was to come.

"You may kiss the bride."

He gave her no time to protest. His human lips reached hers and although his touch was gentle, the kiss was over very quickly. She kept her eyes open, thinking he would ravish her, but his human eyes were closed, and she knew again she had hurt him.

"There is paperwork required, if you care to follow me?" the slightest inflection at the end of the sentence made it a question, instead of the statement it was intended.

"Make any notations you need for your diocese and for your own records, but there is no need for secular forms to be filled. As the lady mentioned, we were married earlier this evening and the paperwork was completed then. I need—"

"There is no need to explain further. A room is waiting…" the Monsignor said. "We will not keep you from the fulfillment of your vows."

"We appreciate your hospitability," Brenda said, for she could not imagine a cathedral kept bedrooms available for anxious husbands and their frightened wives. "I hope we are not inconveniencing anyone."

"It is an honor, Mrs. St. Caspian."

Brenda had never spent much time in a large cathedral, but, following the slow moving monsignor, who released the other priest and led them himself, they passed through long corridors where she was certain the public was never invited. And she wondered if this church performed exorcisms, for while she did not believe the man who had left when Milton entered the church was evil, neither could she dismiss it.

The lighting was dim and indistinct and she felt the pictures on the wall they were gruesome, most depicting private moments of the Savior suffering. The angels looked fat and vainglorious, and she wished she was anywhere but here. She was relieved by the church leader's halting steps.

"This room has been maintained since the building was constructed…"

"I have no doubt we will find everything in order."

"You may take whatever time you require. No one will disturb you here."

"Thank you."

"Will you require refreshments? Breakfast in the morning?"

"No. And we will not stay long. The lady, the child and I must travel somewhere before morning."

It was a broad heavy door, stained a deep, nearly black mahogany. The priest opened it with a fat, ancient key he wore around his neck, then handed it to Milton, without opening the door. "No man has been in this room since it was constructed, and no woman has entered except to clean."

Milton nodded, but said nothing. If he were anxious or eager, he gave no indication.

"In accordance with the covenant…" the priest continued.

"I am certain everything will be fine." The church official left, his slow steps shuffling down the deserted corridor, leaving Brenda standing alone with the creature in manform who had the right to call himself her husband.

Milton swung the door open wide, it moved on well-oiled hinges, to reveal opulence. She paused, the last illusion of safety vanishing, for Brenda knew when he shut the door behind them there would be no reprieve. Deny it as she wanted, she had entered into his bargain twice. For a fleeting second, she was eight-years-old again, facing the monsters chained in the dungeon, knowing she had ten years of nightmares ahead. She became paralyzed and afraid, and he did not say anything, nor did he come closer.

"This room?" she asked. She would do anything, find any topic, to postpone the inevitable.

He moved, silently, comfortable in his human guise, casually touching religious icons on the dresser, running his hands down the velvet of the thick draperies. "It is a covenant between this religion and my kind. In return for the gargoyles protection of their holy buildings, we ask only this in return: marriage by their priesthood's authority and one night on sanctified ground. Each cathedral of certain size and even many of the smaller ones, have a bedroom, never used for mortals. These rooms are often off in a far corner and sometimes used for storage, but the sheets are always clean and our privacy is assured."

Her eyes darted, back and forth, but it was primarily a bedroom, and thus, the dominant piece of furniture was a bed. She found no comfort there.

Brenda swallowed tightly. "You said he would be paid."

"It is considered an honor for a priest to officiate at the wedding and a great deal of the payment is that privilege."

"Bragging rights?"

Milton rolled his shoulders, the same motion a monster had made, stretching his wings, but this time there were none. The action helped ground her in the reality that although he appeared a man, he was not a human.

"If you will, but only to himself, and I am certain, in his prayers to God. It will never pass from his lips a gargoyle and his wife spent the night here, I promise you. There will be no photographers in the morning, no news items anywhere."

In this bedroom, with this thing wearing the signs of his subjugation at his neck, wrist and ankle, Brenda wanted to kick something, slash something, kill something, but instead, gently and silently, she kissed Lorenzo on the forehead. That was what all this was about: making a baby whole and perhaps even conceiving another.

"Is that all? It seems a steep price to pay for bragging rights only in prayer."

"For God himself, it is enough, fulfilling a covenant, made before the Earth itself was formed on the First Day. But for the priest, there is another blessing. In the morning there will be blood on the sheets. It is considered holy blood and can be used for small miracles, mostly healing, a few people, four, or perhaps five."

"My blood?" she asked, as color drained from her cheeks.

"Mine." He shifted, started to move toward her, but turned, and spoke to her over his shoulder, and Brenda knew she had hurt him, deeply and intently, and she realized that had been her intention. And she realized, he would still have his consummation, and perhaps he would have no reason to be gentle, for when wounded, a creature could be expected to attack.

"It will be my blood. I have never made love before and the first time, I will bleed, a small amount only, in similitude… well," he said, as if he would not speak of religion with her, "in honor that the covenant is complete."

"I see." She didn't and didn't want to. "And the gargoyles on top of this building? Should we free them?"

"None are gargoyles, as I am. Each was a representation of a gargoyle. Over the centuries mankind has forgotten we are living, breathing beings. They only remembered holy buildings guarded by gargoyles were kept free from evil, so men were hired to carve them from stone, as if the form of the creature were enough to vouchsafe their welfare and keep destruction from their doors. After I am released from this task, if life still remains to me, perhaps I will seek out other gargoyles, and offer them freedom. Maybe not, for I will still have my obligation to you, and your happiness will come first until I die."

Brenda sat on the bed, lightly bouncing the infant. Lorenzo's eyelids had grown heavy, and he was drifting into sleep.

Brenda never took a drop of alcohol for she had seen too many times how the cares of the job and easy access to the legal numbing effects of a bottle could destroy a cop, but at that second she was desperate for a slug of something very strong. "Can you die? I thought you immortal or are you referring to being killed, like when you were attacked by those beings at the Inn?"

Milton turned around, leaned against the dresser. His legs were not lean so much as muscular, and they went on forever. His hips were narrow, his stomach flat. He finger-combed his hair back from his brilliant green eyes, hair which looked soft enough to drown in. For a second Brenda wanted to see him without clothes. For a second, she wanted to pretend...and be pleasured by a man's loving.

"I am no longer immortal. I am as strong as I always have been, and with the exception of tonight, I will be affected by the HOLD spell, but I will age and die, granted a human lifespan, probably no more than fifty years left to me."

"You're mortal now?"

"When I married, here, in this church, mortality came upon me."

"Why would you do that?"

He smiled slightly, a fleeting movement that soon vanished. It surprised her how a smile, which she had always thought to convey happiness, could show so much pain.

"It is a blessing. Were I to live forever, after promising my heart to you, I would grieve through all the centuries after your death. At least with my release, I will find ease from the pain of your loss, should you precede me."

He approached, stood in front of her, this handsome man dressed in a light gray suit of exquisite tailoring, wearing chains at his neck, wrist, and ankle. When he stopped she waited, not able to think or hope.

He reached out and she stood her ground and refused to cringe, refused to close her eyes, and met his gaze. Milton slowly unbraided her hair, taking the time to do it gently, destroying all the beautiful work Lori had created. It wasn't very often she wore her hair loose for it was silky and wanton and she liked every part of her body under rigid control, but at her wedding she had felt beautiful.

"Shake your head," he said, not so much an order as a plea. She did, tentatively at first, a hesitant, awkward movement then when she saw the way his nostrils faired, watched while he swallowed, nervous and slightly out of control, she did it again. She shook her head until her hair cascaded around her, and the ends brushed the tips of her breasts and he gasped. She felt power of a different sort, one she never expected to experience.

"When you were in the lair and your hair was down, I wanted to touch you."

She could say nothing, for what could she admit—that she found the thought of his caress repulsive, yet seconds ago she had wanted the exact same thing...to touch his hair?

"I knew the dragon and his consort would not approve, and I did not wish to embarrass you before we were wed, for I never thought you would agree to my terms, but I saw your hair down and I ached."

"Did you pull it down? Did you undress me?"

"No. After the battle, I flew you to the dragon lair and the witch tended you with your sister. I used the time to tend to my own wounds. I promise you while you were unconscious and bleeding from your demon-wound, nothing untold happened."

She breathed a sigh of relief.

"I told you, I would respect you, until we were married."

Her jaw ached for she had been clenching her teeth together. "And now that time of respect has come to an end."

"If you must see it that way," he whispered, and the trace of an accent from antiquity reappeared. Brenda decided she could be frightened, or she could accept. Without taking the time to analyze, she decided not to give in to her fear. Instead she laughed and shook her hair again, but this time he didn't stand granite still. He moved, snaking out a manacled wrist and grabbed a handful of her hair. Milton tugged gently until she was forced to move closer. With his free hand he ran his fingers through her long, red hair, up her back, then brushed it from her neck, caressing the silky strands.

"Brenda, I believe strongly, with a knowledge stronger than mere belief, after death we will be reunited."

"Then there is no escape for me." She felt breathless, and oddly unsettled. She wanted what was to happen between them, even if she had no basis for that desire.

"No escape. But I think you knew that as a child. I suspect that is why you have been having nightmares. Your soul has ached for mine. You didn't know how to deal with it, for you thought me a monster, but you always wanted to return to me and when you were old enough, you did."

She did not retreat, and if this were an attack, it was one she offered softly, for she did not screech, did not yell. "If I thought you a monster, it is because you are. And there is no need to put an attractive spin on it, to fit your hopes. I came back to fight my fears and to eradicate them. I have been living with a nightmare, not certain if I were insane."

"You are not."

"My parents think I am. I had this vivid description of creatures chained in a torture chamber, of being bitten by a monster which walked on two legs yet had a beast's head. My parents felt I should be committed."

"You are committed: to what you feel is right."

"That's not what I mean, and you know it."

"It sounds like after all the years of living with your parents, they do not know you as well as I, and I only met you once when you were a child. How could they not see your strength?"

"I do not feel strong now."

"Then you are mistaken, for you are one of the strongest women I know. I am not speaking physically, although you have trained and kept your body well honed. I am talking spiritually. How many other women would make the decision you have, to marry a monster, as I appeared?"

"I did not do it for you. I did it for Lorenzo." The baby was deeply asleep. Moving away, Brenda found a drawer and opening it, discovered it was empty. She placed a blanket in it, then gently placed Lorenzo inside. He was so tiny, born early, with three brothers. Watching him sleep for a moment, she studied his little hands and feet. If anyone was brave, it was Lori. Then she realized her mistake. Although she was uncomfortable holding the incomplete child, he had also acted as a shield, keeping her safe from her husband's advances.

Moving silently, Milton came up behind her. She had no idea he was as close as he was until he spoke, whispering in her ear. "He must have found all that crying very tiring."

She had only to lean back to touch him and she wished she understood her own emotions, for they had never been so bi-polar. She wanted him and feared him. She anticipated the next hour and at the same time dreaded it. Brenda closed her eyes and swayed, slightly dizzy, confused, almost wishing he were a monster, so he could hurt her, take the indecision from her hands, make her the victim and not the wife.

"I hate to take him from here, if he will cry again."

"The dragon was correct. We need him with us, if we find his chakra."

His breath was warm against her shoulder, or so she imagined. Brenda did not like him behind her, where he could be performing all kinds of devilment, like watching her, breathing in her scent, perhaps even reaching out, caressing her—and thereby initiating her into the facets of physical loving.

Her time was running out.

She turned slowly, no longer looking at the sleeping infant, but to stare in his eyes and study him. He was tall, but she was tall for a woman and used to dealing with tall men. He had human eyes now, a deep green iris with small round pupils, dilated in the shadowy dimness of the room. They were clear, bright, inquisitive and met hers without flinching, expressing his openness.

If there were secrets here, or pain in the future, she couldn't read it. Studying him, she thought of his statement that she was strong and she wanted to be strong for him, to be his equal and his companion and for an instant, she forgot to be afraid.

CHAPTER 16

Brenda wanted to touch his chin, his nose, to make sure he existed, and this was not some spell he had placed on her, here on sanctified ground. When her courage mounted, she did reach out but it was not boldly as she would have wished, and it was not his skin she felt, but the coldness of the heavy metal collar he wore at his neck.

"Are people safer when you are chained?"

"No. I have never hurt a mortal. I cannot. Although I look the beast, I am not one."

It was not a large room, but they could have been in a phone booth, for all the space between them. She had the dresser behind her, so she couldn't back up, but she didn't feel peril, nor necessarily trapped. Brenda suspected if she shoved, he would let her go, but she knew if she ran he would catch her. There would be no escaping the events of this night.

He kept his arms motionless at his side, made no move to touch her, as she touched him. Brenda left the sign of subjugation he wore at his neck, and used her hyper-sensitive fingertips to caress his human ear. She had no idea she would find it so erotic. While she traced the outline of his lobe, he shut his eyes, all but purred, but still made no move to grasp her, take her, hurt her.

Brenda felt softness and warmth, neither of which she expected. How could she have imagined a body so muscular could be soft? She found she could not resist touching him, found it hypnotic, erotic. It felt like her fingertips were sending back more than simply tactile sensations, but were also relaying colors and scents and depths of passion she never anticipated. For a fleeting second she wondered if other brides felt this way touching their new husbands, but decided it didn't matter.

Only here mattered. Only now.

She wanted to know everything about him, and in the privacy of this chamber, in this massive church of all places, she would get her wish.

Her pulse raced, and underneath the light yellow sundress she wore, her nipples beaded. That was something else she had not anticipated, and by itself was so exquisitely pleasurable it was almost painful. It felt wonderful. Maybe she believed in gargoyles and maybe she didn't, but he felt wonderful. She felt incredible.

From his ear, she slowly lowered her finger, caressing his neck. A light growth of beard had started, a mere darkening of his chin, which surprised her, for she doubted as a gargoyle he shaved. Lightly she ran her fingernails over his cheek, over the sensitive place above his upper lip. She listened to the rasp. She wondered what kissing it would feel like to her lips.

Still he did not move. With her explorations she grew bolder, and felt the same freedom with her questions.

"Does it bother you, dealing with a soulless being?" Brenda found it odd that she accepted Byron could turn into a dragon and into a teapot, but was having trouble accepting he had no soul. She never thought of souls before. Never. She was not a church goer, and when she dealt with criminals, she only dealt with evidence, procedure, and keeping society safe. She had no time to consider souls. Now, because it seemed so important to Milton the distinction be made between chakra and soul, it was also important to her.

"The dragon?" he asked. His eyelids had lowered, but with her question he opened them. The pupils were wide, his breathing irregular. He liked what she was doing so much, she decided, that she had taken him from his present into pleasure. That was power.

"Yes," she whispered, finding her voice strangely husky.

His voice was sexy, warm and intoxicating, and, she realized, it was exactly his gargoyle's voice. It hadn't changed in volume or timbre when his snout vanished, when his massively alien features disappeared. It was easier to think there never was a gargoyle, only this. But then, what was she doing with a stranger in a room where the bed was so obviously waiting to be utilized?

"No. Dealing with the dragon does not bother me. He is not a creature of this planet, and therefore not bound by the holy laws of Earth, as I am, as you are. Yet he serves Good. Byron fights evil in ways I cannot. I am pleased for this opportunity to help him. I have grown fond of his sons. I wish them all healthy lives."

He moved to the bed, pulled the top bedspread off. It was heavy, ornate, obviously an heirloom. Milton then straightened the pillow, both a delaying tactic and an action to force things to move a shade more quickly. Odd how moving one bed pillow could do both.

"Brenda, I am required to tell you what will happen tonight: in case you did not realize this when I mentioned it before, the HOLD spell will not work here."

"Here, on holy ground?"

"Yes."

"Is that why you insisted on it?"

"No. There is another reason, but I want you to know, if you wish me to stop, if I do anything you do not like, you have only to tell me. You cannot paralyze me, but I give you my word, as much as I am able, to stop should you ask me to."

She breathed deeply, closing her eyes for the moment on possibilities. When she opened them again, he had withdrawn, moved, with his silent gate, across the room, standing now, beside the curtain. His shoulders were slumped and somehow, for the first time since she had known him, he looked defeated. Chained in the dungeon, he had only looked defiant, facing down the dragon, he had appeared invincible. Now his shoulders were rounded and his back sagged. He radiated hurt she could almost see.

"There are two ways we can do this."

This. She did not have to ask which 'this' he meant.

"I can take my time and try to bring you pleasure or I can do it quickly and have it over with the least amount of inconvenience."

"I, um," Brenda said, but she only heard the word pleasure.

"I know you find my touch repulsive."

She would not lie to him. "I do, but I think I could get used to you looking like this." She had no idea if that were true.

When he touched her hair, it had been far better than she anticipated. Milton had taken his sensual assault no further. Brenda could see how tightly he reined in his passion when he touched her. He had been deeply affected and the bed was close, the door locked, yet he had honored her giving her time to adjust, to accept before the union of their bodies.

"I do not know you."

"Is it your wish to know me better?" his voice was very quiet in a room as silent as a tomb.

"Milton," she paused. His given name felt strange on her tongue, for she was not used to calling the monster Milton. He did not turn, he did not look up. Somehow he expected to be hurt this night, and that insight amazed her, for she was the one expecting to be ravaged.

"Milton," she spoke louder this time, a bit more forceful. She wasn't certain any longer whose side she was on: his, her own, the side of Good and righteousness, or the side of cowardice. She only knew somehow, since she studied him since he had moved away giving her breathing room, something deep within her changed. "I wish to know you better."

She looked once at the infant, still sound asleep, then at the bed, high and imposing, before she moved to him, and this time when she said his name, she whispered it. "I am not a coward."

"I never meant to imply you were."

"I intend to honor my commitment."

She could read him better as a man than she could when he walked as a beast, understood the look of hope which brightened his eyes for a moment, before he lowered his lashes. Still, if escape were possible, she would seek it.

"Husband, wife, marriage, the words mean different things to each couple."

"No, you are wrong. The words have meant the same through all the eternities. It is just Satan who would have you think there is leeway within the bonds of marriage to do things which were never intended. Marriage is a blessed institution, and family, which begins with marriage, is the single most important unit to LORD."

Brenda waited, trying to count her heartbeats but they came too rapidly, too out of control for her to seek to calm herself in that manner. "May I hold you?"

He had been hurt, she could see that, for this time he did not look hopeful, only resigned. "What do you mean, precisely?" There was a bitter edge to his question, a sharpness which was ugly. He did not trust her and Brenda could not blame him, for although she had agreed to the marriage ceremony--two marriage ceremonies, she had done nothing honorable or even kind.

"Hold you. I want to learn your feel, your touch."

"Only hold?"

"We have all night. I know you are eager to get started with your quest, but this should not take long."

He bowed his head, a slight acknowledgement. With that, she walked to him, put her right hand in his left, her left hand to his back, as if they were to waltz, some exotic form of ballroom dancing in this holy sanctuary. She swayed, as if she heard music, and her feet moved, a step here, then there, moving in place, but he matched her, his motion coordinated to mimic hers. His hands were warm when she expected to find them cold. His fingers wrapped around hers were strong, confident, and reassuring. What she could feel of his back, through his shirt, his vest, his jacket, was his body, firmly muscled, poised and controlled.

Heavens above, he was normal. That was as much a shock to her as her own surprise at agreeing to marry him.

She shut her eyes, inched closer, until her breasts rubbed against his chest, adding that sensation to the experiences flooding through her. Her body liked this, she knew from the beading of the nipples as they responded not so much to the soft abrasion as the potential. Her skin tingled, felt warm and cold and more than those, incomplete. She wished he would touch her intimately.

Seconds passed, although it could have been minutes, hours, she knew instinctively that as fast as time moved, their relationship progressed from strangers to something more. They would be lovers. It never occurred to her they could be friends.

Inches away from him, she studied his face, made easier because his eyes were closed, lightly, as if he prayed, or as if each experience was so unique, so longed for, that he did not wish to miss a second of the pleasure. "You smell good. Like summer," he said, "wild roses."

"It's the body lotion Lori made me wear. Do you like wild roses?"

"I don't know. I have been chained, locked in a dungeon where daily I fought for my life. I was not allowed out to see the world. But I remember the smell of roses."

She remembered something he had said in the cavern, something she had not believed. "Were there roses in Eden?"

"Yes." Then he grinned, and his features lightened, and he looked boyish. "But they had no thorns."

Ahh, she thought. Eden. She had always thought it a fairytale, an allegory. He was talking about a literal Eden.

"Did you walk in Eden?"

"It was our earliest task, to keep Adam and his wife safe from the evil which roamed the land, for Satan was loose then, and there are many thousands of his minions."

"Then you failed, for they were tempted."

"We did not fail. All proceeded as needed."

"The Fall—" she had no words for it, for Sunday school had been many years ago, and even then she had not believed.

"I did not think on my wedding night I would be talking of Adam and Eve, but it does seem appropriate. They were innocent when they were in the garden, and LORD wanted them to know good from evil, to taste of the fruit, but He could not give it to them. They had to take it. Yet they had no understanding of choice and consequence. They were innocent. The gargoyles kept them from lesser temptations, kept Satan's minions from hurting them, for Satan knew if Adam and Eve died, new life would have to be created, and in his evil, he wanted a hand in that. So, when Eve partook of the fruit of the tree of good and evil, it was what LORD wanted. They had not sinned, they had fallen. There is a difference. In their innocence, they could not have children and they did not have agency.

They only had obedience, and while LORD does want obedience, he wants choice and accountability too."

"That is a different story than the one I was told."

"Yes. It has served the evil ones of this land for man to believe Eve was weak, both tempted and becoming her husband's temptress, but that is incorrect. She was devout and became the mother of all humans who have ever lived."

Then Brenda realized she could draw a parallel. "Was she frightened when they were kicked out?"

"She had an incomplete understanding, and therefore was frightened, and the Gargoyles could not interfere, could not instruct, but the angels were singing when Adam knew his wife for the first time, for with that action, all LORD had planned came to its culmination."

An incomplete understanding. Yes, Brenda realized that was what she was afraid of. She didn't need to know the future, she only to know herself and her husband, and he was a stranger to her.

"Did they miss the Garden?"

"They were busy with their children, planting, and their religious obligations. They did not yearn to return to ignorance."

Adam and Eve. What a crazy turn this conversation had taken from the scent of a rose.

Milton's eyes had darkened. His lips were full, parted. They looked soft, welcoming, and were less than an inch away from hers. She tried to step forward, found herself rocking more than moving so she did not kiss him, even when she thought she might.

"I hope when this quest is complete, no matter what the outcome, I will have the time to learn to cherish the things I have missed." He was not speaking of roses and she knew it.

Brenda breathed deeply, emptied her lungs slowly. "I hope so too."

"You feel good. Never in all the centuries I have been alive, have I felt this softness." His hand in hers tightened a fraction, a comforting acknowledgement turning to a lover's caress. His fingers at her back wandered, from her hip, across her back, up her slender spine to her shoulders. "You are so lovely."

When she was with him, while he was in this guise, she felt beautiful. "It is this dress. Lori thinks the Inn found it."

"The Inn has that ability, but while the dress is attractive, it only enhances your loveliness, does not create it."

She was a woman, had never realized she had such vanity when being held. She cocked her head, an unspoken question. She would not troll for compliments, but if he would offer them, she was standing there, had nothing better to do, so she would listen.

"Your eyes are stunningly beautiful. It was the first thing I noticed about you as you wandered down the stairs into my dungeon. They are bright and intelligent. They sparkle with your laughter, they echo your sorrow. When you smile, you force me to catch my breath, for I cannot breathe in your presence. And your body…"

He let the sentence drift off, but he finished "…will give me great pleasure." This time when she heard his voice she was not frightened, but perhaps enchanted.

"And you are good."

Years on the police force had flushed all innocence from her, but Brenda felt herself blushing. "Don't make me into something I am not."

"You doubt me?"

She could hear his amusement, see his grin, in this handsome man who was simultaneously a stranger and her husband.

Brenda pouted, and her body swayed against his, a seduction more than a dance, the music imagined, fed by their thumping hearts. "I am petty and jealous. I can hold a grudge for an eternity. I don't call my parents enough, even when I know they are worried. I'm short with my friends and abrupt with people I think are lying to me. Maybe I haven't murdered or stolen anything, but I am not good, not in the sense you mean."

"Do you remember the man who left the cathedral when I entered?"

She didn't answer with words. Instead she eradicated most of the remaining distance between them and lowered her head to his chest.

"Evil cannot exist in my presence. Yet, here you are, comfortable. That speaks to your goodness."

"But I am uncomfortable in your presence." This time, holding him, she knew she lied on more than one level.

He chuckled and she heard it, felt it, absorbed it. "No, you're not. You are afraid of the monster, but before you knew what I looked like, you had no trouble talking to me, on your porch, and now…"

"Now…" she whispered.

An invitation.

CHAPTER 17

He moved his hand, the one which had been caressing her shoulder, until it explored her neck, the soft cascade of her hair. She closed her eyes, moved her body even closer, so she touched him, from thighs to forehead. Their bodies meshed, communicated. She ached in ways she had never felt and she knew the meaning of temptation, for in all honesty, she had never felt that either. While all her campus friends were seeking temporary alliances, she kept herself aloof, undefiled. For marriage, to this man.

She did not know love yet, but she realized in a few minutes she would know loving.

"Milton, I give you my word, for I cannot promise for always, for I cannot see the future, and there may come a time when I need to, but I promise never to invoke the HOLD spell against you. And when I say hold tonight, it should be understood I mean 'hold me please, Milton,' for you are my husband now and I am no longer afraid."

His features remained very still, almost granite, his eyes with a deep, palpable sadness, his shoulders still hunched. Then slowly he straightened and when he met her gaze again, he grinned. "You lie. I do frighten you. But less, I think, in this form."

"Saint Caspian?"

"For tonight and the rest of our married life, please think of it only as a surname." Leaving her side, he walked to the light switch and flicked it down, leaving the room in twilight. The drapes at the window were heavy, and very little light entered through the center seam where they almost met.

He approached, and while she stood her ground, she realized she stayed because she wanted to. She yearned for his touch, and she was desperate to plunge the depths of her own passion. Looking at him now, in this room, with her crazy thoughts, she wanted to be a wife and a lover, two things she had never been before.

As he had once before, he rubbed his chin against hers, but this time she felt not his heavy fur, but his smooth skin. She let her eyelids drift closed, let the sensations swirl around her. This close, she could smell his scent, a male musk which had her pulse racing and her breath coming in quick little pants. With gentle hands on her jaw, he raised her chin and nipped, very lightly, at her bottom lip. It did not hurt, but it was provocative and invasive and a prelude, for she smiled. The next time she felt pressure against her lips, it was not his teeth, but his lips and they were soft and sweet and she thought she might melt, right there, on sacred ground.

The kiss was gentle and over quickly, although perhaps that was not true, for although he moved back an inch, perhaps an inch and a half, she knew with that sensitive kiss he had marked her, and she would go through with her part, willingly. Perhaps if he left her now she would suffer. She felt the start of a coil of pleasure, knew she ached for release.

"Please," Brenda said. Please what, she had no idea. Please yes, please no: neither seemed to have any meaning. He nodded and his eyes grew fuzzy. She knew what his passion looked like, and knew too, he would offer her only tenderness.

"Thank you," he said, his response to her statement. Thank you. He had given up immortality. He would suffer should she die, and he had ceded his freedom for joint chains, a quest he had no particular interest in and a wife he had only seen a few times and barely knew. Yet he thanked her.

She felt cherished with his words. A flush of pleasure rose to her cheeks, so she kept her hands bolted to her sides, to keep from drawing attention to her embarrassment, and thereby making it worse.

Milton leaned closer, refreshed the kiss. He parted her lips and inserted his tongue into her mouth, slowly, touching hers, then darting away. A second later it was back again, this time more forceful, mimicking the in and out movement her body craved, even if she craved it somewhat lower.

She liked this kissing, found her body matched his. In this she could be his equal. The trouble with kissing is that it is never enough: It creates other needs.

Her breasts brushed his chest, sensitive, screaming out for his touch. Her body had been kept under rigid control all her adult life, and she had never felt so wanton. She swayed her hips, side to side, afraid to move them front to back, for he was close, close enough that it wouldn't take much for her to know how involved he had become in their simple kiss.

"Brenda, if you would stop me, now is the time."

She almost heard angel harps, the setting so beautiful, her own body so responsive. Her pulse spiked, her breathing quickened. She felt warm and cold and more than either, desired and desirable. That last was new to her, for she never considered herself beautiful.

Brenda stood very still as she considered his words. Her mind flipped randomly from the Voice who had helped her time and again, a Voice she had been attracted to, to the gargoyle, kneeling during their wedding ceremony, a creature appearing to be a monster who cried as three dragons became whole and one suffered. Milton stayed still as she studied him, keeping his face expressionless, although she knew without a doubt he expected her to hurt him, to shatter him into tiny little pieces with her ugly and abrupt refusal. Because she knew she had the power to stop him and she recognized the nascent need in herself to understand the love developing between them, Brenda didn't have to.

She moved deliberately, one foot in front of the other until only inches separated them. With fingers trembling only slightly she held her arms out. "Hold me, Milton. For tonight, for now, put your own HOLD spell on me. I want to celebrate this marriage, here, in this place. I don't understand. There is too much I am confused about, but I know right now, I want to learn all the secrets of your body, and have you teach me the secrets of my own."

"I will hold you," he said, and his voice was low, somber, as if a prayer. "We will find the blessing LORD gave man and woman to find joy in a sanctified union."

She hadn't worn much, a cap-sleeved yellow dress with a scalloped hem Lori had found a lifetime ago. The sundress had an invisible zipper, which started at her shoulders and went low, to the curve of her spine. Brenda held her breath, keeping the air trapped in her lungs as he unzipped it with one single stroke.

Milton did not pull the dress off, rip it from her shoulders, toss her on the bed, as she half feared. Instead, he brought his warm hands under the material, and caressed the silky skin of her back, the broad plains of her shoulder blades and the sensitive indentation of her narrow waist. His touch felt welcoming and right, and for a second, she thought of the gargoyle, with claws at his hands, and the fears she had carried with her for well over ten years. Warmth and desire spread as she found the monster was capable of great tenderness. Curious, she reached out, touched him, his upper arms where thick corded muscles rippled. As a gargoyle, he hadn't worn much in the way of clothing. She was well acquainted with how the upper half of his body looked naked.

Seconds later, deepening a kiss which had her mindless, he put his hands against her buttocks, pushing her closer, deeper against the broad strength of his muscled chest, against the hard invitation of his erection.

Gently, slowly, Milton rubbed his forehead back and forth across hers. "You make me want you, as I have never wanted another, in all the centuries I have been alive."

"You make me want you," she confessed, "when I thought you a beast. When I couldn't imagine how we could ever make love, I still wanted you. I think you spoiled me for any human man, all those years ago when I first saw you, chained in the basement."

He laughed at her confession, for he knew it to be true. Still, he could tease her, and in addition, he could be honest with her. "Lust, in an eight year old? I am glad I did not know that then." He rocked back, forth, on the balls of his feet and gently pushed her stomach again against the rock hardness which was his indication of passion. "It would have made the intervening years very painful."

Brenda grinned and knew, in addition to the desire and the rapidly vanishing anxiety, what she felt was happiness. "It was not lust then, for I didn't know the word. I was raised in a happy family without any kind of ugliness. I didn't understand anything like that, until sex-ed classes in junior high. But then, I thought of the creatures I had once seen, chained in a dungeon, and while I was terrified, and had nightmares, I also realized I was entranced." She stopped, wet her lips with a tongue gone very dry and when she spoke again it was only a whisper. "I thought it was perversion."

He lowered his head, kissed her through her wedding dress, filmy slip and the summer-weight bra she wore, and her nipple hardened. "Does this feel like perversion?"

"Milton, no." But then she ruined the effect, by whispering, "Milton, yes," although her second response was not to his question, but due to the fact he had raised her up, let her plant her legs around his hips, and he still clothed, and she in the open dress and her underclothes.

With firm, deliberate steps, he carried her to the high, antique bed. As he released her, he did so slowly, bringing her down the complete length of his body, letting her feel the effect she had on him.

"I do not leave you," he said. "I prepare the bed."

The sun had set hours before but the light coming in through the parted curtains was red now, giving everything in the room a rose tint. He pulled back the sheets. Brenda could see they were freshly laundered. She thought she smelled lavender.

Nerves began to tingle all through her body. Because of growing apprehension, she could not settle, walking around the room, touching the bedspread, the picture frames. "You would think they expected us."

He loosened the tie, pulled the noose over his head, showing again the broad ring of the ugly metal collar he wore. "They were. For over two thousand years."

While she waited, while she swallowed, he removed his jacket, vest and shirt with mindless desperation.

It was not courage that had her reaching out, placing her palms flat against his chest splaying her fingers against his flat male nipples. It was desire. "I am glad, as a gargoyle, you have such a marvelous physique."

He grinned then, and she knew his eyes were still a gargoyle's. They had not changed. "You do not like my manform?"

"No, I adore your manform."

With a flick of his wrist, the dress slid down her shoulders, down her back and past her hips, to pool on the ornate carpet. With it went the slip, so light and airy she did not miss it. She wore a bra and wisps of panties, open toed yellow sandals, knee high stockings with garters, and hair, her glorious red golden hair. "You take my breath away."

"You make me feel beautiful." It was true. She was with a monster, someone who only hours ago had repulsed her, and she was enchanted. She thought, she was almost certain, what she was feeling was love.

"I am new to this," he said, fingering the closing of her bra. She wondered if he meant female clothing, for he had had no trouble with the zipper, but, as the clasp ceded and the bra snapped open, he grinned. "I have never been with a woman."

"Two thousand years old, and you're a virgin?"

He quirked a grin. "I am actually significantly older than that, but yes. I am a virgin. No woman in all that time has wrapped her hands around my heart, has filled my mind with this budding love."

She thought to call him on his statement, love, how could this be love? But Brenda recognized in herself that was exactly what she had been feeling, was exactly what she was feeling now. This tangled, confused emotion between them was at least the beginning of love.

"Eternity?" she asked, having no idea where the question had come from. He was magnificent, facing her wearing nothing but his slacks and his hopes.

"Eternity," he answered and it was both a vow and a promise.

Unconsciously she raised her arms, covering her breasts with modesty she could not control. "My aunt did you no favors, keeping you chained in the basement."

He bent his head, nipping her neck, her shoulders, then her breasts with dozens of tiny, persuasive kisses. "If she hadn't, I never would have met you, and at the moment, the wait does not seem all that long."

Shockwaves traveled through her, bringing warmth and a new feeling she could only describe as excitement. She was a policeman, knew all about sex, the good and the ugly, but at the moment, with his lips at her neck and her heart thumping almost painfully she only knew want and realized she knew nothing about intimacy.

His hands went to his belt, but Brenda brushed them aside, and with a grin, feeling her own empowerment, worked the buckle herself. She placed the flat of her palm against his groin, watched while he swayed, his human nostrils flaring as the small Adam's apple in his throat bobbed. He was full and heavy and they had been talking of heaven earlier and she knew, with bride's intuition they would find another heaven together, wrapped in each other's commitment.

"Brenda, I—" he said.

"Don't worry," she said, undoing his zipper, then pulling down his slacks, "we will have this over quickly, then we can get on with our quest."

"Ahh, beloved," his head hung back exposing his long neck, and his eyes were shut, and his expression, if she didn't know better, could be described as pained.

She rubbed. She teased, working her fingers up his heavily muscled thighs toward where he wanted her, where she wanted, but she took her time, to feel the washboard strength of his abs, the honed muscles of his stomach.

"Beloved, I think you kill me."

She tingled, feeling hot and cold and very, very needy. "Soon," she whispered, but had no idea what she referred to specifically.

"That is what I am afraid of, that this will be over too quickly."

Brenda pulled down his slacks, his formfitting briefs, waited while he stepped out of them. His toes were long, clean, looked like they would bring her pleasure if she started her tactile exploration of his body there. But she raised her gaze from his feet and her breath caught.

Brenda doubted she ever be able to breathe again.

He sprang forth, full and magnificent, and she cupped his length. He was hot and hard while soft and welcoming. But she did not have much time to explore, for he lifted her onto the bed, and checking her, to be certain she was ready, he quickly entered her. There was pain, a sharp, biting stab, and he waited, a long second followed by another while her body adjusted to his width and length. He moved himself an inch, no more. She cried out, not so much aching as incomplete.

"Do not leave me," Brenda cried.

"Not for a second, for all the moments we will be granted together."

"No, please, Milton. Hold, hold, hold…" he waited, feeling no need to transform, fearing for her if he did, crushed under the weight of marble, impaled, for all the spell wouldn't work here. "Hold me, just like you're doing." Instinctively she moved, sensing what her body needed, what his could provide.

There was pleasure coming, overdue, but at the moment she only felt curiosity and a rampant incompleteness.

"Am I hurting you?"

"How could you when you know how desperately I ache for this?" she rocked again, the mattress giving support, meeting an immovable object, until he too could not deny the rhythm, the dance-steps that would see them to the other side.

He had confessed to her he had made a devil's bargain. He had admitted he had sinned, the worst sin possible, but laying naked beneath him, with the intimacy of their new marriage, with his promise of love, she desperately wanted what he could provide. They matched each other and the tempo increased as male and female joined.

"I feel all explosive," she muttered, her eyes shut, while ribbons of color soared in her and through her and around her. Brenda could only think of Milton, but only thought of him as a man who had brought her happiness.

They gasped together, their lips locking, pleasure rocking their bodies as their hips maintained that glorious movement. They kissed, and planets swirled and stars collided, and their love was joined until they found completion.

Long minutes later, she leaned against him, her head resting on his shoulder. While she lay, replete, she explored his body, touched the heavy collar he wore.

"It never comes off?"

"No."

"Ever?"

"Does it bother you? I have grown used to them."

"As a sign of servitude they bother me," she said, reaching down for his left arm, touching the heavy manacle there too. "Do all gargoyles wear them?"

"Yes."

"Was my aunt evil, to keep you chained?"

"With all respect to her, no. We were kept busy. The Inn sits on several portals, doors to different worlds.

"Almost without exception, most of the creatures which come through are evil. It is perhaps creatures who serve Good are content where they are, or they are kept so occupied they have no time to wander, but I and my companion kept the evil from the Inn, and therefore from the Earth."

"But you wanted to feel sunlight on your wings, enjoy your freedoms." She thought again of roses and the color yellow.

"Yes, but at the moment, with a beautiful woman who is my wife in my arms, I cannot think of a single complaint." He raised up on an elbow, and his grin when he faced her this time was heated. "Now, will you be sore, if we join again?"

Brenda stretched, raising her arms well above her head, extending her legs, pointing her toes. When her stretch was complete, she pushed, forcing him from his side onto his back. Slowly, methodically, she crawled up his chest, straddling him, and kissed him, deeply, passionately. "I think I'll be able to manage one more time."

And their love was coupled again.

***

"Are you ready to go?"

She wanted to complain, moan "Already?" for she did not have his urgency, and she felt boneless and replete, but today she would support him.

She turned on the light as she returned from the bathroom, after having washed quickly and gotten dressed. She stopped, dropped the sandals she was holding until they thumped on the carpet. There was blood on the sheets.

"Virgin blood," he said. "I did not know you were a virgin as well. I should have smelled it on you."

She shrugged, wondered if she should apologize. "It was hard. I had plenty of opportunities. I have been tempted more times than I care to admit, sometimes by men I even admired."

He straightened to his full height, gloriously, magnificently naked, even if the part which had given her so much pleasure in the night had softened. Still she remembered tasting every inch of his long, imposing body with her kisses, needing to explore the new emotions budding within, to understand him until he was so completely a part of her that she could not tell where one ended, the other began. She had been bold in the dark, pleasuring and pleasured. It had been a long night filled with wonderful, unexpected discoveries.

"Yet you were saving yourself for marriage?"

She rubbed her ring finger, wished she had something tangible to solidify this union. "I don't know if it were marriage exactly, more like a commitment, something I felt could be lasting."

"What we have here, Brenda, is lasting."

The room suddenly felt cold, and she shivered, not understanding this antsy feeling creeping through her. "So my Aunt Jan said."

She stepped back, checked the drawer where Lorenzo continued to sleep peacefully. He had not whimpered once during their long night of loving. Now as she watched, his lips puckered, his eyes crunched, although asleep, he would awake soon—and again she knew, be inconsolable. Their interlude was coming to a quick close.

She moved in front of an oval mirror, gilt framed and ornate, where she struggled to braid her hair. "Let me," Milton said, his broad, firm hands gentle on her shoulders.

She met his reflection in the mirror, smiled as a thought intruded, "He's mine! All mine!" of a bride after a night of passion with a man she loved. "I don't want to be a bother. And I'm used to doing it myself, although tonight I seem to be all thumbs."

His breath was warm on her neck, smelled sweet. "I would love to touch your hair again." While they had been intimate, it had sheeted around them, cascading in a brilliant red explosion of silky strands. He braided her hair quickly, professionally, not with the drama Lori had managed, but the quick simple pleat she wore every day. She handed him a hair band and he secured the ends.

He did not bother to get dressed. He stood, and where once stood a naked man, now Brenda faced the gargoyle. She screamed, stepping back, putting as much distance as she could between her and the monster.

"Brenda?"

"You're a gargoyle."

"Yes. Why does that come as a surprise? You knew what I was when you agreed to the marriage."

"But you said—" she struggled, finding the words painful, "—you had a manform, and you were granted mortality."

"Both of those statements are correct. I do not see why you are so upset."

"I thought with the marriage, with the time we spent here, you were through with your curse."

"I can maintain manform only to mate. This is my normal physique."

It bothered her, the things she had confessed, the way she had responded to him. She set her teeth, spoke as she ground them together. "I feel betrayed."

His hands, curled with vicious sharp tips at the end, where empty, held out in entreaty. "I have been completely honest with you."

"When I saw you—"

"That which I am is not so readily dispensed with."

"But your immortality—"

"I told you, it was taken so I will not suffer should you precede me in death. Are you ready to continue?"

"No, I want to go back to my aunt."

"I will do so, but first, I need you. I cannot fight my enemies if I am carrying the infant, and I cannot rescue the ne-chakra without Lorenzo."

"I will go with you, but as soon as this is over, I never want to see you again."

"I agree to your terms. You realize, should you quicken with my child, gargoyle children are not easily disposed of."

She had not thought of that. "I have no interest whatsoever in disposing of it." Even the thought felt ugly. "If I find I cannot raise the child, my aunt would raise your baby. Or my sister."

"It would be acceptable for the witch or the dragon's spouse be made guardian of my child. I will have a document for you to sign, should your body quicken my seed."

"Is not my word enough?"

"Apparently not. Come, we waste time arguing here."

When he had changed, when his wings had sprouted and his hideous snout developed and when she noticed there were claws at his hands and his feet and she knew he wore the collar and the manacles to keep him prisoner, she had been revolted. Brenda tried to remember their interlude, shared just minutes before, when he brought her pleasure she had never known before.

"We have a quest," he said. "We have taken too much time away from it." His shoulders slumped and he looked away.

"Then let's get started. Do you know where to begin?"

"Massachusetts. It is not far, the way I fly."

"Massachusetts." Boston, the Cape. Shopping. Whale watching. Fresh fish and baked beans. Evil?

"I do not know if the chakra will be there, but that is where the trail starts."

Brenda bent down, picked up the infant, changed his diaper quickly, pleased when she noticed it was stained and wet. "Is he starving?"

"Lorenzo?"

"Yes."

"The dragon would not let his own son starve. He will live. I cannot say if he will thrive."

"And you are sure my child will not be born with wings?"

"He will be born human."

"He?"

"Or she. I have no way of knowing if you have conceived yet. Do not borrow worry, Brenda. Let us help Lorenzo first."

Milton lifted her in his arms and carried her though the deserted corridors of the ornate cathedral. They met no one. He launched himself into the air from the broad steps that fronted the door, and why New Yorkers didn't scream or crash into light poles, she had no idea, for they were apparently invisible. Warm and secure in his arms, Brenda flew above the New York Thruway, until they picked up the Massachusetts Turnpike. He landed about an hour later, stretching his wings as his feet touched ground. "I have been too long without flying."

She had used the time to think through her own quixotic emotions, and when she answered him her words were light with humor. "I suppose we could always take a bus."

"I suppose," Milton acknowledged. "At least while we are on Earth."

She liked this image, so she smiled, of this huge, winged gargoyle, with his grotesque face, coming up with exact change, so he could sit anywhere he wanted on a city bus.

Milton landed in a wealthy, upscale neighborhood, large brick houses, well-spaced from each other and the road, perched on manicured yards, with flowers and trees and bushes professionally trimmed. Dawn was approaching, for there was color in the east, the first shades of orange, and the air smelled of ocean.

"Should you change?" she asked the gargoyle.

"Anyone who sees us will see my human guise."

"Anyone but me. Is there Evil here?" she said, indicating the house. Pierce Billova, the mail box said.

He raised his snout and sniffed, and his eyes were long-seeing. A moment later he spoke. "No. This is a false lead. A wizard lives here, a powerful one, but not the one we seek."

She was relieved. "We could knock on the door, ask if he has any information. I don't know anything about wizards, but it might be a small community."

"Your suggestion has merit."

"At least the baby is still sleeping."

"It won't last. Also, I think if his chakra, or ne-chakra were nearby, he would react to it."

"You said there are other worlds?"

"Yes."

"Is there any reason why the wizard we seek would find another world, or is it likely he would stay here?"

"Here, Earth?"

"Yes."

"Every creature, human or not, seeks to stay where it is most comfortable, especially in times of high stress. He, our wer-wizard, was born human, of this I am sure, so he would be more comfortable here. However, given he has or had the ne-chakra, he would also be looking for a creature of evil to bind with it, and he wouldn't necessarily find that on Earth."

"But there are evil creatures here."

"But a mortal evil creature will be no good to him."

"Because it will die?"

"Yes, but also because mortals have souls. It is unlikely he could get a creature with a soul to bind with a chakra. They are not compatible."

"Could a creature with a soul lose a soul?"

His features darkened, and anger overcame him, until, while Brenda watched, he controlled it. "Why do you ask?" his words were terse, growled. He looked more like a monster in than he had since she married him.

In the face of his banked rage, she had trouble recalling her train of thought. "So the evil creature could merge with the chakra."

"Unlikely. It is more probable he will seek a creature of faerie, if he is still on this planet."

"Then we will find the faeries. They should be able to help us, although I am all for knocking on this wizard's door. As long as we have come all this way, we might as well."

Two things happened simultaneously. The infant started crying again, loudly, and with such intensity he could not be quieted, and the door to the house opened.

"The wizard comes, whether we are willing to talk with him or not."

Brenda gasped in fear, for he was dressed in a long robe and he was making unusual hand motions as he approached.

CHAPTER 18

"A gargoyle and his human lover." The words snapped abruptly into the morning and held more than an acknowledgement of what he faced, they held a challenge.

The wizard kept his distance, pausing six feet in front of them. While he did not look tense, his hands were active, moving in continuous arcs, as if he fashioned a weapon they could not see. Beside her, Brenda felt Milton grow tense, and she feared they may have found their enemy, and come unprepared to deal with him.

With her resolve firmly in place, Brenda considered the man, found him attractive, with dark hair cut short and expressive dark eyes. His jaw was firm, thrust forth perhaps in arrogance, definitely in threat. Of his body she could see nothing, for it was covered with the black, flowing robe which reached the manicured grass.

A wizard. Something else to add to her new analysis of the world she lived in. As a patrolman, Brenda thought she had been exposed to everything the streets had to offer: now she had met dragons, gargoyles, creatures of faerie and a wizard. Monsters every one of them.

"Darn," Brenda said, before Milton could stop her. "I wish I had brought my little dog Toto with me. And for some reason I feel strongly I should yell 'Pay no attention to the man in the dark robe…'"

"Cute," he said, and this time, in addition to the arrogance, there was amusement. "I see you're versed in the classics."

Before Brenda could retort, and her tongue was stinging with a reply, Milton roared, spread his wings, and forced himself in front of her, making himself the target of any danger.

The wizard didn't back up, didn't raise his hands in any sort of futile self-defense motion against the clawed, beast which towered above him. Instead he laughed. "Oh dear. Now the neighbors will complain, and I do try so hard to keep a low profile."

"You will answer our questions."

"The gargoyle speaks. I know what you are, although I have never seen one before, at least one not decorating a European church as a waterspout. Your kind is rare."

"Almost as rare as yours," Milton acknowledged, but his answer, was calm, and Brenda was able to breathe easier.

After he spoke, Milton bowed, conveying honor and apology. He held his hands out, palms up, to indicate he was unarmed and folded his wings back, allowing Brenda to step forward, no longer shielded. She would have a talk with him later about his Neanderthal need to protect her.

"We mean you no harm. We ride quest, searching for a wer-wizard, and I realize we have landed here by mistake. You are not the one we seek. I have no quarrel with you, but I will fight to defend my family."

"And, I have no argument with you, if you leave quietly." He turned to Brenda. "You, gargoyle-whore, do you need protection from this beast?"

She tightened her eyes and felt his question hone on her heart like an accurately aimed arrow shaft. She felt like a whore, for isn't that what she was? Hadn't she taken favors in return for sex? There was a marriage, the sex had been consensual, for she had not denied him. She had to believe Milton would have stopped if she had demanded it, but that had no bearing on the discussion. She had her pride. Maybe not in front of Milton, but she could defend herself against this man.

She straightened her spine, knew now why police officers did not wear lace decorated embroidered yellow sundresses for she wished she had the anonymity of her uniform, the security of her badge. "I am no whore. I am a wife and everything I have done—and shared—with this gargoyle, I have done of my own free will."

The wizard looked at her hard, as if trying to unravel her lie, but a moment later he returned Milton's bow respectfully. "Yes, indeed, I believe that. Free will is important to gargoyles."

"It is the creed by which we stand."

The wizard moved closer. A slight breeze rose, warm and from the west, smelling of lilacs, and his robe swirled around his ankles. His feet were bare, his toes firmly planted in the grass. Funny, standing here, facing a wizard, whatever they were, when she knew how evil one could be, Brenda noticed his feet. By comparison, she checked Milton's feet. His toes were long as well. Long and green, they ended in curved, deadly looking talons. A beast's feet. Her stomach sickened. Hoping to hide her reaction, she brought the infant up to her lips, kissing Lorenzo gently on his forehead until she had her nausea under control.

The wizard stopped, advancing no closer, and the look he offered her was compassionate. "Yet, I think you are not wife by any definition you hold sacred."

"She is wife by every definition which I hold sacred," Milton amended.

The stranger's eyes looked deeper, more expressive than green, vibrant and stunning, richer than seedlings brought to life. At the moment she wished she were a painter, and when he had come, he had done so without the covering of a robe. She would love to see him in worn jeans, a tight work shirt, with sweat rippling down his muscles. This was a man she could be attracted to. The gargoyle had no pupils. His eyes were black. She would admit there was intelligence in them, but they were alien, different than anything she was used to. The only time she had seen kindness in them, he had been in human form. Every time she faced him when he was in his natural shape, his eyes offered only anger, danger, or derision.

The gargoyle was her husband. By everything I hold sacred, he had said. But the wizard was surprisingly accurate: not by everything she held sacred. The baby in her arms continued crying, red faced and obviously uncomfortable. She rocked Lorenzo, tried talking to him, humming silly songs she remembered from her own childhood. There were no words her subconscious could fashion, and no silliness she could bring to fore, standing here beside a monster from the pages of antiquity, facing a robed man who studied arcane arts for purposes she could not discern.

"I ask again, do you need rescuing?"

Would it be that easy to escape? "No. I know your offer is honestly meant, and what you see on the surface seems perverted, but this creature and I are united in marriage both by someone with the power of the blessings of the faeries and by a priest on sanctified ground. If I have not given him my heart, that is my concern. I will not leave him, for beyond the giving him my vow, which is not easily broken, we share the same quest. I have given my word and will see it through."

The wizard listened to her intently, with a concentration she found disconcerting. When he finished his silent analysis, he nodded, then moved forward. "It is not me your child objects to," the wizard said, and when he spoke, Brenda's gaze locked with his, and she wondered if he had just thrown her a lifeline and if this safety net she thought of was real or imagined.

The wizard broke his gaze from hers and returned to the infant she held. He set his jaw, his eyes hard, and his hands again spinning yarn she could not see, and faced down Milton. "Still, I think we will do battle. The child has no soul. Have you stolen it?"

Milton bristled, the ruff of fur at his neck standing up. She had seen this action from him before, as he attacked creatures in the dungeon when he had been chained to a wall. The gargoyle placed himself between Brenda and the wizard.

"It is his chakra we seek. He has no soul."

"Chakra, another word I am familiar with, but with which I have no experience. If I may?"

Milton looked at him a long second, then moved aside. "You will not harm him?" Brenda asked as the wizard approached the infant. "He is precious to us."

"Not harm. I only seek to offer him ease." He pulled something Brenda could not see and manipulated it, as if he were tying a large, ornate Christmas bow.

"I will not have you bind this child."

"It can be released at any time," the wizard said, and lifting Lorenzo's left hand, tied something invisible around the infant's wrist. "It will not be like your bindings."

"The boy's mother wears a tie like that."

"What?" Brenda asked, for she still could see nothing. However, whatever it was, it must have been a miracle, for Lorenzo stopped crying.

"This will not make up for what he has lost and its effects will be temporary, but for a while it will provide him nourishment, energy he can assimilate."

"I can't see anything," she said, but Milton took her hand, nothing more than entwining his fingers with hers, and her vision sharpened. Things which had been invisible were now clear. There were bright, neon-colored strips of power floating around the wizard, coiling around his legs, and wrapping themselves around his torso. A few power strands soared nonchalantly around the street, as if too independent to be attracted to him, but the rest were clearly sycophants, drawn to him as if he were the magnet, they iron filings. There was also a small round power strip of brilliant pumpkin orange, very thin, now wrapped around Lorenzo's wrist.

"Lori has one?" Brenda asked. A few power strips, she noticed, approached her timidly, keeping low to the ground, sniffing like dogs, not certain whether to welcome a stranger to their neighborhood. None were so bold as to approach Milton.

"It is my understanding she has worn one since her fight with the wer-wizard."

"Is it a binding? Does it shackle her to him, somehow? Make her his prisoner?"

Brenda directed the question to her husband, but the wizard answered. "Such a use is known to us."

Milton shook his head. "It does not seem to bother her and the dragon has never asked her to remove it, although it is inconceivable he does not see it."

"Dragon. That is what this child is?"

"An incomplete dragon, without his chakra."

"I am not certain I can help you, Caspian," the wizard said, "but I think we search for the same enemy. I too have devoted my vocation for the past year to seeking a powerful wer-wizard."

"Is there any information you could give us?"

"I doubt I have any information you lack. A month or so ago, there was a huge convergence of power, illegally stolen, which I traced to upstate New York. From there it vanished. It was not destroyed, for power cannot be destroyed, but it vanished."

"It went to another world." Milton turned to his wife, and in a casual motion, she never would have expected of him, he gently tickled the baby under its chin until Lorenzo laughed. "While the dragon fought the wer-wizard, your sister freed the powerstrands. I have the story from your aunt."

"Lori can manipulate these things?"

"She is no wizard but in the other land where she was, she was able to access them. She was filled with powers at the time the dragon had transferred to her. It would have been a horrible loss for good, if the wer-wizard had succeeded in his plan, but your sister stopped him."

"I would like the full story one day, but I can see you have no time to tarry, and here, in front of this street, is not the best place for a discussion with a gargoyle to take place."

Wide-eyed, Brenda studied the wizard. "And you lost the trail, then?"

"I did. I was only an hour or so away, when the powerstrands returned."

"It was Lori's doing."

The wizard continued. "I found a witch dead in the forest and there was widespread devastation from an opened portal, but what killed the witch I have no idea, and of the portal, I found nothing. The faeries who would talk with me were frightened and would not elaborate."

"Is he mortal, this wizard we seek?"

"Mortal, yes, but not defenseless. There are powers forbidden to us which he has claimed."

"This I know. You have no name for him, no location?"

The wizard settled his hands at his sides, no longer twisting the powerstrands he manipulated into weapons. "If I did, I would deal with him myself. The powers he seeks do not belong under his dominion. I wish I had more to give you. Although I suspect I have not given you any information you need, I would appreciate it if there is anything you have learned you could share. I too am enjoined in this quest to find the wer-wizard, but I expect for different reasons."

"The wizard you seek, I believe his name is Andrew. I do not know if it is his birth name, or a form of his power-name or an alias, but currently he answers to Andrew."

"Andrew." The wizard chewed the information over. "It is a start. More than I had. Maybe I can help you after all. Three days ago, a call went out, from someone named Andrew, for the lesser creatures of faerie. Since faeries did not appear to be directly related to what I seek, I ignored it, but with what you have told me I might have been too hasty in ignoring it."

"A call to the faeries? Where, and for what?"

"I don't know the answer to either, except a great reward was promised the one which succeeded. I do not know what the task or quest was, and there has been no great disturbance in the forces I worship since, so while this call did originate from him, it does not involve powerstrands."

"Then our quest will take us to the lesser faeries. They are no friends to gargoyles."

"If you find the wer-wizard, be careful. I do not know what your powers are, but I doubt you can destroy him."

"Destroying him is not our primary task."

"Then if you do locate him, I would appreciate it if you let me know, since it is my goal. Evil such as his must not be allowed to reign unchecked."

"For your help, we will do so. We appreciate your assistance with the infant. Come, wife, we will fly."

Brenda felt the touch of his clawed fingers around her forearm, but for the first time, realized she was not repulsed. His hand was warm, and the air cold, the touch was welcomed for that alone, but there was more. In addition, she felt comfort.

Surprising herself, the Brenda looked to her husband and offered him a gentle smile. Then she freed herself, and held her hand out to the wizard. "We apologize if we interrupted your sleep or your work, and we thank you for your information. We will keep in touch."

Pierce shook her hand, clearly aware with his touch, Milton raised his wings and the hackles at his neck rose.

"Your husband is jealous."

"He has no need to be."

"I meant what I offered. If you entered your marriage for other than love, I have powers…"

"No. That is not necessary. For your compassion to Lorenzo, again we thank you."

Milton wrapped his arms around her and effortlessly lifted her. He was in flight the moment later. "You are tempted by his offer to help you escape from this marriage?"

"No." That at least was honest. "I entered into this quest willingly. I will see it through."

"Quest. We talk of different things."

"He did a kind thing for the baby."

"Yes. It was no strain to him, or to the power he worships, but it was a kindness. I did not like to see the infant suffer."

"Are they human?"

"Wizards?"

"Yes."

"As opposed to?" he asked.

"Well, do they come from another world? Are they alien to this planet, like dragons? Like you are?"

"I am indigenous to this planet. I have never known another. But to answer your question, it is my understanding all wizards are human, for they do have souls. How they obtain their power, I do not know. I have been chained for a long time, and no wizard had challenged me before or I would have learned more of them. Is it important to you?"

"No. I am just curious. I have been working the streets for a number of years. I thought I knew just about everything going down, and there is an entire spectrum of beings or creatures which I had no idea existed. Even witches. I thought all women who were accused of witchcraft were simply herbalists or maybe had some form of mental illness. I even thought a few might be Satan worshipers, but all were normal women."

"Normal women?" he asked.

"You're not making this easy."

"I do not see how I can, when I cannot follow your line of thought."

"I did not know there were witches who had real power, that could control and manipulate magic."

"Like your aunt."

She would agree to this, reluctantly. "Like my aunt. I did not believe in fairy tale witches."

"Fairy tale witches?"

It was hard for Brenda to continue this stream of conversation, while being held above a highway, by a flying creature who could be considered 'normal' by no definition of the word as she knew it.

"Fairy tale witches," Brenda said, and she would have hit him, had she not been holding onto the infant with both hands. "Wicked witches, the kind that build gingerbread houses and fatten up young children so they can eat them."

"Don't you think there are things in society so frightening and vile that if the information became public knowledge, life as we know it would be changed?"

"Yes." As a policeman, she had to believe it.

"There are witches who are that evil. Belinda, for all her fixation on the dragon, was one. She was not extremely powerful as these things are measured, however her crimes were legion. The dragon did right in killing her. There are white witches as well, women, born human who have learned to control unseen forces from parallel universes."

"And wizards. Is wizard a male witch?"

"No, they are completely different. As different as pineapples and grapes. You could say both were fruits, but there would be little other points of contiguity. Male and female wizards are called wizards, or werwizards or necromancers, or sorcerers, depending on how they invoke their use of powerstrands. Female witches and male warlocks, or the term witch can be used for both sexes, if you wish to speak in general terms, do not use powerstrands at all. I am certain not all witches can see powerstrands, let alone manipulate them."

"And that wizard was a good guy?"

"A quaint description, but as far as I could tell, he serves Good. I knew as soon as he exited his house he had never done the things Andrew has."

"If we find Andrew, will you tell him?"

"I cannot answer, for I do not know. It will depend on the circumstances. If my quest is completed and if Andrew escapes, he deserves to know so Andrew can be stopped."

"I wish I knew more about these other creatures, witches and wizards and the creatures of faerie."

"If we have time later, I will share with you all I know. If I regain my freedom after this quest is successfully completed, I would like to travel. We could seek the different types of beings together, if you wish."

"I'll think about it," Brenda answered, for at the moment, it was as much of a commitment she was willing to offer. She couldn't help thinking of the wizard. It sounded like he would fight for her, help her to regain her freedom from a marriage she already felt trapped in. The only reason she did not mention it then was she still had the quest to fulfill. The quest she had sold her future for.

CHAPTER 19

Bright moon rays illuminated the ground as they flew beneath it, just past a quarter and edging toward full. Now, as they flew north above cities and towns and small embroidered parks the sun put in an appearance. Early summer was in full blossom here, for the temperature was mild, and she suspected the days would be hot.

His wings worked effortlessly, seemed to cause him no stress.

"Where will we find lesser faeries?"

"The easiest place to locate them is near the Inn. The woods there are heavy with high faeries and the lesser ones."

"Do you know anything about Andrew?"

"He is a former lover of your sister's."

"Are you sure?"

"Yes. I did not participate in the battle, but I can hear, and your aunt and your sister spoke on the subject exhaustively. We know why the wizard seeks the lesser faeries."

"For the chakra."

"Yes. We can hope it has not merged with any creature yet."

Milton flew for a while longer. "You were tempted by the wizard's offer to help free you." He said again, making it a statement.

She saw no reason to lie. "Yes. But it would have done no good. I am married to you and our union cannot be dissolved by whatever power he controls. And I think, although I am certain I don't completely know my own heart, I did enter our marriage willingly. And Milton, I have no complaints about the night we spent together."

"I wondered if you would be that honest with me, and with yourself."

"I'm used to understanding my own emotions. My life has been simple. This confusion is driving me crazy."

"Perhaps you only need to know me better."

"Perhaps," she said tongue-in-cheek, "I need to understand myself better. And I will see the quest through."

"For my help."

"For your help," she agreed.

"You still find me repulsive."

"Do I? Is that what this is about? I ask myself endlessly, how could I not think you a monster? For a second, when I saw your human form, I thought marriage had changed you."

"It did. I am now mortal."

"But you are still a creature who wears his sins so everyone can see them."

"True. It is because I have sinned I look this way. But before you judge me, know no one but LORD was ever perfect."

"I know. But I also have been on the streets for years as a police officer. I know how people look when they sin, when they deny what they have done."

"I have never denied what I have done. It is part of my penance."

"Yet, to look the way you do, you must have done something so horrendous God himself could not bear to look at you and think you human."

"Although you mock, your statement is the truth. That is the reason we were changed. But Brenda, I will not hurt you."

"You already have."

"I shall repeat what I told you before. I have given my word I will not touch you again, in the manner our wedding vows allow, until you offer your permission." She bit her lip and had to be content with that, for she suspected after they found the chakra she would return to her home and her job and would be alone.

While Milton flew, Brenda cradled Lorenzo. The boy was still skeletal, but since the powerstrand was put on his wrist, his color had improved and his crying had stopped.

Although she was honest with herself enough to admit she had always wanted a child someday, she had never felt maternal. In high school, in college, she had only tried to prove her fears groundless by taking any dare tossed her way. She ran track and was captain of the soccer team. She lifted free weights and took every self-defense class she could. There had been no time for casual dating, no opportunity for anything which did not involve increasing her self-image of her courage. Even the weeks before her marriage when she had held Lorenzo's three brothers, her maternal instinct had been limited. She had done it to help her sister, to feel needed, to put off the decision to marry a hideous monster. Now she felt something for Lorenzo she had not felt before: tenderness. It was completely different from her compassion, from her obligation. This she felt in her heart and oddly enough, in her breasts. She wanted to open her dress, let him suckle from her body, wished for the first time she had the ability to do so.

She cared. As a cop, Brenda had tried desperately not to care, except in the most superficial manner—she cared about getting criminals off the streets. She cared about her fellow officers, cared enough to be was there for them, as backup when they called, coming in on her days off, if needed. She cared that the streets were as safe as she could make them, safe for families…other people's families.

This was a different kind of caring. Now, facing a quest and the possibility of meeting up with real evil, she tried to tell herself had no time to dwell on it.

"I love you, little baby," but as she whispered it to the infant sleeping in her arms, she knew she was not speaking to Lorenzo, but her own future child.

"If we had discovered something," Milton said some time later, "we would report at the Inn, but we have nothing, so to do so would be a waste of time. Still, Brenda, I think it might be best if you went to stay with your aunt."

"Why?"

"I will not be able to protect you."

"I do not require your protection."

"It is important I tell you this: if it comes to completing my quest, or saving you from danger, because of the pledge I made, the quest must come first. It is not what my heart would have me do, for I have made an eternal vow with you, but, in the manner of gargoyles, my marriage vow is of lower priority than this arrangement I made with the Dragon."

"Even if you could save me, and rescue the chakra at a later time?"

"Even with that knowledge. I promised nothing would interfere."

"I am sure Byron would not require that degree of dedication from you."

"Although it is to the dragon I made the promise, it is superseded by a higher law. Remember my promise: I will finish this quest without interruption or die in the attempt."

While she could understand his vow on an intellectual level, she was also hurt by it, for when she married, she had wanted a man who would put her first.

They had been flying northward since leaving Massachusetts, and below them, the Adirondack Mountains rose in majesty. The deciduous trees were in full leaf now, the forests thick with early summer growth. Lorenzo was awake, but mesmerized by the flapping of the gargoyle's wings so he made no sound. Below her it looked like the ground swayed, as something white undulated through the trees. Brenda tried to interpret what she saw, and could not.

She pointed, "Look, what is that?"

"Lesser elves, called imps. They are not the kind who were invited to our wedding."

"Are they evil?"

"Not necessarily. They just rarely serve good."

She shivered in revulsion. "It looks almost like a river."

"There are hundreds of thousands of them. They are heading toward the Inn."

"The Inn?" Brenda's voice rose in pitch. "Is Lorenzo's chakra at the Inn?"

"I cannot believe that is their primary purpose in heading there."

"Why? Are they going to attack my Aunt Jan?"

"That is a possibility."

Then Brenda noticed long bouts of flame coming from the Inn. "It's on fire!"

But before Milton could respond, she saw a dragon take flight, and the flames came from him. He circled the Inn, and even from the distance, they could hear his roar. "They are under attack!"

"It appears they intend to fight the dragon and kidnap the children. The dragon was correct. In evil hands, those children would be priceless."

"Andrew could not turn them to evil."

"No, he would have no interest. He would desire their fangs. Each is an extremely powerful weapon."

"On a living dragon." Although the dragon fought, she could see hundreds of thousands of imps scaling the walls of the Inn. Many of them were breaking the windows, trying to gain entrance. There were archers in their hoard, and the dragon was pelted by arrows.

"From a dead one as well. In addition to the fangs, there are other things a dragon corpse could provide to those whose intent is evil. It would do Andrew no good, as dragon entrails are not something a wizard could use, but he could barter with the witches for other icons of power he could use."

"Why are the imps fighting?"

"There is a possibility the Andrew has promised the ne-chakra to the imp commander who captures the dragons or gains him access to the Inn."

"We need to help! Because there is no gargoyle there, the Inn is vulnerable."

"What you say is true. But Andrew would not bring his prize so close to Byron, not unless the dragon was already defeated. No, we travel north a few more miles."

She started to struggle in his arms. "We have to help."

"Our path does not lie that way."

"Milton, can Byron win this fight?"

"I do not know, but it seems unlikely. As you said, there are millions below."

She rushed him, got in his face. "But you could help. I've seen you fight."

"No. Have you understood nothing I've said? My word and my pledge are to hunt the ne-chakra. At this point, even if the dragon is destroyed and the three children kidnapped, I cannot turn from my course. I gave my word."

"I'm not afraid to fight them. Let me go. They are in danger."

He reached out, held her. Although there were heavy claws at his hands, his touch was gentle. "Listen, I will not lose my wife to a fight she cannot win. You are mortal, Brenda. You would only be in the way, a distraction to the dragon."

"Then you fight them!"

"I will not lose my soul by going back on my pledge. I can offer no help to the dragon, your aunt or your other nephews."

She pounded his chest with closed fists. "I hate you! You could help them and you refuse."

"So I do, but I have a quest."

"Then get on with it," she growled. "The sooner we succeed, the sooner you will be able to help them."

He released her and bent his head. "Amen."

CHAPTER 20

Milton flew low skimming the tree tops and landed in a small clearing. His claws dug deeply into the verdant soil to stop his forward progress, his wings cupped to further aid his movement. The tall pines and firs encroached so closely his wingtips brushed the needles and she turned her face into his chest, protecting Lorenzo. Brenda's feet touched the ground, but she still felt uneasy, as if she were flying, or as if the ground beneath her writhed.

"Milton—" Holding the infant with one hand, she stretched her fingers out and touched him on the snout. The texture was rough, course, like she imagined a lizard's skin would feel, and it was cold, but oddly enough, it was starting to feel familiar.

"You're getting braver." His voice held traces of his scorn and what he offered was no compliment. "Just this morning you would rather have died than touch me willingly."

"Yes. No." She had no idea. She wanted to cover her face or to turn and hide, but drawing on the courage he mocked, she did neither and faced him directly. "I used to think myself brave, prepared to face anything, even a bullet, but this—" she couldn't complete the thought with a more descriptive noun, "is beyond anything I ever expected. I don't even believe in dragons or gargoyles."

He would show her no mercy. His top lip curled, highlighting the breadth of his wicked snout. "Yet you always believed in monsters."

She shivered, stung. "Yes. I've always believed in monsters. You saw to that."

He stretched his wings, an action he made when he was about to fly, but this time he only did it to settle them into folds. She felt more foolish, for she had been about to call him back, beg him not to leave her.

"I feel like there are so many things I need to apologize for. A hundred slights—"

With his back turned, she barely caught his spoken words. "I do not seek nor require your penitence."

"And I do want to thank you—"

She clearly heard the snarl. "I do not want your grudging gratitude either."

Brenda took a deep breath, let it out slowly. To their left, the west, an army of hundreds of thousands of lesser imps traveled northward. Their footsteps were light, because the bodies were slight, but there were thousands of them perhaps millions of them so the ground she stood on reverberated, pulsed to the rhythm of their marching. It was almost like a heartbeat.

She needed to explain before he left, before she didn't have the chance to explain.

"I don't understand my own mind. My life is changing in ways I never anticipated—and not just my relationship with you. My sister is important to me. I hadn't realized that. We've never been close. I didn't even realize I cared if Lori lived or died. But as a consequence, what you're doing is important to me. I am willing—"

He cut her off before she could finish. His eyes flashed and he showed an amazing amount of razor sharp teeth. "Are you—willing?"

"I am willing to offer what help I can, but you have to understand, I don't know how to deal with wizards or imps or powerstrands. That by itself is enough to send me into shock. I thought I had seen everything, understood everything."

"What we face is not different from what you have been exposed to. Evil is evil, no matter the guise it wears."

Through the gaps between the trees she could see the army pass. They were close enough she could smell them, making her think of moist decay and things with a hundred legs that lived in darkness and fed on death. Hating the fear she felt and the growing nausea, Brenda studied the imps, finding them even more terrifying close up. If they noticed her, the creatures gave no indication, continuing their mindless march.

Each imp lightly carried a weapon, as if the feel of such instruments of death was so familiar to them they had no need to think about it. The small swords, bows, spears and other pointed instruments she could not recognize were a part of them, an extension of their being. And while she felt she could defeat one or two easily, their numbers were limitless, and she knew defeating them would be impossible.

As the lesser imps wormed their way along the narrow path deeper into the darkening mountain forest, Brenda understood this war was something they looked forward to. They smiled, several of them moved with a bounce. A few of them skipped along. What was it Milton had said, *not the kind of creature which was invited to our wedding*? No, she supposed not.

Most were white, nearly translucent, Brenda corrected, pasty more than a healthy pink color of children and babies, but the colors varied widely through all the hues of yellow and green, and even some that could be considered bluer than purple. They had big, wide eyes, the kind that would stare at her, and scare her if she had seen them in the dark. There was not one she wouldn't consider a monster.

Milton must have read her thoughts. She would have to ask him later, if there were to be a later, if he had access to her brain, if he always knew what she were thinking. If he did, it would be a kind of rape, one she would find far more invasive than the sexual equivalent. "They covet the chakra."

"Yes." Her mouth was dry. She had to dredge moisture from under her tongue to find the strength for her one-word answer.

"It is a great prize."

She thought of her husband, kneeling while the three of Lori's boys joined with their chakras. She remembered how she cried at the beauty of it. If her tongue continued to be dry, such was not the condition of her eyes. She wiped the moisture before it could drip, not wanting the winged, chained monster beside her to think she cried out of fear.

"There are so many." There was no end in sight, either to the beginning of the line or the end. "Are they infinite in number?"

He gave a slight snarl which she could not believe was something as innocent as the clearing of his throat. "You do not understand infinity, if you ask such a question."

She wanted to hurt something, anything, and he was the only one available. She tried to imitate his dripping disdain. "And you do? Understand infinity?"

He smiled, a slow, almost poisonous grin. "I have stood on the cusp of a nameless, spaceless void and witnessed the origin of the cosmos. I have seen the Earth formed from dust and the plants and animals created as day became night over the space of what is called a week. Yes, I understand infinity." His wings mantled, but after a moment he settled. "It may seem as if there is an infinite number of these imps, but as with everything on this planet, there is an eventual end."

The marching continued past her, so many she could not comprehend their numbers. She thought of ants, grown over three feet tall, trained in an army, and carrying weapons. And the analogy for many of them felt correct. They looked like they had a hard carapace, a suit of armor for an outer covering, each and every one in some way monstrous.

"How many do you think there are?"

"A million? A million million? It matters not. What is significant is Andrew has the power to call in this many as allies to fight for his cause, and over the centuries the dragon has become a loner. It is unlikely any will come to his aid. And your aunt…"

"Yes?" she asked when he hesitated.

He met her gaze directly. "Your aunt has always used gargoyles to fight her battles."

"But there must be other beings they could call. Aren't there faeries?"

"Yes, but faeries care only for their own pleasures, and by the time they realize they should join this war, it will undoubtedly be far too late for them to make much of a difference."

"War?" And suddenly Brenda felt like a fool, for this was obviously a war. She simply had not seen it in such a term. "Milton, what will happen if we lose? If Andrew gains control of the chakra, if Byron and Aunt Jan are defeated?"

As she asked her question, she stared down at the ground, noticed his long, talon covered toes dig deep into the soil. No comfort there. No comfort either in looking at Lorenzo. The baby seemed to be having a nightmare, for although his eyes were shut and he slept, he twitched, and his head jerked. Nightmare. Awake or asleep. Nightmare.

"Good has always been able to keep the forces of evil in check. Oftentimes it looks like the Good can be defeated, but over the past millennium this has not been the case. There is always a balance. But if a creature of strength gains the chakra, not an imp, for even with the chakra their powers will be limited, but something with the ability to control a dragon's powers while answering to the wer-wizard, and if I am defeated, there might be a return of the Dark Ages. All human-kind will be affected. Centuries might go by while evil has the upper hand. There will be no music or art for I cannot believe Andrew will be a lover of beauty. There will be no scientific advancements, except those used to torture or exterminate. There will be no safety anywhere, only destruction of the kind you would describe as Armageddon. Good will rise again. This I promise you, but I cannot say when and I cannot say where. It might be eventually all that is praiseworthy on this planet will be destroyed, and the descendants of the followers of Andrew will take to the stars seeking other planets to conquer, and not meet defeat until then. I do not know."

The bleaker he painted the future, the better she felt about their quest. "So it is important we regain the chakra. Not just for Lorenzo. For every living thing."

"For Good."

Brenda wasn't sure it was her imagination, but the imps passing by appeared to be larger, rougher, more substantial. "But the battle will not end if we regain the chakra."

"Correct. This many imps on the march to war will not be turned away even should we snatch their goal from them. I promise you Brenda, should I accomplish my mission, I will help your sister and brother-in-law. I will not leave them to slaughter. I will make it an oath—"

"No, please don't make another oath to me."

He shifted his attention to the north, beyond the marchers, toward the B&B. He removed his arms from around her waist. Odd, she had not realized he was touching her. She had always shied away from him, now, with his hands gone, she felt an ache, a loss.

"As much as possible, you will be safe here."

That she doubted. Her thoughts churned. Too much had happened too quickly and none of it made any sense. Her legs continued to be unsteady; for a moment she feared they would buckle. Her stomach rolled as she contemplated evil and the escape she had been offered a few minutes before from a wizard she had not been able to accept. She inched back, a foot, then another, as much from the invasion she watched as the massive green skinned creature she called husband.

She shivered in repulsion. "They're so..." then her words dropped off, for she could think of a bad enough description.

"Evil," he finished for her. "You are looking at one of the many forms of evil."

Although the imps smiled, she could not equate it with happiness. They sought the acquisition of power, the desire for conquest, but not joy. Blood lust. Although they were small, she had no doubt they understood the concept of strength in numbers. She did not see how Byron, Lori and Jan stood a chance against them. Not when they were protecting three helpless children.

She softened her glance as she studied Lorenzo, now thankfully sleeping. "Is there anything we can do?"

"Do?"

She would have hit him, to find him so clueless. "To help Jan and Byron against this assault."

He exhaled his frustration. "Find the chakra, release me from my oath, and then I can help."

Annoyed, angry, she spoke, almost yelled. "I misspoke. Is there anything I can do?"

"Draw their attention and find out." His voice was low, controlled.

He would not help her if the imps captured her, if they hurt her. He would not help, except to find the chakra. She hated him at that second, more than she had ever hated anything.

"Was it you who bit me, as a child?"

"Brenda, you do not want to go into this now."

"Yes, I do. Answer the question. The scar I carry came from you, didn't it?"

"Yes, I—"

"You tried to kill me?"

"No."

"I am sick to death of your rationalizations."

She was sickened, could not face him, so she returned her study of the army, fascinated in spite of herself. Evil. All these years on the police force, she thought only mankind capable of evil, that animals, plants and machines could only be evil under the direct control of people bent on destruction. She had to revise her thoughts. These things parading in front of her were evil, she had no doubt.

It was her sanity she questioned.

"One day when we can communicate without hostility, I will tell you why I bit you."

"I suppose that's something I will look forward to."

"The answer to your question?"

"The fact there might be a day we can communicate without hostility."

The imps were getting bigger. Of this she was certain. "This can't be real."

"It is." Milton flexed his claws. By his very presence, the imps moved quicker, farther from him. If they sensed him, they had enough self-preservation not to make eye contact. According to his testimony, evil could not exist near him, yet she would swear he, himself was evil. She had left blood on pristine sheets to prove it.

Brenda did not like the fear she felt, the helplessness. She could not fight them with karate, with judo, and although she had no gun, she doubted a bullet could kill them, or if it would, how could she prevail when there were hundreds of thousands? "We need to call for help."

"The police?" he scorned. "The national guard?"

"Why not?" She was used to calling in backup, used to having support of those who had trained as she had, who believed as she did.

"Will you make the call?"

"If I have to." If these things were real, why not? The police should know.

Milton turned around, placed his hands on her shoulders and shook her, ignoring the greater danger. "And what would you say? Would you discuss faerie? Would you try to explain wizards and gargoyles?"

"You seek to protect yourself?"

"Myself? Regardless of what you think, this is not about me. The police cannot help us. Even if you could get them to respond, it is likely Andrew will hear. He will have spells. Their weapons will not work."

"But this is their battle too. You said Mankind was in danger."

"So they are. There is nothing they can do. Do you wish panic? Think what would happen if what we are witnessing now was to appear on your evening news, or discussed in a closed session of Congress."

She suspected he was correct, but was not willing to concede. "Something should stop them. We have to help Byron."

"No. Our only task is to reclaim the ne-chakra."

"If Byron and the boys are killed, it will be a moot quest."

He only whispered "Yes." He clearly understood what she was saying, how he had boxed himself into an untenable position with his vow, and how, even knowing that, he would not break it.

"I hate you! I hate you!" What she hated was her own powerlessness, and her fear he was correct: the police could not stop them. She had been trained to believe law enforcement could stop just about anything. And without help, perhaps they could free the chakra, but have no child to give it to.

Again he read her mind. "All hope is not lost."

"How can you say that? How can Byron defeat this many evil creatures? How can we hope to find the ne-chakra against a force this strong? If Andrew has it, it will be guarded, and neither you nor I will be able to approach undetected."

"Your point is valid. We will not be able to take the wer-wizard unaware."

"And Lorenzo could die."

"I promise you Brenda, even if Lorenzo dies and we rescue the chakra, the quest will not be for naught. It will be worth it to keep it from the wer-wizard."

She curled her top lip into a snarl. "Perhaps I see things differently."

Milton bowed, acknowledging her point. "I can only do what I promised. I cannot do more and I will not do less."

She wondered then of his sin, if arrogance were a greater crime than murder, if stupidity were. Or maybe the greatest sin was in not having the ability to adjust his plans to fit a changing environment.

"If Byron or Lori die, I will blame you forever."

Something must have caught Milton's attention, for his nostrils twitched, and his ears arched and he moved away from her.

In the distance, she could still hear the dragon's roar. There were answering responses, war-chants and insane, violent screaming: evil given voice. The imps she watched moved picked up their pace, and their grasp on their weapons was more intentional, less casual.

She heard explosions, had no idea if the imps and the wer-wizard had plastic explosive or the equivalent, if Bryon were capable of large-scale violence, or even if her aunt, a witch, were invoking spells, trying to keep her Inn safe.

She set Lorenzo aside, under a tree. Wrapped tightly in his blanket, she pushed some deadfall over him, branches and leaves, leaving his face exposed, but otherwise hiding him from the invaders. Although he slept restlessly, he did sleep. Her hands were free, but that highlighted her own lack of weapons.

These imps had long, bony physiques as if their internal organs did not exist, only bone, covered by a shallow layer of skin. They were both whiter and greener than normal skin tone, making her wonder if when cut their blood would run red. Their eyes were pale, bulged from their faces, scanned neither right nor left, looking only to a companion now and then, otherwise, locked ahead on the goal they approached.

They marched without any kind of unity, an army only in their single-minded purpose. There was a stench about them, similar to woodlands and gardens, but of those gone to rot. Bile rose in her throat.

"Are my aunt and Lori in danger?"

He did not pretend to lie, but perhaps that was what she hoped for when she asked her foolish question.

"Why do you ask when you know?"

"Just answer."

"Yes, they are in danger, but there is a greater risk than simply losing their lives. The Inn sits on the nexus of several worlds. Andrew would covet that property, but it is still my impression the dragons are his primary goal, and conquering the Inn will be an added bonus."

"He wants Byron and the boys?"

"Dead or alive, if he can get them in their natural state. Byron killed in manform will do the wer-wizard no good, but, as you can see, it is unlikely Byron will revert to his human guise. Not while the battle rages. Now stay here."

"You smell something, don't you."

"An old enemy. Brenda, stay down."

Turning away from her, Milton growled. His feet were bare, the long, ugly talons dug deep ruts into the forest soil. "You cannot fight him, and he will take great pleasure in hurting you, for he will know how such an action will hurt me."

"He?" she asked, her lips forming the word more than any actual speech. Coming out of the forest, was a second gargoyle, identical to Milton in every respect.

No, that wasn't true. Superficially he looked like her husband, but there were distinct differences. While Milton's snout was long, pointed, had almost a canine aspect, this other gargoyle's was rounder, more ape-like. Milton's face was triangular and this monster's face was round. He had no fur on his head, no ruff at his neck.

"Longfellow!"

"My brother. How good to see you again." Longfellow stepped into the sunlight, his muscles corded, moving soundlessly through the tall grass.

Milton stretched out his wings. "I do not find pleasure in this meeting. If you step aside, we do not need to do battle."

Longfellow laughed. "Ahh, but I think it has been inevitable for centuries."

"You serve the wer-wizard now?"

"I do. He has promised me the chakra."

She could see Milton quiver, had never seen revulsion so sharply etched into a single action.

"A chakra is no fair exchange for a soul."

"Yet Brother, I think you realize I have been losing my soul for centuries. It is black now. I will shed it as soon as the ne-chakra hatches."

"It hasn't hatched yet?"

"No. I understand the others hatched, but aided by their proximity to the fetal dragons." He looked past Milton, into the darkness where Brenda stood. "After I defeat you, I will take the infant. Perhaps he will encourage the ne-chakra to hatch so I can proceed with my experiment."

Moving quicker than Brenda could follow, Milton crouched, jumping forward, and Longfellow mirrored his action. They met six feet off the ground, a combination of claw and teeth and wings battling to stay aloft. She had expected there would be circling, a sounding out between them, bullies taunting each other until a breaking point was reached, but that was not the case.

With a crash, they fell, not a long drop, but a significant one, for she felt the impact in her feet, heard the sound. Before Milton could stand, Longfellow attacked.

The other gargoyle held his snout open, reaching for Milton's neck, his long talons slashing. Brenda screamed, watched as Milton kicked with enough force to send Longfellow flying. Blood flowed from the open wound, and the battle continued, tooth and claw.

Brenda watched with sickening fascination as the two fought. She could no longer separate them. There was only wings and claws and blood, so much blood.

Occasionally an imp would stop, watch the battle, but then hurry on, toward the Inn, and the prize that awaited there. She grew desperate for dragon fire, for it was the only weapon she could think of which she might employ.

"Brenda, put the HOLD spell on us. Separate us, and destroy him."

"I promised you once I would never do so."

"You can release me, later."

"No, Milton, do not ask it of me." But she saw how he bled and she knew she would do as she was told.

"HOLD!" she screamed. Milton became paralyzed, turned into marble, in the exact position he had been, his hands outstretched, his wings spread behind for balance, his feet firmly planted on the ground. But Longfellow continued to move.

"You did not stop!" she screamed.

"No." He grinned, showing teeth, dripping blood. "My soul is so black it is worthless, and the HOLD spell has no effect on me. I do thank you though, for your thoughtfulness in stopping him. We are evenly matched. This fight could have gone on for centuries. Now, I can destroy him."

Brenda ran forward, to do what she had no idea, while Longfellow swung a cudgel at Milton, first at his legs, then at his arm. The sound of the crash was deafening.

"Release!"

Milton came back to life, but he was at a disadvantage, his arm and his leg broken. He crumpled down, sinking into unconsciousness or death.

It was then she saw the approach of those hideous black monsters, the things she had fought against with Milton outside the Inn, the day they were married. Snarling, crawling on all fours, they approached. Brenda ran back toward the tree, grabbed the baby, and started to run. She did not see the creature that hit her, she only felt a sharp stab of pain at the base of her neck as she passed out.

CHAPTER 21

The old woman, Maria Consuela Gonzales had worked as a caretaker at the cathedral for over thirty years. She scrubbed and waxed floors, dusted and polished miles of oak and mahogany furniture. She had a routine, which varied little. She pushed her cart through the dim corridor, going through the offices, emptying wastepaper baskets, vacuuming carpets. It was hard work, not because the priests and parishioners were slovenly, but because over the years her bones had grown brittle and her joints throbbed. She would stop, move away from the city, live with a granddaughter who promised her food and warmth and ease, but she could not. Once, as a tiny child in Mexico City, she had been promised by her abuela she would live to see a miracle. It was the reason she was so devout, why, when she worked, she never complained, and made sure no greasy fingerprint soiled her windows, no muddy footprint marred her granite floors. When this miracle occurred, she wanted her cathedral to be spotless.

Over the years she had seen much which might have qualified, people absolved of their sins with a deathbed confession, lives of depravity changed for the better, families reunited with the return of prodigal sons, but she still did not believe she had seen that which had been foretold. So she pushed her cart carrying her cleaning supplies through the dimly lit corridors, stopping at a locked door.

From the key ring she wore swinging at her hip, she located the key. Thirty years, and she believed she was the only woman, the only person, who had been in this room. On the rare occasions when she missed work for more than a day or two, the funeral of her oldest son, a treasured return to her homeland to see her parents' gravesite, and her own brush with death, cervical cancer, which had been caught early enough to be healed, the room was untouched. Other than a speck of dust here, and the changing of sheets never in need of changing, there was little to do. Hers was not to question. She knew this task was vital, even if she never knew why.

She slipped the large, round key into the old fashioned keyhole, and turned, but before she could put her hand on the knob and open the door, the monsignor was there.

"Not today, Senora. I will see to this myself."

She was stunned, speechless. "No man—"

He smiled at her, then laid a warm, comforting hand on her gnarled fingers. "Today it is my honor to see to the room. Later, if you wish, you can return to finish."

She bowed her head. "As you wish, Father."

She pushed her cart down the hall, saw him waiting, hesitating until she was out of sight before he opened the door and went into the sanctuary himself. She turned the corner, waited a dozen heartbeats before looking back. He was gone, vanished inside.

He found her an hour later finishing up at the nave. "You may go in now," he told her. "At your convenience."

"I will go at once."

He was holding linen close to his chest, wadded fabric she recognized as the sheets from the bed.

"Should I wash that for you?"

"Not this time sister."

She reached out, touched the bedding, then pulled her hand back. She gasped, "Oh," then looked at her fingers.

Pain, her constant companion, left her, and the twisted bones, the throbbing joints vanished, leaving whole, unblemished skin. The healing traveled up her arms, to her shoulders, across and down her back, to her hips, and her legs, leaving her pain-free.

She pulled in a deep breath, her first in decades without appreciable pain. She struggled, managed to find a pew and sit. "What?" she asked, gasping for breath, "what happened?"

"A miracle, Sister," she was told. "A miracle."

And it was her miracle, for she was the first.

She would not be the last.

***

Brenda moaned, her stomach rolling in sickening waves, her pulse pounding in her temples with the intensity of war drums. She coughed, feeling the rise of bile in her throat, before she had the courage to try and open her eyes. She had been unconscious, remembered being attacked, remembered falling.

She rubbed her neck, felt clotted blood from a wound which had bled freely. Her body ached, not only at the base of her neck, but from scratches on her hands and knees. The pretty yellow dress she had put on--was it only the day before?--was now shredded, nothing more than a rag, covered in dirt, leaves, twigs, and blood.

She stretched her legs, checking for wounds. She had been dragged, and there were scrapes, at her knees and heels, but although she found them painful, she had no doubt they were superficial. She moved her fingers, her wrists, her shoulders, again finding only aches, not wounds like the one on her neck.

Her vision was blurry, and the thousand aches she felt were multiplying, becoming less specific. She lowered her hands down her stomach, and her fears rose.

"You were not raped," Milton said. "While I would not put such an action past Longfellow, other than rough handling bringing you here, you are untouched."

She leaned back, exhaled, stunned with relief. "Where are we?" She decided her eyes were open, but the lighting was poor, nearly non-existent.

"The dungeon at the Inn," he responded. As he spoke, she recognized the place making his words unnecessary. It was here she had been bitten as a child, here she had seen him swear at Byron after her aunt had recaptured him. It was here she had released him and thought herself righting a significant wrong.

She knew now she was mistaken.

Had she followed Byron's orders, and left Milton chained by his ankle, his wrist and his neck, maybe their situation would be different. If there had been a gargoyle on the premises, Andrew and his minions would not have been able to take the Inn. She would not be married. She would not be here, a victim herself.

She straightened, tried to stand, got only as far as her knees before dizziness and waves of blackness forced her back into a sitting position. She tried breathing through her nose, but the scents that reached her made her uncomfortable. They made her think of dark things, of slimy things, of things better left undiscovered. It was not the scent here before. This was new. Already Andrew was controlling the Inn, turning it into something dark.

It bothered Brenda to think when Milton had been chained here, the scent was somehow comforting.

She did not like the direction her thoughts were taking. Instead, she gingerly touched her neck, shivered at the blood, looking black in the dim light. From what her fingers could determine, the wound was about four inches, ran from just under her right ear almost to her shoulder blade, a straight line, parallel to her spine.

"The wound is not life threatening."

"It hurts."

"Yes, but you are alive, and it will heal. There is no neurological damage. The garntz only captured you. They did not use you for sport. You were lucky. They like to play."

Lucky. Yeah, let me count the ways.

Brenda clamped her eyes shut on the vision his words evoked and let her bitterness flow from her. She was alive and basically unhurt. She supposed for that at least, she should be grateful.

The cellar, the dungeon, whatever this place was, looked different. She decided that was because of her change in status. When she had been here before when the chains hung empty, and then later Milton was chained, she had come in a position of power, able to come or go at her own discretion. Now she was a prisoner.

"Milton." She would have railed at him, blasted him with her temper, accused him of being responsible for this disaster, but she had no heart within her to do so.

As before, he was chained but with a difference. His arms were high above his head, with his weight on his broken legs. She was about to speak, about to go to him, when she heard a sound, the whimpering of a baby.

"Lorenzo!" Brenda reached for the infant. She quickly ran her fingers over his tiny body. His diaper was soaking but he was unharmed. The whimpering continued, another moment, then he stopped, as if he lacked the strength to continue. "He weighs almost nothing."

"He cannot thrive."

She kissed the baby on the top of his head, then slowly got to her feet, holding the infant, and went to Milton. This would be hard, but she felt she owed it to him. "I'm sorry. The HOLD spell, I never meant to hurt you."

His head had been hanging low on his shoulders, indicative of his pain, his exhaustion, and perhaps lack of hope, but he raised it and made eye contact with her. His words came in pants a few at a time as he struggled to get the thought out. "It is not your fault. It was done at my command. No blame will attach to you."

Brenda could see the compound fracture of his arm, with shattered bones protruding from his skin, and although most of his weight was on his legs, she could see how they were obviously broken, the bones bent at unnatural angles.

She hated him. Didn't she hate him for the way he had fooled her with his statement of mortality, with his refusal to help Byron and Lori and Jan when they were in trouble? But now all she knew was compassion for the way he suffered. She would not think her emotions any deeper than empathy. It was not love she felt. She refused to acknowledge that. She reached out toward him, her hand quivering, her heart so torn she had no idea what she thought or felt.

"Is there anything I can do to help?"

"No."

"Can you heal yourself?" she asked, and all she could remember was her statement she hated him.

"Not from this position." His healing came from his saliva, and hanging he could not reach the wound in his arm.

"If I put the HOLD spell on you, would that help?"

"You think to control me?" His words came out as a snarl.

Her eyes dripped, and her vision which had become unreliable now swayed through a watery mist. "No, I only want to ease your suffering."

"That cannot be accomplished by turning me into marble."

"Milton, for everything I've said, for everything I've done, I'm sorry."

He stared at her with what she could only believe was hate. "Everything?"

Brenda desperately tried to come up with a response, to free her honesty from things she believed before and might not believe any longer, but before she could speak, she heard sounds coming toward them. Footsteps echoed loudly in the cavern, heightening its immensity, as they moved closer. It was not the firm positioning of boots, but the tapping of claws on bedrock. Longfellow appeared, folded his arms across his chest, and laughed.

Brenda sickened as she noticed him and wondered how she could ever have thought this monstrosity looked like her husband. This was evil made manifest.

"So you are awake. I told Andrew it would not take long."

"Where are Jan, Lori and Byron and the other children?" Brenda demanded. She had a chain around her ankle, loose enough it brought no pain beyond the psychological. She despised being trapped. She could move within a six foot arc, and approached the monster at the end of her tether. Longfellow stood fully in shadow, the light, coming from no discernible source, shining on Milton and her prison.

"Unfortunately they left. The dragon took them from here, when it was obvious he could not win in a pitched battle against Andrew and the imps. We are searching for him. He will not elude us much longer. Andrew has a special treat in store for him when he is captured. However, there is something I must do first. Something you should be honored to watch."

"Whatever it is, we have no interest," Brenda spat.

Longfellow ignored Brenda and instead spoke to Milton. "Ahh, but I believe you do. Certainly the child does."

"Do not do this!" Milton bellowed. "By all that is holy, I beg you, do not do this!" He strained to the length of his chain and Longfellow only laughed.

The other gargoyle moved toward the stairs, where he retrieved a large, round egg. Brenda knew what it was immediately, had her conclusion confirmed by Lorenzo, now fully awake, screeching a high-pitched wail.

"Brother, I cannot tell you how long I have wanted to do this." Longfellow set the ne-chakra egg down, then with two fists, grasped at his chest, and pulled something black yet transparent from his body.

Bile rose up in her throat, and Brenda had trouble swallowing it down. "Your soul?"

Milton struggled against his chains, railing, screaming. "I beg you, stop before it is too late! Nothing is worth the loss of your soul."

Milton slumped, head down, defeated. His words echoed, "Soul, soul, soul."

For an instant, Longfellow looked like he might reconsider, and perhaps the infant's howls and Milton's pleas had reached him, then, with the most evil look Brenda had ever seen, he smiled. "I have no more use for it. But I do have need of this." He ripped the baby from her arms. Lorenzo's scream intensified, although this time, it had hope. His ne-chakra was close, so very close. Brenda, who was bound, could only watch, struggling to the length of her captivity. Longfellow set the baby beside the ne-chakra, and within seconds the egg started rocking.

"No," Brenda whispered, tears dripping unchecked. "No, please." But her pleas were to no avail. The egg cracked.

When the chakra appeared, the small transparent image of a complete dragon, it trumpeted and started walking toward Lorenzo. "I beg you," Brenda said but Longfellow picked it up, and shoved it down his throat until he swallowed it. Brenda turned, retching dry heaves for what seemed like an eternity, and Milton raised his snout and bellowed, an animal in pain.

For Lorenzo there was no comfort. Not now, probably never, for although small, he would know he could never be complete.

With a triumphant roar, "Mine!" Longfellow flapped his wings, once, twice, then took to the air. Seconds later he disappeared into the darkness surrounding them.

Time passed, but Brenda paid no attention. Milton offered to lick her wounds, to heal them, but she wanted nothing to do with him, so she kept her distance answering him only with her disdain. Longfellow had left the baby, so she tried to comfort Lorenzo. He was inconsolable, after having been so close to his chakra and then denied it.

Her stomach rumbled and she grew lightheaded. She couldn't remember the last time she had eaten, beyond a sip of dragon tea after she had been wounded in the cave before she was married. She suffered, but realized from the way he hung with his weight on his legs and his broken arm, Milton must be in considerable pain. She wanted to take back the words she had yelled at him, for she didn't hate him, but the words refused to come. Instead she stayed as far from him as her bonds would allow, and spoke only to the infant.

"Is there any way you could shut that monster up?"

She hadn't heard anyone nearing, but when she looked, she saw a stranger approaching, a man dressed like Pierce Billova had been, in a long flowing black robe. She found it odd she was beginning to recognize wizards by dress alone.

"You must be Andrew," Milton said.

"That is what I am called."

He was younger than she expected, probably not more than his late-twenties. He twitched and she knew instinctively he was uncomfortable, and being so close to Milton nothing as evil as he was could be unaffected.

"Let us go." Brenda demanded, straining at the length of her chains.

"No, it amuses me to keep you. While I hold you, I can be assured the dragon will be vulnerable, for he will do anything to get you back, perhaps even negotiate one of his sons. He has a soft spot for that witch he married."

"My sister is no witch."

"Actually, she is," Milton said.

Andrew turned from Brenda and concentrated on Milton. "You may yet be of use to me."

He showed his teeth. "I will never help you."

"Perhaps not, but there is something of a black market for actual gargoyle water spouts. How would you like to spend eternity on a building, situated so the rain will drain through your body?"

Milton snarled, snapping his massive jaws as he strained the length of his chains. "You'll not get away with this."

Andrew rubbed his own forearms, as if the action was keeping his skin from crawling. He curled his top lip, trying to appear superior, in control. He may have frightened off Jan and Byron and his family, but around a gargoyle he was massively uncomfortable. "And you will stop me? I think not."

Muscles in Milton's neck stood out in sharp relief as he pulled, the brace around his throat keeping his prisoner only inches from Andrew. "Where is Longfellow? Put him by me, so I can strangle him with my bare hands."

"He is indisposed at the moment."

"Turn him into a water spout?" The sentence dripped Milton's repugnance.

Andrew tried to smile, and Brenda thought the action not quite successful. "No. He has lost his soul, so that particular option is no longer open. He merged with the chakra."

"Then I have another reason to kill him." Milton reached out, dragged his claws only inches from Andrew's face.

He stepped back, tried to make it look casual, not at all a strategic retreat. "Although I find this conversation delightful, and I do enjoy watching you suffer, I must be going. Now that I have taken over the Inn there is much I need to explore."

"Enjoy your victory while you can," Brenda shouted. "Byron will see you shredded into a bloody pulp."

"But not your, what is it I hear, your husband?"

She understood his mocking, but she answered quickly, without taking time to think. "He is more of a man, more of a lover than you'll ever be. He understands tenderness."

"Tenderness? Milton? Of all the adjectives you could have come up with, I'd have to say I never expected that one. And Brenda, when I take a woman, I take her, if you know what I mean. I've no use for tenderness. And I think I'll try for Lori again. I've an interest to have her struggling under me, if only to rile the dragon."

"I hope your sick perversions give you comfort at night, for that will never happen."

"No? How about I take you, here, now, to show you how I'm effected."

"It will be the last thing you ever do, you miserable slime."

Andrew stepped back again, and Brenda knew it was Milton's presence keeping her safe.

"I've work to do, discovering all the secrets of this Inn. Of course it is impossible for me to open all the rooms up for habitation to those who would have the most interest here. You do realize I cannot invite my friends while a gargoyle is alive on the premises?"

Milton snarled, baring teeth. "Bring them to me. I will offer them welcome."

Andrew laughed, a grating sound. "Even that has its possibilities. But realize, your presence here is also keeping most of my enemies away. I have need of you until I consolidate my power. Then we'll see."

He was not tall, Brenda decided, five six or seven perhaps, but his body was concealed, so she had no idea if he were muscular. His face was expressive, magnetic. It was not that he was handsome, but he was so supremely confident of his victory, success sheeted off him. It was charisma, she decided, and knew had the situation been different, she would be drawn to him.

"This is working out much better than I expected. Soon I will have four dragon carcasses, and with them I will be indestructible. I will control all the portals in and around the Inn. And, no less a treat, I get to personally destroy the witch Jan Pikorski, a goal of mine for some years."

"I think you're counting your dragon carcasses before they've happened. You will never defeat Byron."

"Ahh, but your faith in your brother-in-law is misplaced. He is outnumbered, a hundred thousand to one. Yes, a single imp is no match for a mature fighting dragon, but with the numbers I bring against him, he stands no chance. He cannot rest, he cannot eat, he cannot tend his own wounds. It will not be much longer before I am a supreme ruler over all creatures of faerie and all wizards will bow to me."

Andrew waved his arms and vanished. She gasped, blinked, thought again she was losing her mind.

CHAPTER 22

Time passed slowly. Eventually, exhausted from crying, Lorenzo fell into a restless sleep. For the hours it had taken, Brenda had cooed, sang, and rocked him, all without result. He felt lighter, less substantial, as if he were fading away and would vanish as completely as Andrew had. His color was poor, not only his skin tone, but his eyes were losing the rich gold tone so reminiscent of his father. Places which on a healthy baby should be a pink, were distinctly graying.

Even with him asleep, Brenda continued to hold him. Her thoughts were not on 911 police response or on turning her back on this and returning to her career. Instead she thought only of the infant, and even when she was certain she did not believe, she prayed, her eyes closed, her thoughts feverous.

"Poor Lori. Poor Byron."

"He is asleep. Set him down." Milton's voice held his own pain and exhaustion, but beyond that, the compassion was thick enough even when she wanted to scoff, she couldn't.

"I feel so helpless." At least holding Lorenzo she felt she was doing something, anything.

"You don't like feeling powerless."

It annoyed her that he changed the adjective. She did not now, nor had she ever, equated the two words. "I want to help." Needing her hands empty to punch the air, to avoid waking the child, she set the baby down on the cold floor, then stood and stretched. Lorenzo did not stir. If she could not see his tiny chest expanding then contracting, she could easily fear the worst.

"Milton," even his name felt foreign on her tongue. In her mind, he was the thing, the creature, the Voice. Milton, naming him personalized him, somehow gave him dignity. "I can't help but think all this is my fault."

Chains rattled, his body twitching. "This," he said, giving the word an odd inflection, "is a lot of things, none of which are your fault."

Her nerves were wired, her joints ached. She was too hoarse from trying to comfort the baby to even moan. "I can't help but think because I was here, Jan was distracted. That she could have prevented Andrew from stealing the ne-chakra. I responded…badly…when you came to tell us of the theft. Maybe things would be different if you had not been offering me assistance in Albany. Maybe—"

He would not let her finish. Even wounded, bound, and helpless himself, he would let none of the blame stick to her. "I have free agency. I chose to aid you in your police work. That was not your fault. And the ne-chakra was already stolen when I came to the kitchen. There is no way that can be construed as a result of any of your actions."

She rubbed her face with her hands. "Milton, tell me the marriage was the right thing to do. Tell me this is all going to come out all right."

"I will not lie. I do not know how things will resolve but I swear to you on all I hold sacred, this marriage has a purpose, and it is for the best, for all eternities. Even if I die this hour at the hands of my hated enemies, the time I have spent with you has been the highlight of my life and we will be joined in the hereafter. That I promise. We shall not be separated."

Oddly, the thought which had sickened her before, no longer caused the same reaction. "I want so much to help." She had no idea when he had ceased being a thing of horror to her and had started to become an ally. She stood, back, arms, heart aching. Tentatively, she reached out, touched the chains that bound her. "When I was here before, I was able to release you."

Blood dripped from the open wound in his arm. Slowly now, but each drop fell into a puddle, indication that he had bled heavily as he was being chained. "Yes."

"Could I again?"

"Perhaps."

She turned, approached him, her eyes flashing. "Why didn't you remind me? Why did you stay there, suffering, when I could have given you ease?"

"Is that what you want, Brenda, to give me ease?"

She back-stepped, wondered if she had painted herself in a corner. She was certain his question referred to something completely different than loosing his bindings, perhaps helping him to find freedom. "I don't like to see anything suffer."

"Not even a monster like myself?"

"Milton," she raised her hands, pulled, found she was able to release the chains so he no longer hung. He fell to the ground, and she found herself holding the heavy cold metal chain which had been around his arms.

"I thank you." His tongue lashed out, licked his wrists, the open wound on his arm.

"Why didn't you ask me to help? We have been here hours."

When he looked up, Brenda realized there was blood on his snout. She grew nauseated, thinking of how many times she had seen that sight: blood of the evil he fought, his own blood like now, even her blood.

"I told you I would ask nothing of you again."

"Don't be a fool, Milton. You should always ask for what you want or need. I may not be able to help you, but I can't read your mind. You need to ask."

"As you wish," he responded. "I am honored by the boon."

She did not want his honor. She wasn't sure what she wanted, except the baby made whole and perhaps to understand her own quivering emotions. She thought she wanted never to see him again after this was over, but more and more she realized that was impossible. She had come to like, even cherish their evening talks. And he was her husband. Disgusted by where her thoughts took her, Brenda bent down, tried to get the chain at his ankle to release. She pulled but she could not make any progress in regaining his freedom.

He grasped her hand, her impulse was to fight, but she felt he was not trying to force her to do anything. She looked where he indicated, at the chain she was trying to break. It was secured its entire length with gold powerstrands, similar to those she had witnessed in Massachusetts.

"Andrew?"

"He does not wish to lose his prize so easily." Still touching him, she realized the chain around her own ankle was similarly locked. There were no strands around Lorenzo, except for the orange one the wizard Pierce had placed there.

His chain was now as long as hers, probably granting him a twenty foot circumference. He crouched down, continued licking his wounds. And her heart felt full as if she had come to a shocking revelation. Yes, she felt compassion for him. Yes, she was grateful to him for all the times he had helped her as the Voice.

But this was something different.

She hoped...and feared...that what she was starting to feel for him was love.

***

Byron settled the two boys he held into a pallet of branches. They fussed for a few seconds, then settled back into sleep. "We will be safe here."

"For how long?" Arthur asked. He still held his sword Excalibur out, anticipating an assault at any minute.

"An hour, maybe more. Long enough for the babies to be fed, for us to catch our breath. Then we must move deeper into the forest."

An alien rainforest surrounded them, thick, almost impenetrable, but they had a dragon with them, and what he couldn't push through, he could burn.

Arthur shoved the sword into the scabbard, an angry, fluid movement that showed his frustration. "I don't like not being on Earth."

"You are a creature of Earth," this from Jan.

"If you'd like to go back, I can show you the portal," Byron said, almost amused. He sat beside Lori rocking one infant while she nursed two.

"Arthur, sit down. Let me tend those wounds. Whatever possessed you to fight those demons by yourself?"

He had a dozen cuts, none life threatening, all painful. They had bled freely. Jan dug through the carpetbag she carried, came out with a pile of red towels she wrapped around the most egregious of his injuries. "We are thankful for your help. We wouldn't have been able to get out with this many supplies without you preventing the hoard from entering the kitchen.

He laughed, feeling better as the towels started their healing magic. "Look at the bright side. Now you won't have as many dishes to wash."

Jan exhaled, more in exasperation than frustration. "Yes I will. They seem to multiply like hydra-heads. When one breaks, two dirty ones take its place. When we get the Inn back, I'll need a month or more just to set the kitchen to rights, and who knows what the rest of the building is going to look like. Lori, are you ok?"

Her eyes were bloodshot and she'd lost significant weight, for feeding three hungry infants was taking a toll, but she had given up crying. She doubted she had any tears left. "I'm just tired and worried about Lorenzo. I'm not hurt, if that's what you're asking."

Jan laid food out beside Lori, sliced purple halchatze Lori loved, even if these were raw and they were better cooked.

She had three babies but her heart ached for the fourth. "Byron, do you ever think we'll see him again?"

Byron wrapped an arm around her, as gentle a man as he was fierce as a dragon. "I trust Milton. He will see the boy whole, or if not whole, at least safe. As soon as you finish feeding the boys, why don't you try for a nap?"

She was exhausted, body and soul. She had been through a lot, but grief itself can be exhausting. "I can't sleep."

"I'll stand guard," Arthur promised, his hand on the familiar sword hilt. "Take some time to hold her so she can rest."

Arthur moved out, and although he expected to be alone, Jan followed. "You could be safe now. This is not your fight."

He was a man of Earth, had lived there for centuries. This alien land held no comfort for him, even if he believed Byron when he said it would take Andrew some time to find them here. "Safe? Worried about you? I think not. Jan, anything you're involved in, I want to be involved in."

"What are you trying to say?"

He reached out, took her hands. She was not old, not like he was, but there were creases at her eyes and her hands showed signs of the hard work she forced upon herself. "I'm saying I love you, and I have for years."

Tears freshened at her eyes, but from joy. "Oh, you idiotic man, to wait until now to tell me."

"I tried to tell you before. I don't think you were listening. Jan, you need help. I want to be there for you, all your days and nights."

"I, um, don't know what to say." But she did know what to say, for although he was on watch, she kissed him while the cat which was named for his long dead wife twined between their legs.

***

"Can you get those bones to heal with that magic saliva of yours?"

Milton's tongue forked out, swiped at the compound fracture of both bones in his forearm, which was already looking better. The bones were knitting, the skin regrowing. It was still red, still painful looking, but it was definitely healing. "Yes. And I would heal your wounds, should you let me."

He had blood on his long, alien snout, blood on his tongue. Brenda shook her head slowly, not to wake the baby. "Take care of yourself first."

Holding Lorenzo tenderly, she paced the length of her chain, one direction then the next, trying to ignore Milton, trying to ignore her jumbled, confused thoughts. The baby was slight, his weight almost non-existent. His eyes were unresponsive, half-lidded. She should have left him with his parents. She never should have entered into this bargain, but she loved the baby with all her heart and couldn't stand to put him down. Honestly there had been pleasure between her and Milton: a wife's pleasure found only in the arms of her husband.

Those thoughts gave her little comfort. She was a modern woman, used to caring for herself, used to relying only on herself. She had not written love into the equation of her life, had never considered a woman's need could grow so deep after losing her virginity.

On one of her circuits, she noticed something at the limits of her vision, thin, black, ethereal. Nausea rose in her throat as she realized the twitching thing was the soul Longfellow had ripped out. How many times since before she met Milton had she considered her soul? Never? Had she ever believed it actually existed, had mass, and could be ripped from the body? A soul. She wondered if her own were turning black for she was cruel to this man who was her husband, had taken no time at all to set about understanding him, when he had dedicated his life, for as long as it took, to help the pale, suffering infant in her arms.

The soul shuddered slightly, spasmodically, although there was no breeze, as if it were being blown.

"It's alive?" She had not realized she had spoken aloud until Milton answered.

He gave a long, drawn-out keen of anguish, before he spoke. "Not for much longer. A soul cannot exist outside the body. It is the most sanctified gift given to us by God."

"Soul." The word felt funny on her tongue, sacred, but clearly not understood. She was not a church-goer, had never been, not since she had been bitten as a child and had discovered her parents refused to believe her. She looked at the proof and denied. "There is no such thing as a soul."

He scoffed but did not look up. "You find yourself married to me, and you believe that?"

She started to speak, realized she had nothing to say, so she clamped her mouth shut. She wanted a gun, two weeks sleep, to never have come to wish her sister and new brother-in-law well all those weeks ago. She wanted revenge and freedom, and oddly enough, to be held in a man's arms in love and tenderness.

She liked that last thought least of all.

She thought perhaps she should pick a fight with Milton, he was the only one available, and it could be argued, successfully she supposed, he was the cause of all of her problems, but she watched him, crouched down, his heels on the cold stone, his broad, green-scaled wings spread around him, licking wounds, and knew she did not have the heart to hurt him any more than she already had.

She wished Lorenzo would cry again. Although it had been painful, it had been obviously a sign of life. Now she had nothing in her arms but desolation, a body wilting away.

She kissed the baby once on his forehead, found him cold, unresponsive. How many ways could a human heart break?

"I'm willing to concede that you believe you have a soul, and many religions describe it. I'm even willing to say in people who are evil, their evil does not necessarily come from their bodies, but from something inside of them. Ego, id, soul, whatever you want to call it."

His eyes were dark, unfathomable. There had been love in them once, when he lay on top of her, when he had been buried so deeply in her body that pleasure rippled through her strong enough she had wondered if it might kill her.

"That's a start."

She slumped down beside him, hoped he hadn't noticed, hoped he thought her sitting. She had very little dignity left. Still, she wanted desperately to understand. "I fight to defend laws, property and people. I have no time to attribute actions to sin."

He gave her the start of a grin, the transient understanding he knew, somehow, he was getting through to her. "Yet a good deal of your work deals with motivations."

She sighed, shifted the infant and rubbed her eyes, but there was blood on her hands and dirt so deeply engrained she wondered if she would ever feel clean again. "Motivations." She gave the word ugly inflections. "Only in catching the bad guys, to discover who had a reason to perpetrate whatever crime I'm investigating, to narrow down our search. Personally I don't care why someone did something. I leave that to the lawyers and the criminal profilers. If someone is hurting someone else, I don't care why, I only want to find some way to make him stop. I'm not a psychologist and certainly not a priest. I'm willing to say they've got their place, but unless they agree with what I already believe, I think they're a waste of time."

"A waste of time. Maybe one day, when things do not pressure us so, we will have to sit down and discuss what you think is the purpose of life."

She would like that, for she clearly had no idea what the purpose of life was, and knew if she did have an opinion it would be diametrically opposed to his. Church and sin and forgiveness. It all fit somewhere, but not for her.

Brenda realized how petty she had been, in her less than subtle ways she was unkind to Milton, so while she rubbed her ankle, she tried to reach him. "Are you in pain?"

"I am doing much better. I thank you for your aid. I do not mind being chained."

She doubted very much that was true, or even if true, it was only because other things bothered him more. "Will you kill Longfellow?"

He stopped swiping his tongue along his lower legs. She could no longer see the shattered bone, and although red and painfully puffy, the skin, like that of his arm, was unbroken. "Kill him. He is my brother. For centuries we fought together against evil and now it is up to me to stop him, if I can. Killing Longfellow has become part of the quest, Brenda, but more, it would be a mercy. He will be judged for his actions and we cannot let Andrew gain control of the chakra."

"I know you believe that." She stretched her legs in front of her, realized no matter how she sat, there was no way she could be comfortable, mind or body. "God, I feel dirty."

She was not sure if it was her swear word which was the name of his deity which had him looking up, or her complaint. "Let me help."

"What? How?"

Slowly, so not to startle her, he reached out, cupped her hands. "I know you still find my touch repulsive, but I promise you, I will not hurt you."

How many times had he promised her that? And how many times, as a direct result of his actions, had she been shattered?

Milton moved the infant to the floor then his tongue flicked out, a fast movement, long and repulsive, narrow, pointed, but where it made contact with her skin, the blood, the mire, the thousand little cuts were gone.

"You think I would rather have your saliva on my hands?"

"Peace, Brenda. Peace be with you." He licked her again, and she shut her eyes, not wanting to see what devilment he was up to, but with her eyes closed, she only felt warmth, comfort, cherished. Slowly her hands, in his, relaxed. From there, she was able to release some of the tension in her shoulders, down her back. With her eyes shut, the action was sensual, almost sexual. The repulsiveness vanished, leaving only a lethargy she yearned for, and a buzzing in her blood she did not.

His tongue was at her neck, at the wound there. Pain dripped away, vanishing. She closed her eyes and sighed. "Can you tell me?"

"Tell you what?"

She turned, made eye contact. "You said you committed the worse sin imaginable. I would imagine you meant murder?"

"I have never taken a life in anger or without just cause. I have never committed murder."

"But—"

"Actually, there is one sin worse than murder."

That she could not believe. "What?"

"It is a long story."

"Andrew is off surveying his new domain. I doubt he'll be back anytime soon. We cannot get the chains off and Lorenzo is sleeping." She would not use the word unconscious. "We have time. I'd like to know of the worst sin imaginable and how you committed it."

CHAPTER 23

He sat on the cold stone floor, pulled his wings around him, as if they were a king's mantle. "If you wish. As my wife you should understand." She watched as his eyes tightened, and she saw his pain, almost felt it, sharper, more intense than what he felt as he hung on two broken legs. "Before this Earth was created, before there was even the separation of darkness and light, we, all who are heir to human, lived as spirits with God."

"I don't believe…" she said.

"It doesn't matter. I am telling you what happened and every word I say is truth, small 't' because it actually happened, and Truth capital 'T', meaning knowledge from LORD and God the Father. As a test, God asked the assembled masses how were we to deal with this new world He planned to create. Two options were put forth. The one presented by Satan made a lot of sense, but it was the one by LORD that God accepted. Satan rose in anger because his plan was rejected, and in his fury, he took one-third of the hosts of heaven and left the presence of God. It was called a war, although I doubt you would recognize it as such. When Satan and his minions were banished from the sight of the LORD, a small group of us realized we had made a mistake, chosen the wrong path, and our belief was in goodness and divinity and not following evil."

"You chose to follow Satan?"

"It was a long time ago. He spoke persuasively. I, and many like me listened."

"What did he say?"

"I will start with some background: No one who is heir to human is perfect. All born into mortality will make mistakes. This is accepted and expected, and although most would not see it as such, it is a blessing. Agency, the ability to choose between good and evil, is a gift from God. As a result, what you call mortality, life on this Earth, is a crucible. All who live as human are given bodies here on Earth to have their spirits tested. None will be tried by God beyond his or her own ability to endure. People must learn to recognize the differences between right and wrong, and to learn to choose the better part.

"Satan's argument was following death all should return to the glory of heaven, and none should be lost. Think, Brenda. Wouldn't that be magnificent? Everyone could live here in paradise, in peace, with no contention, no sin, and return to heaven to live with God."

"Not that I believe this fantasy," she said, "but that sounds a hell of a lot better than what we've got."

His tongue flicked out, but he did not heal more of himself. "Hell. You name it correctly. Since no unclean thing can exist in God's presence, Satan's plan was to not allow sin into the world. There would be no choice, only blind obedience and the innocence which existed in the Garden.

"There would be no sin, and all people who lived would return to live with the Father. This sounded like goodness to us. We listened and were beguiled. Before the Earth was created, before the plants sprouted from the first seed, and the first creatures formed in the waters, we realized we made a mistake, and in humility we returned to the presence of the LORD, and asked forgiveness. Yet, because we had chosen to follow Satan, if only for a minute amount of time, it was impossible for us to be granted mortality, and allowed to be human. There was no room for us in the plan put forth by the Son and accepted by the Father. We still had our souls, but we had no chance to be born and die, to accept or reject the grace of salvation. So we begged to be allowed to serve LORD's greatest creation, man. We wanted to offer our support. If we could not be mortal, at least we could repent throughout the millennia of the wrong choice we had made. This was found acceptable. We were given a task. We could destroy evil when we came across it, because for a few seconds we had been evil ourselves, we could recognize it in its many guises. And, we could guard holy buildings and keep them safe. For Satan would not suffer grand cathedrals to be left to divine glory. Satan would destroy all of what was considered Right and Beauty. And so Gargoyles were set around churches and cathedrals. And because people forgot, and because we looked evil, it was rumored we were decorative water spouts, reminders of the other things LORD has created and which were found displeasing in his sight. And while we were rarely allowed inside the cathedrals, we were always allowed outside, to serve."

She chewed on his words, tried to decide if they made any sense. "What was the other plan? The one God accepted, the one you did not originally accept?"

"This world was given free agency. Each person would have the ability to choose for him- or her-self between good and evil. There would need to be a Savior to take the evil in the world or else no one could ever return to God, and there was the need for all the other things religions speak of, repentance, sacraments, and remembrances."

"So, we could have been mindless automatons under Satan or thinking beings in need of help."

"Exactly."

She rubbed her ankle where the metal band rubbed her skin raw. "There's a lot to be said for being mindless automatons."

"I know you joke, but you can see why for less than a fraction of a second I was beguiled?"

"I can see. And the HOLD spell?"

"Our penance, one which we had to verbally accept. Because we betrayed the LORD once, there was fear by some of the angels that we would betray Him again. We agreed to stop, to show our obedience. Other than Longfellow, it is my understanding no gargoyle has ever strayed from goodness."

"And now Longfellow has lost his soul?"

"It is there. It pains me more than these wounds pain me to see it discarded." He licked at the wounds at his legs, then looked over to her. "Did Longfellow merge with the chakra?"

"I don't know. He swallowed it. Opened his mouth and swallowed it, but it was not like the merging I witnessed with the three children."

"Maybe that is why Longfellow is indisposed. He cannot assimilate the chakra, and he cannot rid himself of it. I am certain he told the wer-wizard he has merged with it, but I think if he had, he would be here, lording it over me."

"But you said a chakra is not as powerful as a soul."

"It is far more powerful—when used for evil."

***

Brenda Larwick St. Caspian never thought the first time she would make love would be in an ancient cathedral, in a hidden bedroom in fulfillment of some mysterious rite.

She never thought the second time would be in a dark underground cavern she always thought of as a dungeon, while she and her lover were both chained.

Given that track record, who knew where she would make love for the third time, if she managed to live that long.

It happened slowly, unexpectedly for both of them. Milton had told her he was going to die...

"Die?"

The chains rattled. "Andrew cannot let me live with what I know about him. You saw how uncomfortable he was in my presence. If I am correct in my assumptions, he intends to make this Inn his headquarters, and to do so, he cannot allow me to remain. Longfellow has no reason to want my life to continue."

There was nothing she could give him, except, perhaps comfort. It was the first time she had reached out to him willingly. She touched him, lightly, on his chest, above his male nipple. His flesh was warm, her fingers chilled. It felt good.

It was her intention a single touch, not a caress, but a touch would be enough. Except beyond her conscious control, she splayed her fingers, placed her palm flat against his body, could feel the rippling of his heart.

Milton stayed completely still. If it weren't for the pulse she saw as well as felt, she would have wondered if she had inadvertently turned him into a statue again. For some reason she could not fathom, her other hand reached out, and she kneaded, ever so lightly. His flesh was responsive.

And it was no longer a gargoyle's.

"Brenda?" it was a whisper.

"Yes," she said, knowing what she was agreeing to as she said it. Yes, and she wanted it, and him. Desperately.

She reached up, cupped his neck with both hands, using force, as if he would fight her, as if she expected to be rejected. Instead he let her position him where she would, let her lips meet his.

She expected a gentle kiss, a sounding between the two of them, but instead fever grew, flashed, flared, burned. He still did not touch her, not with anything but his lips, his tongue which had gained access to her mouth, his breath which was sweet and bathed her in what felt like promise.

She had never been on fire before. Every nerve ending sizzled, every inch of her begged for his touch, and still the kiss continued and he kept his hands lowered, unmoving.

She grew bold, brazen, broke the kiss long enough to feast at his neck, his throat, the long, tasty bones of his clavicles. His skin was sweet too, though how that was possible, she had no clue. He had fought, turned to marble, been defeated and was chained, suffering in a torture chamber where he expected to die and she tasted the tangy, slightly intoxicating taste of crisp, tart apples.

"I want…" she said, but had no idea how to finish the statement.

He offered no help. He had participated in the kiss, there was no doubt, leaving her breathless and coiled tighter than any spring, and he had moaned when her lips left his, a throaty moan of pleasure, but still his hands were limp at his sides. Her breasts tingled, yearning for his touch, even when she had no idea that was precisely and exactly what she needed.

Lower down, at the joining of her thighs with her body, where he had initiated her into the pleasures of loving after her second wedding ceremony, moisture sprung to life.

And still he did not touch her.

She reached down, found as a man this time, he still wore the loincloth he wore as a monster. Working feverously, she removed it, found him hard and bold and very big. She cupped him in her hands, rubbed him, liking the feel, liking the way he moaned again.

She had no experience with foreplay, except what she read, what she heard secondhand from the bragging of cops in locker rooms or on boring stakeouts, perhaps shared to impress her. She found the sack hanging behind his shaft, cupped it gently and he rocked, as if she had electrified him. The thought gave her power. He liked that. Brazen, not quite knowing what she was doing, she lowered her head, cupped his male member with her lips, sucking him deeper into her mouth. The flavor here was intense, sharper than apples. It tasted of brandy and was as heady. She grew drunk on what she sucked.

Still he did not touch her.

"You do not want me?"

"How can you say that, when I want you with every fiber of my being?"

"But—"

"I promised you I would never make love to you again unless it was your idea. I will not seduce you. Brenda, if you want…whatever it is you want…you will have to ask me. In this I cannot presume."

She should hate him. She did hate him. Instead she stood, slowly removed the yellow dress. She slipped out of her panties and the bra. She threw her shoes aside and removed the stockings, which were long ago ruined.

Her lips were tender, from his kissing. She liked the way they felt, somehow tingling, somehow experienced. She smiled. She liked the way that felt too. Slowly, she brought her index finger up, watched him as he watched her, and traced her lips.

She stood, naked, in the bright glow of light which came from no discernible source, her nipples erect. It was crisp, not cold, and from somewhere, occasionally there was a slight breeze, but she doubted cold aroused her nipples, doubted it was the breeze. Her stomach felt all flip-floppy, and she could feel her blood rushing, feel it in her fingers, in her heart, in other parts of her anatomy, specifically at the apex of her legs. She could hear the blood rushing in her ears. She liked the way her knees felt more than a trifle unsteady.

Her waist was narrow, her legs shapely, her back straight, her stomach flat. All because she exercised religiously, kept her body toned. She spent hours at the gym and jogged almost every night because she wanted to be fit for her job. Now it was obvious having an attractive body had other significant benefits.

"Do you still hurt, Milton?"

His nostrils flared and he met her gaze with a heat she was surprised did not cause her to spontaneously combust. "Do you ask of my injuries?"

She lowered her hand, cupped herself at the junction of her thighs, covering the patch of hair. She waited for she knew he watched.

"Yes."

He swallowed. The action might not have been as obvious in a gargoyle, but in his manform, it spoke volumes. His legs were long, corded and muscular. Although he stood with his feet apart, at the moment they looked like they would not hold him. They seemed sturdier when he hung suspended by chains. "The bones have knit. They give me no additional pain."

She extended a finger, pushed it inside herself, found the nub he had discovered for her earlier. With her other hand, she fondled her nipples. They had never been sensitive before. "You are not in pain now?"

He shifted his weight from foot to foot, but made no move to approach. He was erect, his manhood stood, straining, as if in reaching, it might close the distance his legs and his mind would not complete.

"I am in pain now."

She removed her hand from where it had been intimately engaged, brought the finger under his nose, watched his nostrils flare as he caught her scent.

"Milton—"

"Do you seek to torture me, as Andrew does?"

Was that what she was doing? Shame washed over her, but the reaction was short-lived, for that had never been her intention. "No. I'm sorry, that's not what I meant at all. I needed to know you would not break your word. That I would be safe."

"My word will always be honorable."

"Then love me, Milton. Please."

She thought he would jump her, grab her, take her. He was ready, and judging by the cream on her finger, so was she. But again he surprised her.

"Wife," he whispered. "My wife." He lowered his mouth to hers again, and as he moved closer, that part of him which was straining, was trapped between them.

She met his kiss, his kisses, then giggled as she rubbed her stomach back and forth. "That's not where I want it."

"Show me what to do," he begged. "For I am new to this as you."

He had had no trouble on their wedding night. It seemed unlikely he had forgotten the fundamentals this soon.

She raised a leg, jumped up, her arms around his neck. The chain around her ankle rattled. It would be the music they would make love to. She felt him then, intimately, thrusting against her womanhood, seeking, but not yet finding entrance. He would not do it. She knew as well as she knew her own name if this union were to find completion, she would have to position him, would have to show him the way.

He rubbed, a mere shifting of his hips. Sparks flew behind her eyes and her body felt hot and cold and shivery, a thousand emotions none of which she could put a name to. Her thoughts were jumbled, raced around inside her brain. She only knew desire, and in her desire, lack. He held her weight easily, moved slowly, but not how she wanted him to move. Too much inside her was incomplete.

"Milton, please..." and she wrapped her fingers around him again, and brought him home.

***

Two hours before:

Arthur swung his sword, decapitating three imps simultaneously. He was coated in blood, and surrounded by piles of bodies, six and eight deep. He knew if he ever laid down the weapon he would feel exhaustion, but it did not trouble him while he fought. He was too well trained a warrior, had survived too many battles. The blade sang its ritual song of death as if it fed on carnage. It probably did. More than once over the centuries had he believed the weapon sentient.

In the sky above, the gold dragon flew, flames belching from its mouth, and thousands of imps, perhaps millions, turned into part of the inferno raging around them.

Still more came. They crept in through windows and doors, tried to climb up the outer walls using only their fingernails and determination. A dozen different types of lesser elves, each armed, each attempting to claim for itself the prize, little realizing their deaths meant less than nothing to Andrew, who only saw them as a distraction.

"Jan, I can't keep them much longer," Arthur said. He bled from half a hundred cuts.

"I'm ready." She had her hands filled with packages, had more on her back. These things they would need for a long exile. "Byron is coming in." Behind her, Lori wore a sheet strapped around her shoulders and waist, a ridiculous affair except it held three infants, leaving her hands free to carry supplies, diapers and wipes and long, sharp carving knives that could be used as short swords.

"Where are we going?" Arthur demanded. He brought up the rear, keeping the death-toll of imps mounting. At least he fought only imps, not the wizard, or the cunning other creatures of faerie which would not die so easily on his blade. The women opened the downstairs door, started moving out. Arthur could not turn his head and look. To do so would prove fatal.

"I've got a place," Bryon the man said, but then Arthur had to duck as a blast of dragonfire spurted behind him, turning hundreds of imps into torches, giving them a few minutes breathing room. "Come with me."

Byron led them down the stairs toward the landing, to a freestanding door which he opened and jumped through. Lori and her children, Jan, Arthur and the cat Genevieve followed. Byron shut the door behind them, blowing flame again to seal it temporarily. It would give them time to catch their breath, to clean their weapons and regroup before Andrew discovered where they had gone. There, off the first landing down the stairs in the Inn, heading for a gigantic cave, they bounded into a rainforest jungle.

***

"It might be for the best if we got dressed." Brenda might have drifted off to sleep, she only knew she had been cuddled against a man, and now, who knew how much later, she was wrapped in a monster's embrace.

"Dressed?"

"Wake up, Brenda. It is open here. Andrew or Longfellow or any of a million imps could approach without a moment's notice."

Mortified, she quickly put her underclothes and the filthy dress back on, thinking if she ever got out of this alive, she would burn them. How pretty the dress had felt when she first put it on. Now she felt soiled, body and soul.

Brenda's eyes were wide as she scanned the darkness surrounding them. "We could have been watched."

"We were not."

"Anyone could have come while we were…occupied."

"Yes. Such a possibility did not seem to bother you a moment ago."

He was hateful and despicable to remind her.

The baby woke, started crying, and although it was lethargic, it was a sign he still lived. Brenda picked him up, brought him to her chest where she rocked him. Her breasts, which had felt full under Milton's ministrations, now felt useless. She had no food to feed him, and Andrew had left nothing suitable for an infant. "We will find your father, little one, your mother and your brothers." But the pledge brought him no comfort. Although he was too young to understand, he would not want to be surrounded by complete dragons, when always there would be an ache inside of him.

"Your empathy is your greatest attribute."

Milton stood, his body alert. His hands, coiled into open fists, for should he fight, he would do it mostly with the long, lethal nails at the ends of his fingers.

"There is someone coming." Brenda did not have to make it a question.

"It is the wer-wizard."

Andrew dropped a tray of fruit within the circumference Brenda's chains. Starving, she picked up an apple and a banana and ate. She had finished the apple before she thought of Milton, and moved the tray so he could also eat.

Andrew studied Lorenzo, his concentration riveted on the small orange band on the infant's wrist. "You have been in touch with another wizard?"

"We have. Since it is unlikely there is a tenet of your profession you have not violated, I would imagine all of your brothers are looking for you."

Andrew threw back his head and laughed. "I hold all the power now. Let them come."

Milton clawed open a pineapple. He lifted his head, juice dripping down from his jaw and chin. "You better pray they will kill you quickly and without making you suffer."

"I would not think my chances against them so poor. I will be ready when they come."

Andrew approached Brenda and she coiled in revulsion, but when he spoke, she recognized it was not depravity he had in mind. "Would you mind if I provided another powerstrand for the infant? That one has nearly lost all its potency. It needs to be replaced."

Milton snarled, but unfortunately from where Andrew stood, his chain was not long enough to attack the wizard.

"It is unlikely you provide it to be kind."

"You are correct. I have found a buyer for the baby."

"A buyer? You are selling the child?"

"A faux dragon is something of a rarity. To a collector, it is the equivalent of having a real gargoyle waterspout."

Brenda snarled. As a cop she had been trained never to give her emotions free rein, but she was livid, and terrified, and lashing out helped control the fear.

"Instead of providing Lorenzo with a powerstrand, how about you release the ones on our chains, so we can settle our differences here and now?"

Andrew studied her, and the look was approving. "You have Lori's spunk."

"I will take that as a compliment, for I never thought you would spout anything but evil, but how do you know her?"

"Your sister was my lover for almost a year. Did she not tell you?"

She would have spit if she could have dredged up the saliva. "I bet she curses your name in the dark now."

"I am sure she does. You don't look much like her. Your coloring is different, not just the hair, but the skin as well. She is much paler, more delicate."

"Yeah, well, red hair will do that to you."

"Your jaw is stronger. Hers looks so fragile. I often thought it would take nothing to snap."

"You're a sick, twisted little bastard, aren't you?"

"If it pleases you to think so. I'm wondering now if I made a mistake giving the chakra to Longfellow. I never suspected I would get my hands on an infant dragon. Of course there are advantages to having a gargoyle with a chakra, almost unlimited advantages, but perhaps I was too hasty. I would like a set of dragon fangs."

"Since you do not have any, Byron is still alive."

"Yes. He left, with that long impressive tail between his legs, taking his family. He is no longer on Earth. I have my minions checking portals, but so far without success. Little worry. Eventually he'll get tired of hiding out and come looking for me." Andrew laughed again. "I intend to be ready."

CHAPTER 24

After Andrew disappeared, Brenda crawled to her husband. Milton kept himself occupied swiping his tongue between his toes. While they had been making love, his tongue with its healing magic had been busy. All the bruises and aches she had were healed.

"Milton, can Andrew hear us?"

"I do not know. It is my understanding some of these powerstrands can be used to transfer sound, but I have no idea if he is interested in listening in on our conversation. Why?"

"He said the powerstrand on Lorenzo had weakened, needed to be recharged."

"He did."

"Could the ones on our chains be weakening?"

"Perhaps."

"Could you let me see?"

He took her hand, and the strands became visible again. She almost screamed in frustration, for the frighteningly beautiful powerstrands remained intertwined with the chains, but then she looked closer. "They look lighter now than they were. Less substantial."

She pulled on the strand attached to his ankle, felt her desperation rising, but she could not get the chain to snap.

Moments later, Milton added his strength to hers, the muscles standing out starkly against his naked chest as he pulled with all his strength. For an instant Brenda stopped and took the time to appreciate the beauty of his body.

Beauty...but he was a monster. A monster, yes, but the fact no longer seemed to matter. He was honed to perfection. Wings, claws, horns, and even the manacles he wore as indication of his past shame somehow became unimportant. Even more so, Milton had transformed himself in her eyes, become attractive, seductive, alluring. And not just in his manform.

In his gargoyle form.

His shoulders were broad, his muscle definition stood out in stark relief. His stomach was flat, hard, tapered to a narrow waist. He was so beautiful. She wondered when he had stopped being repulsive to her, and when she had started to become attracted. Certainly longer than half an hour ago, or what passed between them would not have happened.

"What? You're smiling."

"Nothing," she said, meaning nothing she would admit to. Brenda doubted she could explain to him something she did not understand herself. He would make love to her as a man, but it was the gargoyle who at the moment was causing her pulse to race. Brenda resumed her task, working beside him, working together. Unexpectedly, the chain snapped open.

He raised his long broad snout, sniffed the air, then, without a word, took off running toward the stairs, his wings spread out behind him, his claws making tapping, scratching noise against the bedrock.

"Wait, don't go."

He half turned to face her, which meant half of him was still poised to flee. "I am free Brenda. I must continue the quest."

She moved closer, a step only, for she remained restrained by the ugly, hated chain. He was abandoning her to Andrew and his monstrous friends. Her fear rose, as did her anger. He was leaving her alone, taking his freedom as if she meant nothing to him. She would not admit her fears. She had too much courage, too much self-respect. "Stay. Eventually someone will come. We can take them by surprise, if they think we are still chained."

He spread his broad wings, brought them back to his chest. The look he gave her was sad, perhaps apologetic. "Killing or destroying imps and demons is not directly involved with my quest."

"Take me with you."

"I cannot. At this point you would only slow me down. I told you Brenda, if there came a time when I could work on my quest or save your life, what I would have to choose."

"You cannot leave me!" she hollered. "You cannot."

But he spread his wings and a moment later was gone.

Brenda screamed as Milton gained altitude, his wings flapping as he passed all those layers of stairs, heading for the kitchen.

Andrew appeared almost instantly, dressed in his black robes, his feet bare and filthy. His hair was unkempt as if ravaged, and his eyes, it took her a moment to realize what she witnessed. His eyes showed madness. The rage on his face so visible he spit. "He got away?"

"Yes."

"How did he manage that?"

She had been betrayed by the creature she called husband, but this was her enemy, more human looking, but far less human. Brenda straightened her spine, drew courage oddly enough from the one thing she had in abundance: her fear. "Your power is not as strong as you would believe."

His nostrils flared, and he drooled spittle. "I am invincible. I control the nexus. I have defeated the dragon and the caretaker witch. I had captured the gargoyle and his human lover."

Oddly enough, she thought of Milton, this time more compassionately. If she could keep Andrew occupied, maybe she could give Milton the time he needed to complete his damned quest.

She felt power. Not good cop bad/bad cop, because at the moment she was no cop at all. She was a woman in love. She faced her captor with defiance. "You will have nothing because you are nothing."

He reached out, and when she thought he would strike her, instead Andrew grabbed a hold of her hair, pulling until she screamed. "You are coming with me." He tugged on the chain and it broke effortlessly, as if made of paper.

He shoved her, not toward the stairs which would lead to the kitchen, but to one of the freestanding doors at their base. "Where are we going?"

"To see Byron. To see if that pretty wife of his will negotiate for her sister's life."

"What about Lorenzo?"

"I do not need him, and it is unlikely Lori will want him, he is that close to death. We will leave him."

"You can't be that cruel."

He dropped his head back on his shoulders and maniacal laughter erupted from his throat. "Ah, but you see, I can."

    ***

With insanity dripping from every pore, Andrew dragged Brenda to one of the three the free standing doors. She was a cop and over the years there wasn't a personal defense class she missed, so as he started feeling confident she would remain his victim, as he was about to push her through the door, she pivoted on her heel and kicked out. Her feet were bare, but that didn't matter. She put all the force of her terror and her frustration into the kick. She caught him high, in his stomach, and Andrew went down hard with a whoosh. With his breath knocked out, she hit him again, his nose, his neck. She needed to incapacitate him and the rage within would not be easily placated.

He was amazingly strong, supremely resilient. After her first kick, he met her, blow for blow, had her blocking his attack. She would have won. She was the better hand to hand fighter, had more experience in personal defense, but his hands and his feet were not his only weapons. He waved his hands in movements which to her only reeked of frustration, but a powerstrand locked around her ankle, pulling her down. Without Milton's support, she couldn't see it, but she could feel it. It tightened, painfully, and felt somehow soapy, which should have made it comfortable, but instead burned, as if made from acid.

Another then another crept over her skin, invisible spiders, scorpions, fire ants. It felt like creatures stolen from the depths of her terror, slippery, monstrous things making free with her body, a personal invasion. This battle she could not win.

Brenda thought if she could knock Andrew out, she could stop the assault, but she no longer had the power to move. She was a prisoner again. Slimy, worm-like invisible powerstrands crept over her stomach, across her breasts.

"Get them off me!"

Speaking became impossible as Andrew twisted his hands yet again and something thick tightened around her neck.

Andrew pulled himself to his feet, lorded over her. His words remained choppy. He hadn't regained his equilibrium from the fight. "I really don't need you alive. I had hoped to trade you, but it's no skin off my back if you die here instead."

The invisible powerstrand tightened. Her lungs screamed, desperate for oxygen. Black spots danced in front of her retinas.

"Do you yield? And before you answer, know I am leaving you tied. You won't get the chance to escape again, but perhaps the dragon values you. Perhaps he will trade. Do you accept my terms?"

She thought of Milton on his quest and she hated him afresh. He abandoned her to this monster. It was because of him she was here. But even as she thought that, Brenda knew her accusations were groundless. She wasn't here because of Milton. He was not where she should cast her blame.

The powerstrand loosened and Brenda gasped, pulling in a grateful breaths of air. Her throat was raw. Every bone and muscle on her body ached. Even chained she had not felt this debased.

"Come now, Brenda, you must know hostage negotiations. Do you agree to my terms?"

She tried to sit up, found herself still restrained, but worse, she looked around. The cavernous expanse was filled with vile creatures, hundreds of thousands: the heavily armed imps they had noticed when they first landed in the area, and other, larger, less easily defined monsters. They all drooled, eyed her as if she were the main entrée in a dinner given in their honor.

Andrew noticed where she looked. "Yes. They serve me. At my whim, I could hand you over to them. Would you like that?"

She continued pulling in great draughts of air over a throat that continued to burn. "You're despicable."

"Yes, I suppose there's no denying that." He roared with laughter, his breath back from her assault when she thought she had a chance to escape. "Now, all those years on the Albany police force, you must know when you're, for want of a better phrase, outgunned?"

"You speak like you know me."

"Ahh, but I do. You see, I've been planning my assault on this Inn for years. I sought the easiest way in. I thought perhaps you, but I realized Lori would make the better introduction to Jan."

"Lori must have gone home and vomited after every evening she spent with you."

He laughed again. "No, I can assure you, she didn't. I really can be quite charming when I want. Are you ready to come with me, or should I leave you here…for their entertainment?"

She looked around, debated the lesser of two evils. "I'll come."

Andrew twisted his hands again, and the majority of the slimy strands slid off her body. He made a pulling motion, and her throat closed while she were being garroted.

"I'll just leave this one. You understand."

He pulled her to her feet, his touch as repulsive as the invisible strands which had slithered over her body. "We're going this way. It took me ever so long to find where the dragon escaped to. There's literally any number of exits, so I started sending out field teams to locate him. I got lucky. Of course he fried my minions, but as you can see, I've really no shortage."

Andrew pushed her through the free-standing door into another world. How she knew this, Brenda had no idea, but the door, which appeared to have nothing behind it, dropped them into a rainforest. One moment they were in the cavern and one step later, a forest appeared, lush with green growth, with the sounds of a thousand different hidden species chirping, singing, or roaring.

"Dragon!" Andrew shouted, maintaining his tight, painful hold on Brenda's hair. "Dragon!"

In the sky, the great gold and bronze dragon flew. She could see it through the infrequent breaks in the canopy. Fear rose unbidden, even knowing it was Byron and she had learned to trust him. There was something primordial about seeing him, some instinctive terror buried so deep in her genes she could not control her reaction.

Andrew laughed, feeling his power. His chest expanded as he took in great gulps of the moist, verdant air, and he appeared larger, more formidable. He was in his element here, supreme ruler. Evil and insanity sheeted off him in waves so strong she nearly could see them.

He pulled her hair tighter and Brenda had to bite her lip to prevent herself from crying out.

"Dragon, I have something you might find valuable. I have come to negotiate."

The beast settled not fifty feet from them. It swung its sinuous neck back and forth, releasing steam as it moved a step closer, then another. It was massive. Had it been this large in the cavern? Certainly surrounded by the majesty of this primordial rainforest the beast should appear somehow diminished instead of the reverse.

Still, Brenda wanted to shout, "Run Byron. Don't listen to him. It's a trap!" But she kept her mouth shut. Whatever this ambush between titans of antiquity was, she would let it play out.

Release her, and we will talk, not before.

The voice was familiar, brought her sharp images of Byron kneeling, crying at the cradle of a boy who could not be made whole. Byron. For a split second Brenda could understand why her sister loved him.

With his free hand, Andrew flexed and contracted his fingers, probably hoping to create fear. Brenda for one was terrified enough without the physical manifestations.

"That is what I want to talk about. I am willing to trade Brenda for one of your other sons."

And Lorenzo?

"Dead. But you can have your sister-in-law."

"Where is Milton?"

"He has fled."

Is this true, Brenda?

She wanted to lie. She wanted to tell the truth. She had no idea before this second how closely related truth and lies could be and how both…and neither…could offer comfort. Milton. Hadn't she started to love him? Hadn't there been tenderness between them?

"Yes, he fled. We were chained. When he got his freedom, he left me."

Milton had made many promises to her, and that one he kept. Even if he could save her and go after the chakra later, he had to put the chakra before her.

"Will you make the trade, Dragon? This human for one of your sons?"

The roar bellowed loud enough to have Brenda covering her ears. *You have already killed one. I will not give you another. No father would countenance such an action.*

"Then will you watch while I kill her? Will you let your wife observe as I murder her sister?"

The dragon walked awkwardly through the trees on heavy legs. *What else do you require?*

"You have gems. Bring me all your jewels."

That can be arranged. Let the maid go.

Andrew pulled the powerstrand he had dragged around her throat, and Brenda felt it cutting off the oxygen. She found herself growing lightheaded, her body desperate for a breath. She had her hands to her neck, but she could not feel it, not see it.

But she had been trained in physical combat, so she lunged out, kicking with her anger and her experience and an emotion she had never felt before—hate. In all her years on the police force, with all the felons she had dealt with, never before had she hated. The dragon roared, but she refused to move back, refused to allow Byron the chance to kill Andrew, when she could already feel the wizard's blood on her hands.

Move away, Brenda. Let me finish this.

CHAPTER 25

Byron had chosen his exile carefully, something Andrew had not realized. There were no powerstrands here. Andrew looked around, his chanting growing mindless. There was no way he could mount a defense. He was powerless. Gripping the one powerstrand he had held to her neck, he twisted it, then vanished.

***

A familiar yet sickening smell led Milton to the kitchen. Centuries he had lived below, sniffing the delicious scents which originated here, but lasagna, stews and éclairs were not the prey he was interested in tonight. This hunt was different, and Milton was honest with himself. It had been inevitable for eons.

Stacks of dirty dishes still covered every square inch of floor space, of the table, of the counters. He gave them no mind. His enemy was here, somewhere. He could smell him, hear him.

Milton moved with concentrated stealth through the chaos, holding his claws out defensively. There would be a fight and it promised to be ugly. He and Longfellow were matched: opposites but equivalent. He could hear a hundred million imps traveling through the Inn, going through the rooms, looking for treasures or perhaps only causing mischief.

And still, his heart was broken. After his original sin, the planet's only original sin, he thought himself never capable of such evil, but abandoning Brenda had been evil. Perhaps for the second time he had chosen wrongly. He had no idea how he could make it up to her, for marriages were sacred and their union should have come first.

Longfellow crouched in a corner, head low, wings covering his back. His face was in dark shadows, hidden. He was not moving. Milton crept closer, his nose active. There was no sign of decay. He doubted the gargoyle was dead. They were not easy creatures to kill. No, Milton was trying to sense something else.

Nothing smelled like a trap. That kind of deviousness was generally beyond Longfellow. His brother always preferred the direct approach.

"Longfellow!"

There was no need to yell, his enemy was only a few feet from him, but he shouted his defiance, moved closer. Longfellow shifted his wings back and looked up but Milton gave him no time to prepare. Milton jumped, slashing at his throat with his talons, digging his teeth deeply into his forearm, then tearing, ripping. They fought, but it was short and bloody and decidedly one-sided. For the first time in all the centuries they battled, Milton was clearly the victor.

He held his hands on either side of Longfellow's throat, watching the life slowly ebb. "I don't want to kill you." But he lied. Longfellow was beyond redemption, and he sought his death. Still he had killed his brother, a fratricide as ugly and sinful as anything which occurred between Cain and Abel. This Milton would have avoided had it been possible.

Tenderly he cradled Longfellow, watched as the life drained from him. "The chakra was never yours."

"But it is mine." The words were whispered, for there was no air in his lungs, and his lifeblood flowed freely into the slate tiles of the kitchen. His eyes were sunken, dulled with pain.

"It was never yours." The words were spoken with a reverence of something holy happening. How could he possibly hate his brother and love him equally? How was it possible? And was this quixotic mix of emotions something his wife would understand?

"Would you help me?" The sentence was broken, spoken over gasps and bubbling of bright red blood from his throat.

Slowly, painfully, Milton understood. Saying a prayer so intrinsic it was part of his very nature, he tightened his grip, then twisted his hands, breaking Longfellow's neck.

For a full minute, sixty seconds only, he allowed himself the luxury of grief. Milton raised his snout and howled, low and deep, spilling out his anguish. But he had a task to complete, one which could not be denied any longer.

Mindless, intent only on finishing his quest, he flew back down the stairs to Lorenzo, and gently lifted the baby. Although still breathing, the infant was limp, non-responsive. His eyes were half-open, dulled, sunk deep in his skull. His breath was slight, the chest barely moving. Byron had stated the child would not die, but Milton understood mortality, knew death was only moments away.

He flapped his wings and flew back to the kitchen, cradling his precious burden. In the few seconds he was gone, fifteen or twenty small imps had reached Longfellow, were digging their talons into the blood, lapping it off their claws. Milton roared, and they vanished, taking their grating, chattering noise with them.

He looked at his mortal enemy, his brother and knew although it sickened him, he would have to continue the imps' work, and further desecrate the body. He set Lorenzo down. The baby twitched, a spasm, or perhaps a death throe. Lorenzo made no sound, no other motion. Still, Milton had to try. He had given his word, had betrayed his wife. Yet, clearly he understood perhaps it was already too late.

He would reunite the chakra with Lorenzo or he would see it destroyed. He said a prayer. He was a creature who understood the power inherent in speaking to divinity.

On his knees, Milton tore open Longfellow's chest with his claws, ripping him to bloody shreds, then inched back to the fetal dragon. For a long moment, nothing happened. Milton hung his head in frustration, in unbelievable sorrow. Then, slowly, the chakra, in the form of a transparent dragon, rose from Longfellow's chest.

Milton's voice exhaled on a whisper. "He never merged with it."

The chakra raised its snout and trumpeted. It slowly walked across the desecrated body, directly honing in on its other half. Milton remained kneeling, felt his eyes tear. Maybe all this had been worth it.

With infinite patience, and a beauty which took his breath away, the ne-chakra merged with the child. Lorenzo's eyes drifted shut, but Milton could see he breathed better, color already reappearing on his cheeks. Seconds later, Lorenzo looked up to Milton and smiled. He filled his lungs with air, and gave out an ear-splitting bellow.

"Yes, I know you're starving, little fellow. Let's see if there is anything in this mess for you to eat."

A man pushed his way into the kitchen, but it was a dragon who spoke. *Gargoyle, we fight!*

"No, Byron. Can't you see that's Milton?" Lori ran to her son. "Is he—"

"He is whole. He has merged with his chakra. He is only hungry."

Lori grabbed the baby, brought him to the breast she had already bared. The infant latched on, suckled greedily. "Andrew told us he was dead. We came to destroy the Inn and everything in it." Her rage drained. "Byron, look at him. He's so perfect."

Milton looked past Brenda to Jan. "Innkeeper, I would ask a boon."

Speak.

"What do you need, Milton?"

"I would like to take the body, find someplace to bury it. I cannot choose consecrated ground, but he should have rest somewhere."

"Go, take him with my blessing. You have done a very great service for us. If there is anything I, or those I serve can ever do for you, you've only to mention it."

He had started crying when Lorenzo merged with his chakra, realized in the intervening span, he had not stopped. "When the time is right, would you speak over the grave? I know it would mean nothing to Longfellow, but I would find great comfort."

"I would be honored. Take your brother, Milton. When you need me, I will make myself available."

Behind Jan, Brenda watched her husband lift the bloody corpse and head for the back door. In all that time, while he did look at her long enough to realize she was there, he said nothing.

"Mercy," Jan said, "with all that's been going on, I've still got these dishes to do."

***

"I need to go through the Inn," Byron said, "make sure every last imp is gone."

"And get the boys."

"Not until I am certain the Inn is safe. Lori—"

"Don't worry, Byron, I'm happy now. I need to take some time with Lorenzo, make sure he's alright."

"Brenda—" Byron said.

She wiped her eyes, had no idea how she found the strength to stand. "Is the Inn safe?"

"Byron will make sure all the invaders are gone."

Invaders. But there was one who left of his own free will, one Byron didn't have to chase out. "I don't want to talk now." I don't want to talk ever, she finished silently to herself. "With your permission Aunt Jan, I want to shower for about two hours, then put some clean clothes on. I've never felt so filthy."

Filthy. How many definitions did that word have? Did she feel filthy because she could argue she had been used? Or was it because, somehow, she had fallen in love?

"There will be food, when you're ready. And Brenda, we do need to talk."

She crunched her eyes, letting her pain roll through her. She did not have the fortitude to turn around. "I know you think so."

Without bothering to wipe her eyes again, Brenda leaned over Lori lightly caressing Lorenzo's downy cheek. The child still looked sickly, but he was alert and feeding. He was whole now, complete.

"We'll never be able to repay you," this from Byron who had shifted back into his human form.

"I am not looking for repayment."

"Nevertheless, it is always a good thing to have a dragon owe you a favor."

"In case you ever need anything torn into a bleeding mass." Lori spoke lightly, a ribbing to her husband sprinkled with her love but stopped, for she realized who and what Brenda's husband was, and Jan, already on her hands and knees, worked at cleaning up a bloodstain.

"Thanks. If I need anything torn up into a bleeding mass, I'll think of you first."

"Brenda, after you shower, would you come up and chat? With everything that happened, we haven't had a chance to talk."

"No, I don't think so. After I shower, I'm going to leave. I want to sleep in my own bed, and I've been away from work too long." She gave a long look around the kitchen, the dishes still piled up to the ceiling, the bloodstain, the memories of drinking dragon tea, and having Milton's claws prickling against her throat. "I don't have really happy memories of this place."

Because she felt like crying, and she had no idea why, except it might be exhaustion, she kissed Lorenzo on the top of his head, then hugged her sister. "Lori, enjoy your family. I can see you've found true love. You know I wish you every happiness."

"And you, Brenda, what you gave up for us—"

Dressed in filthy, torn rags she straightened her back. She felt like a victim, but had no idea if it were because Milton had betrayed her, or because he had left without saying anything. "I was not forced into making any decision." She stared down at the blood on her hands, Andrew's. Her own blood and her husband's had been licked clean. Maybe when she showered, she would remove all traces of him.

"You have to know without you, without Milton, we would not have defeated Andrew, and Longfellow would still have the ne-chakra."

"Andrew was not defeated."

Jan looked up from her scrubbing. She had to be as exhausted, as shattered as the rest of them, but her smile was radiant and life twinkled in her powder-blue eyes. "Andrew was defeated. He may still live, but even though that is unlikely to change in a moment, it's of no import. He suffered a major upset here. The Inn is safe. I shudder to think of the evil he could have perpetrated using this place as his base. He does not have control of Lorenzo's chakra, and the dark faeries who flocked to him will not so readily answer his call again. No, a lot of good came from this. I will try to find some way to thank Milton, and Brenda, you will always be welcome here."

"Here, yeah, swell. Just the place where I plan to raise my family."

"Your family?"

She rolled her eyes at the question. "I was speaking facetiously."

"Was it horrible, your time with Milton?"

"No." She wouldn't lie. "As much as he could, he tried to be a gentleman." And there had been beauty and inexplicable pleasure when wrapped in his arms. Yet he betrayed her every chance he got. Twice he left her to fend on her own. Three, if you consider when he left just five minutes before.

"Maybe you need time to get to know Milton better."

"Yeah, I'm sure that's it." She ground the words out, feeling the need to weep, not understanding why. "There's no need to tell him where I've gone. I know he can track me."

"You'll not stay for the funeral?"

"Funeral?"

"For Longfellow?"

"Longfellow meant nothing to me. He was just another greedy, ugly monster. I wouldn't bother to cross the street to spit on his grave. I've got work to do. I might make detective. It's what I want." Even if she could no longer remember why she had wanted it.

Brenda ran upstairs to the bathroom, shampooed, and scrubbed and washed, but doubted she would ever feel clean again.

Or ever feel sane again.

And she cried, bellowing out her anguish under scalding water and shampoo bubbles and hoped Byron was too busy and Milton too far away to hear.

"Then go," Aunt Jan said as Brenda hefted her purse on her shoulder at the front door less than an hour later. "But know you will always have a home here, any time you want it."

"Thank you. I'm sure you mean well."

Brenda dug in her purse, located her car keys.

"You can stay. There should be food available. I don't know what, but the kitchen should supply a meal. You probably haven't eaten in days."

The thought of food sickened her. "If I get hungry later, I'll stop and get something. I promise."

"Please," Lori said, "stay." She still rocked the child in her arms, not yet able to put him down.

"No." She looked at her husband, who had been in the kitchen when she came down after her shower. "I can't."

"Well, know we love you, and we're thankful for all you've done.

Really, Brenda, for everything."

With arrogance, or perhaps humility, who could tell any more, Milton walked around Lori to stand in front of Brenda. "I will walk you to your car."

"I don't need or want your assistance."

"Would you rather have this discussion here, in front of your family?"

She shrugged, and wordlessly, she walked out.

It was a beautiful dawn, the sky was a rosy pink, and all around, signs of life, birds singing their heart out, a pair of gray squirrels involved in a complicated game of chase, and half a dozen chipmunks playing what might be hopscotch.

"I never want to see you again."

"We are married. That is not going to change. It was done for all the days of this planet and for all eternity." As if those were two separate things.

"Fine, then we're married. Twice. I remember. It was only yesterday, or the day before, after all."

"Three days ago."

So much happened in three days.

She opened the car door, tossed her keys and her purse in the driver's seat, then with both palms flat on the hood lowered her head. "I understand why you did what you did. You told me your priorities. I know you would never save me. I was prepared for that."

"Yet still it hurts."

"It hurts."

"But Brenda, you did not need rescuing. And you would have resented me all the days of your life if I had rescued you."

"Yes. So, you're damned if you did, damned if you didn't."

"Yes. And I have been damned before."

She wondered if it were raining, for splotches of wet appeared on the hood. She wiped her eyes, refused to turn and meet him.

Milton continued, in his warm, comforting voice, the Voice that had helped her catch countless criminals, save unknowable lives.

"I never thought I could hurt this badly again."

"Use your magic tongue."

"My healing saliva does not work on broken hearts."

She needed a tissue. She needed…something she couldn't understand. Yeah, she was one tough cop now. "I never want to see you again."

"I do not know if I can respect that wish. You might be pregnant."

"What?" Her hand went to her belly.

"It was twice, after all."

"Do you think, do you know...?"

"Nothing yet. It is a secret your woman's body will tell you first."

"Milton, I don't know anything right now. I only know I've been through more than I'm ready to handle. Please, don't bother me."

***

She went back to work, and the Voice still came to her. Maybe not as often, but with enough frequency her reputation continued to grow. She made detective, her partner with her, and while she went to briefings, they were given no direct assignments, only allowed to cruise Albany, bringing in whatever felons they could find.

At first she wanted to ignore the Voice, wanted nothing to do with him, but he would not be silenced, and if he wanted to help keep lawbreakers off the streets, at least that benefited everyone.

But when she finished her shift, when she sat on the rocker swing on her front porch exhausted and aching, the night remained silent, and no words came to her, not from him and not from her own heart. Once, twice, or rather every single second, she thought of calling out, begging, but she bit her tongue and kept her confusion locked in her heart.

***

It was a dinner, not anything fancy, and although there were candles on the table, they were fat red-glass things, and their flame wobbled with drafts came from hidden recesses. The tablecloths were red checked, the napkins real linen, and Brenda felt she could gain two pounds simply by breathing in the mouthwatering aromas where oregano and garlic were prevalent. The restaurant was small, very crowded, but intimate nonetheless. The lights were dim, the tables closely placed, the food incredible, heavy in artery clogging sauces. The salads were fresh, the cheese and the wines aged to perfection.

Brenda was dressy-dressed, open toed heels stolen from Lori, who swore she'd never need fancy out to dinner shoes again, for she was raising four hellions, and when would she ever have a minute to herself, so Brenda might as well enjoy them. Her dress was short, low, black, and fit perfectly. She wore a necklace of amethyst, semiprecious stones, a gift from Byron, for her help in rescuing his son's chakra. When she refused to accept anything costly, she agreed to this, because it was pretty, and dragon forged, and it made her feel somehow invincible wearing it.

Her nails were done, and heavens only knew when the last time she had taken an afternoon to pamper herself, but they made her fingers look slender, poised, graceful with their buffed, polished tips, and she wished for a second she had a ring, to further set off her fingers, but then remembered she was married, and she clearly didn't want to go there.

Her date was attractive, attentive, and as far as friend-of-a-friend dates went, the night was proving to be extraordinary. He too was a cop, not her precinct, but he understood her hours, her frustrations and her passions. She really should have married a cop.

If she considered herself married at all, which she did not for longer than ten or twelve seconds at a time.

They nibbled on appetizers, crab stuffed mushrooms, deep fried mozzarella sticks and their salads arrived, with a basket filled with steaming hot garlic breadsticks so delicious she knew she would be happy if she ate nothing else.

"Do you believe in miracles?" he asked.

She coughed, the bread wedging in her throat. She had to take a sip of wine before she could trust herself to speak. "Why do you ask?"

He crunched into radicchio and raspberry vinaigrette. "It was in the paper today. I wasn't certain if you caught it or not."

Since she had been back from her adventure, she had been swamped at work, having as much success as before in catching all the bad guys. "I haven't had a moment's peace to look at a newspaper in ages. Why, are there miracles happening?"

"So it seems. A bishop, at a major cathedral in the city, is performing all kinds of miracles. There is talk of canonizing him."

"Really." And this should interest me because? She wanted to ask, but was afraid if she did ask, she wouldn't like the answer. She had dealings recently with a bishop from a New York City cathedral. It had to be a coincidence.

He set his fork down, held up his wine glass with two hands as if participating in a holy ordinance. "He has been healing people, hopeless cases, causing complete remissions. He's up to fifteen so far. All the dying are flocking to him like he is the Second Coming."

"I can imagine." The bread and the wine no longer looked good. She decided to try her luck with the salad. "Do you think it's some kind of hoax?" That would be the most obvious answer, and the only answer she could live with.

He set his wine down, leaned back in his chair. His look softened. "No. Apparently all fifteen have complete medical histories, which are well documented from accredited hospitals. And they now have a clean bill of health."

"Is there a pill?" Please let there be a pill.

"No. A bloodstained cloth. He won't say where the blood came from, and won't let a DNA analysis be done. He doesn't want to disturb the mojo."

"Can you blame him?"

"So, you never answered my question, do you believe in miracles?"

Brenda thought, choosing her words carefully. She had no intention of letting this evening end with the two of them entwined in her sheets, but neither did she wish to scare him off, when there was a possibility of a relationship which might prove worthwhile. "I always wanted to believe in miracles," she said, twirling greens around, without having the courage to take a bite. She had lost her appetite. "I want to believe a blood stained cloth can heal those near death, that saying the right thing, and doing the right thing will cause everything to be better, but this world doesn't work that way. Too much is too harsh, too random."

"But don't you think miracles could balance out some of the randomness, make the playing field a little more equal?"

"You believe in miracles?"

"I believe in these miracles. One of the fifteen was my daughter Stacy. She had leukemia. We were counting days until her death, because traditional treatments weren't working. She's fine now. This priest visited her in the hospital. My ex-wife was there. She stepped out for a minute, to throw up. It wasn't the flu or even a cold. She's been taking Stacy's sickness really hard, and Stacy's respiration was almost nil, and her brain was shutting down, and Jackie needed five minutes to herself, and when this priest asked if he could sit with Stacy for a minute, she agreed, seeking only to escape long enough to pull herself back together."

Brenda dropped the fork, twirled her fingers with her date's, a joining of compassion and empathy, rather than anything even remotely sexual. "And?"

"Stacy was sleeping when she got back, and Jackie stayed beside her all night, thinking it would happen any minute."

It. How horrible death was, that it was easier to speak of using a random pronoun than the clinical term.

"I joined her about a half hour after the priest left. I was going to take an unpaid leave. Losing a child isn't easy."

Brenda thought of Lori, and how she had suffered with Lorenzo's 'illness'. "Losing a child is never easy."

"When Stacy woke in the morning, her color was good, and her vitals were incredible and she was hungry. Her blood count came back up and there was an improvement. Not an incredible improvement, but a significant one. The doctors let Stacy eat. Not a lot, something, because they want to keep her spirits up as much as her WBC. And she kept it down, and they let her eat more, and they kept checking her blood, and it's back to normal now. Completely normal."

"I'm so happy for you. Is she home from the hospital yet?"

"No. No one is quite willing to release her. She was in a coma, so she can't say what the priest did, and Jackie had left the room, and we wouldn't have even known where to look for him, if we hadn't seen him on the television, fielding questions about the other miracles.

"I don't think Jackie and I can ever get back together, the divorce was final before Stacy got sick, and her illness has been a strain on both of us, so we're not ready for any kind of commitment to each other, or to anyone else."

"I understand. Please, accept my congratulations to you and your family. If there are miracles, I'm glad you were able to benefit from it."

Their entrees arrived, but neither was interested in food any longer. "I'm sorry," he said. "I thought I could do this. I have everything to live for now, and a date—"

"A no pressure date," Brenda finished for him, "might be exactly what you need, in a few weeks."

"Thanks."

He stood, put money on the table. "Please, finish eating, if you like, or I could escort you home."

"My neighborhood isn't so rough I need a cop to walk me to the door." She raised, kissed him chastely on the cheek. "Whatever happens with your family, I am glad your daughter is recovered."

"The doctors aren't using recovered, they're using remission, which is a good, solidly acceptable medical term, but she's cured, and no one can explain it."

"Go. Take her to a ballgame when the hospital releases her, or on a hot air balloon ride, or something totally, ridiculously fun. She has her childhood back."

"Have you ever come close to dying?"

"Yes."

"On the force?"

"No. No, it wasn't job related. It changes you. Even if it isn't you, but someone you care deeply about, coming close to dying changes you. Makes you see life differently."

"I hope I can see you again, Brenda."

"At the station, perhaps," she said, for although she had no intuition, she knew she would never see him again.

"Yeah."

"I am glad he left. I did not want to have to rip his heart out."

"Milton," Brenda said, startled. "I thought you could only maintain your human form while mating."

He raised an eyebrow, and cocked his head.

"You've come after me to mate?" She left the table, pushed her way through the restaurant until they were on the sidewalk. "That will be a cold day in—"

"You forget, I've been there. I can tell you the current theory that hell is blazingly hot is not entirely accurate."

"Don't tell me, it is really very cold."

"Occasionally it is well below freezing."

"I don't believe this conversation."

"And I don't believe my wife was out on a date with another man."

"I left you. You know that. I packed my things, waved farewell and drove away. Or didn't you believe me when I said I never want to see you again?"

"You are my wife. You do not have that option."

Why was her heart singing? Why was she ecstatic to see him? And Brenda realized she had gone on that date for one reason and one reason only: she had wanted to make Milton jealous. Still, she could be obstinate, and admitting she wanted him, perhaps even loved him, was hard to confess. She pushed the button, unlocking her car, opened the door, slid behind the wheel. Brenda realized he could quite easily shatter the passenger window to get to the door latch, or for that matter, pull the door off its hinges simply to be perverse, so with a push of a button, she unlocked his door, let him sit in the passenger seat.

She had suspected in the small confines of her car that he would be too large, too invasive, too close, but he fit comfortably, and her body reacted predictably to his nearness with an increased breathing rate which clearly did not have its origin in fear. No, what her body craved from his was quite a bit more visceral.

I thought you could only maintain your human form when you were mating. Yeah, she thought. Oh, yeah.

Brenda wrapped her hands around the steering wheel, took a deep breath, prepared to lie. "I entered into the marriage under coercion. I am certain a good lawyer would have no trouble seeking an annulment or a divorce."

He looked at her. She was afraid his look would turn cold, divisive, and she understood she deserved it, but his look remained compassionate, and his large, human hands, hands that had given her such pleasure, remained still, folded in his lap.

"Do you want the child to die?"

"Child? Lorenzo?"

"Stacy."

Since she met him all those years ago when she had been a child, had anything made sense? "What are you talking about?"

His lips were full, sensual. She remembered them at her breasts, and worse, between her legs when her pleasure had been so mindless. He might have been sexually inexperienced, but based on her direct knowledge, he had all the moves down.

"If the miracle of our union is voided, then the miracles which have arisen from it are also voided. Not that I think it is likely, but you do seem determined, and I have learned not to underestimate you."

Brenda wondered if she should leave, that no evil thing could exist in his presence, so she tightened her fingers on the steering wheel, a subconscious defiance he wouldn't get rid of her that easily.

"You would kill that child because you were mad at me?"

"I am not mad at you, and I would have nothing to do with the voiding of any miracles. But Brenda, I need you to think. You know what the miracle is the priest has been using."

"Blood," she said. Her throat was dry, her heart thumped erratically and her mind was back to a hidden room when he had unlocked the pleasures of her body.

"Consummation blood, of a marriage set to last forever. Mine and yours."

He still didn't move, and his look remained kind. How had this conversation gotten so off-track? How come she could not reconcile the fact what her brain wanted and what were mind wanted were two completely different things?

"Milton, I don't want anything to do with you. I want my life back. I don't want to kill Stacy, or anyone. I want to work my shifts and I want to go back to my house and sleep alone."

"I am your husband."

She took a deep breath and lied again. "You are a monster," she countered. Did she want him to be a monster? Is that why she was baiting him? Now when she tightened her fingers on the steering wheel it was so she wouldn't touch him in honesty and in compassion.

"And how do you define monster, Brenda? I really would like to know."

With that he opened the car door and slipped out, leaving her alone in the late evening in the middle of July, knowing if there had been a monster in the car in the last few minutes, it had been her.

CHAPTER 26

Quietly, without telling anyone, she followed the news stories of this priest from New York. The newspapers and the internet were saturated with the facts, the speculations, and the rising count of miracles. People flocked by the thousands to the cathedral, bringing their sick, their dying, their hopeless cases. While the priest tried to keep a low profile, Brenda saw he struggled to avoid the notoriety, he was up to thirty-one confirmed cases of miraculous cures. Thirty-one lives saved because of her marriage. Thirty-two if she counted Lorenzo, probably thousands more, since Andrew was prevented from his planned domination of worlds.

She wasn't pregnant. She cried when she realized it, tried to be rational, tried to convince herself it didn't matter, she didn't want the responsibilities of a child, and the timing would be wrong. She had grown very adept at lying to herself.

She even bought a pregnancy test, although she never needed it. Sometimes when a woman's body tells her something, there is no need to verify with store-bought proof.

A loud bubble gum bubble popped, so invasive that startled, she almost went for her gun. She shook herself from her musings, looked over at her partner who grinned snidely like he should have canary feathers between his teeth.

"So, Larwick, are you going home?"

Her hands shook. She wasn't sure she could drive. With the start of her period, she'd come to several decisions, vital, correct decisions, but still painful. It was never easy asking for forgiveness.

"There's paperwork."

"You've been staring at that computer for about thirty minutes now. You're worthless here. Let me finish up. That kid is safe because of you."

Kidnapped little boy, sex offender. Had they arrived even twenty minutes later, the paperwork would have been written up much differently.

She thought of an Inn in upstate New York and a man she never wanted to see chained again, even when he still wore the signs of his subjugation at his neck, wrist and ankle. "Do you mind if I go?"

"Please. Go. Quickly. With my blessing."

"Sal, I don't want your blessing, but I'm going." She grabbed her purse, kissed him lightly on the crest of his balding pate which surprised her and had him roaring with laughter.

She wrapped a shawl around her shoulders, for the wind stolen from Canada had picked up and brought with it a chill. Maybe summer was never going to get a toehold in this year. Dark clouds hulked and occasionally thunder lethargically grumbled, for the storm was coming and thunder, as everyone knows, is impatient. Still, Brenda sat on the rocker on her porch, kicking it back and forth, listening to the squeal of metal on metal for thunder is not the only thing which likes to grumble. She didn't have long to wait before the Voice appeared.

"Do you wish to be alone?"

Her heart tripped, beating fast and loud. She took a second to analyze the feeling, then, fearful he would take her pause for reticence or reluctance, spoke her heart. "No. Milton, please, sit beside me."

"As you wish."

He appeared, this huge hulking gargoyle with horns and a fourteen foot wing span, and her heart beat faster and her body responded by secreting hormones in secret places that left her uncomfortable and edgy.

She had a hundred things to say to him, complete conversations she worked through her mind day after day, night after night. Now that he sat beside her, she found the words would not come. She only found it somehow glorious that he was there.

"Thanks for saving that little boy's life."

"No problem. It would have been ugly. Had you not been there, I would have saved him."

"He," the boy, "wasn't the first."

"No. He," the murderer, "had a long run of slaughter."

"He's off the streets now." Brenda cringed, realized this conversation was becoming more awkward. What did you say to the seven foot monster you loved?

"I spoke to Pierce Billova last week."

Pierce Billova? Ah, the other wizard. Funny, she'd almost forgotten him.

"I told him about Andrew. I've done some research, found some things but Pierce said he would take over. My interest was never in fighting a wizard."

"No," she said, not sure if she meant it as agreement or not.

"He asked after your health, and about Lorenzo. I was able to reassure him Lorenzo is healthy and putting on weight, and his family now knows happiness."

His family now knows happiness. Why did that hurt, in the center of her chest, almost have her crying, when she wanted desperately for Lori and Byron and their boys to be a happy family? Obviously Milton had been unable to tell Pierce Billova she was part of a happy family.

A single fat raindrop splatted near her feet, left a round puddle on the porch. "We won't be able to sit out here much longer."

Great. Now she was talking about the weather. Could this miserable conversation get any worse? "Are you hungry? Could I get you something to eat?"

"Your aunt fed me a few hours ago. I'm fine."

"So, how have you been?"

"I am fine. I'm staying at the Inn, you know."

The wind picked up, turning the leaves on the red maples surrounding her house inside out. The wind was heavy with moisture. If she were smart, she'd go inside, make sure all doors and windows were closed and locked.

She wasn't smart.

"No, I didn't know. I'd think that would be the last place on the planet you'd be interested in staying."

He shrugged, and the wind whipped his wings. They fluffed and he settled them back down.

She needed to do something with her hands, found them restless. "I'm keeping in touch with Aunt Jan and with Lori, but they don't mention you."

There were three inch nails at the ends of his fingers, claws she'd seen rip bodies apart. They were clean, no sign of carnage, but she had seen what they were capable of.

And she remembered the tenderness of his human appearing fingers.

"I asked them not to. Occasionally, now, they listen to what I say."

"So, what are you doing?"

"I thought of traveling, but I decided the work I do there is important. When I am not here," checking on you, she inferred, "I am keeping the Inn evil free. Many imps and other creatures who were made welcome by Andrew, or who heard the Inn was open for corruption are only arriving now. I am kept busy."

"If it makes you happy, I'm glad."

"Jan has oddly enough decorated the cavern for me. There is a bed and dresser now. I am allowed upstairs to eat."

"No chains?"

"No chains."

"So, she's finally treating you like you have a soul."

"Yes. And like a family member."

Family member. Ahh, yes, her husband. "I'm not pregnant."

"I know."

"I—" she swallowed, wondered if she even knew what she had in her heart, and worse, if she had the courage to speak her heart. She took a deep breath, spoke very quickly. "I would like a child."

"His child?"

"His? Oh, the man from the dinner. No. No. Your child."

"Do you know what you ask?"

"Milton, I'm not sure I love you. Well, I think I do, but I'm not sure. I want to take the time to get to know you better. I want to explore this marriage and to make it real. I want—" she didn't know what to say, or how to say it. "Milton, I want everything."

"I am what I am, Brenda. I cannot change that."

"You've been forgiven. Can you forgive me, for the things I've said, for the way I've treated you?"

More rain slashed, coming in hard, perhaps with hidden shards of ice crystals. They were going to be soaked.

"Yes, Brenda, I can forgive you, but there is no need. I understood you lashed out because you were confused and you felt trapped. You are a woman who always does the right thing. What does your heart tell you now?"

"Heart? It's my brain I want to listen to."

He moved, little more than a shifting, so his wings covered her, enveloped her like an umbrella. Without being sexual, it was one of the most sensual things he had ever done for her. Brenda looked up, she'd been staring at her hands. He faced her with his body as well as his eyes and there was tenderness there.

She thought of the healing miracles from a blood stained sheet, but that was hardly the only miracle. There was a little dragon complete, and a young boy safe with his parents. There were dozens of criminals off the streets, but none of those were the miracles she considered.

"My heart tells me I can love you. I fell in love with you long before I ever saw you, when you were just a voice to me, when you would help me with work that's important to me. Even then, I wanted what we had to be much more."

He took her hands in his, but his weren't hands. They had sharp, deadly claws at the ends, and his skin was greenish, leathery. He wore signs of his past life at his neck, one wrist, one ankle. Shackles he wore willingly.

"Milton, I don't know what you would like. I don't know you at all, not really, but I would like to take the time sharing my life with yours, getting to know you, to give this…" what word would be appropriate here? She had no idea... "this marriage between us a chance to turn into something I could trust. I would like a ring," she said. "I want tell everyone we're married. I think, all things considered, I have been ashamed of my own feelings and never of who or what you are, and I don't want to feel that way anymore. And I want—"

"Yes?"

"This may sound funny."

"I cannot know how to react until you tell me what it is you want."

"I want a broad ugly bracelet, like the one you wear. I want it on my left wrist, like yours and I want it so it can never come off."

"That's not necessary."

"I think it is. We're bound to each other, Milton. We have everything it takes to make this marriage real. Every time I get a day off, I'll spend time at the Inn. I want to do what I can to support you."

"Support me?"

"The work you do, stopping evil."

"And?"

"And I want a baby, but more, I want the intimacy, the tenderness we found together on the night we were married." And when they were chained in a dungeon with evil imps possessing the Inn.

The hand holding hers was no longer scaled, no longer green. It was warm, hard, like a man's. And it was a man who stood, lifted her up into his arms, and carried her to the front door.

She was charmed, enchanted, and just a tiny bit annoyed, for she was a modern woman, used to doing things by herself, for herself. "I can walk, you know."

He grinned and his warm, human eyes sparkled. "I know. But since we are starting our marriage at this moment, I thought you would grant me this boon."

Then his head lowered and his tender, invasive lips met hers for a kiss that would keep them married for all the days of the Earth and for all eternity.

THE END

BETSY J. BENNETT'S AUTHOR'S PAGE

My name is Betsy J. Bennett and write fantasy/paranormal romance. I often tell people that I write because my characters are far more interesting than the people I know, and that's true, but there are other reasons. I write because I see these people. I know their stories, their problems, their search for love and I have to tell it so readers can see it. I also write to avoid depression and possible homicide charges. When I write I'm happy with the world around me. I can not always control my worlds, but they always lead me to fascinating places and take unexpected turns which always turns out happily.

Betsy J. Bennett's Books

The Dragon's Roost Bed & Breakfast Series

Book 1	**A Dragon's Tea**
Book 2	**A Gargoyle's Vow**
Book 3	**A Wizard's Spell**
Book 4	**A Ghost's Chance**

Santa Takes a Wife
Yes, Virginia.

The Frog Kiss

Her Puzzle

Strangers in the Night

Left Star of Orion's Belt

All books are available on AMAZON.com

www.ingramcontent.com/pod-product-compliance
Lightning Source LLC
Chambersburg PA
CBHW020559180626
46810CB00007B/2577